Willow Place

Joan Clinton Scoggins

Joan Scoggins
306 Warthen St.
La Fayette, GA 30728-2529

JOAN CLINTON SCOGGINS

Willow Place

JOAN CLINTON SCOGGINS

A Division of WINEPRESS PUBLISHING

Front cover photography provided by: Linda Wilson Capps

Printed in the United States of America

Packaged by Pleasant Word, a division of WinePress Publishing, PO Box 428, Enumclaw, WA 98022. The views expressed or implied in this work do not necessarily reflect those of Pleasant Word, a division of WinePress Publishing. Ultimate design, content, and editorial accuracy of this work are the responsibilities of the author.

Unless otherwise noted, all Scriptures are taken from the Holy Bible, New International Version, Copyright © 1973, 1978, 1984 by the International Bible Society. Used by permission of Zondervan Publishing House. The "NIV" and "New International Version" trademarks are registered in the United States Patent and Trademark Office by International Bible Society.

Scripture references marked KJV are taken from the King James Version of the Bible.

Scripture references marked NASB are taken from the New American Standard Bible, © 1960, 1963, 1968, 1971, 1972, 1973, 1975, 1977 by The Lockman Foundation. Used by permission.

ISBN 1-57921-707-9
Library of Congress Catalog Card Number: 2003107323

About the Author

Joan Clinton Scoggins was born in Aragon, Georgia in September of 1929. She currently resides in La Fayette, Georgia with her husband of fifty five years. Joan is the second child of Clarence and Rebecca Ann Clinton. She has three sisters and one brother. She was married to the love of her life, Max Scoggins, on November 17, 1947. They have two sons, Phillip and Gregory, five grandchildren and four great grandchildren.

Joan worked in the Cherokee Regional Library of Walker County, Georgia as well as the Media Center of the Department of Education in La Fayette, Georgia. An avid reader, Joan has also been a writer since her high school years. Poems, short stories, family history, and daily ledgers are among her treasures.

Joan has been a Christian for more than fifty years and has chosen to use her giftedness in writing as a tool to bring others to Christ. She has written plays and skits for her church and for the past twenty five years she has had a letter writing ministry to the elderly.

"Willow Place" is a wonderful Christian love story whose readers will be swept away with suspense and anticipation, and whose hearts will be blessed.

If you would like to write the author you may do so by e-mail at <u>jcmscoggins@aol.com</u>

Acknowledgements

The desire to write a book since early high school years lay dormant until shortly before my 73rd birthday. On July 8, 2002, I chose a pencil with a sharp point, a legal pad and began one of the most fulfilling, enjoyable endeavors of my life. My husband, Max, who allowed me to write, undisturbed, for at least eight hours each day for three months and listened to my progress, page by handwritten page, was my faithful encourager. He kept me up-beat by saying, "Joanie, your book is good." Our son, Phillip, of Columbus, Georgia edited my book and typed it into the computer. He volunteered, unselfishly, for the task, which took many hours. He said I had a God given talent for writing and was glad to see me extend it by writing a book that will minister to its readers. Our second son, Gregory, of Brenham, Texas read Willow Place, did some additional editing and prepared it to be submitted to its publisher. This required much of his time. He was very complimentary of the drama in the book, loved the Christian message which should be well received by its readers, he commented. Our granddaughter, Rebecca Lee Wilson, of Goose Creek, S.C. read "Willow Place," loved its characters and the mysteries that unfolded. She created a web page www.willowplacenovel.com for me as a gift.

My neighbor and special friend, Jane Crawford Collett, read "Willow Place" in 40-page hand written increments until it was finished. She attached little notes to what she read. One of them said . . .

> "I feel very acquainted and almost kin to some of your characters . . . I've cried with them, I've smiled and laughed out loud. I have been especially touched so warmly by some of the examples of how close one can be to God, to 'talk' to Him so personally! Thank you for sharing your talent, emotions and Christian love in *Willow Place*."

Upon finishing the book two more close friends read the handwritten copy. They were Barbara Perkins Marshall and Vivian Hobbs. Some of their comments . . .

> "We have loved every single page, anticipating each person's next move, next love, next trip. What a joy it has been to read *Willow Place*."

Paul Chambers, friend and retired Superintendent of the Chickamauga, Georgia Board of Education, encouraged me years ago to write a book. Thanks for your faith in my writing ability and for your and Pat's long standing friendship.

This positive support and encouragement has been priceless on my book-writing journey. My parents, Clarence and Rebecca Ann Clinton, were avid readers as long as I can remember. They would have been so proud that I have written a book.

Chapter 1

OCTOBER 6, 1855

A gentle breeze was blowing the weeping willow branches of the trees standing on the banks of the huge lake. Savannah Baldwin, sitting on the porch of the stately home place never tired of the beauty of her favorite of all trees. Reflecting on her surroundings, she heard the front door open and turned to see her granddaughter, Elizabeth, carrying a tray of lemonade and a plate of almond scones. Elizabeth was the one person Savannah adored most in the world.

Elizabeth realized her grandmother had awakened early from her nap and hoped that she was not ailing. Setting the tray on the round, wrought iron table she spread a yellow linen napkin across her grandmother's lap. Putting a scone on a small cut glass plate she set it on the table beside her grandmother's chair and poured her a glass of lemonade.

"Aren't you up a little early from your afternoon nap, Grandmother Savannah?"

"Yes Elizabeth, I am but I had so much on my mind I simply was never able to go to sleep."

"What on earth do you have on your mind that would weigh so heavily, pray tell?"

Elizabeth seated herself in the chair across from her adored grandmother who had a look of consternation on her face.

"There is something I need to tell you, Elizabeth. It concerns your mother and father, God rests their souls. It isn't a pleasant story but it's important that you know."

Elizabeth wondered what on earth she could be talking about. She noticed that her grandmother looked a little pale. Her eyes looked tired with a pained expression.

"You have stirred my curiosity considerably. Please tell me what you are talking about."

"Now is not the time. It's a long story but I feel tired and a little chilled. I'm about ready to go to my room. We will finish this talk after breakfast in the morning."

"I doubt I'll sleep a wink tonight for wondering."

"It can wait one more day, Elizabeth, dear. Let me tell you how special you are to me. You have been a bright spot in my life since you were born 19 years ago. Never have you been a disappointment but you've always brought me joy. I don't know what I would have done without you when your grandfather died three years ago. You've been more like a daughter to us than a granddaughter. I hear the old grandfather clock striking six." She stood up, laid her neatly folded napkin and plate on the table and said, "Even though it's a might early I'm going inside now, maybe have a glass of warm milk and then I'm off to bed."

"Sleep well, grandmother. We'll have our talk in the morning."

But that talk never happened. Instead, Savannah Elizabeth Baldwin, at the age of 70, died in her sleep on October 7th. The shock of her death left Elizabeth devastated. Her grandfather, David Baldwin, whom she lovingly called "Dandy", died just ten days after her sixteenth birthday. He was 73. And now the last of her family was gone, leaving her alone.

Elizabeth's father, Alex Sloan, was killed in a fall from a horse when she was hardly three. She had very little memory of him except he used to smother her with hugs and kisses and called her princess.

Chapter 1

At the time of Alex's death, Elizabeth, her mother Victoria, and her father Alex, lived in Charlottesville. After the funeral the Baldwins brought Victoria and Elizabeth back to Willow Place to live. The Baldwin home was an imposing two-story brick structure with plenty of room for the two of them.

David Lee Baldwin was a lawyer and later became a judge. He and Savannah were saddened to see the heartache reflected in their daughter's eyes. She was barely able to function. They comforted her as best they could. Their granddaughter Elizabeth was such a pleasure to them. They showered her with love but were careful not to spoil her.

The Baldwin's had been members of the First Wesleyan Church in Richmond for years, so parishioners were very sympathetic to Victoria in her loss. They reached out to her and Elizabeth. Pastor Will Davis and his soft spoken wife, Madeline, were long-standing friends of the Baldwins. They loved young Elizabeth. She blossomed and grew in her new surroundings.

Victoria adored Elizabeth. She took time with her, giving Elizabeth her bath each day and brushing her hair. She read to her and they took walks together.

But as time passed, Victoria was not able to eat and grew weaker and weaker. She became listless and finally was unable to care for herself.

Victoria had worshipped Alex. They had been blissfully happy. He was a loving husband and a doting father to Elizabeth. Victoria found that she simply could not cope with her loss. Even with the loving support of her parents as well as the parishioners and Pastor Davis, she was unable to pull out of the deep depression which had engulfed her. Two years to the day after Alex's death, Victoria died quietly, of an apparent broken heart.

Chapter 2

*U*nexpectedly her grandmother Savannah was now gone from her. Elizabeth was in a daze, a state of utter disbelief. But she simply must pull herself together and make arrangements for her beloved grandmother's funeral service.

The days blurred, but somehow she got through them. The funeral was simple which her grandmother would have wanted. The church was full of those who loved her. Pastor Davis was gracious in his eulogy of "Ms. Savannah" as he always called her. Elizabeth would never forget the support of those around her. They had all suffered a great loss too, but their every thought was of her.

Two weeks after the funeral, Elizabeth was sitting on the front porch admiring the weeping willows. She knew better, but it was almost as if they were weeping for her beloved grandmother who loved these trees so much. Today their name "weeping willows" seemed to fit so well.

Sitting there she began to mull over in her mind what her grandmother had said to her the day before she died . . ." There is something I need to tell you, Elizabeth. It concerns your mother and your father. It isn't a pleasant story but it's important that you know. It's also a long story."

What could it have been? She remembered the urgency in her grandmother's voice. Was the story forever buried with her grandmother? Would she ever know? How could she ever know?

Elizabeth was startled out of her deep thoughts by Emma O'Riley the Baldwin's cook. Emma was the first generation out of her homeland of Ireland, and spoke with a sharp Irish brogue. "Elizabeth lassie, I've just made a kettle of hot chocolate. Would you like a cup?"

"Yes, Emma. Sounds delicious. Bring yourself a cup and sit with me for a while."

Elizabeth thought . . . *how fortunate I am to have Emma. Hmm, I wonder just how long she lived with my grandparents. I know she was here when I came. Wonder why she never married? She is still a very attractive lady.*

She reached for her cup and said, "Thank you, Emma. Come sit beside me. May I ask you a personal question? Why have you never married? With your strawberry blonde hair and those emerald, green eyes you must have had many beaus."

"Thank you for being interested, lassie." With a twinkle in her eye she said "I loved a boy named Michael Kelley once. He said he loved me too. But he left Richmond seeking a better life. He said he would return for me but he never did. My love for him has never faded. I've often wondered what happened to him. He was a big, rugged Irishman with a boisterous laugh. But he was as gentle as a lamb and a good person. I wonder what my life would have been like had he returned for me. I will never really know," Emma said with resolve and a tear in her eye.

Elizabeth patted Emma's hand and said, "Thank you for sharing this with me. Sometimes I would like to hear more about this Michael Kelley."

Both sat quietly sipping their hot chocolate, reflecting on the beauty that surrounded them. With winter approaching they would soon have to enjoy this tranquil scenery from inside. Elizabeth wondered if they would have an extreme winter this year after the mild one of last year.

As was usual in October she spotted three deer on the far side of the lake. They were standing very still looking all about. Somehow it always excited her when she saw deer. They were graceful and so inaccessible. She always wished she could just walk up and touch them. Already something had spooked them and all she could see were their white tails as they disappeared into the brush.

Her attention was drawn to movement under the old oak tree near the north end of the house. Several squirrels were busy hiding acorns for the winter. They were industrious little animals and fun to watch.

Emma laughed out loud at some of their antics.

Finally Elizabeth decided the time had come for her to ask Emma some questions or at least to share some of her muddled thoughts with her.

"There is something I need to talk with you about, Emma."

"What is it? You look troubled, child."

"Do I Emma? I am troubled. It is about a conversation Grandmother Savannah had with me the last day of her life. She said she had something important to tell me about my mother and father. She planned to tell me the next morning after breakfast. But of course she died in her sleep that night. Oh, Emma, what could it possibly have been? How will I ever know? I do know that she kept a journal. Perhaps there is something revealing there. I need to go through her things but I can't bring myself to do that just yet. Emma, my parents have been dead for ten years! Why would grandmother have waited so long to talk to me? Why? Why?!" Elizabeth said imploringly. "It's all such a big mystery. My mind is in such turmoil."

"Elizabeth, I can help you with this mystery, but you must first understand some history. I came to work for your grandparents when your mother, Victoria, was ten years old and I was twenty. I came from a poor but hard-working family from Ireland. Judge Baldwin hired me to cook for the family. I also helped Mrs. Baldwin take care of your mother.

"Over the years your grandparents began to treat me like family. Victoria was such a pleasure. Why that child loved me like a nanny, much to my delight. They insisted that I attend church with them and sit in the family pew.

"Your grandmother and I became close friends. She respected me and she would share many personal things with me."

"Oh Emma, I'm so glad grandmother had you as a friend and confidant."

"With your grandmother, I feel our close friendship was born out of necessity. She had to have someone to talk with and I was available. Your grandparents went through some hard places. Your mother was an only child. What I am about to tell you, Elizabeth will come as quite a surprise to you, but your mother was married to a man before your father Alex. Her first husband, John Lee Morgan, was killed before you were born. When they were married, John Lee whisked her away to Charlottesville. Your grandparents did not hear from her very often and got to see her even less. But what you need to know will be a shocking story to you. It is long. After prayerful consideration, your grandmother decided to confide in me. It is good that she did. The only reason she would ever have revealed the past to you was because of a letter she received from Williamsburg just a month ago."

"I feel almost frightened, Emma. I have a feeling this is going to change the way my life is now and I'm not too sure I want that. But I must know."

"Since it is so near lunch time I'll go inside and warm some Irish stew I made yesterday. I'm sure Sadie and William are ready to eat by now. Sadie has been cleaning upstairs and William is still raking leaves."

William and Sadie Clark came to work for the Baldwins ten years ago. Her grandparents said they felt God had sent the Clarks to them. They came from good stock, as Elizabeth often heard her grandfather say.

While Emma prepared lunch Elizabeth pondered all that she had heard. *I wonder just what else will be revealed to me. I really do want to know . . . don't I?*

Chapter 3

After lunch Elizabeth and Emma settled in the parlor. A sudden chill filled the air so William had made a fire in the fireplace. He predicted a heavy frost for the night.

Emma leaned back comfortably in her chair in front of the fire. Elizabeth was sitting on the couch with her legs curled under her looking expectantly at Emma.

Searching her mind for what Savannah had revealed to her the story began to unfold.

When Alex Sloan, the man you have thought was your father all these years, died tragically and you two came here to Willow Place to live, Victoria told your grandmother, Savannah, the whole sordid story of her life while she was married to John Lee Morgan.

Your mother met John Lee here in Richmond. She and your grandfather Baldwin attended a stage production at the Richmond Opera House. John saw her there and was transfixed by her beauty he told her later. After the play was over he followed them to their carriage, however, Victoria's father had stopped to speak to a colleague for a few minutes. Victoria walked the few steps on to the awaiting carriage. John stepped to the carriage door, tipped his hat and introduced himself. Victoria said she had never seen such a strikingly handsome man. His black hair and deep blue eyes were accented by the dark tan of his skin. His engaging smile was very disquieting. Victoria told her mother he bowed to her and asked her name. She was so startled she involuntarily told him. With the tip of his hat he told her that he *would* see her again and with that he disappeared into the crowd.

Savannah said his pursuit of Victoria was relentless. She was completely swept off her feet by his charm. Within six months they were married by the justice of the peace, and John took her to Charlottesville.

In the early months of their marriage John was very attentive to Victoria. He showered her with gifts, took her to the nicest restaurants and to the theater quite often. She could not believe her good fortune to have someone so gentle and kind to love her.

But soon after, things began to change. John became moody and despondent. The least thing made him angry and he became verbally abusive. Victoria said she did not know what he did for a living. He would leave and stay gone for weeks. She never knew where he went and dared not ask. However, she said he never left her without money. They lived in an exclusive part of Charlottesville in a lovely old colonial home. It was completely furnished when he took her there and they had servants. But they really had no friends. John told her they didn't need friends.

It seems one of his favorite people was an older colored man named Garrison Wheeler. He was John's driver.

Victoria said John's temper became so bad she was deathly afraid of him. He was insanely jealous of her. She dared not look at any other man when they were out.

Savannah was horrified to learn that when her precious daughter was expecting their first child, in a fit of rage, John shoved her down and kicked her so hard she lost the baby. After hearing the horror stories, your grandparents never understood why Victoria did not leave John and come home.

Emma paused and said, "This is not a pretty story for you to have to hear, Elizabeth."

"My poor mother. She was alone, frightened, and terribly abused. It breaks my heart. This revelation is almost more than my mind can comprehend."

"If you want me to stop all you have to do is say so, lassie."

"No, Emma. Please don't stop. I want to know the whole story."

Well, Victoria told her mother when she was expecting you in 1836 that they had gone to the Charles Inn in downtown Charlottesville. John told her he had to meet a man there to take care of some business. They went upstairs to the second floor. Victoria said she made the mistake of asking him what the business was about. He became so angry that she would dare question him about *his* business. He told her she was to be seen and not heard and shoved her recklessly backwards. She was standing so near the open stairway that she lost her footing and was falling when Alex Sloan, the owner of the Inn, who was coming up the stairs, caught her in his arms. He steadied her, turned her loose and she stepped back up to the landing. Victoria said it infuriated John that Alex had touched her. John lunged at Alex, who stepped aside, and John tumbled down the steps to his death.

Victoria said that she fainted. When she awakened Garrison Wheeler was cradling John's head in his lap. He looked at Victoria and told her that "Mr. John" was dead. After the authorities came and ruled John's death an accident Garrison took his body to their home in John's carriage. Alex drove Victoria home. He helped her with the funeral arrangements. She really had no one and was in such a state of shock after John's death that Alex felt compelled to help any way he could. She didn't seem able to make even the simplest decisions. In the weeks to come Alex visited her regularly. Her dependency on him pleased him very much.

Soon it became apparent to Alex that Victoria was with John Morgan's child. By this time he had fallen in love with her. He told her if she would marry him he would love this baby as though it were his own. They were married two months before you were born.

There could not have been a father more proud. He cherished Victoria. Their love was a strong and binding cord.

Victoria told her mother that Alex made her a card for their first Valentine's Day. He had taken all the words from the Song of Solomon. She proudly showed it to Savannah, commenting on the personal message it conveyed.

"Thou art beautiful, O my love.
How fair and how pleasant art thou.
Many waters cannot quench love.
Neither can the floods drown it.
I am my beloved's, and my beloved is mine."

Victoria, you are my special Valentine on this February 14, 1837.

Your husband, Alex

"Elizabeth, when Savannah told me all of this she took the Valentine from Victoria's Bible and showed it to me. She said that the two years they had together were the happiest years of her life."

"There is still a big part of the puzzle that you have yet to hear. Your grandmother received a letter recently. It is very revealing. But we will have to finish this tomorrow. We both need a rest from this," Emma declared.

Elizabeth's head was spinning. So many thoughts collided within her mind. *I am not a Sloan but a Morgan. Did my real father have a family in Charlottesville? What business was he in? Why did he behave as he did? Was he truly just devilishly mean, or could something have happened to his mind?* She knew one thing. She was exhausted! What would this letter reveal that Emma spoke of? She felt such empathy for the mother she barely knew.

Chapter 4

$\mathcal{E}$mma had supper prepared by six o'clock, and everyone enjoyed the meal. William bragged on the wonderful flavor of her baked chicken, which really pleased Emma.

Elizabeth realized just how tired she was and went up stairs early to prepare for bed. She needed some time alone for reflection on the days events. With so many questions consuming her thoughts she reached for her Bible and turned to Psalm 91 which spoke of the safety and security of believers. She began to read:

> "He that dwelleth in the secret place of the most high shall abide under the shadow of the almighty. I will say of the Lord, He is my refuge and my fortress: my God; in him will I trust. He shall cover thee with his feathers, and under his wings shalt thou trust: his truth shall be thy shield and buckler. For he shall give his angels charge over thee, to keep thee in all thy ways. They shall bear thee up in their hands, lest thou dash thy foot against a stone."

Elizabeth prayed, "Lord, you know that as for family, I am alone. I am facing the unknown in my life, but I am going to trust in you for strength and guidance. In the beautiful book of Psalms is written, 'Thy word is a lamp unto my feet, and a light into my path.' I cherish your word, Lord, and I thank you for your many blessings. Amen"

Elizabeth awakened early, but she felt more rested than since the day her beloved

Grandmother died.

She refreshed herself and slipped into a simple black dress. After making her bed she went downstairs to the kitchen.

Selecting a warm bran muffin and pouring herself a steaming cup of hot chocolate she asked Emma if she slept well.

"That I did, lassie. How did you rest after yesterday?"

"Surprisingly well, thank you. Emma, how could we manage without the strength of the Lord? I realize I am not yet 20, however, from good teaching and training by my grandparents I feel a little older and perhaps a little wiser than my years. Last night before going to sleep I read in Psalm 91. After my prayers, I snuggled way down in my feather bed. You know I could almost hear 'Dandy' reading one of his favorite scriptures to me . . .

'Hear O Israel: The Lord our God is one Lord: And thou shalt love the Lord thy God with all thine heart, and with all thy soul, and with all thy might. And these words, which I command thee this day, shall be in thy heart: And thou shalt teach them diligently unto thy children, and shalt talk of them when thou sittest in thine house, and when thou walkest by the way, and when thou liest down, and when thou risest up.'

"Then Emma, he always took me by the shoulders, looked me straight in my eyes and would say, 'Elizabeth Ann, you must always love the Lord with all your heart. And remember, too, that He loves you!' He always chuckled at the little rhyme he made.

"Oh, Emma, how many times he read me that scripture from the sixth chapter of Deuteronomy. He and grandmother taught me so much about the Lord and his ways. I miss them terribly."

By this time Emma was wiping tears on the corner of her apron skirt. She was a small lady, not so short, but pleasantly thin. She looked rather frail.

What would I do without her? Elizabeth thought.

Chapter 5

*A*fter a nourishing breakfast Emma and Sadie cleared the table, washed and dried the dishes, swept and mopped the spacious kitchen till all was in its place.

Elizabeth retreated to the library where William had a roaring fire going. She walked over to the window and looked out towards the lake. William was right. There was a heavy frost on the ground. It looked almost like snow. On the lake there were geese that were on their way south. A little late, she reasoned.

Elizabeth heard the click of the library door. She turned around as Emma entered ready to finish their talk and end this mystery.

"Sadie and I finished in the kitchen. She is going to prepare us a light lunch today so we may finish our talk.

"Elizabeth, I asked that we talk in the library because your grandmother Savannah placed the letter she received from Williamsburg in the family Bible. I'd like you to get the letter and read it for yourself. It will finish clearing up the mystery.

Elizabeth walked across the room to the round William and Mary lamp table that her grandmother loved so much. It was a wedding gift from her parents, a cherished family heirloom. This is where the large, old but well-preserved family Bible had been as long as she could remember. Inside the front cover was an ivory-colored business envelope. In a distinguished penmanship it was addressed to:

Mrs. David Baldwin
306 Willow Place
Richmond, Virginia

With trembling hands Elizabeth took the letter out of the envelope, unfolded it and examined the heading. It read:

Morgan Shipping Enterprise
2021 Shipping Lane
Williamsburg, Virginia

President, John Lee Morgan, Sr.
Vice President, Zachary S. Bainbridge
20 September, 1855

Elizabeth walked back to a chair near the fire. She was trembling all over. Was it a sudden chill from the cold or anticipation from what she was about to read? She sat down and adjusted the woolen shawl around her shoulders. Then she raised her eyes from the letter she was holding to meet Emma's eyes. Emma leaned forward in her chair and inquired, "Lassie, are you alright?"

"Yes, Emma. I'll be fine. I am ready now to read this letter. Will you listen as I read it aloud?"

She did not wait for a reply but began to read . . .

Dear Mrs. Baldwin,

I pray you accept this letter in the spirit with which it is written.

It is my understanding that your daughter, Anna Victoria, was married to my son, John Lee Morgan, Jr., and from that union a child was born. You will no doubt question my knowledge of this. And you rightly should.

Chapter 5

In August of this year I was summoned to Charlottesville by an old colored man. He said he had information about my son, John Lee.

I had heard nothing from my son since he left home some 21 years ago.

John Lee was an independent young man. He asked for a sizeable loan and told me he wanted to see what he could do on his own.

He was our only child. His mother, Catherine, and I had no reason not to trust him. We are people of means. What we had would be his one day, after all. We never imagined the day he left home at the age of 24, we would never see him again.

Needless to say, I immediately went to see this man. When I arrived at the address he gave me, I found him at his daughter's house in very needy circumstances. He is 67 years old and a sick man. His name is Garrison Wheeler. He said he feared he is not going to live, and before he dies he wanted to take care of some old business that was long overdue.

He told me he was a driver for my son for three years. He lived in quarters off the main house and served my son well. John Lee didn't have any real friends and became very comfortable with Garrison, confiding in him when he would become depressed.

John Lee told Garrison where he was from and gave him my name and address, "Just in case," he remarked mysteriously. Garrison was acquainted with your daughter, Victoria, whom he greatly respected and admired. He was aware and saddened that John Lee mistreated her. Garrison said one night, in a rage, that John Lee pushed Victoria down and then kicked her, causing her to lose their first child.

On May 2, 1836, Garrison said he drove my son and Victoria to the Charles Inn. John Lee had been very depressed for days. He had told Garrison that Victoria was with child. He was afraid he would not be a very good father. They had been at the Inn about twenty minutes when John Lee accidentally fell down the stairs from the second floor, and was dead when Garrison got to him.

Garrison said Victoria remained in Charlottesville and had a baby daughter about six months later, but she remarried before the baby was born.

Mrs. Baldwin, this child would be the daughter of our son, John Lee. You cannot imagine the joy Mrs. Morgan and I felt to think that we might have a granddaughter.

After some detective work, we were given your name and address.

My question to you is, will you be willing to see us regarding this matter? We no longer have a son. But our hearts are filled with so much love to give this miracle granddaughter. She would be our only heir.

Please answer this letter with haste, and forgive its length.

Sincere regards,
John L. Morgan

Chapter 6

*E*lizabeth sat quietly for such a long time. Still holding the letter, she thoughtfully gazed into the fire. Finally she broke the silence and said, "Well Emma, it appears I have a letter to write."

Emma saw a resolve about Elizabeth that she was glad to see. Really, she expected no less from this precocious young woman.

Elizabeth walked over to her grandfather's desk and sat down in his big old leather chair. She said, "Emma today is October 23rd. It has been a month since Mr. Morgan wrote this letter. I am sure he has great expectations for a reply. I am going to send him a telegraph to let him know a letter is forthcoming."

"That is a good idea, lassie."

"Thank you, Emma, for being mine and grandmother's friend and confidant. If it weren't for you I'd have no knowledge of the past. I will be forever grateful."

"I believe the Lord had a hand in this revelation. He is to be praised, child."

"Indeed He is!"

As Emma rose to leave Elizabeth said, "Please ask William to come into the library."

She turned her attention to the task at hand. Brevity would be best, she reasoned.

Dear Mr. Morgan,

My grandmother Baldwin received your letter dated September 20th. You will receive a reply shortly.

Elizabeth Sloan

After William left for town to send the telegraph Elizabeth reached for her grandfather's well-worn Bible on the corner of the desk. She turned to Proverbs, one of her favorite books. She read from the third chapter, noting her grandfather had underlined verses five and six . . .

"Trust in the Lord with all thine heart; and lean not unto thine own understanding. In all thy ways acknowledge him, and he shall direct thy paths."

Elizabeth pondered these profound scriptures as she had done many times in the past. She needed direction now to answer Mr. Morgan's letter. She bowed her head and began to pray . . .

"Lord, I do not pretend to have the wisdom to pen this letter, so I am going to trust in your wisdom to direct me in this important undertaking. Please guide my heart and thoughts. I thank you now Lord for the help I know I will receive from you.

Amen."

She picked up the pen, dipped it in the ink well, and began her letter to Mr. Morgan.

Richmond, Virginia
23 October, 1855

Dear Mr. Morgan,

I am Savannah Baldwin's granddaughter, Elizabeth Ann Sloan.

Grandmother died unexpectedly in her sleep on the seventh of October.

She had received your letter dated September 20th, two weeks earlier.

Because Grandmother shared your letter and other pertinent information with a mutual friend of ours, I have been made aware of its existence and have read your letter. Needless to say, I do not know well how to respond to these revelations. However, I am willing to meet with you. I will ask that you make the arrangements for our meeting.

I am respectfully yours,
Elizabeth Sloan

Elizabeth knew she had many decisions to make. It had been almost three weeks since her world had been turned upside down by her beloved grandmother's death. She felt so alone. However, she must begin to face the future with a positive attitude.

Chapter 7

November 2, 1855
Williamsburg, Virginia

The long awaited letter had finally arrived. John Morgan opened the envelope. In his haste the single page dropped to the floor. He quickly picked it up and read the letter from Elizabeth, John Lee's daughter. She was willing to meet with them! He must hurry home to share this news with Catherine. He took long strides into Zack's office holding the prized letter in his hand. Zack Bainbridge was the young vice president of his shipping company. He had been with him in this capacity for five years. John had hand-picked him from several applicants to apprentice in the business. His confidence in Zack's ability proved to be well founded. Zack also knew about this new-found granddaughter of John's and Catherine's.

"Zack, I have here in my hand a letter from my granddaughter, Elizabeth, from Richmond. She has agreed to meet with us. I am going home to tell Catherine the good news. Will you have the carriage brought around while I get my coat and hat?"

"Indeed I will, John. I can only imagine your excitement over this news," Zack replied.

As John entered the front door of his home, Simpson, their butler, looked astonished at Mr. Morgan's hasty entrance.

"Sir, is there something wrong?"

"No, Simpson, but do you know where Mrs. Morgan is?"

"Yes sir. She is reading in the sunroom. Shall I tell her you are here?"

"No, no Simpson. I'll go to her."

So as not to startle Catherine, John knocked lightly on the door.

"Please come in," Catherine called out, looking to see who it was.

"Why John, it's you. What are you doing home at this hour?"

"Catherine, I have good news. We received the letter we've been expecting from Elizabeth and she says she will meet with us. Here is the letter for you to read for yourself."

When she finished reading it, she said, "Poor, poor child. What a shock the death of her grandmother must have been."

"Her letter is not very revealing, Catherine. She is agreeing to meet with us, but what if she rejects us?"

"Oh John, we simply must not entertain such thoughts."

"Well, she really gives us no encouragement, except to say she will meet with us," John said thoughtfully.

Catherine replied, "But she could have said no. Besides John, you know how much we've prayed about this. If it is God's will we have nothing to worry about."

John looked lovingly at Catherine. She was a tower of strength to him.

"Yes, my dear. You are so right. He has surely permitted all of this to come about for a reason."

"John, today is November 2nd. If our son were alive, he would be 45 years old. What could be more fitting than to receive Elizabeth's letter on her father's birthday. We must be sure to tell her this when we meet with her."

John lamented, "It is still so painful to think of him. He was a good boy growing up. We educated him well and taught him the right way to live. We will never know what went wrong in his life. Had it not been for Garrison Wheeler feeling a need to be in touch with us, we might never have known anything about his life after he left home. And we certainly would not have known about Elizabeth. Just think, she is a part of him . . . a part of us. Garrison never gave me an answer when I asked him why he did not notify us when John Lee died. He could have, you know."

"I know, John, I know."

"Well, Catherine dear, we must make plans. I would very much like for Elizabeth to come here. Maybe a change would do her good. At least she said I could make the arrangements. I will go now, purchase a train ticket, and send it along with a letter of invitation to come here for a visit."

John stood, gave Catherine a hug and kiss, then walked briskly out the door to his waiting carriage.

Chapter 8

NOVEMBER 16, 1855
RICHMOND

William brought the carriage around to the front door and loaded Elizabeth's baggage. Elizabeth was checking to make sure she had her train ticket and the telegraph she had received from John Morgan two days earlier. In it he said he was sending a business partner to ride with her from Richmond to Williamsburg. He would feel better about her having an escort, even though it would only be a two hour trip.

Elizabeth was mumbling to herself . . . *Let's see now, this gentleman's name is Zachary Bainbridge. I remember his name was listed on Mr. Morgan's letter head. And he will be wearing a yellow scarf. Hummm.*

Emma asked, "Were you saying something to me, Elizabeth?" as she entered the foyer.

"No Emma, I was only thinking out loud. Is my bonnet on straight?" she asked as she turned to look in the mahogany framed mirror hanging above the long, slender matching table in the foyer.

"Yes, lassie, that it is. And might I add that you look stunning."

35

"Why thank you, Emma. I hope I have chosen well what I should wear to meet the Morgan's for the first time."

The front door opened and William said her baggage was loaded. Elizabeth gave Emma a hug and kiss, and said she would see her in about three weeks.

William drove around the beautiful lake. The dusting of snow the night before clung to the willow trees and sparked like icicles in the early morning sunlight. They circled half way around the lake, then entered the long driveway leading to the main road which would take them into Richmond.

They arrived at the train depot half an hour early. The Chesapeake & Ohio would arrive at 8:45 A.M. William unloaded Elizabeth's bags, setting them on the loading platform. Then he helped her out of the carriage.

"Goodbye William. Take care of Sadie and Emma while I am away. I'll let you know when to meet me on my return trip home."

"Don't worry about a thing, Miss Elizabeth. I'll take care of things just as if you were here," William replied. He stepped back into the carriage, snapped the reins and drove off.

Elizabeth looked anxiously around the platform to see if she could see Zachary Bainbridge.

Zachary had come to Richmond on Tuesday, the day before, on a business matter for Mr. Morgan, and had stayed the night at the Downtown Richmond Hotel. He had arrived quite early and was inside the depot out of the cold. Watching out the window Zachary saw Elizabeth as she stepped down from her carriage. Could this possibly be Elizabeth Sloan? This vision of loveliness? He watched spellbound as she stood looking at the people on the platform. Her hair was as black as raven's feathers, and she had a perfect widow's peak, giving her face the shape of a heart. She was wearing a deep green velvet dress with a matching bonnet and hand muff.

Her green wool coat, buttoned snugly, accented a tiny waistline. As she moved toward the door of the depot she looked like a dream walking. He could not take his eyes off her. As the door opened he turned around. Would she notice that he was wearing a yellow scarf?

Chapter 8

Elizabeth stepped inside the door, stopped and looked the room over to see if she could recognize Mr. Bainbridge. She was given no description, only that he would be wearing a yellow scarf.

Her eyes stopped on the man standing near the window. He was the most handsome man she had ever seen . . . and was wearing a yellow scarf! She expected a much older man, perhaps in his fifties. But this man, this Zachary Bainbridge, was in his twenties. His hair was a silvery blonde, and his glorious tan implied that he surely must sail a lot. He looked to be over six feet tall with square, broad shoulders and narrow hips. He was impeccably dressed. Their eyes met and both seemed frozen in time. She finally diverted her gaze and began moving toward him.

She extended her hand and said, "You must be Zachary Bainbridge."

He thought, "How can one be so perfect?" Her eyes were azure blue and wide set with long eyelashes and perfectly shaped eyebrows. She had a beautiful smile with lovely deep dimples in each cheek that made her look invitingly impish. Her skin looked like peaches and cream.

"Well, are you?" Elizabeth said.

"Am . . . Am I what?" he stammered.

"Are you Zachary Bainbridge?!"

"Yes . . . yes I am. And you are Elizabeth Sloan, I presume?"

He reached for her hand, bent over and kissed it. Elizabeth's heart raced and she could scarcely breathe. She pulled her hand away quickly . . . *Look at you, Elizabeth. You don't even know this man and you are letting your emotions run away with you.*

"Yes I am. And could we please sit down?" . . . *before my legs buckle beneath me, she thought to herself.*

They moved over to a long bench up against the wall. After she was seated he placed her hat box to her right and seated himself to her left. Then he removed his watch from his vest pocket, noting the time. They had fifteen minutes before the train would be arriving.

"Did you have a pleasant ride into town, Miss Sloan?"

"Very pleasant, thank you." *Did he hear the tremor in her voice?*

"How far from Richmond proper do you live?"

"Willow Place is five miles west of the city."

"Did you have much snow on the ground?"

"No, just a little dusting. But the trees at Willow Place shone in the sunlight as though covered with icicles."

There was a long pause and each looked around the room trying to think of just the right thing to say.

"Did you arrive in Richmond on the evening train yesterday, Mr. Bainbridge?"

"No. No, I came in on the morning train. Mr. Morgan sent me early to take care of a business matter."

"Oh, I see."

They sat in silence. Zachary was still stunned by her beauty. The Morgans were in for a pleasant surprise by this granddaughter.

What made her think Mr. Bainbridge would be an older man? Perhaps because he was vice-president of Morgan Shipping, she reasoned.

Suddenly the C & O engine whistle sounded and shattered the silence.

Zachary stood to his feet, picked up Elizabeth's hat box, and guided her by her elbow through the door and onto the platform.

Elizabeth trembled again at his touch. They stood by their bags until a Porter came to load it into the baggage car. Then they walked to the steps of the train. Zachary stepped aside for her to climb aboard. He followed close behind. They walked only a short distance down the aisle before choosing two seats.

Zachary placed her hat box next to her and sat directly across from Elizabeth. Both had window seats.

He removed his cape and top hat, laying them in the seat to his left. There were not so many passengers as to fill all the seats.

The train seats were not very comfortable. Zachary knew it would be a long, tiring trip for Elizabeth. But it would be his good fortune to have her to look at for almost two hours!

"Oh my, I seem to have dropped my handkerchief," Elizabeth exclaimed as she leaned over to look for it.

He said, "Yes, there it is right by your foot," and he leaned down to pick it up for her. In doing so their faces were just inches apart and their eyes met. Elizabeth felt again that they were frozen in time. But she quickly straightened up and said, "Thank you, Mr. Bainbridge," as he handed her the handkerchief.

The conductor called out, "All aboard!"

The train began to slowly move. As it gained speed, she watched the countryside disappear as though it were moving instead of the train.

At 10:45 A.M. the train pulled into the Williamsburg Depot. By this time she and Zachary Bainbridge were more comfortable with each other. She had learned that he has an older brother, Thomas, who is twenty-seven and married, a younger brother, Benjamin, twenty-three. He also has a sister, Rebecca, who is twenty-one. Ben and Rebecca still live at home with their parents in Norfolk. Both his parents celebrated their fiftieth birthdays this year.

Zachary had also told her he was an avid sailor with his own sailboat. He and his two brothers have spent a lot of time sailing on the James River.

Mr. Morgan had shared his knowledge of Elizabeth and her mother, Victoria, with Zachary. Elizabeth told him she was the only one left in her family except for two great uncles, who were brothers to her Grandfather Baldwin, which lived in Charlottesville. And a great aunt who is her Grandmother Savannah's older sister, who lives in Roanoke.

Elizabeth told him of her love for Willow Place and the city of Richmond. She mentioned that she attended stage productions at the Richmond Actor's Theater as often as possible, and that horseback riding around Willow Place was one of her favorite pastimes.

They enjoyed the scenic route along the James River and saw some sailboats, even in November.

The conductor came down the aisle informing the passengers they were nearing Williamsburg. Elizabeth became apprehensive about meeting Mr. and Mrs. Morgan. She retied the satin bow on her bonnet and smoothed the skirt of her dress.

The train had begun to slow down and came to a sudden stop.

Zachary picked up her hat box and stepped aside as she stood up. He descended the steps ahead of her, turned and took her hand as she stepped down to the platform.

Mr. Morgan had sent his carriage for them. The Porter loaded their baggage, and Mr. Bainbridge assisted her into the plush carriage. The driver mumbled a quick "giddy-up" and the carriage began to move.

Chapter 9

*B*oth Elizabeth and Zachary were quiet and reflective. The Morgans lived southwest of Williamsburg in Jamestown facing the James River. It was about a twenty minute ride by carriage from the train depot. Elizabeth made mental notes of land marks along the way.

The carriage driver pulled up in front of the Morgan home. It was an elegant, white wood structure of the federal townhouse design with three stories. It had porches across the front of the house on each level. Four windows lined the wall on each story. The porches were supported by four large, round columns. They sat on pedestals and were topped with cornices and frieze. Dark green shutters were on either side of the windows. There were two dormers projecting through the sloping roof. A cupola topped off the house. The front door was wide and heavy with a double cornice above it. The front yard was rather small but well kept with varied shades of green shrubbery.

Elizabeth realized at this moment that the Morgans were well-to-do. She should have known from the fact that he owned a shipping company! She became very uncomfortable, and her apprehension at meeting them only grew worse.

Zachary stepped down from the carriage and assisted Elizabeth. He took her arm and guided her up the steps onto the porch. He stepped to the door and lifted the heavy brass door knocker, letting it fall several times.

The door swung open. Zachary smiled and said, "Good morning, Simpson. This is Miss Elizabeth Sloan. Miss Sloan, this is the Morgan's butler, Simpson."

Simpson bowed and said, "The Morgans are expecting you. Please come in."

Turning to Elizabeth, Simpson said, "Mrs. Morgan said you would want to freshen up before lunch. Please wait and I will have Millie show you to your room. Mr. Bainbridge, Mr. Morgan is waiting for you in the library. He asked that you join him there."

With that he disappeared. Zachary squeezed Elizabeth's hand and said, "You will like Millie." Then he left her.

She heard a warm, friendly voice say, "Good morning miss. I am Millie. Come with me, please." Millie led the way up a grand suspended staircase to the second floor.

Elizabeth didn't know if it was her sense of humor or her nerves inflicting the thought, but she giggled and said to herself . . . *I guess I could say I'm making a "ceremonial ascending" of this grand staircase to the second floor of this lovely mansion!*

At the top of the stairs they turned left and, coming to the third door off the hallway, Millie opened the door and stepped aside for Elizabeth to enter.

"This will be your room, Miss Sloan. Simpson is having your baggage sent up. There is fresh water and towels on the wash table and also a bar of lilac soap. Do you need me to assist you in any way?"

"No, Millie, thank you."

"I will unpack your bags later. After you freshen up, please ring the bell. I will come and show you to the library where Mr. and Mrs. Morgan, and Mr. Bainbridge are waiting for you."

"Again, thank you Millie. I won't be long."

Millie left the room closing the door behind her.

Elizabeth caught her breath, in awe, as she looked around the room. The walls were off-white with same colored draperies which were open allowing the morning sunlight to shimmer across the floor.

Against the opposite wall stood a white, French Provincial bed. The bed spread was made of heavy white cotton and had a hand-embroidered candlewick design of tulips and ribbons, with a six-inch border of crocheted lace fringe. The wash table, chest and dressing table were French Provincial. There were two chairs covered in gold and silver patterns of brocade. A large picture of a romantic river scene, framed in white, was hanging over the bed. "This is definitely a room for a young lady," Elizabeth said aloud. She had never stayed in a room such as this before.

She removed her bonnet and refreshed herself with cool water on her face from the marble basin. Combing through her long hair, which was naturally curly, she smoothed it into place. She walked over and pulled the cord to ring for Millie.

At the foot of the stairs Simpson was waiting for Elizabeth and Millie. He nodded to Elizabeth and said, "Please, follow me." He knocked and then opened the door to the library for Elizabeth. When she entered, Mr. and Mrs. Morgan as well as Zachary stood up.

Mr. Morgan extended his hand to her and said, "Welcome to our home, Elizabeth. This is Catherine, my wife and John Lee's mother, of course."

Catherine walked across the room quickly and said, "Elizabeth, we have anxiously awaited this moment," extending her hand to Elizabeth.

"Thank you," Elizabeth replied with a nervous smile and quick curtsey.

"Zachary says you had a pleasant trip from Richmond. We are happy you had this time to get to know one another, somewhat. Catherine and I have sort of adopted Zack. He came to work for me five years ago and has been an invaluable asset to the business. We truly love him like a son."

"John, I'm sure these children are starved. I asked Virginia to have Martha set the table in the sunroom for our lunch. I'll ring for Simpson to tell her we are ready."

Simpson appeared at once and was given instructions.

"Elizabeth dear, we have talked like magpies and haven't given you a chance to say a word. How was your room? Will you be comfortable there?" Catherine asked.

"It is a very lovely room and certainly more than adequate. Your home is so impressive. Have you lived here very long?" In this house, I mean?"

"Let us walk to the sunroom. I am sure Virginia will have the food ready to serve by now." Catherine took Elizabeth's arm and led the way.

"To answer your question, we have only lived here for six years. John felt he couldn't pass up the opportunity to buy this house when it was put on the market. We have loved living here."

"Zack, my boy, speak up and get into the conversation. We can't let these women folk get ahead of us," John interjected with a chuckle.

"Sometimes if one listens . . . one learns more, and I certainly want to learn more," Zachary said, casting a broad smile Elizabeth's way.

"Why, Mr. Bainbridge, just what do you wish to know?" Elizabeth replied, feigning innocence.

"Now that you've asked, I'd certainly like to know more about you, Miss Sloan," Zachary said.

"And so would Catherine and I," John added.

The food smelled delicious. Elizabeth realized how hungry she was. Could that possibly be blue crab salad, her very favorite? Indeed it was.

They finished a sumptuous meal and adjourned to the parlor. Zachary asked to be excused so that he might return to the office.

Chapter 10

"Well, Elizabeth, the time has come for us to talk about why you are here. First, we want to thank you for coming to Williamsburg," John said.

"There are things we feel you should know about us. First, we are born again believers. We strongly believe in seeking the Lord's guidance for our lives. We certainly sought His guidance regarding this situation. You need to know that our financial means are independently secure, and Morgan Shipping is not affiliated with any larger controlling unit. Morgan Shipping is *our* family owned company. I say that for no other reason but to give you the facts. We believe God has blessed our efforts. This is the reason we gave John Lee a substantial amount of money when he asked to try a venture on his own. We had the money to grant his wish. I remember, he laughed and said he did not want to play the part of the prodigal son. In light of what happened, how ironic that he should have said that.

"Elizabeth, your father, John Lee, was a very normal little boy. He showed unusual intelligence at a young age. He was a rough and tumble lad, mischievous at times but never mean-spirited.

"His mother and I had such high hopes for him. When he left home we expected that he would invest his time and money in a business venture and return home in a couple of years to tell us about it.

"You cannot imagine the anguish we have suffered. We did not try to locate him at first, but later we did try. We hired a private agency to find John Lee, but unsuccessfully. We did not know that he died three years after he left home until I just recently visited Garrison Wheeler."

"Do you have any questions?" John asked.

"I have no questions thus far, Mr. Morgan. But tell me more about your visit with Garrison Wheeler," Elizabeth said.

"Well, we received a letter from him on August 15th. Actually, he had someone write it for him. It was one paragraph saying he could give me information about my son. He gave me his address in Charlottesville. I went most of the way there and back by train, the rest of the way by stage.

"Elizabeth, Garrison was a very sick man. He said he had gone to an old fashioned revival about six months earlier and saw his need for salvation. He repented of his sins and gave his heart to the Lord. In the months that followed, the Lord impressed upon Mr. Wheeler to get in touch with me. If you remember, I wrote in my letter to your grandmother all that he told me. After he said his peace, he turned over and went to sleep.

"They were living very poorly . . . He, his daughter and her husband. His daughter had three children, all grown. They seemed like decent people but could not earn enough to get ahead. I made some financial arrangements to help them before I left Charlottesville. It was the least I could do for someone who was a friend to my son."

"What do you think happened to cause your son, my father, to do the things Mr. Wheeler said he did?" Elizabeth asked.

"I wish I knew, Elizabeth," John said with a sigh. "I wonder if something happened to his mind. But supposing won't get us answers. We simply have to let the past rest and move forward.

"However, I am convinced that what Garrison Wheeler told me is the truth. I wish it weren't, but he had no reason not to be honest with me.

"Changing the subject, Elizabeth, but when I first saw you I was stunned. Your resemblance to John Lee is striking. You have his hair, his eyes, even his dimples! My love for you is kindled by your likeness of him. I feel I have found new meaning to life. I do not ask you to return that love now. But please give us a chance. You would make me very happy indeed if you could find it in your heart to call me grandfather."

Catherine was drying tears from her eyes. She said in a trembling voice, "Elizabeth, I have kept quiet and let John share our hearts. We discussed what we felt needed to be said to you and agreed he should speak for this home. Now I want to say that I, too, love you. You are a part of John Lee . . . and a part of us. From being with you these few hours I believe you are an angel God has sent to us. We want to earn your love and respect. And I, too, hope you will come to the place that you will want to call me grandmother."

Elizabeth was overwhelmed by all she had heard. She remembered a scripture her "Dandy" had taught her in first John: "Beloved, believe not every spirit, but try the spirits whether they are of God." She felt a kindred spirit with these two beautiful people. She knew in her heart they were exactly who and what they said they were. They were truly believers! And they were her grandparents. Oh how she needed them in her life!

She stood to her feet and held out her arms to them. They came to her and the three of them embraced and cried tears of joy.

Elizabeth then kicked off her shoes and playfully asked, "May I go up stairs, crawl up in the middle of that beautiful bed and take a nap?"

Both her grandparents laughed heartily. Catherine said, "I will call Millie and she will turn the bed down and help you get into your night gown."

"No, no, Grandmother Catherine. I will do it myself."

With that she bounded out of the parlor with her shoes in hand and raced up the stairs in her stocking feet. Her grandparents heard her say loudly . . . "Now that was an 'unceremonial ascending' of this grand staircase!!"

Standing at the foot of the stairs, John and Catherine hugged each other, laughing joyously.

Catherine looked into her husband's tanned, handsome face and exclaimed, "John, we have found a treasure!"

Chapter 11

The next two weeks were spent getting acquainted with each other. They spent hours talking. John only went to his office when it was absolutely necessary. Elizabeth and Catherine would sit on the floor of the sunroom and chat away like school girls. Indeed, they were kindred spirits. Elizabeth was surprised that both her grandparents were only sixty-five. She had pictured them as being much older.

Grandmother Catherine was Elizabeth's same height, five feet six inches. Her hair was snow white and she wore it in a very becoming upsweep. She had soft brown eyes, making her look even younger than her years. Catherine loved sailing and was tanned from the sun. She had remained active in her later years and was slim and agile.

Elizabeth's Grandfather John was a tall man, a little over six feet. His broad shoulders were beginning to be a little stooped. His hair was more black than gray. He had aristocratic good looks and exhibited much of the warm courtesy, dignity and gesturing grace of a true Virginian. He seemed to have a "partnership with the ocean" as he spoke lovingly of sailing and shipping. He said it was in his blood. Elizabeth thought he was one of the most interesting people she had ever met . . . and he was her grandfather!

Elizabeth told them about Willow Place and her great love for it. She spoke of her growing up years and how "Dandy" and her Grandmother Savannah had been more like her parents than her grandparents. Elizabeth spoke softly and lovingly of her mother, Victoria. She was so young when her mother became very ill and died. But she remembered being loved and held by her mother.

Elizabeth told them that she barely remembered the man she thought to be her father, James Alex Sloan. But learning of her mother Victoria's undying love for him, she nurtured a respect for the man he was. She said she felt more like her name should be Baldwin than Sloan. She could not connect with that name since she never really knew him that well.

In sharing with each other these past two weeks, Elizabeth's new-found grandfather said he wanted to make a proposal to her.

"Elizabeth, I have been thinking about what you said about the name of Sloan. Would you consider having your name legally changed?"

"What do you have in mind, grandfather?" Elizabeth said.

"Well, since no blood runs in your veins from Alex Sloan, and your true blood line is from the Baldwins and the Morgans, I am thinking of Elizabeth Ann Baldwin Morgan. I realize it would take some getting used to. Your long-time friends in Richmond would have to get used to it. But, Elizabeth, your life is different now and will continue to be. Is it too difficult a thing to ask of you, my dear? Do you think me selfish?"

"Dear, dear grandfather. I could never think of you as selfish. It is a surprising suggestion but certainly not unreasonable. You are right. My life is different now. The last two weeks have been quite a revelation for all of us. It has changed all of our lives forever. To assume the names of both my grandparents is very appealing to me."

"Then I have your permission to start the legal work right away?" John asked.

"Yes. Will it take long?"

"Perhaps a month. Maybe sooner."

Catherine spoke up, "I feel as if I am dreaming. The Lord has been so gracious to us since John wrote the letter to your Grandmother Baldwin . . . uh, Grandmother Savannah I believe you call her. I only wish she could have lived to know about all of this."

With a far away look in her eyes, Elizabeth replied, "Yes, and so do I."

Catherine added, "Elizabeth dear, I also have a question for you."

"Yes, grandmother, what is it?"

"I have been thinking of having a cotillion in your honor to introduce you to a few of our friends. It might require you staying a week longer than you planned. Today is November 29th. I would have to get invitations sent. It will take some doing, but I think we could be ready by December 16th. People expect to go to parties at Christmas time. You could plan on going back to Richmond on December 18th and still be there for Christmas. What do you think of my idea?"

"Thank you for your thoughtfulness, grandmother. But I really do need to get back home. Suppose we schedule the cotillion for February. That would give you time to plan it without rushing and would give me a good reason to return. Besides, I want to spend as much time with you and grandfather as possible on this trip. When Zachary was here for dinner night before last, he asked if I would go to dinner with him tonight. I accepted his invitation. I have enjoyed the few times we have seen each other since I've been here. I will be going back to Richmond on Saturday, so I feel I must spend my time as wisely as possible between now and then. Do you mind terribly if we wait?"

"No, my dear," Catherine replied. "I think you are right. We will plan a proper party for you then."

"It is getting late and Zachary will be here soon. I must begin to get ready. I should have told you earlier that I would not be here for dinner tonight. I hope it will not inconvenience your dinner plans for this evening," Elizabeth said.

"No, we had planned a light meal of leftovers. Go with our blessings. Remember, Zachary is a wonderful, unattached young man, Elizabeth."

She replied, "Yes, I know. I know."

Chapter 12

*Z*achary was right on time. He arrived exactly at 6:30. This is one thing that impressed Elizabeth. She was a stickler for promptness, always had been.

They said goodnight to the Morgans and hurried to the awaiting carriage. The full moon shone so brightly it hardly seemed like nighttime.

"Elizabeth, we are going to a favorite restaurant of mine. It is called Cuisine by the River. Their food is excellent. I have a favorite table with a view of the river. With the full moon we will be able to see it reflecting on the water."

"It sounds delightful, Zachary."

He was right. The food *was* delicious. The large window framed the James River like a picture. The silvery moonbeams added to its charm.

Conversation flowed easily between them that night. It was as if they had always known each other.

They finished their meal and Zachary reached for Elizabeth's hand. Their gaze was fixed on each other. She began to tremble inside and was powerless to move her hand. She found the moment much to her liking. When they left the restaurant, Zachary asked their carriage driver to go down by the river. It was surprisingly warm for the last of November. There was a garden area with a bench facing the river. Zachary dismissed the carriage driver, asking him to return in an hour.

Zachary waited until Elizabeth was seated. Then he propped one foot on the bench, leaned on his knee with his forearm and said, "Elizabeth, I want to talk seriously with you. I think you know I am very fond of you. Our acquaintance has been brief but I have never seen anyone like you nor known anyone like you."

Raising his hand in a gesture to quiet her as she was about to speak, he continued, "No, Elizabeth. Hear me out. When I first laid eyes on you in Richmond you were like an apparition. I could not believe you were real. But you were. And since I have spent time with you, I find your inner person is as beautiful as the outward."

Zachary changed his position and perched on the edge of the bench facing her. "Like you, Elizabeth, I have been raised in a Christian home and cannot imagine life any other way. It is a great treasure to find someone whose Christian principles are so strong. What I am trying to say is my feelings for you go far deeper than just a passing fancy. Dare I hope that you might be interested in me? Or is there a special person in your life already?"

Elizabeth stood to her feet and walked a few steps away from him. Turning she said, "Zachary, I would be less than truthful if I did not tell you that I felt drawn to you from the very beginning. It's been a magnetic feeling. I find you equally attractive. But Zachary, you will have to admit that our relationship has been in a romantic setting from the start. Everything has been perfect. Romance, as such, is not always real. It can mask true feelings. Remember my mother and father? He simply swept her off her feet. Then look at how it ended. I have to be sure. You do understand, don't you?"

"Yes, I understand," Zachary said. "But I feel that God has had something to do with this."

"If He means a future for us, Zachary, then it will happen. Can we trust Him for that?"

"We have no choice, do we?"

Chapter 12

"Zachary, as you know, I plan to leave for Richmond on Saturday, December 10th. Grandmother wants to have a cotillion for me in February. I will be returning then. We can write in the mean time. We will see how we feel when the reality of everyday living resumes. True love of two people will always pass the test of time."

"Do you always have to be so right?" Zachary said.

The carriage rounded the corner. They must be getting on their way.

Chapter 13

*E*lizabeth awakened early and lay in bed for a few minutes stretching and yawning lazily. She looked around the room that had been hers for the past two and a half weeks. She loved the brightness of it. She got out of bed slowly, tip-toed across the room, opening the draperies. The early morning sun felt warm through the windowpane. She put on her pale blue "robe-de- chambre." It had a front button closure, was loose fitting with long, slightly gathered sleeves and gathered frills at the cuffs. The sleeves had a button closing. Her Grandmother Savannah had given her this robe last year for her birthday. Elizabeth loved it. She slipped her feet into her matching booties, warmly lined.

There was a knock at the door.

"Come in. Good morning, Millie."

"Good morning, Miss Elizabeth. Mrs. Morgan says breakfast is being served shortly."

"Thank you, Millie. I'll be right down."

Her grandfather rose to his feet when Elizabeth entered. He gave her a kiss on the cheek, turned to Catherine and said, "Your granddaughter is a vision of loveliness, just like her grandmother!"

Elizabeth blushed and asked, "Grandmother Catherine, is he always such a flatterer?"

It was a leisurely breakfast with good food and conversation.

Finally, Elizabeth excused herself to go get dressed for church. Before she left, her grandfather said, "Elizabeth, your grandmother and I would like to talk with you this afternoon if we may."

"That will be fine, grandfather."

Elizabeth chose to wear her navy blue silk dress with matching color lace at the neck, long fitted sleeves, and a silk ribbon belt. She especially liked the unlined, long skirt. The deep stiff hemline gave it a look of fullness. Most of the gathers of the skirt were to the back making Elizabeth's figure look smooth and flat.

She put on her matching bonnet with pleated edging on the narrow brim. She tied the ribbons to one side under her chin and wrapped her short gray cape around her shoulders. She tried to walk lady-like down the steps but really wanted to slide down the bannister! Maybe someday.

They arrived at the church early. The parishioners were friendly. Her grandparents were introducing her to so many of their friends she scarcely heard their names. Reverend Perkins was genuinely warm and friendly. He had a firm handshake. She liked him.

Just before Reverend Perkins spoke, he had the congregation stand and sing "Nearer My God to Thee." It was one of Elizabeth's favorite hymns.

The sermon topic was "How to Better Understand God's Word."

The reverend opened by saying, "It is said the Bible is a rich treasure house of truths. Yet many people do not know how to unlock its rich storehouse because they are not using the right keys."

He spoke so eloquently, giving the congregation the keys that would unlock the treasure house of God's word. He took his text from the books of John, II Timothy, and the 17th chapter of Acts. He commented that to read God's word without knowing Jesus Christ as our savior would only lead to an outward, intellectual knowledge of the Bible, devoid of joy and the peace that comes with salvation. The message was inspirational and thought provoking.

Elizabeth enjoyed the service. But she felt a sense of homesickness for her church in Richmond. It would be good to get back there.

Riding back home in her grandfather's carriage, Elizabeth remarked to him, "I've been meaning to tell you what a nice carriage this is, grandfather."

"It is a nice carriage. The advertising brochure called it a Landau. It was designed in 1743 in Bavaria, Germany. It has a removable top and a raised seat outside for the driver, as I'm sure you've noticed. I've always had a fascination with carriages. I feel there are many things that can be done to make them more comfortable. I bought this one in your hometown of Richmond from a business acquaintance."

"Could it be Mr. Payton Randolph? He owns a carriage manufacturing company in Richmond. My Grandfather Baldwin bought our carriage from him."

"Yes, it was Mr. Randolph, and he certainly does good work. When I bought this Landau I looked over his operation. I was very impressed."

"Leaving the carriage talk, Elizabeth, may I ask what you thought of the church service this morning?" her grandfather inquired.

"Oh, I was going to tell you how much I enjoyed the service. The people were very gracious.

Your choir group sang beautifully. I especially liked "In the Garden." It lifted my spirits! You are blessed to have Reverend Perkins as pastor. He made his message so interesting. Time went by quickly. The Apostle Paul's life was quite a journey! Reverend Perkins made him come alive to us, don't you agree?"

"Yes, and we are indeed blessed to have him here at First Wesleyan," her grandmother added.

They had finished lunch and were comfortably seated in the sunroom.

"I am going to miss your sunroom. The view of the James River is so calming. The occasional sailboat that goes by lends a romantic touch. Everyone should have a sunroom and a James River!"

"Elizabeth," her grandfather spoke up, "that brings me to what we want to talk with you about. You have been in our home and in our hearts for only 18 days, but it seems like a lifetime. Your easy spirit and laughter has filled this home of ours. From our long conversations with you, we believe we know your values and they certainly agree with ours.

"Again, we have a proposal to make. We would be two of the happiest people in the world if you would consent to move here to Williamsburg and make this your home. What we have is yours. To prove what I am saying, I have an appointment with my lawyer tomorrow. I will be rewriting my will to include you. Except for some charities, you will be our sole heir. Oh Elizabeth, *please* say you will consider our offer."

Elizabeth could not see for the tears that filled her eyes. She tried to speak but could not. It took her a few minutes to gain her composure.

"I'm completely overwhelmed by your generosity. Your proposal is very tempting. I have loved being here. This is the grandest home I have ever been in. I have been awe struck by the beauty of it all. At times, I've felt I needed to pinch myself to see if I am dreaming.

"How do I tell you what I must without seeming ungrateful and causing you pain? Let me begin by saying I would have felt no differently about you if you lived in a small house on a back road and could barely make ends meet. You are beautiful people to me. You are my grandparents. Grandparents who *want* me, who *love* me, *unconditionally*. This is what makes you special to me. I'm happy for you that through hard work and good management you are people of means, but that has no bearing on my feelings for you.

"However, I must decline your invitation to come here and live. You see, Willow Place is my home. I can't tell you how I love it there. It holds so many *good* memories for me. I love Richmond. That is where I want to live and marry, raise my children and grow old. You might not understand me being so young and having such deep feelings. But I was raised by my Baldwin grandparents who instilled old-fashioned values in me.

"I'm not rejecting you in my life. I *want* you, and must *have* you in my life. We need to spend as much time together as we possibly can. You must come visit me at Willow Place. It is not grand, but it is good! I pray you understand. And I certainly want to come back here as often as possible. We are family now. Our lives are very much connected. Distance can't change that. Please try and understand my decision."

"Dear Elizabeth, perhaps we have been unfair to ask you to come here to live," Catherine said. "We simply cannot imagine our home now without you. Your grandfather and I have been revitalized since you've been here. Now it seems like a selfish idea, and that we are thinking only of ourselves."

"Elizabeth, I am taken aback by your insight to life. How can we be so blessed as to have you in our lives? I can assure you that as long as we live, you will be a part of us," her grandfather declared.

"Now, my dear and special grandparents, I have a request."

Looking surprised, her grandmother said, "*Anything,* Elizabeth. What is it?"

"I want to slide down the bannister on that grand staircase!!!"

Following her, they laughed as she bounded out of the sunroom, up the stairs. She gathered her full dress between her legs, sat astride the bannister and swoosh . . . down she came. She exclaimed, "I'm gonna' do it again!"

What a joy this granddaughter was to them.

Chapter 14

DECEMBER 6
TUESDAY

*E*lizabeth was in the parlor awaiting Zachary's arrival. The door opened and Simpson showed him in. On first sight, she always marveled at his good looks. He was wearing a black high-neck, snug-fitting sweater under his tweed jacket. He looked like a winter-time sailor!

He spoke in his deep resonant voice, "Good evening, Elizabeth. I've missed you."

Her heart began to race, so she had to get their conversation on a safe subject.

"Zachary, we have seen each other several times since I have been here. You have told me about your family that lives in Norfolk. I've enjoyed hearing about your brother Thomas' two children, Joey and Heather. I know you love them very much. You've told me about your love of sailing and your dream, someday, to own a large sailboat. But you haven't said much about your job with Morgan Shipping. Do you like working there?"

"Indeed I do. It has been a very challenging job. John placed a lot of trust in me when he hired me. He gave a young man a chance of a lifetime and I'm deeply indebted to him."

"He says the same thing about you. In his words, he never has to worry when you are in charge of a shipment. He knows it will be handled correctly and fairly. He chuckles and says often times customers ask for you over him. He says you have strengthened Morgan Shipping. My grandparents are very fond of you, Zachary."

Changing the subject, Elizabeth, but do you realize in just four more days you will be gone?"

Zachary lamented.

"Yes, and it makes me sad to think of leaving people I have grown to care for so deeply."

"Then do you have to go? You know you could stay here and make this your home. Your grandfather shared with me the proposal he was going to make to you. Has he talked with you about it?"

"Yes, he did just this afternoon. But Zachary, I had to say no. You see, I have a home. It is a part of me. It has been a stabilizing force in my life and represents my Baldwin grandparents who raised me as their own. Upon my Grandmother Savannah's death, it became mine. My home is surrounded by beauty and space. Do you know why it is called Willow Place?"

"No, Elizabeth. Of course I don't," Zachary said.

"Because it has many huge, healthy and lush weeping willow trees . . . my very favorite tree in the whole world! When I look out in the morning they are the first things I see . . . so graceful, so wispy, so green . . . And so romantic! At least to me they are. It's like I told my grandparents, I want to live there, marry there, raise my children and grow old there."

"You feel very strongly about this, I see. I can *imagine* your grandparents' disappointment. I would like to see this place that has such a hold on you."

"Oh, Zachary. I'm so glad to hear you say that. You must come for a visit. Will you?"

"My dear, you can count on it."

Chapter 15

DECEMBER 10
SATURDAY

*E*lizabeth hugged first one and then the other of her grandparents. She touched their faces, lovingly, and brought herself to bid them goodbye. She looked each of them in the eyes and told them how important they were to her.

"I will return for the cotillion in February," Elizabeth reminded them.

They promised her they would not cry at her departing, but their newfound Granddaughter had carved a special place in their hearts. She continued to wave to them until she could see them no longer. She turned to look at Zachary who was going with her to the Williamsburg train depot. He was staring straight ahead. Elizabeth could see the muscles tightening in his jaw line as he seemed thoughtful and almost aloof this morning. Her leaving was difficult for him she knew. She remembered what he said to her last evening after dinner at her grandparents' house. He didn't stay long but spoke openly and passionately.

"Elizabeth, permit me to tell you how I feel. Considering that we've known each other such a short time I've tried to be discreet. But I am twenty-five years old now, and have never been frivolous with my emotions toward women. When I marry I want it to be for life. So I've guarded my feelings for just the right person. To say 'I love you' might seem too forward. But my heart betrays me, and what must be said cannot be contained any longer. So, Elizabeth Ann Sloan, I love you with all of my heart."

Those words swirled around in her head most of last night. And as they resounded again in her mind, she thought how the last two months had changed her life forever. Now she was gloriously happy and had found new meaning for a life that was full of loss when she came here. As for family, she came to Williamsburg without one. Now, she has doting grandparents whom she loves without any reservations. And yes, she has found a man so dear she longs to spend the rest of her life with him. But she has to be cautious. She simply could not make the same mistake her mother, Victoria, had made. Self discipline had always been so easy for Elizabeth until now. Tears stung her eyes and rolled down her cheeks.

"Where is my handkerchief? I must have dropped it." She leaned over to look for it.

When Elizabeth spoke, Zachary turned to look at her. He saw the tears and leaned over himself to retrieve her handkerchief from the carriage floor. Their heads bumped together.

"I seem to remember this happening before," Zachary said as he reached for her arm and tucked it under his, holding her hand.

They pulled into the train depot with some time to spare. The Porter unloaded Elizabeth's baggage and the carriage driver pulled away, parking near the door to the depot. Elizabeth had her ticket so they decided to sit in the carriage rather than go inside.

Zachary said sadly, "The day I've dreaded so has finally come and the girl of whom I have grown so fond is returning to her Willow Place."

Elizabeth responded, "I've been thinking about what you said to me last evening, Zachary. It was going over and over in my mind most of the night. I've always relied on my good judgment when making friends and I'm seldom misled in my judgment. The fact that my grandparents have known you intimately for the last five years, and grandfather knew you even before that as a fellow sailor, makes me feel that I am right in my judgment of you. I feel very free to tell you that I love you, too. But I will tell you again, I'm going home to Willow Place and resume my life there. I'm very involved in the First Wesleyan Church in Richmond. Christmas is near and that is a very important time for the children of the church. I always help with their programs. In the mean time, we can be in touch by letter. I will be returning here on the eighth of February."

"Elizabeth, to have heard you say the words 'I love you' is all I ask for now. I will prove myself to you. You will not regret the confidence you have placed in me."

The sound of the train whistle jarred them back to reality. Elizabeth reached for her hand bag, preparing to alight from the carriage. Zachary touched her arm gently and reached for her chin. Cupping it in his hand, he leaned forward and kissed her upturned face and then moved to her beautiful lips and kissed them gently but with the warmth of his great love for her.

Taking Elizabeth by surprise, the moment left her breathless and light-headed. This was her very first kiss.

Zachary stepped out of the carriage and assisted Elizabeth. He felt as though he was walking on air.

Elizabeth was wearing the same green velvet dress she wore the day he first saw her at the train depot in Richmond on November 16th. That day would forever be *their* day.

The train pulled away from the depot and Elizabeth looked out the window at Zachary until she could see him no more.

Zachary said to himself, "I won't be there to pick up her handkerchief if she drops it, and I know she will!"

Chapter 16

Sunday, the eleventh of December, Elizabeth awakened in her own bed. She went to her bedroom window, looked out over the lake and watched the early morning sunshine dancing on the water. There was a brisk breeze blowing the skirts . . . as she called them . . . of those gorgeous weeping willow trees. How many times had she done this very thing but it always seemed brand new. She drank in the beauty that surrounded her.

Elizabeth had been so glad to see Emma, Sadie and William, her faithful friends. They had a grand homecoming meal prepared for her when she arrived yesterday. She had so much to share with them when the time was right.

Sunday morning breakfast was oatmeal, toast and a cup of coffee.

Elizabeth went straight to the Sunday school area. She hoped her very special friend, Jane Abigail Adams, had arrived. She loved Jane's name; loved the way it sounded when she said it altogether. They had been very close for the past two years.

Jane was a schoolteacher. She was petite, feisty and fun-loving. At school, during recess, she would pull her full-skirted dress between her legs and jump rope with the girls. Jane had even been known to draw a circle and play marbles with the boys! She had taken some of the kids fishing at Willow Lake and could bait a hook with earthworms as good as anyone.

Elizabeth heard someone call her name. She turned around to see Jane with outstretched arms. They gave each other a big hug.

Jane exclaimed, "It seems you've been gone a year! But you got back just in time. Planning for the Christmas program is now getting underway."

"That's one reason I was anxious to get back. Oh Jane, Christmas is so special . . . for many reasons. But my first Christmas without Grandmother Savannah will also be sad. That is why I must be busy."

"I know, Elizabeth. The past two months must have been difficult for you. The trip to Williamsburg has been a mystery to so many who care for you. I can't wait to hear about it. It's time for Sunday school to begin and we must get to our classes. See you after church," and Jane hurried off.

After the service Jane asked Elizabeth to go home with her. It was always a treat to go to the Adams' house. They lived close to the church on Charter Street. Mr. Adams was a jovial man and a teaser. Mrs. Adams was just as feisty and full of life as Jane. They had four other children, three boys and a girl, all younger than Jane. Jim, Jr. was 17, very lean and muscular.

Joe, 14, was almost as big as Jim. Josh was the one who touched Elizabeth's heart. He was 12 and all boy, very funny and always happy. Little Jenny didn't have a chance. At age eight, she was spoiled by them all.

After lunch, Elizabeth helped Jane tidy up the kitchen. It was a blustery, winter day but they bundled up and walked to a small park nearby. Sitting on a bench, Jane said, "I'm listening!"

Elizabeth began her story of the events that happened after her grandmother's death. She covered as much as she could in the time they had together. Jane listened intently, desiring to know as much as possible about the life-changing events that had happened to Elizabeth. She was mesmerized by it all, especially about this Zachary Bainbridge.

This had been a great release for Elizabeth. She had needed to share all of this with someone . . . someone who would really care and Jane Abigail Adams was just the person!

Elizabeth reached into her deep dress pocket and brought out her Grandfather Baldwin's gold pocket watch to check the time. It was 5:30 . . . almost church time, and it was getting dusky dark. They must hurry.

After church the Christmas program committee decided to meet Monday at 5:00 P.M. Service had ended a little early and Elizabeth was glad. She was more tired than she realized. William climbed in the driver's seat of their carriage. Elizabeth, Emma and Sadie sat close together on the ride home. It seemed to be getting colder. Elizabeth felt very content. These were dear and comforting people in her life.

After the Christmas committee finished a successful planning session on Monday, Elizabeth and Jane lingered for a talk.

"Jane, I've been thinking about doing some volunteer work at the East Richmond Hospital after Christmas. I'd like to use my time wisely and feel that I am contributing to my community. What do you think?"

"Why Elizabeth, that's an excellent idea. Phillip has a doctor friend that's on the staff there. Phillip can ask him if they need anyone."

"Speaking of Phillip, I have missed seeing him these past two months since grandmother died. I had hoped he would be at church yesterday. What is he doing these days?"

"Oh, you know Phillip Gregory Maxwell III . . . he is into a little bit of everything, from lawyering to politicking. But this weekend he is bogged down in a land dispute case and had to spend time doing research. We plan to see each other on Tuesday night. I'll ask him to inquire if they need help at East Richmond."

———————

Elizabeth heard the jingle of the bells before the sleigh arrived at Willow Place. It was Monday, the nineteenth of December, and the snow measured six inches. It had snowed late yesterday and last night. About lunch time the snow had stopped falling and the sun was shining brightly. However, it was still very cold out.

Elizabeth wasn't expecting anyone, but she heard laughter, then a loud knock.

Emma opened the door and in rushed Jane, Phillip, and a man she did not know.

"Hi Elizabeth, Miss Emma. Can you believe all this wonderful snow?! We sent the school kids home early today, those that made it. Phillip came by in his sleigh and brought his friend, Dr. David Blake. We decided to drop by and see if you would like to sleigh ride with us, Elizabeth?"

"Why yes," exclaimed Elizabeth, "I'll be right back." Emma, please offer them some of your spicy, hot apple cider." As she bounded out of the room she called over her shoulder, "It won't take me but a minute to get my coat and mittens. Don't leave without me!"

"Elizabeth loves sleigh rides better than most anyone I know," Emma said as she came back with cups of hot cider.

Jane turned toward Phillip and said, "I told you she would be downright giddy about going!"

Elizabeth ran down the stairs all bundled up. Her cheeks were flushed. She said, "It is a pleasure to meet you Dr. Blake. I'm afraid in my excitement I wasn't very proper."

"My pleasure, Elizabeth, if I may call you that."

"Emma, don't look for me until you see me coming!"

They all four crowded through the door, flew down the steps, jumped into the sleigh and were off. They sang, stopped for a snowball fight, and marveled at the beauty that surrounded them. They saw three rabbits sitting very still in the snow until the sleigh approached. Then they hopped away. The squirrels chased each other up and down the trees, falling into the snow occasionally. Phillip spotted five dear in an oak grove. Then they stopped in Richmond at a small restaurant for hot chocolate, a ham sandwich and some pound cake.

"What a fun day this has been, and so unexpected," Elizabeth said contentedly.

"By the way, Elizabeth, Phillip told me you might be interested in some volunteer work after Christmas at East Richmond Hospital. Are you still interested?"

"Yes, I am."

"We could certainly use your services in the children's ward. You can stop by and the head nurse will be glad to talk with you about it."

"Then I will do that on Monday the 28th."

"Ask to see Nurse Kim Thomas. I will tell her you are coming," Dr. Blake said.

They were standing outside the restaurant. The sun had really warmed things up and they had left their hats and heavy coats in the carriage.

Fun-loving Jane said, "I'll race all of you to the carriage!" and she was off like a race horse out of the starting gate.

Phillip said playfully, "You don't play fair, little Jane," and he sprinted right behind her.

Then Dr. Blake was off and running, so Elizabeth dashed right behind.

All of a sudden Dr. Blake slipped and took a nose dive right into the fluffy snow. He looked so funny falling that Elizabeth started laughing. To her it was hilarious! Not watching what she was doing, the next thing she knew her feet were tangled up and she fell backwards into the snow too. She sure enough laughed then!

Dr. Blake was on his feet by this time. Standing over her, looking magnificent in his black jacket and green plaid scarf, he chided, "Uh huh . . . that's what you get for laughing, my dear!"

He reached down with both hands and said, "Take hold and let me help you up." He gave a quick tug and literally jerked her into his arms. Looking her right in the eyes he exclaimed, "*You* are a beautiful woman!" After steadying her on her feet he turned her loose.

With a gleam in her eye she said, "Race you," and away she went. Her long black hair bouncing against her red wool sweater as she ran made him more aware of what a lovely creature this Elizabeth really was.

Phillip, who had observed this scene, turned to Jane and remarked, "Hmm . . . that looked interesting."

Of course, he had no way of knowing about Zachary Bainbridge.

Elizabeth snuggled in between the warm blankets on her bed. As tired as she was, she could not go to sleep. Her mind was spinning. She thought of Jane and Phillip. They seemed a perfect match. Phillip was a nice young man . . . about five feet ten inches tall, just right for petite Jane. His hair was as blonde as the sun, thick and wavy. But it is his laughing blue eyes that draw the most attention. He has a wide mouth and a cleft chin, really quite handsome.

Dr. Blake's face kept popping up in her mind. He was a lot of fun!

She finally drifted off into a peaceful, dreamless sleep.

Awaking refreshed, Elizabeth went downstairs to the kitchen for breakfast.

"Good morning, Emma. What's for breakfast. I'm starved!"

"Good morning, Elizabeth. I have the small biscuits with ham you like so much and an egg omelette. I just put them in the warmer on the stove."

"Where are William and Sadie?"

"They ate earlier. They both had chores that needed doing."

"Emma, today is the twentieth of December. We've made some progress on decorating our Christmas tree but we need to finish it today. Do you think we could all do that together this afternoon?"

"That we can lassie. I'll tell Sadie and William. You brighten our lives so by including us in such special things."

"Special things are meant to be shared by special people, Emma dear."

William had a roaring fire going in the fireplace. Sadie had found the box of Christmas decorations that were saved each year.

Elizabeth lifted the lid from the box. A nostalgic feeling swept over her. She remembered her Grandmother Savannah's dainty hands lovingly lifting the ornaments from the box last Christmas.

Chapter 16

"Emma, do you and Sadie remember all these ornaments from years gone by as I do?"

"Oh yes, lassie. Several of them Judge Baldwin brought back from a trip to New York. Mrs. Baldwin always said they were her favorites."

"Miss Elizabeth, I remember the first Christmas after we came to work for Judge Baldwin. You were just nine years old. Judge Baldwin would hold you up in his arms and let you hang these ornaments on the tree. You would be delighted and his eyes would just shine," Sadie recalled with a smile.

William spoke up saying, "Christmas time was very special to him. Your grandfather always had to go with me to choose the tree for the house. He would say, 'It's got to be just right for Elizabeth.' My how he did adore you."

Elizabeth loved hearing these stories.

When the decorating job was finished they sat around the fire, popped corn and drank hot apple cider while admiring the beautiful tree and talking over old times.

Chapter 17

Nighttime had fallen on Christmas Day . . . her first without her beloved grandmother. The Christmas program at church proved to be a blessing. The children came through as they always did. Christmas morning service was very sacred. Pastor Davis, always so well prepared, painted a beautiful picture with words of that very first Christmas. The glorious Christmas carols still rang in her head.

She let her mind travel back to Williamsburg. She had purposely stayed busy since returning from there. The longing to see her grandparents this Christmas season was very painful. Her longing to see Zachary was almost unbearable.

January 1, 1856 . . . the start of a brand new year. *What would this year bring to her and those she loved?* Elizabeth wondered. Many changes, without a doubt.

On Monday, January 2nd, Elizabeth went to work at East Richmond Hospital. She reported to head nurse Kim Thomas.

"We desperately needed someone in our children's ward, Miss Sloan. We are so happy to have you as a volunteer."

"I'm glad to assist any way I can."

"Your main duty will be to try cheering up the sick children. Reading to them is always a welcomed diversion from their discomfort. But some are too sick for that. They need someone to sit with them while their parents can't be here. Some just need a cool cloth placed on their foreheads. I believe from our conversation on the 28th that your perceptive ability will guide you. If you find you have questions any of our nurses can help you. Now I will show you to the children's ward."

At the end of the day Elizabeth found that time had passed so quickly. Her buggy was parked in the hospital stables and she was on her way to it when she heard someone call her name. She turned to see that it was Dr. David Blake.

"Say, beautiful woman, how did you like your first day as a volunteer in the children's ward?"

"It has been quite an eye-opener. It takes a day like this to let one see into the world of suffering some people bear. I am thankful and humbled by it, I can tell you."

"That is a very good report. It is a pity you aren't a nurse. You would be a dandy. By the way, after our tumble in the snow, I think we are well acquainted enough that you can drop the doctor, outside the hospital, and call me David."

"That seems like a fair request."

David was smitten by this creature. Where had she been hiding? He had been on staff at East Richmond for the past two years, but their paths had never crossed until the sleigh ride on December 19th.

By this time they had reached her buggy. The stable boy hooked Charlie up to the buggy and David helped Elizabeth up. "Are you going straight home?" he inquired.

"No, I'm going by the mercantile for a few items first."

"It is just now three o'clock. I have one more patient to see and I will have finished my shift. I had hoped to see you today but only caught a glimpse of you as you passed through the door coming outside. Could we possibly meet at the café for a cup of coffee? We should both be finished about the same time."

"Sure thing. I have some questions I'd like to ask you. See you in thirty minutes," and with that she rode off.

Chapter 17

Elizabeth opened the door to the café and David was already there with two cups of steaming coffee on their table. He rose to his feet and pulled out her chair for her to be seated.

"Hmm, the coffee smells delicious. Been here long?"

"No, I just walked in minutes ago. I'm curious, what are the questions you had for me?"

"Do you know the little girl about five years old named Emily in room 43? She has pneumonia."

"Yes, oh yes. We've been worried about her," David said.

"What can you tell me about her, about her family?"

"She comes from an impoverished family. Her father works at a saw mill. It is hard work and long hours. He makes very little money. He and Mrs. Everette have two other children, both little girls. One is four and the other is seven if I remember correctly."

"What caused her to have pneumonia?"

"She was a premature baby and had a struggle in life from the start. Emily was very sick before they brought her to us. We are making some headway in her case we believe. The whole family is undernourished as you can imagine. This doesn't help."

Elizabeth responded, "Then this answers my question about why she is alone most of the time. Her father works long hours and her mother has two other children to care for. How sad."

"Elizabeth, we do what we can for our patients. In my kind of work, we see a lot of heartache and sadness. But we also see a lot of good things happen for people. Nor can we get too involved with people's problems. If so, we would become so over worked we would be very little good to anyone. And remember, the Lord himself said, 'ye have the poor always with you.' Don't think me brutish. It is the truth. Now, brighten up that beautiful face and give me a smile. There . . . That's much better."

"David, did you have a particular reason for wanting to see me? I must be starting back home."

"Elizabeth, I can't deny that I am attracted to you. I guess I just wanted to be in your presence. It has been two weeks since we went on the sleigh ride excursion. I have missed you. Is there a chance I might see you on a regular basis?"

"David, I am flattered. I certainly enjoyed our time together with Jane and Phillip. I must tell you that there is someone else. He lives in Williamsburg. We have not yet made a commitment to each other but I believe it will happen."

"Well, I might have known someone like you wouldn't be available. But since there is no commitment, could we at least be friends and see each other on occasion?"

"Again I say that seems like a fair request."

⎯⎯⎯

Elizabeth had signed up to work three days a week at the hospital for four hours a day. She would not go back in until Wednesday at 11:00.

She had been waiting for some mail from her grandparents and from Zachary. It had been twenty-four days since she left Williamsburg. She had written her grandparents a note on the twelfth of December telling them what a lovely time she had and how much she missed them. In her note to Zachary she reminded him of her invitation for him to visit Willow Place.

She road Blazer out to the main road to their mail box. Swinging down from the saddle, she hurriedly opened the box, and found a number of letters. There was one from her grandparents and one from Zachary!

Her heart began to race just knowing that he had held this letter in his hands. Remounting Blazer she rode back to her favorite place on the lake underneath the largest weeping willow tree. She tied Blazer to a hitching post her grandfather had put there for her. He knew how she loved to ride Blazer to her special spot and sit under her special tree.

Elizabeth held the letter to her heart for the longest before she opened it. The envelope had a faint scent of Zachary from his shaving lotion.

She carefully opened the letter and began to read . . .

Chapter 17

Tuesday, 13 December
Williamsburg

Elizabeth, my love:
You have been gone four days. Since when did four days constitute an eternity? For me it has been just that.

I have gone back to Cuisine By the River to find you but you were not there. I've been back to our bench in the garden by the river but you were not there. I feel I am chasing an elusive butterfly!

Then I remember the touch of your lips against mine and I know you are real. But I long to see you, to touch you, to smell the fragrance of your hair and to hear your sweet voice.

By the time you receive this it will be into the month of January. Then I will have to wait at least three weeks to receive a reply, if you answer immediately.

I agree with your statement, "True love will stand the test of time," but my longing for you will only be stayed when I see you again.

Faithfully yours,
Zackary

Elizabeth read it over and over. In her mind she could see his face, his eyes . . . a deep violet blue that pierced her heart when their eyes met. And she, too, could still feel the warmth of his lips on hers during that one fleeting kiss.

The old saying "absence makes the heart grow fonder" was proving to be true.

She turned her attention to the letter from her grandparents. They told her how much they missed her and how they were anxiously awaiting for February 8th to come.

Enclosed was the official certificate of her name being changed to Elizabeth Ann Baldwin Morgan. This meant so much to them.

Now she would begin to make changes in all of her legal documents.

She must go now. She had some letters to write! Elizabeth remounted Blazer and rode like the wind circling the lake. The cold wind blowing in her face felt so good. She took Blazer to the barn and asked William to take off the saddle and rub him down.

Entering the house through the kitchen, she called out, "Emma, where are you?"

"I'm in the pantry straightening up the shelves, lassie."

Elizabeth stuck her head in the door of the large, well-stocked pantry and said, "Emma, I'd like you, Sadie and William to meet me in the library in an hour. Will you tell Sadie for me? I just told William when I took Blazer to the barn. I'll be waiting in the library."

"I'll tell Sadie. We will meet you there in an hour."

Elizabeth knew the time had come for her to tell them what had taken place in her life. She had the official document showing that her name was no longer Sloan but Morgan. Her friend Jane was the only one she had confided in fully about the Morgan's and their desire to have her come to Williamsburg to live. They also needed to know about Zachary. However, before their talk she needed to write a couple of letters.

She sat in her Grandfather Baldwin's leather chair behind his massive old desk and began to write to Zachary.

Chapter 18

JANUARY 23

WILLIAMSBURG

Several pieces of mail were delivered to Morgan Shipping this Monday morning. John Morgan was flipping through it. His eyes fastened on the matching ecru envelopes with cockle edges where they were sealed. He recognized the stationery from the short note they had received from Elizabeth after she returned to Richmond from Williamsburg. One letter was addressed to him and Catherine. The other one was addressed to Zachary.

John walked quickly down the hall and into Zack's office, waving the letters in the air.

"Zack, I can't think of a better way to start off a Monday morning than this!"

He handed him the letter from Elizabeth. Zachary's whole countenance changed. He turned it over and over in his hands wanting to rip it open quickly and yet wanting to savor the idea of it.

"I'll leave you alone to read it, Zack. I'm so anxious myself to see what our little girl has to say," John said as he left the office.

Zack walked across the room and closed the door. He then sat down behind his desk and turned his swivel chair toward the window. The morning sun was just topping the trees in the distance. He continued to hold the letter in his hand as though, somehow, he might connect with the hand that had written it. He slowly opened the flap, careful not to damage the envelope, realizing Elizabeth had sealed it with the moisture from her lips. He began to read . . .

JANUARY 3, 1856
RICHMOND

My Dear Zachary:

I just received and have read your letter dated December 13th. I felt your presence from just holding the envelope you had touched. You can't know the pleasure hearing from you has brought me.

I have kept myself very busy. I am doing volunteer work at the East Richmond Hospital in the children's ward. It's been quite a learning experience and has helped time to pass more quickly.

Has it only been a month since we said goodbye at the train depot where I received my very first kiss? When I close my eyes I can still feel the softness of your lips.

I will see you on February 8th. Dare I say how I really feel about that? I think not. I will say that I am not an elusive butterfly.

I am very real, my dear Zachary.

Affectionately,
Elizabeth

After reading the letter the third time, Zachary opened his door and walked down the hall to John's office. He knocked and walked in.

"What would we do without the U.S. mail?" Zachary said with a pleased smile on his face.

"I was just thinking the same thing. However, I do wish it moved a little faster! Catherine will be so pleased that we heard from Elizabeth. She is very involved in the planning of the cotillion for Elizabeth. I haven't seen her as excited about anything as she is about this party."

"Do you realize it is only sixteen days until Elizabeth will be arriving?" Zachary noted enthusiastically. "Would that I could just sleep until then."

John responded, "We haven't really discussed how you feel about Elizabeth. I believe you care a great deal for her. I realize you haven't known her very long. The two of you seem to be approaching things cautiously, which is wise.

"Yes, John. We have agreed to be cautious. However, my head tells me one thing and my heart tells me another. I sometimes find myself in a dream, riding to Willow Place, sweeping Elizabeth up in my arms and riding off to some romantic hideaway. Then reality hits me squarely in the face that this could take much longer than I want it to."

John responded, "This brings me to share something with you I have had on my mind even before Elizabeth came into our lives.

"You know how interested I've always been in carriages. Well, I had some correspondence recently from Payton Randolph. He owns Randolph Carriage Manufacturing Company in Richmond. He says it is a lucrative business but he is wanting to sell it. He is in his seventies and wants to retire. He said he would give me first choice at buying it if I am interested."

Zachary inquired, "Well, are you?"

"Catherine and I have been talking about it. Since Elizabeth has come into our lives, it changes the way we look at a lot of things."

"I can identify with that."

"What I'm thinking of doing would involve you, Zachary."

"Please continue . . . I'm listening."

"I, too, have been thinking of getting out of the shipping business. I have had several businessmen ask me if I would be interested in selling. Shipping is a big business. I have been doing it for
forty years, since 1815. I'm sixty-five and I feel I need to be in something less stressful. I would like to develop some ideas I've had for
years about building carriages. They are our most widely used means
of overland travel, especially going to and from our homes to all
our local destinations. Of course, we still have horses, wagons and
the stage coach. But a good carriage is very important to a family.
Now, do you wonder where I am going with this conversation?"

"I'm still listening."

"Zachary, what do you think about me changing the family
business at this time of my life?"

"Hmmm . . . Well, John . . . Henry David Thoreau, a favorite
writer of mine, said . . . *'If one advances confidently in the direction of
his dreams, and endeavors to live the life which he has imagined, he
will meet with a success unexpected in common hours.'*

"If this has been an interest of yours for years, then why not
pursue it? You can afford to venture out in a new direction."

"Do I hear a note of approval? This is where you would come
in, Zachary. I would like for the two of us to go to Richmond in
March and look the business over, see exactly what Payton has
there. We would need to look at his books and the physical plant
and decide if we would be interested."

"You say if *we* would be interested . . ."

"Yes Zack. I want a partner. I am willing to make it well worth
your time if you agree that we are interested. Payton has a man
who is capable of running the business until we become familiar
with the operation, and he's willing to continue working there after we take over."

"You are wondering why I am perhaps being so hasty. Well, I
think you and we know that Elizabeth intends to live in Richmond.
These past two months have been the longest and loneliest ones for
us. Elizabeth brought laughter and joy into our home and she was
our delight. Catherine and I are not so young anymore. We want to

spend what time we have left near Elizabeth. If she won't come to us then we must go to her. My young friend and associate, what do you think?"

"John, few young men have been as fortunate as I. You took me into your business and taught me shipping. I feel I had the master teacher, and with our business knowledge, I feel we can apply it to the carriage industry and we would be successful in our venture. You can count me in. Oh yes, have you thought of how you might miss the James River and the Bay area, not to mention sailing?"

"That would not be a problem. We would sell the big house on Warthen Street but we would keep the smaller house on the river. We could all use it for sailing vacations.

"So Zack, you can plan on a trip to Richmond in March. And if we buy Payton out, you will be moving there to learn the business. I would have to come back here and finalize the sell of the shipping business and our house. I must say you have been very calm about all of this. I suspected you would be turning cart wheels by now."

"If only you could see inside me! My heart has been turning cart wheels since I received the letter from Elizabeth. And now, the prospect of moving to Richmond, being near Elizabeth, and learning a new business!

Chapter 19

JANUARY 25

RICHMOND

*T*his was Elizabeth's fourth week at the hospital. Little Emily Everette had been dismissed and was doing surprisingly well. Elizabeth had gotten to meet Jim and Maggie Everette, Emily's parents, at the hospital. She was impressed with them and had a great desire to help them in some way.

The Baldwins had been long-time neighbors of Henry and Bessie Smith. The Smith's were in their early sixties now, and were genuine friends of the Baldwin family. Their place was three miles south of Willow Place and not as large. But they did have a house on their property that was soon to be empty. Mr. Smith had to have help with the work at his place because in the last few years he had suffered terribly with rheumatism. Elizabeth had seen the Smiths at the mercantile in Richmond about three weeks ago. They said the family who currently lived and worked on their place were moving from Richmond in a couple of weeks and they would be in need of some help.

As they were leaving the store Mrs. Smith said, "Elizabeth, if you hear of anyone who needs work please let us know. The mister here is going to have to have help and real soon."

Elizabeth thought of the Everette family but she had not yet visited them. She needed to know more about them.

On Friday, January 20th, she decided to call on them. She drove her buggy down Long Hollow Road to the very end of the street. She passed several homes in poor condition, with boarded windows and broken screen doors before coming to the Everette's.

Elizabeth stepped on a flat rock placed on the grassless ground in front of the door and knocked The door swung open wide and Mrs. Everette smiled and said, "Good afternoon, Miss Morgan. Emily, look who's come calling." She stepped inside and invited Elizabeth into a spotless house.

Emily's face lit up. She ran and gave Elizabeth a hug. She exclaimed, "Miss Morgan, you've come to see me just like you said you would." She had a look of awe on her face.

She turned to her two sisters and said, "This is the lady who was so nice to me in the hospital."

"And these are your other two little girls that I've heard so much about, Maggie?" Elizabeth asked as she stooped down in front of them. "Yes, indeed they are. Sara is seven and Julie is four. Say hello to Miss Morgan girls."

"I have brought a sack of fruit for all of you. Maggie, I also have a sack of supplies in the buggy. I'll bring them in."

Then she told Maggie about the Smiths and their need for workers on their farm. She asked if they would be interested in working for the Smith's and moving to the little house.

Maggie wept until her shoulders shook. She was so overcome she could not speak. Her three daughters pushed up against her, their eyes very wide. She patted each of them saying over and over, "It's alright girls, it's alright."

She regained her composure and said quietly, "Miss Morgan, Jesus told his disciples in his teachings something that has become dear to me, something I have had to rely on many times. He said, 'And all things, whatsoever ye shall ask in prayer believing, ye shall receive.' He knew his disciples were being sent out to work for Him and there would be many times all they would have to depend on would be their Lord. He let them know he *was* dependable.

"Our situation has become desperate. I have asked the Lord diligently to send some relief. Jim has needed a better job but doesn't have enough time off from work to look for one. It appears our Lord has taken another family's need and supplied our need. I know Jim would gladly accept Mr. Smith's offer."

Elizabeth was so moved she could hardly speak. From what she had witnessed in this home she did not think her going to work at the hospital was a coincidence.

Elizabeth left the Everette's home and drove her buggy straight to the Smith's house. She hoped they had not found someone else for the job.

Mr. Smith was in the yard when she drove up. "Why Miss Elizabeth, what brings you out here in such a fizzy?"

Elizabeth climbed down from the buggy and extended her hand to Mr. Smith.

"Good afternoon. I believe I have some good news for you."

"And what would that be, Miss?"

"First, have you hired anyone for the job you had coming open?"

"No, can't say as I have. Been real worried about it, too. The family jest pulled out day afore yestedee movin' to her poppy's place down in Petersburg. Me an' Bessie jest gotta' have some hep."

"I believe I've found just the right people to help you, Mr. Smith. Their names are Jim and Maggie Everette. They have three little girls, ages four, five and seven. Mr. Everette works for the Patton's at their sawmill. He works long hours and gets very little pay. They are clean people and will take care of your renter house. They are Christian people. I just talked to Mrs. Everette before I came here. Her husband was at work but she said they would be grateful for a chance to work for you and Mrs. Smith."

"This *is* good news! It's an answer to prayer as a matter of fact. When will they be a commin'?"

"That's up to you, Mr. Smith. I can tell them tomorrow. When would you want them?"

"Tha sooner tha better. And I shore do thank you, Miss Elizabeth. You're a good neighbor. Tell 'em the house has four good-sized rooms. The kitchen has a wood burnin' cook stove. I won't charge them for livin' there and I'll settle on a price fer their labor when I talk to 'em. Now the furnishins ain't much to brag about but beats nothin'a tall."

"I'll see the Everettes first thing in the morning. Since it will be Saturday, maybe they can begin moving tomorrow. Thank you, Mr. Smith. Give my warm regards to your wife. Goodbye for now."

She climbed back into the buggy, snapped the reins and said, "Let's go Charlie."

Elizabeth decided to ride back to the Everette's and give them the good news.

She would also send William over on Saturday morning with the wagon to help them move.

"Do unto others as you would have them do unto you" really felt good!

Chapter 20

JANUARY 28
SATURDAY

*T*he sun was shining brightly this morning. A couple of inches of snow had fallen in the night, just enough to remind everyone how pretty the landscape looks dressed in white. Jane Abigail Adams stretched energetically. She must get a move on!

She bounded into the kitchen, rushed over to her dad and gave him a quick peck on the cheek. She grabbed her mother, whirling her around the kitchen for a few steps.

"Good morning, good morning," she sang out as she filled her plate with Virginia cured ham, biscuits and gravy from the stove warmer.

"Hmm . . . you must have a date with Phil," her father reckoned.

"How'd you know?"

"It's not your usual Saturday morning entry into the kitchen, so I knew somethin' was up. I do like it when my Janie girl is happy."

"Well she's happy this morning, father. You're right, I do have a date with Phillip."

"I'd be dancin' round the kitchen, too, if I had a date with the likes of Phillip Gregory Maxwell the Third," her mother Mary Beth sighed, rolling her eyes in mock adoration.

"And just what may I ask is wrong with me, your adoring husband, James Russell Adams?" Jane's father chimed in as he pulled Jane's mother into his lap.

"I haven't time for this", she chided. "I've got work to do! What are your plans, Jane girl?"

"We are going horseback riding in this heavenly snow. By we, I mean Phillip, Dr. Blake, Elizabeth and I. Mother, I hope you don't feel I'm abandoning you. I realize you need my help on Saturdays. But I really wanted to do this today. Do you mind terribly?"

"Of course not, child. Working with the children at school all week and then helping with the chores here at home . . . you deserve a day off every now and then. You have my blessings."

Jane finished in the kitchen then dressed for the day. She put on wool socks, boots, her new brown tweed riding skirt with matching brown sweater, a short warm jacket, grabbed her leather gloves and flew out the door. She went to the barn to see if her brother, Jim, Jr., had her horse Rowdy ready to go.

About that time she heard horses' hooves coming toward the barn.

Phillip called out, "Jane, we are here. Are you ready?"

Jane came out of the barn leading Rowdy.

"Where have you guys been? Kinda' draggin' your feet aren't you?" she remarked impishly. Phillip let out a whistle. "If you didn't look so gorgeous I would challenge you on that statement." He turned in the saddle and looked at his friend David. "I have a question for you. Have you ever seen anyone so lovely? Just look at that dark brown hair with matching color eyes, her olive complexion that is forever tan, and that turned-up nose . . ."

"Enough of that, Phillip Maxwell! Whoever heard of matching color eyes?"

They all three laughed good-naturedly. Jane all but leapt on Rowdy and they headed to Willow Place.

David enjoyed the company of these two friends. Their time together was a relaxing break from his responsibilities at the hospital.

———

Elizabeth could not make up her mind what to wear. She looked through her chest of drawers for the second time. Finally, she chose a black woolen riding skirt, a white cotton blouse with a round collar and a red sweater. Her short black coat would do nicely. Her leather riding gloves were in her coat pocket.

She walked through the snow to the barn. William had Blazer saddled and ready, and she mounted and rode out of the barn to the front of the house. She heard laughter and saw 'Dumas' "three musketeers" approaching!

"You three sound like you're in a good mood."

"We couldn't have picked a better day to frolic in the snow, beautiful woman, could we? David remarked in his flirtatious way.

They rode four abreast heading south past the Smith's place. There, repairing a fence for Mr. Smith's milk cows, was Jim Everette. Maggie and her tag-along daughters were feeding chickens nearby.

Elizabeth had not told these three the story of the Smiths and the Everettes. She took this time to do so.

David stared at Elizabeth in disbelief. She is not only beautiful, he thought, but she is also a caring and giving person, even more than he realized.

"Elizabeth, you are a remarkable person. I once read somewhere that a real friend is one who walks in when the rest of the world walks out. I believe this is what you did for the Everette family. Your good deed reminds me of the scripture in Proverbs that says, 'He that hath pity on the poor lendeth unto the Lord; and that which he hath given will pay him again.' Your day of blessings will be remarkable, I predict."

"I did not tell you the story for self praise, but to make you happy for little Emily and her family."

"You see the clearing up ahead? Let's let these horses run!" And away they went!

The sun had almost melted all the snow. The wind felt good against their faces and the sun felt warm to their backs. They rode like the wind for a couple of miles. Coming to a small grove of apple trees they all dismounted and tied the horses to some lower branches of the trees.

Jane and Phillip walked hand in hand up a small hillside and sat down in the grass. The sun had melted the night's snowfall.

Phillip looked very thoughtful. He stretched out on his side and propped on his elbow facing Jane. "I've been thinkin' 'bout something a lot lately and I'd like your thoughts on it."

Jane looked at this perfect specimen of a man. She thought, *could he possibly be going to say what I think he is?*

"Of course you know I have a law degree from William and Mary. And I've been practicing real estate law for almost two years. But I'm more interested in politics than real estate. A friend of mine says he saw an advertisement for a political science teaching position at William and Mary. I have the credentials for the job. I'm thinking seriously about applying for it. What do you think?"

I think I could ring your neck, Phillip Gregory Maxwell, III, she almost said.

Instead, she smiled and thoughtfully replied, "You know the saying 'nothing ventured, nothing gained.' You are young. Why not explore life's alternatives? If you find you do not like teaching you will always have your law degree to fall back on."

He stood to his feet and exclaimed, "I'm going to apply for that job! I knew you could help me decide. I was almost sure it was the right thing to do. I guess I just needed a little shove."

He pulled her to her feet and gave her a big hug. Then he examined her face up close. "You are a beautiful little pixie, Janie. You could cause a man to lose his head."

"I'm at least glad you noticed. Far be it from me to cause you to lose your head."

Hand in hand they walked on to the top of the hill.

Elizabeth sat down, raised her arms, clasped her fingers together and rested her hands on the back of her head. She leaned back against the trunk of an apple tree.

David was leaning his shoulder against a tree and chewing on a piece of straw. He was staring at Elizabeth again.

She became uncomfortable and started to stand.

"Don't move. Stay just like that. I want to remember you this way."

But she stood to her feet and said, "Let's walk over here. There used to be a small creek where we could water the horses. It really was more like a branch. It might be dried up."

David took her by her shoulders. He looked deep into her eyes. She was very close to him and could not move. His eyes were so dark they almost looked black. He had a square chin and perfectly shaped lips. She looked up at his hair. It was as black as hers.

Suddenly she removed his hands from her shoulders and stepped back.

"Elizabeth, you might step back away now, but surely you feel the attraction between us. You are beautiful. Anyone who looks at you knows that. But what you have inside is even greater than your outward beauty. I've watched you with those children at the hospital. Yours is a gift. You exemplify it to everyone. You have endeared yourself to me. I don't know about this guy in Williamsburg, but I know how I feel. Do I have a chance with you?"

Elizabeth was so surprised by this confession! She felt guilty that she had agreed to see him occasionally. She had meant it to be a friendship, nothing more. He was attractive and she liked him as a friend very much. But nothing more. What could she say to him?"

"David, it will probably surprise you to know I had no idea you had thoughts of me other than friendship. That is the truth. Yes, you are an attractive man. You are so much fun to be around and are a *good* person I have great respect for you. Do you feel I have misled you? I told you from the beginning there was someone else, remember? If I have caused you to be hurt I am so sorry."

David's countenance changed quickly from serious to jovial as Phillip and Jane walked up.

"Are you two ready to ride?" David asked them.

"Yes, I've got a little more research to do on my land dispute case."

"And I have some lesson planning to work on for my school kids."

"What about you, beautiful woman? Wanna race?"

They all mounted their horses and rode like the wind again.

Elizabeth *needed* the wind in her face.

The four of them reigned in at Willow Place and were saying their goodbyes.

David rode across the front lawn a few yards. He turned around and looked at Elizabeth's home place. It was a rectangular-shaped house, two stories high, made of red brick. There was a chimney on each end of the house. The porch was centered in the middle with six large white columns on each side of the porch. He counted nine windows across the front of the house including five on the second story and four on the first. The white front door was oversized and was crowned with a wide cornice. Quite impressive.

David then danced his horse Buck around facing the lake. He could well understand the name

Willow Place. Elizabeth had to be beautiful to fit this setting! He agreed with what a writer had once said, 'The genius of the Old South is rural!'

He rode back across the lawn and said, "Goodbye Elizabeth. See you at work Monday." They waved to Elizabeth as they rode away.

She took Blazer to the barn, unsaddled him and gave him a good brushing. When she finished she gave him an apple. "Blazer, you are such a good boy. Your coat is so shiny. William takes good care of you. He will feed you later." She laid her cheek against his neck and gave him a big hug.

She went in the back door calling out, "Is anybody home? Where is everyone?" She walked through the dining room into the hallway and to the parlor. Emma was putting clean slipcovers on the parlor chair.

"Where is William? What's for lunch? What time is it anyway?"

"One question at a time, lassie. William has gone to check on the Smiths as you asked him to do. I sent the Everettes some stew.

"I hope we are having stew" Elizabeth said. "I'm starving!

"Do you think we could eat without William?"

"Miss Elizabeth, you treat us just like family. Of course we can eat without William. You can do anything you want to do whenever you want to," Sadie chided mildly.

."Sadie, I do not look at you, William and Emma as hired help. I see you as my dear friends who are willing to do kind and helpful things for me. You earn the money you are paid and the living provisions are a part of your salary. I can't imagine my life without the three of you. You are truly my family here in Richmond."

Tender hearted Sadie was wiping tears and blowing her nose.

———

Elizabeth retired early. As she curled up on her side in bed, she relived her encounter with David. Was she guilty of leading him to believe she cared for him? She was friendly, loved people and enjoyed her time with him. She felt badly about the whole ordeal. One thing she knew for sure . . . she had completely lost her heart to Zachary Steven Bainbridge.

———

In his room at the Butts Boarding House, David had retired for the night and was lying sleepless in bed. He thought about his conversation with Elizabeth. He had known her for only five weeks but she had crowded his thoughts during this time as no other had. But she was right. She had told him from the beginning there was someone else. It was not like she had broken an engagement! If things had worked out for them it would have been great. But he needed to move on. He did not want her to feel badly. He would ease the tension at work on Monday. But . . . she truly is a beautiful woman.

⚊⚊⚍⚏⚍⚊⚊

Jane sat in the chair next to her bed. She had on her flannel gown and warm robe. She had her leg crossed and was shaking her foot nervously so she could think better. She thought, *Phillip Maxwell, you make me so angry. Why are you so dumb? Can't you see I'm blindly in love with you. What a team we would make. When are you going to wake up?* Then she said out loud, "Please Lord, let him love me. Please let him want me!"

⚊⚊⚍⚏⚍⚊⚊

Phillip turned the wick on the lamp down and then blew it out. He slipped between the bed covers and stretched out on his back. He had finally finished the research on the land dispute case. Now he turned his thoughts toward Jane. She is a special little "pixie" and he loved her. If he applied for and got the teaching job at William and Mary College in Williamsburg, he would have to move. Of course, he would want to take Jane with him. By Jove, what if she wouldn't want to move? *What if she doesn't even love me? I guess I'd better be finding out.*

⚊⚊⚍⚏⚍⚊⚊

Monday morning when Elizabeth entered the hospital David was waiting for her. He pulled her inside the empty waiting area.

"I need to talk to you, beautiful woman."

Elizabeth's heart sank. She hoped this was not going to be difficult.

"Yes David. I suppose after Saturday we do need to talk."

"I've been doing a lot of thinking about us. You are correct. You did tell me from the beginning there was someone in your life and that you expected there would be a commitment. Your beauty and your intelligence plus an incredible personality just overwhelmed me. If it were not for your 'someone else' I believe there could have been a future for us. However, I don't want to spoil a good friendship. Can we forget about Saturday and remain friends?"

"Indeed we can, David. Thank you for being such a gentleman."

Chapter 21

JANUARY 30
MONDAY

*P*hillip was waiting for Jane after school let out for the day.

"Hi Pixie," he said teasingly. "Come on, let's go for a ride. I have something to ask you."

Oh no . . . not again she thought. But she could not resist this man.

"Where are we going?"

"Wait and see."

They were riding out toward Willow Place. They rode in silence. The suspense was killing her. She wondered if he was going to ask some more advice of her.

They got to the road that turned off to Willow Place. Phillip circled the lake. He stopped and lifted her out of the buggy. They walked to one of the many benches lining the banks of the lake. They sat down. Phillip perched on the edge of the bench.

"Jane, I want to ask you a question. But the place to ask you had to be beautiful and special, just like you. I could think of no prettier place than here. So, on this Monday, January 30th, 1856, on bended knee I ask you . . . Jane Abigail Adams, will you marry me?"

Jane was shocked speechless. Her heart was racing so she almost felt faint. Did she hear what she thought she heard? She was taking no chances so she replied breathlessly, "Yes, Phillip Gregory Maxwell the Third, I certainly will marry you."

He reached down with his strong arms, lifted her to her feet, held her very close and gave Jane her very first kiss. It was everything she had imagined it would be. Then Phillip, methodical as he was, said, "Now we've got plans to make."

Jane, the romantic that she was, replied enthusiastically, "I'll have to choose my wedding dress. Will we have a church wedding or an outdoor wedding? Do we want a large wedding or a small wedding? What do you think about" . . . Phillip shushed her and said, "Jane, my little pixie. We don't have to make these decisions in two minutes! We will have time to plan these things. The planning I'm thinking about is moving from Richmond to Williamsburg. If I were to get the job at William and Mary it would mean moving. Now, would you be willing to do this? Think about it. It will mean leaving your family, your friends, your teaching job here, and our church. This will be quite a drastic change for us. Think carefully before you answer me."

A thoughtful and serious look creased lines in Jane's face. She sat very still staring into space. Then she placed her hand on Phillip's face, turning it so she could look directly into his eyes, and said, "Phillip, my love, I know my friends describe me as feisty and fun-loving, perhaps overloaded with enthusiasm. That is my personality and I like it. But I am not a fly-by-night person. Marriage is very sacred to me. God instituted it in the Garden of Eden. His Son has given us instructions in Matthew concerning this institution. He says we should leave father and mother and cleave to each other and instead of two we would be one. Leaving familiar people and places will be painful, but I am more than willing to go to Williamsburg with you. I have absolutely no reservations about this. I believe that our life together will be good wherever we are."

His laughing eyes seemed to almost close as he smiled broadly saying, "I should have known you would feel this way."

"Now, with that all settled, let's go share the good news! I saw Elizabeth's buggy go by not too long ago. She probably wonders why we are here. Do you want to tell her now or do you want to tell your parents first?"

"Yes, I would like to tell Elizabeth while we are here. Besides, you will have to *ask* my father, you know. When and *if* he gives his consent we will tell mother," she said teasingly.

"What do you think *your* parents will say?" Jane inquired.

"They will be delighted. After meeting you last summer they both liked you immediately. Mother even commented, 'Phillip, Jane will make some man a good wife.' And you know how mother's intuitions are. Yes, they will be delighted. This weekend we will ride down to Petersburg and tell them the news."

The happy couple stood at Elizabeth's front door, waiting for an answer to their knock.

Emma opened the door.

Jane said, "Hello, Emma. Could we please see Elizabeth?"

"Yes, Jane. I'll tell her you are here."

About that time Elizabeth appeared in the foyer and exclaimed, "Jane, Phillip! Do come in out of the cold. What may I ask are you doing at Willow Place? I saw you were sitting under the willow tree when I rode in an hour ago. You must be frozen."

"Frozen? You mean its cold outside? I hadn't noticed. We have some good news to tell you. But we can't stay long. Mother doesn't even know where I am."

"Yes, Jane. She does. I went by your house and told her I was going to pick you up at school. She knows."

"My dear Phillip. You think of everything."

"So come on in. Emma, is there some hot chocolate left?"

"Yes lassie. I'll bring some into the parlor."

"Wait Emma. Elizabeth, may we sit at the kitchen table? I love Emma's kitchen. There is such inviting warmth there."

"We certainly may."

Emma had poured three steaming cups of hot chocolate and placed a plate of oatmeal cookies before them.

"Emma, please join us. This is such happy news. We wish to share it with everyone. Is that alright, Elizabeth?"

"I was going to suggest the same thing. Emma is my dear friend and confidant," Elizabeth said warmly.

Phillip said, "Well folks, we really need a sounding of the trumpet to precede my announcement, but we will have to do without it, I suppose."

He looked at Elizabeth explaining, "I'm sure you wonder why we came to Willow Place this afternoon. I wanted to bring Jane to the prettiest place in these parts and Willow Place was it. On bended knee, underneath the biggest and prettiest willow tree by the lake, I asked Jane Abigail Adams to marry me."

Elizabeth and Emma turned at the same time to look at Jane.

"And I said yes! Phillip made me the happiest girl in the world."

Elizabeth stood to her feet at the same time Jane did. They met halfway around the table, laughing, exclaiming happily and hugging one another. Phillip propped his chin in his hand and, leaning on the table, smiled contentedly at the girls. He loved them both. Elizabeth was their closest friend. He looked at Emma who was wiping tears from her eyes. He could see she was happy for them but yet he caught a fleeting look of sadness in her eyes that disappeared as quickly as it came. Hmm?"

"We must go now. I can't wait to tell my family. Thank you both for such southern hospitality and your love."

As they headed to Jane's home Phillip remarked, "I wonder about Emma. Jane, do you know anything about her?"

"No, not much, now that you mention it. She came to work for the Baldwin's when she was only twenty, I've heard Elizabeth say. She is now fifty-five. I know because I was with Elizabeth in September last year when she bought a gift for her birthday. She has always attended First Wesleyan Church. She came with the Baldwin's. I know she was loved and highly respected by Judge and Mrs. Baldwin. They always treated her like family. You heard Elizabeth say she was her dear friend and confidant. Mrs. Baldwin also confided in her. That is how Elizabeth found out about her past. If Mrs. Baldwin had not shared this information with

Emma, Elizabeth might never have known. Why do you ask?"

"When you and Elizabeth were hugging at the table a strange thing happened. Emma was wiping tears and looked happy, but a fleeting look of sadness swept over her face. I wonder what it meant and thought you might know."

"No, I don't but my curiosity is stirred."

"Jane, things have happened so fast this afternoon. I wanted the setting for my proposal to be perfect. And it was. Let me tell you now why I want to marry you. When I first saw you my heart ceased to be my own. Your personality, particularly, charmed me. After I got to really know you I've found you to be a person of character and integrity. You are intelligent, easy to talk to, and fun to be with. And little Janie, I see the fruit of the spirit . . . gentleness, goodness, joy and longsuffering, to mention a few, shining forth as a beacon to those around you. In fact, you are the kind of woman I want to be the mother of my children. And today I found out just what those red, sometimes pouting lips feel like against mine. You have completely stolen my heart."

Jane was left breathless and somewhat dizzy from Phillip's declaration of his love for her. No wonder she wanted to be his wife!

The horse was turning onto Goose Creek Road where she lived. They circled behind her house and stepped down from the buggy. It was dusky dark by this time. Phillip took both her hands and looked down at her.

"Now it is my turn to tell you how I feel," Jane whispered. "I *did* love you the first time I ever saw you. You were new in town and had just become a boarder with Mr. and Mrs. Parker. I saw you walking up the street toward the library. The sun was shining on your blonde hair and your sky blue eyes were squinting against the brightness of the sun. Your broad shoulders looked as if they could hold up the world. The confidence in your walk gave you a look as if you *owned* the world! I had just crossed Jefferson Street coming from the library and almost bumped into you. I was never the same after that. I made it a point to find out all I could about you . . . without your knowing. The more I learned the more I liked you. I can tell you now you never had a chance, Phillip Maxwell. I have longed for this day to come."

Phillip knew a display of affection in public was improper, so he looked all around and didn't see a soul. He pulled Jane very close to him and kissed her gently and lovingly. Then he quickly let her go. They joyfully ran around the house to the front porch and entered the door. Phillip said, "Let me speak first."

They entered the parlor where Jane's mother and father were sitting.

"Good evening, Mr. Adams, Mrs. Adams. I've finally brought your daughter home. I have something I want to say. Would it be possible for the boys and little Jenny to join us?"

Good evening, Phillip and Jane girl. Mary Beth, would you ask the children to please come to the parlor?"

"Yes. I won't be but a minute."

Mary Beth came back with the children in tow. They each spoke politely to Phillip and found them a seat. Phillip thought to himself what well-mannered children they were.

"Now young Phillip, what do you have to say?"

All eyes were on Jane and him. He felt a little self conscious. He shifted his weight, then he began . . . "This is the most important day of my life and I want all of this family to be a part of it. This afternoon I asked Jane if she would marry me. She said yes. Now I am asking your permission, Mr. Adams and the approval of the rest of you. I love her very much. She has said she loves me . . . and so we are asking for your blessings."

They all looked at Jane. She was absolutely glowing.

Jane's father looked at her and asked, "Has Phillip spoken the truth?" with a mocked sternness in his voice.

"Oh father, of course he has!"

"Well then, you have my blessings."

With that Mary Beth crossed the room, hugged Jane and said, "I'm so happy for you, Jane girl. Phillip, you will be welcome in our family."

Chapter 21

The boys began to clap and then little Jenny joined them. They crowded around the young couple with hugs pats on the back and many questions. They were a united, happy family.

Chapter 22

Virginia, please have Martha serve me and my guest in the breakfast room for lunch today. We will remain there after we have eaten for a work session. Simpson, when my guests arrive please show them into the parlor. The ladies are due to arrive at eleven in about fifteen minutes.

"Yes, Mrs. Morgan. Very good."

Catherine was thoughtful as she watched the flames leap high in the fireplace. She loved this room. It was a sturdy room. Good furniture. The rococo console table by Bernard Van Risenburgh was her favorite. John had given it to her for her 60th birthday. Millie kept fresh flowers in the cut glass vase that sat in the middle of the table. The light that came through the windows gave the room a bright, clean look. They had chosen comfortable seating and spent lots of time here.

Her mind turned to the upcoming cotillion for Elizabeth. She admitted it had consumed most of her waking hours for the last month. She hoped the Lord didn't think she had gone overboard!

But, oh how she wanted to share this wonderful person who had come into their lives with some of their closest friends. And she wanted the sharing to be special.

Her thoughts were interrupted by Simpson's knock on the door. He announced her guests were here and her very best and trusted friends came chattering in.

Judy walked straight to the fireplace extending her hands to the flames. She was always cold! Judy was petite, had black hair with a sophisticated grey streak in front on the left side. Catherine thought her best feature was her dark brown eyes, offset by perfectly shaped eyebrows.

"I'm glad you have a warm fire going, Catherine. Could I please have some hot coffee?"

"By all means. Let me ring for Martha. I would like a cup myself."

Sharon said, "And so would I."

Mary chimed in, "Make it four."

Sharon walked over to the book shelf. She was an avid reader.

"What new books do you have, Catherine? Hmm . . . here is one by Emily Bronte that I haven't read called Wuthering Heights. Have you read it?

"Oh yes. Sharon, you will absolutely love it. Take it and read it."

"Thank you. I shall."

Sharon was tall, had dark brown hair and eyes as brown as chestnuts. She had a vivacious personality. Her laugh was contagious. People loved being with her.

Mary was knitting furiously. She had to always be doing something. Last month she had finished a sweater for Russell . . . Rusty as she affectionately called him. Now she was knitting herself one. She was a true blonde with long legs. She kept herself trim and was quite an equestrian.

Catherine looked at each of them, admiringly, as they all drank their coffee. They and their husbands were hers and John's dearest friends. How blessed they were.

"Ladies, are you ready for an early lunch so we can finalize the plans for the cotillion?"

In unison they all said, "Yes."

"Then I hope you won't mind lunching in the breakfast room. It is toasty warm there. After lunch we can remain at the table to discuss what each of us has accomplished in planning this special party."

"Virginia makes the best clam chowder I have ever eaten," Sharon remarked as she savored a bite.

"And her green salads are great, especially with this delectable, homemade salad dressing. I'd love to have the recipe," Mary declared.

Judy chimed in, "I *know* about her apple dumplings with the juicy filling and crispy crust. That will be our dessert, won't it Catherine?"

"Knowing you were coming, Judy, Virginia said it was the only dessert to fix!"

Martha quickly cleared the table when the ladies were finished.

Catherine thanked everyone for being so willing to help her. Then she asked the group to share what had been accomplished.

"Mary, what did Mr. Wellington at the Wellington Hotel say about decorations?"

"Since it will be a Valentine cotillion, he said it will be no problem. He has nine cherubs to place on column stands all around the ballroom. The round guest tables will be covered with white linen cloths and overlaid with white, fine lace. The backs of the chairs will be covered with white linen slipcovers. He will use eight tables for the guests and four for the food and drinks, plus one for the center piece. They will be placed in a semicircle around the ballroom.

"Catherine, Mr. Wellington and I talked about centerpieces for the tables. I like using low bowls with floating, fully opened red roses. What do you think?"

"An excellent idea."

"Also, the serving tables will be skirted just like the guest tables. We will have five white wicker baskets filled with greenery and a sprinkling of red roses placed randomly. It is all arranged with Mr. Wellington and the florist. So you can mark that off your list."

"Mary, I knew I could count on you."

"Judy, what did you find out about the food?"

"I spoke with the maitre d' about what we should serve. Since we all agreed not to have a sit down meal, he assured me he would have a table laden with hors d' oeuvres. He will use several meats, cheeses, select breads, shrimp, blue crab salad and lady fingers. I know his work. It will be delicious. I asked especially for strawberry cake as dessert.

"I also told him we wanted a hearty fruit punch, no alcoholic beverages, and hot coffee. Your food is all taken care of."

"I could not have done better myself."

"Sharon, I'm anxious to know about the music for the evening."

"I can tell you now, we are in luck. The group I told you about was already scheduled for that evening, but they had an unexpected cancellation! They contacted Mr. Stratford at the Stratford Theater to ask if we would still want them. He booked them then and there.

"Norman and I went to a concert they gave at the Stratford six months ago. We were so impressed. They call themselves Classic Harmony. The group has five violinists, two violists, one harpist and three flutists. They play selections from Strauss waltzes and polkas, plus other classical and contemporary music. We are all in for a real treat."

"Ladies, how can I ever thank you? You volunteered to help me and with your coordination skills and I foresee a perfect party for Elizabeth."

"What did you decide about the final guest list? I know you have already mailed out the invitations, but did you change it from the last listing?" Judy inquired.

"No, I kept the list as it was after we decided to cut the list in half! I agree that a smaller party will make it more intimate and enjoyable. There will be thirty-two of us if everyone can come."

"What did you decide about Cordelia Fuller? I know you had some apprehensions about her. Did it have something to do about Zachary?" Mary asked.

"I did invite her. I knew her parents, Judge and Mrs. Fuller, would expect it. I have never been sure exactly what the problem was but Zachary steers clear of her. With Elizabeth there I'm sure there won't be a problem. I invited her current beau to keep her occupied."

Sharon stood up and said they should be going. The buggy was waiting outside for Judy, Mary, and Sharon.

"With this remaining lemonade let me offer a toast to my volunteer cotillion committee. Without your help I could never have gotten this planned so perfectly. The party is two weeks from tomorrow."

Chapter 23

FEBRUARY 5
SUNDAY
RICHMOND

*E*lizabeth choked back tears as the congregation sang the wonderful old song Amazing Grace. What a worshipful spirit prevailed in the service this morning. Pastor Davis stepped to the podium and said, "You have heard of a musical medley. This morning I am going to read a 'scriptural medley' from Psalms." In his deep, comforting voice he began to read:

"I will love thee, O lord, my strength. The Lord is my rock, and my fortress, and my deliverer; my God, my strength, in whom I will trust; my buckler, and the horn of my salvation, and my high tower. The Lord is my light and my salvation; whom shall I fear? The Lord is the strength of my life; of whom shall I be afraid: O magnify the Lord with me, and let us exalt his name together. O taste and see that the Lord is good: blessed is the man that trusteth in him."

Elizabeth left the service feeling a renewed strength. She was excited about going to Williamsburg on the eighth to see her grandparents again. She was also anxious to see Zachary. She trembled at the thought. However, she felt that she needed exactly what she had received in this morning's service before going to Williamsburg, somehow.

After a light lunch Elizabeth said, "Emma, I am going to ride Blazer down to the Smith farm. I want to see for myself how they and the Everettes are doing. I will be gone to Williamsburg for almost two weeks, you know.

Elizabeth reined into the Smith's first, and knocked on the front door. Mrs. Smith answered her knock.

"Come in, Miss Elizabeth. Everyone is in the sitting room around the fireplace."

Elizabeth heard little girls' voices before she entered the room. Mr. Smith jumped up and said, "Miss Lizbeth, what ya doin' this fer down?"

"I wanted to check on my friends."

Emily, Sara and Julie were all stretched out on their stomachs with their chins propped up in their hands as they gazed into the fire. All three of them said in unison, "Hello, Miss Elizabeth."

Jim and Maggie Everette were eating an apple. They smiled warmly and said hello.

Henry Smith sat back down after Elizabeth was seated.

"I want to thank you again for bringin' tha Everettes into our lives. These younguns have brought me 'n Bessie more pleasure than we've had in years. My rheumatism is even better!"

Bessie smiled and exclaimed, "Why, it's been just like Christmas ever since they came."

Jim Everette remarked in his very deliberate manner, "Miss Morgan, it was a great day in the Everette family's life when you came along, first at the hospital, then at our home on January 20th. It has been only fourteen days since we moved to the Smith farm. Already there is an improvement in our health. The Smiths have been more than generous to us. I have been able to work reasonable hours, getting enough rest. We are certainly eating so much better with fresh milk, eggs and fruit especially. We have thanked God over and over. We have thanked the Smiths and we want to thank you again for helping us."

Maggie agreed with a "that's right" every now and then while Jim spoke.

"You all might think you are the only ones blessed in this, but I can say that my cup runneth over as well!" Elizabeth said.

"Mrs. Smith, Emma wants to know if you have a dozen eggs you can spare."

"I sure do. Since Maggie and the girls have been feeding the chickens they seem to be outdoing themselves lately."

Elizabeth said her goodbyes. Today has been a very good day.

Chapter 24

FEBRUARY 8

*T*he clickety-clack of the train passing on the railroad track became somewhat monotonous to Elizabeth. They should reach Williamsburg in thirty minutes.

She had relived every moment of hers and Zachary's time spent together from their first meeting to their last goodbye. She remembered what he said to her on December 10th, the day she came back to Richmond.

"I have never been frivolous with my emotions toward women. When I marry I want it to be for life. So I have guarded my feelings for just the right person."

She wanted to believe that he meant what he said. This trip should dispel all doubts. It would be wonderful to see him, to touch him, to have him hold her. She felt almost like a princess going to her very own ball!

The train came to a stop. Elizabeth hoped Zachary liked what she was wearing. The blue wool gabardine suit with the shawl collar and long A-line skirt was one of her favorites.

She looked down as she descended the steps of the train car. Before she knew what happened she was stepping into the arms of Zachary Bainbridge! He swung her around, out of the way of the other passengers, set her down at arms length but still holding her and exclaimed, "You are finally here at last." Then he gently pulled her back into the circle of those big, strong arms and gave her a warm and tender kiss.

"You certainly swept me off my feet, Zachary Bainbridge."

He pushed her back again, looking her up and down, gave a low whistle and said, "You are just as lovely as I remember."

"It's good to see you again, Zachary. It's been a long time. I'm looking forward to my time here."

As they drove up in front of her grandparents' house, she saw them standing on the porch.

"Elizabeth, Elizabeth, you're finally here! It has been so long." her grandmother exclaimed.

"It's been one month, twenty-nine days, two hours and twenty-three minutes to be exact," Zachary chimed in with a boyish grin.

"Doesn't your old grandfather get a hug?"

They all laughed joyously as they entered the house.

It was lunchtime and Martha announced it would be served in the breakfast room.

When they had finished, Zachary reluctantly said, "I really must get back to the office. We have a big shipment going out early in the morning. I have to tie up some loose ends to get it ready. By the way John, did Mike tell you they got the problem solved on the steamboat that is to take the shipment to Savannah on Friday?"

"Yes, Zachary. He said a main shaft had broken. They got a new one and finished the repair work about two o'clock this morning. We have some good men working for us."

"I'll see you tonight then if the dinner invitation still stands."

"Of course it does," Catherine said. "We will eat at seven o'clock."

"Elizabeth, I know you would like to freshen up and perhaps even rest for a while. Let's meet in the parlor at three o'clock. We must make every minute count. I have so much to tell you."

When she got to her room there was a fresh vase of red roses, her favorite. There was a note propped up against the vase. It had her name on the small envelope in Zachary's familiar handwriting. She eagerly opened it and began to read.

My Dearest Elizabeth,

I cannot take you to a garden in February, so I'm bringing a part of the garden to you. I hope you like red roses as much as I do. Their soft petals remind me of your perfect lips.

Welcome back to Williamsburg. I am expecting good things to happen.

Faithfully yours,
Zachary

"Could one be so thoughtful, so perfect in so many ways, and not be everything he appears to be?" Elizabeth thought.

Was she trying too hard to prove his intensions? Surely after her visit this time she would have a proper perspective. One thing she knew for sure, she was madly in love with him.

Elizabeth knocked on the parlor door and entered. The fire in the fireplace had a magnetic attraction. She walked straight to it.

Her grandmother was sitting close to the fire and said, "How did you like your bouquet of roses?"

"Grandmother, they are beautiful! Zachary is so thoughtful."

"He was like a school boy when he came in with them. He asked me to place them in your bedroom along with the note. He was afraid the florist wouldn't have roses in February. But they told him because of Valentine's Day, they always had roses in February."

"Elizabeth, I can't tell you how happy we are to have you here. We have missed you terribly."

"I've missed you and grandfather, too. I have tried to keep busy back home. Volunteering at East Richmond Hospital four hours a day, three days a week has been good for me. Working in the children's ward is very fulfilling. I've met some interesting people there."

"I'm very proud of you, Elizabeth, for doing volunteer work."

"By the way, grandmother, I will need to shop here for a dress to wear to the cotillion.

Hopefully I can find just the right one. Do you mind going with me to look?"

"Mind? I can't wait! We will go to Schumann's tomorrow. They will have exactly what you are looking for I feel sure."

Catherine talked to her granddaughter about the party plans and told her how much fun the planning had been. Before long they both were sitting cross-legged on an area rug in front of the fire talking like school girls.

"Elizabeth, you have told us how much you love your home which you call Willow Place. Tell me about your life there."

"Oh grandmother, I'm so glad you asked and want to know about my beloved home. Let's see . . . where to begin. Hmm. When mother and I first came there I was a very frightened little girl. My mother was so sad. She cried a lot. My Grandfather and Grandmother Baldwin seemed to have insight into what mother and I needed. The first morning after we arrived . . . it was August 15, 1840 I've been told . . . Grandmother Savannah carried me to the kitchen and gave me buttered biscuits with honey. It was so good and just what this frightened little girl needed to start the day. She then held me very close and told me how happy she was that I had come to live with them at Willow Place. She read me a poem called 'Mary Had a Little Lamb.' I found out later it was written by Sarah Josepha Hale in 1830. My, how I loved that story within a poem. It is my favorite to this day.

"After she dressed me, my grandfather scooped me up and took me outside. Carrying me across the front lawn to the big lake where ducks were swimming, he showed me the beautiful weeping willow trees and told me if I would listen carefully, the willows might whisper to me as the wind blew their wispy leaves. I remember all of this because it became a ritual with us every morning. My grandparents took time with me. They made me feel secure.

"As I grew, grandfather exclaimed one morning, 'Elizabeth, you are a dandy!' I really didn't know what a dandy was. Later I learned that it meant "Just Great!" But it sounded like an endearment at the time so I said, 'Oh no, *you* are a dandy.' I almost always called him Dandy after that.

"Grandfather raised horses at Willow Place for several years and when I was seven he gave me a pony. He and I would ride around the big lake together. He rode Molly and I rode Midge. What wonderful memories we built!"

"How large is Willow Place?" her grandmother inquired.

"It is a 40-acre farm five miles out of Richmond. The lake covers three acres. It is prime land. As you look around you see rolling hills covered with many shades of green hardwoods and pines in the summer. From a distance they look like a lush carpet. Then in the fall they are covered, just like Joseph, in their coats of many colors! I might also add that in July and August we have many gorgeous blooming bushes and wildflowers around the lake. In the spring we have white and pink dogwood trees. They compliment the wispy weeping willows.

"I can almost picture the place from your description, Elizabeth. No wonder you love it so."

"My sweet Dandy died on November 12th, 1852 just ten days after my sixteenth birthday. He had given me this beautiful, purebred dapple-gray horse named Blazer. It was love at first sight both for me, and Blazer. He is my pride and joy. He carries me fast as the wind over my beloved Willow Place."

"Elizabeth, your birthday must be November 2nd, right?"

"Yes, Grandmother Catherine. That's right."

"Do you know that was your father's birthday, too?"

"No, I did not know that! Remember, I only learned of his existence five months ago."

Elizabeth saw such a sad look in her grandmother's eyes. Suddenly it dawned on her the depths of her grandparents' suffering. She had been too caught up in how this revelation of the past had affected her that she had not realized the depth of pain they had suffered at losing their only son whom they adored. Yes, they had great joy in having her come into their lives but this joy was born of pain. She rose to her feet and went to the chair where her grandmother was now sitting. Elizabeth knelt before her grandmother, leaned over and rested her head on her shoulder and her grandmother held her very close.

"Dear, sweet Grandmother Catherine, how very much I love you. I do so *need* you in my life. Also, I hope you see things in me that remind you of my dad, in a sweet and wonderful way, so that it will bring you joy and not pain."

They both wept together. A bond was formed between the two of them that day that Elizabeth hoped would never be broken.

As they dried their tears and her grandmother regained her composure, she took Elizabeth's face between her hands and said, "You can't know the pleasure your dad brought to us. He was not a spoiled, only child. He was very considerate of us, his parents. He thanked us on many occasions for the life we had provided for him. He worked hard to learn about the shipping business. He loved working on the loading docks. The harder the work, the better he liked it. He remembered us on our birthdays, always. He was not hateful, nor spiteful. He was gentle with children. We went to church together as a family.

"I can't imagine what happened to John Lee. The person Garrison Wheeler described is not the John Lee that we knew. I am a mother talking, but I can't help but believe something happened in his mind. We will never know. But I have good memories of my son. You are a gift to us from him. We cherish you, Elizabeth. And we thank our Heavenly Father for the *revelation* of your existence."

They embraced again feeling the love flowing from one to the other.

"My goodness Elizabeth, it's almost time for John and Zachary to be here. Let's freshen up a bit."

"What a wonderful afternoon we have shared. Grandmother, I feel as if I've always known you! You are right, we do need to wash our faces."

Chapter 25

*D*inner was over and they had moved into the library. Elizabeth looked at her grandparents in a whole new light after her talk with her grandmother that afternoon. She felt very protective of them and hoped they never had to suffer pain again. She wished she could take them to Willow Place to live with her feeling a great need to stay close to them.

"Elizabeth, what did you and your grandmother do this afternoon?" her grandfather inquired.

"We talked and talked, grandfather. It was a wonderful afternoon. I feel such a need to be close to you both. I wish I could take you back to Willow Place with me."

"Elizabeth, we will pray about our future. I am sure God will chart a course for us to follow that will be right for all of us. We don't like our times of separation from you either. What a difference you have made in our lives," her grandfather said.

He opened a table drawer and took out a box of dominoes. "Would you like to play a game with me anyone?"

"Zachary spoke up and said, "After our last game, John, I'm surprised you would challenge me again so soon!"

They all laughed.

"Let's go in the breakfast room and play on the table in there," John said.

They had a fun night being together. It was obvious just how much her grandparents loved Zachary. They really did treat him as a son. In fact, both of them called him son on many occasions.

Elizabeth's grandparents excused themselves a little before time for Zachary to leave so he and Elizabeth could have some time together. They walked hand in hand to the parlor. The fire was still burning in the fireplace.

Zachary stood, looking down at Elizabeth. "You really are here, my elusive butterfly. I wish I could catch you in a net and keep you here always. My how I've missed you."

"It's so good to be here, Zachary. I've missed you, too."

"Do you think we could go to dinner at Cuisine by the River tomorrow evening?"

"Perhaps. Grandmother and I are going shopping in the morning. Grandfather is going to meet us for lunch. He said he might take a couple of hours off from work after lunch to be with us. I simply must spend time with them, Zachary. I *want* to spend time with them. Since we three will be together tomorrow afternoon, you and I can go to dinner tomorrow evening.

"Would you permit me to kiss you goodnight, Elizabeth?"

"How could I say no when I want you to?"

He tenderly drew her into his arms and gave her the sweetest kiss so far. His kisses, literally, took her breath away.

Thursday morning was bright and sunny. They got to Schumann's early. The sales lady was very helpful and Elizabeth found exactly the right formal. Her grandmother's approval of the dress meant a great deal to her.

They ate at The Sandwich Shop near Schumann's. John joined Catherine and Elizabeth for lunch. Elizabeth was surprised at the inside of the restaurant. It was well decorated and all the tables had linen cloths and napkins. The all male waiters were dressed in black and white. Their food was extraordinarily good, as was their time together.

Chapter 25

Zachary picked Elizabeth up at seven o'clock. Soon they were back in "their" Cuisine by the River. They had a leisurely dinner, and their conversation was interesting and light hearted.

Again Zachary wanted to talk about their future.

"Elizabeth, can't you see what we have is more than an infatuation? We've spent two months apart and our feelings for each other have not dimmed but seem to have intensified. I so desire to make a commitment."

"Zachary, I have told you that I love you. But we have known each other for only three months. It's just not long enough. We need to spend more time together. We can't stay in close touch by mail because mail moves so slowly. I'm sorry Zachary, but I must have more time. Is this going to change things between us?"

"No, Elizabeth. I would wait for you forever. But I do have John's permission to tell you something. He is so unselfish. He could have already told you this since you have been here, but he wanted me to tell you 'at just the right time' as he put it."

"What is it Zachary?"

"Do you remember when you were here last, your grandfather told you of his fascination with carriages?"

"Yes, I do remember."

"Well, on January 23rd we both received our letters from you. After we had read them, John began talking to me. He said there had been something on his mind for quite some time, even before you came into our lives, and he wanted to share it with me.

"He had some correspondence from Payton Randolph in Richmond. Mr. Randolph wants to sell his carriage business and retire. He is in his seventies. He has given John first choice at buying it. John is negotiating with him now to buy the company."

"This is interesting news. What would grandfather do with the shipping company? At sixty-five he wouldn't surely try to run both businesses, would he?"

"No, he says shipping is so stressful that he wants to do something less demanding. He is going to put Morgan Shipping up for sale. He has had inquiries from several businessmen in the past about buying the business, so he doesn't anticipate any problem selling, and he thinks he will have enough profit from the sale to invest in the carriage company."

"Zachary, where would that leave you? Would you stay on with whoever bought it? Would that be part of the deal?"

"No, Elizabeth. He wants me as a partner in this new venture. He said he would make it well worth my time. With our business background we would have no trouble running the business after we become familiar with the operation. Mr. Randolph's head foreman will remain with the company. He will be our teacher and Mr. Randolph will be a consultant. It will be a considerably smaller business than Morgan Shipping."

"When do you expect to take over the company?"

"Elizabeth, John and I have train tickets for Richmond on Thursday, March 2nd. We will meet with Mr. Randolph and his attorney on Friday, March 3rd. John is taking our attorney with us. If there are no problems with the contract, the deal will be finalized Friday. And that isn't all. He wants me to go prepared to stay in Richmond. He will return to Williamsburg, to officially put Morgan Shipping up for sale as well as their home. When all of this is done, your grandparents will be moving to Richmond! His words to me were . . . if we can't bring Elizabeth here then we will go to Elizabeth."

"Zachary, it is hard for me to comprehend all you have told me. This is dizzying! It most likely means that I will leave to go home on February 18th and you will be *moving* to Richmond just twelve days later!"

"It is a lot to digest, I admit. But it means you and I can see each other practically every day. I have hardly been able to sleep since knowing about this. Do you think I waited for 'just the right time' to tell you?"

"Zachary, I am in such a state of shock. I'm happy and overjoyed. My mind is whirling round and round. I'm thinking, my grandparents are going to be a *daily* part of my life. One hour ago, we were worlds apart as far as I knew. What a wonderful Valentine's present!"

Chapter 25

The days seemed to fly by. Elizabeth and her grandparents had so much to talk about. She was concerned about their having to give up their beautiful home in Williamsburg. Both said they would be relieved to sell. The house was much too big. They used so few of the rooms. The older they got, the more they saw the need to scale back.

They were very excited about going to live in Richmond to be near Elizabeth. She assured them Willow Place would be their home until they found a home of their own.

Chapter 26

FEBRUARY 14, 1856
TUESDAY

John, Catherine and Elizabeth arrived at the Wellington Hotel early. They had their dresses and accessories delivered to the room John had reserved for them. The Morgans had chosen the Wellington for its old Southern charm. It had a winding staircase leading from upstairs into the ballroom downstairs. Elizabeth would be making her entrance to the party down these steps. It wasn't what Elizabeth preferred but she would do it for her grandparents. She knew this was important for them.

They also arrived early so they could see the ballroom, and make sure everything was perfect. When they entered the room, they all three caught their breath in awe of its size and beauty. The decorations were exquisite. The ballroom had a narrow balcony overhead with a two-foot white balustrade. It was in a half-moon shape and extended over the entrance area of the ballroom. Two large white columns on either side, supporting the balcony, framed the entrance to the ballroom through which the guests would pass.

The walls were done in pale blue. From the ceiling there was a two-foot border around the room, framed in white with white wooden appliqués, which allowed the blue walls to show through.

The windows were curtained with tieback, pale blue, velvet draperies with white sheers.

The room was encircled with eight-foot white cherubs, each holding a red heart.

Several Chesterfield Victorian sofas in blue and silver brocade lined the walls. In between the sofas were console tables and Belter chairs of the Rococo Revival style.

The white wicker baskets, placed randomly, filled with greenery and a sprinkling of red roses gave the room a feeling of romance for sure on this Valentine's Day.

The guest tables in a semicircle grouping were perfectly done.

Tears came to Elizabeth's eyes. She could not believe her grandparents had done all of this for her. She was happy but she felt so unworthy of all of this attention.

As the guests started to arrive, they were totally surprised by the fairytale beauty of this place. They could not help but stop and stare in awe.

The ladies' gowns were stunning. A variety of styles and colors lent an extra measure of beauty to the occasion.

The men looked magnificent in their evening attire. There were also a variety of ruffled shirts, formal coats and neckties.

Catherine had selected a deep rose-colored, velvet dress. It had a scalloped neckline with long fitted sleeves. The gathered skirt was made full by a crinoline.

"Grandmother, you chose the right color for your snow white hair. You look gorgeous!" Elizabeth said as she lovingly kissed her on the cheek.

John was handsome in a black cutaway coat and slim-cut pants. Elizabeth straightened his black bow tie and buttoned a button he had missed on his white, ruffled fronted shirt.

"You will be the handsomest grandfather here tonight," she said with adoration in her eyes.

When Zachary arrived he could not have looked more dashing. Elizabeth liked his form-fitted waistcoat. His plain-fronted, white shirt with the black silk ascot tie accentuated his tanned skin. *My, my, this blonde, blue-eyed handsome man is to be my escort for the evening,* Elizabeth thought with satisfaction.

John and Catherine stood at the entrance to the ball room to greet their guests as they arrived. The Fullers and the De Lays came in together and were the last to arrive.

Crossing the room, John paused to tell the Classic Harmony group to play the fanfare as soon as he and Catherine reached the bottom of the stairs.

The music sounded and the band director announced:

"Ladies and gentlemen, we present to you Miss Elizabeth Ann Baldwin Morgan, the granddaughter of John and Catherine Morgan."

When Elizabeth walked down the wide stairs, she looked elegant. She was wearing an ice blue, silk gown. The scooped neckline and fitted bodice was flattering to her perfect figure. The gathered skirt with yards of chiffon billowed around her, accenting her movements as though she were gliding.

Her black hair was in a sophisticated upsweep with tendrils framing her face. Her dazzling smile as she looked down at Zachary standing at the foot of the stairs made her dimples very conspicuous.

When she reached the bottom of the steps Zachary bowed, took her hand and said, "May I have this dance?"

They circled the ballroom floor to the enchanting strains of Elizabeth's favorite, The Blue Danube Waltz.

The music stopped and another fanfare sounded. John Morgan announced:

"Ladies and gentlemen, you are our honored guests at this party for our Granddaughter Elizabeth. As your names are called please come forward. Then feel free to dance to the music of Classic Harmony.

"Steven and Barbara Bainbridge, Thomas and Joyce Bainbridge, Benjamin and Rebecca Bainbridge, Dr. Russell and Mary Parks, Anthony and Judy Waller, Norman and Sharon Wallin, Steve and Rebecca Wilson, Matthew and India Jones, Scott and Libbi Dixon, Andrea Ashton and Max Hammond, Dr. Robert and Sara De Lay,

Judge John and Rose Fuller, Cordelia Fuller and Daniel Pierce, Reverend James and Barbara Perkins."

----∞∫∞----

John and Catherine watched with pleasure as their guests danced to the beautiful waltz music. They especially noticed Elizabeth and Zachary. They could hardly take their eyes off them. Her raven tresses so close to his very blonde hair as her forehead touched his cheek was such a pleasant contrast. They were a dashingly handsome couple.

After several dances Elizabeth said, "Zachary, let's go sit with your family for a while."

They made their way to their table. Steven and Barbara, Zachary's parents greeted them warmly.

"Elizabeth, your cotillion will long be remembered by all of us. It couldn't be more perfect.

Your grandparents have been good friends to Zachary. We have enjoyed our association with them over the years. Their finding you is nothing short of a miracle. We hope to get to know you better in the months to follow," Mrs. Bainbridge said.

"Zachary is a fortunate young man indeed," Zachary's father said as he patted Elizabeth on the arm. "We know that he is very fond of you."

"I appreciate your kind words and I, too, want us to become better aquatinted," Elizabeth replied.

She looked around the Ballroom at the many couples. Everyone had been very friendly.

Matthew and India Jones were especially nice. Maybe she could get to know them better.

Scott and Libbi Dixon had gone out of their way to be friendly. Scott had brought her some punch and Libbi was very complimentary of her dress. She liked them.

Elizabeth had never heard more beautiful music.

"Zachary, if this group ever comes to Richmond in concert we should be sure and go hear them."

Chapter 26

As the evening wore on fewer couples were dancing and more were seated at their tables, nibbling on food, listening to the music and chatting with one another.

Kreisler, the band's leader called Elizabeth and Zachary up to a front table and said they were going to play a special medley of songs just for them. During the next pause in the music, Kreisler asked that the ballroom floor be completely cleared. He took Elizabeth and Zachary by the hand, had them to stand and said, "This waltz is just for you two. And when we finish we are going to ask all of you to join in and dance the Virginia reel!"

Zachary and Elizabeth glided over the dance floor as though they were on air. It was as if they were in their very own world with no one else around. It ended all too soon it seemed.

Everyone joined in the Virginia reel. It was great fun!

Andrea Ashton came up to Elizabeth and said, "I understand you live in Richmond. Is it very different from Williamsburg?"

"It is different in Richmond. We don't have the hustle and bustle of riverboat shipping. I think we live at a much slower pace."

"I'd like to visit Richmond someday."

"If you ever do come, please let me know so we could get together."

"I surely will."

The guests had become more relaxed and less formal and were engaging more and more in conversation.

Someone else called Elizabeth's name. It was Rebecca Wilson and her husband, Steve.

"Hello, Elizabeth. We are so glad to finally meet you. Your grandparents are dear friends of ours. Steve and Zachary went to school together. What do you think of your party?" Rebecca inquired.

"It's wonderful, Rebecca. I never dreamed it would be so special. This is such a beautiful and elaborate grand Ballroom. However, it is the people who have made this party really special. My grandparents have a host of wonderful friends."

Steve said, "Zachary told me he had met a special and beautiful lady, Elizabeth. He certainly wasn't exaggerating."

"You are very kind to say that. I hope I can get to know you two better."

Elizabeth felt a tap on the shoulder. It was India and Matthew Jones. India was such a lovely name, Elizabeth thought.

"Matthew and I want to tell you how much we are enjoying your party. Isn't this Ballroom the most elegant place you've ever seen? We will never forget this Valentine's Day, will we Matt?" India said as she smiled at him.

"That's for sure!" Matt replied. "I'm glad we were invited."

"Thank you for saying hello. It means a lot. I hope to see more of you two."

Elizabeth went to the table where Thomas and Joyce Bainbridge were sitting and joined them for a while. She let them know Zachary had spoken to her lovingly about Heather and Joey, their two children.

Rebecca and Steve were filling their cups at the punch table when Cordelia Fuller came up.

She nodded and said, "Hello, you two," as she reached for a cup of punch. "Well, I see Zachary is leading another girl astray. This Elizabeth really thinks she has herself a catch. I think I'll just break up this little romance. I can make up a story about me and her precious Zachary that would fix his wagon for good!"

"Cordelia, you wouldn't *dare* do such a thing!" Rebecca scolded.

"No, I guess I wouldn't. Just forget I said that," she said and walked away with her cup of punch.

"You don't think she is serious do you Steve? Do you think she would dare do a thing like that?"

"No, she has a chip on her shoulder because she has always had her eye on Zachary and he has never paid her any attention at all. Her pride is hurt more than anything and she's jealous of Elizabeth's good looks. Don't worry about it, Rebecca. I think Elizabeth can take care of herself."

"I thought Cordelia had run off to Norfolk to live with her aunt and uncle. That was right after she fell for that man from Norfolk who came here to visit her brother Charles. When did she get back? What happened to that beau? Steve, she is a troublemaker wherever she is."

"She came back about six months ago, according to Charles. She only stayed with her aunt and uncle about four months. Charles' friend lost interest because she was so pushy. Now don't worry about her, Rebecca. She is really quite harmless."

Cordelia circled around the tables looking for Zachary. She did not see him. She turned back toward the punch table and spotted him walking in that direction. She retraced her steps, hurriedly, and got there at the same time.

"Why, hello Zachary darling. Do you still love me?"

"Cordelia, behave yourself!"

"I've just been thinking how I can send Miss Elizabeth packing back to Richmond. When I get through telling her about us she won't want you anymore."

"Cordelia, there is no *us*. There never has been and you know it."

"Yes, unfortunately I do know it. But she doesn't."

"Cordelia, don't you go near Elizabeth. Do you hear me?" Zachary said in an angry voice.

"Why, hello Elizabeth. Zachary and I were just getting a fresh cup of punch," Cordelia said very sweetly and walked away.

"Who is that young lady, Zachary? Is she a friend of yours?"

"No, she isn't. She is Judge Fuller's daughter. She's rather to be pitied. Let's have another cup of punch. It's very good, don't you think?" Zachary said rather nervously.

"Yes, it's delicious as well as the food. Grandmother and grandfather can be very proud of the party. Their planning has made it a huge success."

Zachary took Elizabeth's arm and led her back to a table.

Sensing the cotillion would soon be over, the couples had all moved back onto the dance floor. Zachary held Elizabeth ever so tightly as though he was afraid of losing her. He whispered softly into her ear, "I love you so, Elizabeth. I could not bear to lose you."

He seemed to be acting strangely. At that time her grandfather tapped Zachary on the shoulder. He wanted one more dance with his beautiful granddaughter.

"Elizabeth, you have made us so proud tonight. Our friends have felt your warm sincerity. You are stunning in your party dress. After the next two songs we will bid our guests goodnight. Have you had a good time?"

"Grandfather, this is the grandest thing that has ever happened to me! I feel like Cinderella. You and grandmother have been too good to me. I can never repay you for such a wonderful party."

"Oh yes, Elizabeth. Our reward is having our granddaughter in our lives. That is all we ever need from you! Your grandfather and I love you, dear Elizabeth."

He took her back to her table and went to find Catherine. Zachary was talking to his sister, Rebecca. She had gorgeous auburn hair.

Elizabeth stepped out into the hotel lobby to catch her breath. Someone called her name. She turned and there stood Cordelia Fuller.

She said, "Elizabeth, may I talk with you a moment? Could we step behind that screen please?"

Elizabeth followed her.

Cordelia said almost in a whisper, "There is something I feel I should tell you. It is for your own good. You seem to care for Zachary Bainbridge. But I don't think you really know him. Six months ago he courted me, told me he loved me and wanted to marry me. I felt like he was rushing things. I told him I needed some time. He said he would have me one-way or the other. He became abusive, even angry and tried to force himself on me. I was horrified and had to leave town for months due to the stress. I went to Norfolk and stayed with my aunt and uncle. I feel terrible telling you this. But you seem so nice. I just hate to see him hurt someone else as he hurt me." She wiped a tear from her eye. "I found out that there was another girl before me that he mistreated. He is terrible, really terrible! I felt I had to warn you." And with that she left.

Elizabeth felt faint. How could such a wonderful, fairytale evening end like this? She knew she must go back inside the ballroom. Her grandparents would be looking for her. She squared her shoulders, lifted her chin and walked into the Ballroom.

Zachary came toward her and asked, "Elizabeth, are you alright? You look a little pale."

"I'm fine. Just a little tired."

Her grandfather was ready to make an announcement. The musicians played another fanfare.

"Dear friends and family, thank you all for coming to Elizabeth's party. It will be a Valentine's evening we will never forget. Valentine's Day is to spread love and love has been very present here tonight. The Morgan's are fortunate to have you for friends. We bid you all a very pleasant evening and thank you for coming. These wonderful musicians will play one last love song before we go."

Zachary wanted one last dance with Elizabeth. Inside she felt like a wooden puppet as they waltzed around the ballroom. Her heart felt as though it had been completely crushed.

It was late. Zachary had come in his own carriage and wanted to drive Elizabeth home. She said she would ride with her grandparents telling him she thought this would please them.

Zachary said goodnight, reluctantly. He lifted her chin for a goodnight kiss and was barely able to brush her lips with his before she quickly said goodnight and stepped into her grandfather's awaiting carriage.

On their way home in the carriage Elizabeth laid her head on her grandfather's shoulder.

They all talked excitedly about the party, and agreed that it was perfect. Little did they know that inside she felt as if she were dying.

When they got home Elizabeth excused herself and went straight to her room. She undressed quickly and slipped between the warm blankets and cried a river of tears. Sleep eluded her.

The words she heard pounded in her head . . .

"Cordelia, don't you go near Elizabeth. Do you hear me?"

"Is she a friend of yours?"

"No, she isn't."

"She is to be pitied."

"It's for your own good."

"You don't really know him."

"He said he would have me one way or the other."

"He became abusive, even angry."

"He tried to force himself on me."

Elizabeth whispered to herself, "My Lord. Oh, my Lord. Not Zachary. Please God, not my Zachary. He is too sincere, too kind and gentle. I've seen nothing about him to back up her accusations. He was angry when he told her not to come near me. But maybe he had reason to be.

"And Lord, he told me in December, the day I left to go to back to Richmond, 'I have never been frivolous with my emotions toward women. When I marry I want it to be for life. So I have guarded my feelings for just the right person. I love you. I'll wait for you forever.'

"Were these all lies? Were they, Lord? What *am* I to believe? I don't know this Cordelia. She might not be an honest person. But why would she tell me this if it were not so? She seemed truthful.

"I'm so mixed up, Lord. So hurt. You are going to have to help me know how to handle this. I love Zachary. But Lord, I can't have my life wind up like my mother's. Help me. Please, Lord, help me."

She lay in bed all night trying to decide what she must do. She did not want to tell her grandparents any of this. She simply could not. They loved Zachary. They loved him like a son. And surely, after five years of working with him and having him in their home so often, they would know if he had done something like what this Cordelia had accused him of. And she said it all happened just six months ago!

She did not want Zachary to know about this because, if it weren't true, he would feel betrayed by her lack of trust. But how could she act as though nothing had happened?

Whom could she trust? She needed to trust someone. She needed to get to the bottom of this. She must know in her own mind if Zachary is an honorable man.

Her mind and body were so tired.

The sun rose and she could not face the day. She must be alone. She simply must be.

She heard a knock on the door.

"Come in. Good morning, Millie. Will you please tell grandmother I am not feeling well. It's just a headache. I did not sleep well last night. I guess all the attention at my party was too much. I plan to stay in my room and rest today. I'll let you know if I want anything to eat. Right now I feel I can't eat a bite. Tell her not to worry. I'll be fine."

"I hope you get to feeling better, Miss Elizabeth. If you need anything, just ring."

Elizabeth thought to herself . . . *today is the 15th. I will be going home Saturday the 18th. I will stay in tomorrow also. Then I will only have one more day to pretend things are alright. I almost feel as if my world ended last night.*

Chapter 27

*E*lizabeth opened the draperies and looked outside. The sun was shining. The world outside her window looked perfectly normal. But inside her heart, her world had been shattered. She had relived the events of last night over and over. Because she wanted to believe in Zachary so badly, she felt this Cordelia person might be a troublemaker and be misrepresenting the truth. Then she would remember how innocent Cordelia looked when she was telling her of Zachary's behavior. She *even* cried . . . *why, why would she tell such a thing if it were not true?*

Then she would remember Zachary's warm and tender kisses, his gentleness. He had never shown a mean nor aggressive spirit toward her.

The more she thought the more muddled her mind became. She shivered and realized she needed her robe. She closed the draperies, walked back to the bed and crawled back in between the warm blankets. Out of sheer exhaustion she fell into a restless sleep.

Late in the afternoon she heard a light knock at her door. She called out, "Come in."

The door opened a few inches and her grandmother peeped inside.

"Elizabeth dear, are you feeling any better? I've been concerned about you."

"Come on in, Grandmother Catherine. What time is it?"

"It's a quarter past three. Aren't you hungry?"

"No, grandmother, I'm really not."

"But you need to eat something. Virginia made some fresh clam chowder. Could I have Martha bring you a tray?"

"That would be fine. A small cup of soup and maybe a glass of milk."

"What do you think is the matter, Elizabeth? You seemed fine yesterday and last night."

"Oh, grandmother, I'll be fine. I guess all the excitement for a plain country girl was just too much! I didn't sleep well at all last night. I have slept some today. Do you mind terribly if I stay in bed now and plan no activities for tomorrow? I'm sure I will feel stronger Friday. We will make up for lost time then."

"The most important thing, Elizabeth, is that you get to feeling better. Rest will help you more than anything."

"Thank you for understanding."

"Zachary came by at lunch. He was sorry you are not feeling well."

"Tell him for me that I am some better and will see him on Friday. Tell grandfather not to worry. I'm a Morgan and I'm strong! I'll bounce back in no time."

"Yes dear. I'll send Millie up with some warm water so you can freshen up. Martha will be up with a tray. Rest well, Elizabeth. I won't disturb you again tonight. I'll check on you in the morning."

Millie came with the water. Elizabeth washed her face. This made her feel better. Then Martha came with a tray.

"Miss Elizabeth, if you will eat you will get your strength back. As you know, Virginia's clam chowder is a delicacy. She made this just for you."

"Please thank her for me, Martha. I'm sure it is delicious. I will eat some of it, I promise."

She did and it made her feel better.

She began to take stock of things. In two more days she would be going back to Richmond, back to Willow Place. She always felt safe there.

Then in twelve days, if things went as planned, Zachary would be coming to Richmond to live. Her grandparents would come as soon as the sale of the business and their house was finalized. This is reality. This *is* going to happen. She might as well lay her feelings aside. She dearly loved Zachary, if he is really the man she believes him to be. She wants to move slowly with this new revelation. She must find a way to verify what Cordelia told her to see if it is true. But she reminded herself she simply could not reveal any of this to her grandparents. They deserved to be happy about this new move they were making. Their happiness was of primary importance. She would find a way to learn the truth. And if Zachary was like Cordelia said, then she would cross that bridge when she came to it.

She reached for her Bible and turned to the book of Psalms. Her eyes fell on these verses in Psalm 91 and 94:

"I will say of the Lord, He is my refuge and my fortress: my God in him will I trust. For he shall give his angels charge over thee, to keep thee in all thy ways. They shall bear thee up in their hands, lest thou dash thy foot against a stone. But the Lord is my defense; and my God is the rock of my refuge."

Elizabeth prayed, *Lord, I take comfort in your word. I accept you as my refuge and my fortress. I will trust in you for this problem. Please do send your angels, Lord. Help me to find out the truth. Give me comfort and strength. Thank you for your blessings and grace. Amen.*

She really did feel better. She got back in bed, blew out the lamp and soon was in a deep, restful sleep.

Today is Thursday the 16th. She decided to get a warm tub bath and then dress and go downstairs. She didn't want to go out, but she would at least spend some time with her grandparents. She rang for Millie to come and assist her.

"Good morning, Millie. Would you please prepare a bath for me?

"Indeed I will, Miss Elizabeth. I'm glad to see you are feeling better this morning."

"Millie, I'll be going back to Richmond on Saturday. I want to thank you for the many things you have done for me on my visits here, the good baths you have provided for me, the way you have helped me with my clothes. You've kept my room so clean. You are a special person and I will miss you when I go home."

"Why Miss Elizabeth, you are so kind to tell me this. You have made my job easy and most pleasant." Elizabeth dressed carefully and took pains with her damp curly hair. It was almost dry when she finished dressing. She wore a simple cotton dress. It was pink with a round neckline. Tiny pearl buttons extended down the front to the waistline. She loved the warmth of the long, fitted sleeves and the comfort of the full skirt. The soft pink added a glow to her cheeks. She wanted to make a good appearance after feeling so poorly yesterday.

Downstairs she found her grandmother in the sunroom. She slipped through the door and said, "Good morning. What's for breakfast? I'm starved!"

"Why, Elizabeth. Look at you. I don't have to ask how you feel. You look absolutely radiant. I've already had breakfast. But let's go to the kitchen and see what Virginia has in the warmer."

"Hmm, Virginia, this omelette is delicious, not to mention the ham and your biscuits. One of my favorite treats is honey with hot buttered biscuits."

"Thank you, Miss Elizabeth. I love to cook for someone with a hearty appetite."

After breakfast they went to the parlor. They heard the front door open. John walked in and asked, "How are my two favorite girls? Elizabeth, it's good to see you up and looking so well. Are you feeling as well as you look?"

"I'm much better, thank you. Why are you home so early?"

"Why, I came to see about my favorite granddaughter."

"Have you two eaten?"

"We've had a late breakfast," Catherine answered.

"Then I'm going to ring for Martha and have her bring me an apple dumpling and a cup of hot coffee to the parlor."

"Just how do you know Virginia made apple dumplings to-day?" Elizabeth inquired impishly.

"Because I smelled them cooking when I left the office."

"Oh, grandfather!"

The three of them curled up around the fireplace in the parlor for the afternoon.

"Since you were feeling poorly after the party, we haven't had a chance to ask you what you thought of it. Was it as much fun as you hoped it would be? Her grandmother asked.

"It was even more fun than I anticipated. I felt like a real storybook princess. I've never seen such a magnificent place as the Wellington Hotel. The decorations carried out the Valentine's theme perfectly. Grandmother, the live red roses floating in the bowls of water on each table was one of the things I especially noticed. A simple center piece but so elegant. The food and punch were superb. The music . . . oh, the music! Never have I heard anything quite so beautiful. They played this one song twice called 'To Each His Own.' Zachary and I call it *our* song."

"Your grandmother and I were made to reminisce as we listened to their music, their captivating strings and flutes. And I might add, they played your grandmother Catherine and my song from our youth, 'One and Only You'!"

"That's wonderful. What great memories!"

"I also met some of the dearest people. I say dearest because they were your friends, and to me that makes them dear. So many of them were young. I was impressed but not surprised because you two are so much fun to be with. You are much younger than your years.

"I watched as you stood together greeting the guests. I am very blessed to be your granddaughter."

"Maybe it seemed a little extravagant but we had the party just for you. It was a way for us to introduce you to some of our friends and have them meet you. If you enjoyed it then we are happy," her grandfather said as he took her hand and kissed it.

"We watched you and Zachary as you waltzed to the Blue Danube, all alone on the ballroom floor. You were a striking couple. Did you two enjoy the evening?"

"Yes, we did grandmother. Zachary was very attentive and sweet to me. He is a most attractive man. I thought so when I first met him on November 16th in Richmond. It was a 'fairytale' night for us."

"By the way Elizabeth, things are moving smoothly as far as our buying the carriage company. We do not foresee any problems. Also, word has gotten out that Morgan Shipping is up for sale. Three businessmen who are very interested in buying the company have contacted me. There should be no problem selling. I'll be putting this house up for sale in a couple of weeks. It appears that we will be residents of Richmond within a month!"

"Goodness, you two will be very busy then after I go home. Our lives have been turned upside down in the past six months!

"Grandfather and grandmother, I have been thinking about something. Remember how you made proposals to me, first about my name change, then the invitation to come here to live? Well, I have a proposal for you two.

"You know how I feel about Willow Place. As I have mentioned before, you are welcome to stay there until you find a place of your own. I have plenty of room and I know you would be comfortable there.

"Now for my proposal. I told you I have forty acres of land there, which includes my house and the lake. Nothing would make me happier than for you to build your own home on the other side of the lake from me. I will be glad to deed you whatever land you will need. You can think about this and decide after you see the place."

"Elizabeth, I can't imagine a more pleasant experience than sitting on my front porch, looking across a beautiful lake and seeing the home of the most precious person in the world to us. You have just made the prospects of our moving to Richmond more exciting than ever. We accept your generous offer. You do agree, don't you Catherine?"

By this time Catherine was wiping tears away.

"Oh John, whatever have we done to deserve such happiness? Elizabeth, I'm convinced the day you were born God knew about

this very day. He is a giver of perfect gifts . . . His life for our re-
demption, and a precious granddaughter like you. We feel honored that you would want us so near to you."

"Then it is settled. Grandmother, you need to come with grandfather and Zachary on the second when they come to Richmond to
meet with Mr. Randolph. That way both of you can see Willow
Place. You can plan on staying a few days and even attend church
with me at First Wesleyan on Sunday. What do you think?"

"John, would I be in the way? If not, I would love to go with
you."

"Catherine, since when have you ever been in the way? Of
course you should go!"

Chapter 28

The carriage moved briskly along Warthen Street. The driver turned onto James Street for a few blocks and then onto River Road, which would take them to Williamsburg Train Depot.

Zachary looked at Elizabeth. Smiling he said, "It seems to me we've done this before! The difference, however, is twelve days not two months until we will be together again . . . hopefully for the rest of our lives."

She looked up into those magnificent blue eyes. She thought, *he has the most magnetic personality. When I am with him the whole world seems right. How can I believe he is anything but honest? But what if I'm being deceived? My mind is so tired. How am I going to find out the truth?*

"Elizabeth, what is it? You seem so far away. You've seemed this way since the party was over. Is it that you are still not feeling well?"

"I've just had a lot on my mind. So much has happened in the past six months. My whole life has changed. It's been a good and positive change, but a change nevertheless. I really am a creature of habit. I'm not a very adventurous person."

"I like adventure up to a point. But I also see wisdom and strength in stability. I so admire the person that you are, Elizabeth. I've found you to have very high standards. You know your own mind."

If you only knew, Zachary, just how divided my poor mind is right now, she thought to herself. They pulled up to the train depot. The carriage driver placed her baggage on the dock, then parked the carriage near the passenger platform.

The train whistle sounded. Zachary held the carriage door open and helped Elizabeth down. He reached for her chin, tilted her face upward and searched her deep blue eyes for the look of adoration he had once seen there. Did he see a hint of sadness?

She smiled her dazzling smile and all fears melted away. He gathered her in his arms and held her ever so closely. Then he gently kissed her perfect lips, trying to freeze this moment in time until he moved to Richmond for good.

Reminiscent of the cotillion Zachary whispered in her ear, "I love you my beautiful princess."

She surprised herself by answering, "And I love you, too, my handsome prince."

She looked out the train window at Zachary standing on the platform. He was waving a handkerchief in the air at her. She looked down and, sure enough, she had lost her handkerchief!

Zachary held it to his face and could smell the wonderful fragrance that she wore. This is one handkerchief she would not get back.

Chapter 29

Faithful William was waiting for Elizabeth when she arrived back in Richmond. When he got her baggage loaded into the carriage, he patted her shoulder and said, "Miss Elizabeth, we've sure missed you. The place is just not the same when you're not here."

"And I've missed you, William, and Sadie and Emma. I hope I won't have to leave again for a long time. I have some news to tell all three of you when we get home."

After they had eaten supper that evening Elizabeth inquired, "Are you ready for some good news?"

"Yes, lassie, but the best news is that you are home. We've all agreed. We aren't going to let you leave us again!"

All of them laughed.

"My news just might mean that I won't have to leave again. My Grandfather Morgan plans to sell his shipping business as well as their home in Williamsburg and come to Richmond to live. He is presently negotiating a business deal here that will enable them to do this. My friend, Zachary Bainbridge, will be involved in this venture and will be moving here also. If everything goes as expected, the deal will be completed on March 3rd. Within the month of March they are planning to be living here in Richmond!"

"You must be very excited, Miss Elizabeth," Sadie remarked.

"That isn't all of the news. My grandparents will be here in our home for a few days visit on March 2nd. They will go back to Williamsburg to finalize their business there. Then they will come back to Willow Place to live with us until they build their own home. I have suggested that they build across the lake here at Willow Place."

Sadie jumped up and exclaimed, "We must get busy and clean the house from top to bottom. I've just been waiting for an excuse to clean the guest room thoroughly. Miss Elizabeth, aren't you glad that you bought that new bed spread and had new draperies made for that room this past spring? Goodness, what time is it?"

"Now, now Sadie. Calm down. We won't start anything tonight. Besides, you and Emma keep this place shining all the time. There should not be much extra cleaning to do at all!"

"Good morning, Elizabeth," Kim Thomas said as she met Elizabeth in the children's ward. "It is so good to have you back."

"I'm glad to be back. I've missed my volunteer work. Have you been very busy?"

"Yes. We've had several influenza cases and three cases of pneumonia. All were very serious. Remember Mr. Billings who was here a couple of weeks before you left on your trip?"

"Sure. He was the small man about eighty-six years old if I remember correctly."

"That's right. Well, he had a setback and we were unable to bring him through it. He was a dear little man. He didn't want to be a bother to anyone.

"We also had a real scare with little Jacob Hobbs. He is six years old and the picture of health. He had a stomachache for several days. His dad said they had a basket of apples stored in their cellar. Jacob admitted to eating several of them. They just knew his tummy ache came from the apples. Unfortunately, he had appendicitis, and by the time they got him here it had ruptured. Dr. Blake did emergency surgery. He did a masterful job. But even so, we almost lost him. We had to pack him in ice to keep his temperature down. He was a real little fighter. The whole staff felt this made the difference in his recovery."

Elizabeth worked extra hours her first day back. Near the end of the day she heard someone call her name. She turned around and it was Dr. Blake.

"Welcome back, beautiful woman," he said almost absent-mindedly. "How were your trip and your party?"

"It could not have been nicer. My grandparents are wonderful people. I am blessed to have them in my life. But, as I'm sure you know, it's always good to come home after a vacation."

"You missed a busy time here at the hospital. We really could have used you."

"Yes, Kim told me how hectic it was."

"Elizabeth, my eyes were opened to the real Kim Thomas. I've known her for the two years we have worked together, but I've never seen anyone so caring and supportive these past two weeks. Did she tell you about Jacob Hobbs?"

"Indeed she did. He gave all of you a real scare, didn't he?"

"Yes, but Kim stayed right with him. He was such a fighter and she was by his bedside the whole way. She has always showed undivided dedication to the field of nursing, but somehow this was different. You should have seen her with little Jacob. It was as though she willed him to live and refused to let him give up."

Elizabeth saw a look of admiration in his eyes when he spoke of Kim that seemed to go beyond professional interest.

"Do you know if there is anyone special in Kim's life? I mean, does she ever talk to you?"

"Most of our conversations are about the work here at the hospital. Her responsibilities keep her very busy and focused. With your aggressive personality, David, I'm surprised you haven't asked her yourself."

"Well, there is something about her that puts you at arm's length. But I *am* interested enough to remedy that!"

"Good for you!"

On Tuesday, February 21ˢᵗ, Elizabeth again visited the Smiths and the Everettes. These two families seemed to go together. Emily looked healthy and robust. The change in her diet had put some weight on her. Maggie said she had not been sick once since they came to live on the farm.

Henry was getting around better and was pleased with Jim Everette's work . . . saying that Jim is the best help he'd ever had, not to mention Maggie.

Bessie had become a grandmother to Sara, Emily and Julie. She really adored those little girls. It was a good visit.

Elizabeth went to the school to see Jane. They didn't get a chance to talk at church Sunday. After the last of the children left, she and Jane sat down for a real visit.

Elizabeth filled Jane in on all the happenings of her trip to Williamsburg. She was careful not to tell her about Cordelia's accusations against Zachary. Elizabeth didn't want anyone to know. She had a plan hopefully to get to the bottom of it, but that would take some time.

Jane wanted to hear all about the cotillion. Elizabeth told her in great detail. She also told her about the business venture her Grandfather Morgan was negotiating. But didn't tell her it involved Payton Randolph's Carriage Company because Jane's dad was employed there.

"Now Jane, tell me what has happened with you and Phillip. Did he follow through with the idea of teaching at William and Mary?"

"As a matter of fact he did. He is waiting for a reply from the college now. Oh Elizabeth, I'm so happy. Phillip is everything I ever dreamed of for a husband."

"Have you set a date for the wedding?"

"We have talked about Saturday, June 3ʳᵈ. If Phillip gets the teaching position, we will have to prepare for the move to Williamsburg. Classes wouldn't start until the middle of September. But we will need to get moved and settled before then. I really have only three months to make my plans. The end of the school year involves a lot of work but I'm glad to be busy."

Chapter 29

"Well, Janie, I best be going. It's always good to talk to my special friend."

"Yes, thanks for coming by."

"Give my regards to your family."

Chapter 30

Monday, February 27th was a slow day at the hospital. Emma had sent a basket of oatmeal muffins to work with Elizabeth to share. Mid morning Elizabeth knocked on Kim's office door.

Kim called out, "Come in." Looking up from her paper work she said "Good morning Elizabeth."

"Good morning, Kim. I have a basket of muffins Emma sent along. I thought you might like one."

"Thank you. I'm starved. I see she even sent some butter. Buttered oatmeal muffins remind me of home."

"Where is home for you Kim?"

"Right here in Richmond. I've lived here all my life."

"Do you have brothers or sisters?"

"Indeed I do. I have four brothers and two sisters. I'm the oldest at twenty-five. The youngest are twin brothers who are twelve."

"Then your parents must be young."

"Yes, I suppose so. My father is forty-six and my mother is forty-four. With a large family like mine I have been a nurse most of my life! I've always been interested in the world of medicine."

"May I ask a personal question?"

"You may."

"Is there a special someone in your life?"

"Yes, there is, but he doesn't know it. Elizabeth, you have impressed me as someone who can be trusted, and sometimes a girl needs someone to confide in. Do you mind?"

"Of course not Kim. I am flattered you feel you can share with me."

"The special someone is Dr. Blake. We came to East Richmond about the same time. He was so focused on his work to begin with and had time for little else, not even small talk or pleasantries. He was all business.

"I wanted to learn all I could. I spent all my spare time studying, determined to do honor to the field of nursing and hoping he might notice. But he never has. I felt if we had the love of medicine in common it might create an interest on his part. But I seem to have empty dreams."

"Don't be too sure, Kim. It might interest you to know that Dr. Blake asked me last week if I knew whether there was a special person in your life! So quit being so 'all business' when you are around him and tell him what a great Doctor he is. Let him see the woman in you for a change."

"Oh really Elizabeth? He asked you that? Oh my, what shall I say the next time I see him?"

<hr />

Elizabeth awakened to a rather warm February rain. She sat for a while and watched as the rain pelted the lake. The wind was blowing the silhouetted willow branches to and fro creating a rhythmic pattern.

She dressed and went downstairs to the kitchen. The fire in the cooking stove gave off a soothing warmth.

"Emma, where are you?"

"I'm right here," she replied as she emerged from the pantry.

"Has everyone eaten but me?"

"Yes lassie. Sadie is putting the finishing touches on the guest room. I'll declare she has cleaned that room until it sparkles. William has gone to the barn to check on the horses."

"It's only two days until our company will be here. I believe we have everything ready for them."

"That we do, lassie. That we do. We will feed them well while they are here."

It had rained steadily all day. Elizabeth hoped it would clear up. She had enjoyed the day. The rain was needed. She liked sitting inside by a warm fire and watching the rain fall. At bedtime it was still coming down, heavy at times.

She read her scriptures, said her prayers and snuggled between the warm blankets, very thankful for her home and family.

The morning dawned bright and crisp. The rain was gone and everything looked fresh and clean. Elizabeth enjoyed the buggy ride to the hospital. She would work today, March 1st, and would not go back until the eighth.

As she was reading to a little girl who had fallen against a stove and badly burned her arm, Kim came into the room. She checked the girl's burns, applied salve and re-bandaged her arm and hand ever so gently. When she finished Kim turned to Elizabeth and whispered, "When you have time please check with me before you leave today."

"Yes, I will."

Shortly before time for her to leave Elizabeth saw David talking to Kim. He was smiling when he walked away.

"Did you want to see me, Kim?" Elizabeth inquired.

"Yes. Let's step into my office. I wanted to tell you that I played 'coy' with David and it seemed to work. He actually flirted with me yesterday! Just now he asked if he could take me to dinner. Of course I said yes."

"Kim, this is good news. I'll be very interested in how things progress. Oh yes, since my grandparents are coming in tomorrow and will be spending a few days I won't be in again until March 8th."

"Elizabeth, thanks for being my friend."

"Believe me, Kim, it's my pleasure."

Chapter 31

March 2

The train whistle sounded and Elizabeth jumped nervously. She was very excited as well as anxious that the three people she loved most in the world were coming to her part of the country. She was trying to be positive about Zachary. Since leaving Williamsburg it was almost as though she had never met Cordelia Fuller. Elizabeth had about talked herself into forgetting the whole thing.

She had no qualms about her grandparents liking Willow Place, none at all. It was like Grandmother Catherine's sunroom and grandfather's James River. Everyone should have a Willow Place.

The train was pulling into the depot. William looked very handsome today. He had dressed sharply for the occasion and had cleaned the carriage until it glistened. Their prize Morgan named Dolly had been brushed until her coat shined. She was rigged with their finest leather harness trimmed in silver. Elizabeth hoped her grandfather would notice.

She waited for the train door to open. Several passengers stepped off ahead of her grandparents and Zachary. Then she saw them.

"Over here, grandfather!" Elizabeth called out.

They spotted her quickly and she gave them welcoming hugs.

"Grandmother Catherine, how was your trip?"

"It was pleasant, thank you. I read part of the way, napped just a little, and enjoyed the scenery. Then we talked about our new venture, and before we knew it we were here."

"Grandfather, William will get your baggage. Did the trip tire you?"

"Not a'tall, granddaughter. I'm too excited at the prospects of owning my own carriage company."

Zachary had waited politely. But now he reached for Elizabeth, gave her a quick hug and kiss on the cheek and whispered, "Till later."

William loaded all of their baggage, then drove around to the platform to pick up his passengers.

Elizabeth insisted on introducing William to her grandparents and Zachary. William looked a little embarrassed but her grandfather put him at ease by exclaiming over Dolly. He looked her over, patted her neck, remarking whimsically what a fine "Morgan" she was.

"Now look here! What a fine carriage this is, Elizabeth. I know this came from Randolph Carriage Company. It's in perfect condition."

"Yes, grandfather. William takes good care of everything. I never have to worry about maintenance. I don't know what I would do without him. Grandfather Baldwin bought this carriage in 1851, a year before he died, so it is five years old."

"It is proof of a very fine product," her grandfather said positively.

"Elizabeth, we will take Zachary by the Richmond Hotel so he can leave his baggage."

Finally they were on their way to Willow Place. Elizabeth almost held her breath in anticipation of their seeing the lake and willow trees. She wished it could be spring so the flowering shrubs could add their color to the setting. But in a couple of months it would be in full bloom and they would see how majestic it really is.

She looked from one face to the other as they started the ride around the lake to the front of the house.

"My, my, my! So *this* is Willow Place," her Grandmother Catherine exclaimed. "No wonder you don't wish to leave it."

"Grandfather?"

"You hardly did it justice, Elizabeth. It's unbelievably beautiful."

"Zachary?"

"I think I'm falling in love all over again, Elizabeth. It's hard to drink in all of its beauty . . . much like its mistress.

"We haven't had a very cold winter this year. You'll notice the pendent branchlets on the weeping willows are already producing their new growth of leaves," Elizabeth pointed out. "By the middle of April they will be lush and green."

William pulled up in front of the house and assisted them out of the carriage. As William unloaded their baggage they stood looking at the architecture of the stately Baldwin home. Its red brick, white columns and tasteful trim made Elizabeth proud. This home represented two of the dearest people in her life and she would never leave it.

"Elizabeth, you have every right to feel as you do about Willow Place. I wish I could have known the Baldwin's," her grandfather said reflectively.

"I'm glad you shared some of your growing-up years with us. Now that we see the place these events come alive to us. You had to be a very happy child."

"Yes, Grandmother Catherine. God in His wisdom permitted this to be. Even though I was not allowed to have a mother and father to raise me, my Baldwin grandparents nurtured me so that I've always felt complete, nothing lacking. They could not have loved me more if I had been their own child."

Elizabeth turned to Zachary, took his arm and said, "Now let's all go inside."

Emma opened the door for them. They entered into the foyer. To the left on the front of the house was the formal sitting room. To its left was the library. From the foyer to the right was the formal dining room, and to its right was a breakfast room. Straight ahead was the stairway to the second floor where the bedrooms were located. In the back part of the house were the kitchen, large pantry, sewing room, an extra bedroom and the much used parlor.

Elizabeth led them through the formal sitting room on to the library where there was a roaring fire and plenty of comfortable chairs and sofas. Emma followed them. When they were seated Elizabeth introduced Emma to John and Catherine Morgan.

Emma said, "I'm pleased to meet you."

Elizabeth turned to Zachary and then to Emma, "this is Zachary Bainbridge, a business associate of my grandfather and my friend."

"You've each heard me speak of Emma many times. Yes, she works for me as she did for my Grandfather Baldwin and Grandmother Savannah. She has been with my family for thirty-seven years. I was three years old when I came here. I do not consider her a servant. She is family. She has been a part of my life as long as I can remember. Emma is kind enough to cook for us and help with the cleaning. We eat at the same table every day, as do William and his wife, Sadie. They live in the small house on the property. They, too, have been a part of the family for years. Sadie does most of the cleaning, but she and Emma work together to keep things going. Emma's bedroom is downstairs here in this house. We live a simple, happy life, and we like that.

"Emma and Sadie will gladly assist you any way they can. I know you are tired from your trip and would like to freshen up and perhaps rest before supper tonight." Elizabeth laughed and said, "Yes, we call the evening meal 'supper' here in the country."

"Elizabeth, this will be a wonderfully relaxed atmosphere for us." Catherine said happily. "And, yes, we would like to rest and then freshen up as you suggested."

Sadie knocked at the library door and entered. Introductions were made, then she took the Morgan's upstairs.

Zachary said, "I prefer to spend some time with you, Elizabeth, if I may."

"By all means," Elizabeth said as she sat down on the sofa in front of the fireplace. Zachary joined her.

"Elizabeth, I have been taking in everything here at Willow Place since I arrived this afternoon. Your way of life here is different. It is slower and certainly a quality life style. You know your own mind and have strong Christian values. Willow Place seems to run smoothly. As we would say on the docks in the shipping business, this is a 'well-oiled machine.' And that is a compliment. I am *so* impressed. And, as I've watched you and listened to you this afternoon, I have never loved you more. My very heart beats your name, Elizabeth."

She sat spellbound. Zachary seemed to really understand her. If she did what she wanted to do, she would ask him to hold her close and never let her go.

But is this the way her mother's courtship went with her father, John Lee? It must have been because he had swept her off her feet quickly. Why must she be haunted by the past?

"Elizabeth, you are so still and quiet. Did I say something wrong?"

"No. No, Zachary. What you said to me is beautiful."

"Then might I have a 'welcome home' kiss? This *is* my home now . . . Richmond, that is." He stood to his feet, took both her hands and gently pulled her up, gathered her into his arms and held her for the longest time.

Elizabeth laid her head against his strong chest, closed her eyes and prayed, *"Lord, I love him so much. What must I do? I am so afraid. What if Cordelia Fuller is telling the truth about his aggressive pursuit of her? I cannot, I must not make a mistake with my life as my mother did. You must lead me. I have to know that Zachary is the person I want him to be for my life."*

Zachary finally tilted her chin upward and pressed his warm lips against hers. He was so gentle, so tender. In spite of her fears she was deeply in love with him.

"Do you feel like a walk around Willow Place, Zachary?"

"I thought you might never ask!"

"First let's go by the kitchen and see how long till supper."

"Emma, are you there?"

Emma came through the pantry door carrying some clean dishtowels. "I'm right here, lassie," she replied and did a little curtsy to Zachary.

"Zachary and I were thinking of taking a walk. How long is it till supper?"

"It's four-thirty now. We will be ready to eat by 6:00 if that's alright."

"That will be perfect, Emma. Please ask Sadie to tell my grandparents that supper will be at 6:00 . . . and see if they need any assistance."

"I will, lassie, I will."

Chapter 32

Elizabeth and Zachary walked hand-in-hand across the front lawn towards the lake.

"Do you ever go boating on the lake?" Zachary asked.

"When Dandy was alive we did quite often. But since he died I haven't had the boat in the water at all," Elizabeth replied.

"This spring we will have to revive the tradition. Would you like that?"

"Very much, Zachary. We also have geese to visit the lake when they migrate north after the winter. Last year we had two white swans that came for several days. I so hoped they would stay. They just seemed to go with the willow trees. But they left as mysteriously as they came."

"Elizabeth, I am sure after tomorrow I will be very busy. If we acquire the carriage company, it will mean some long hours for the first few months. We will have a lot to learn. John has already told me he will lean heavily on me. Our seeing each other won't be as often as we would like. I just want you to understand."

"I certainly will understand. I want you to be there for grandfather. I'm very glad he has you to lean on."

The two walked all the way around the lake. Elizabeth pointed out several of her favorite places. From the west side of the lake they looked back towards the east to the green fields and pasture land. The white fencing against the green grass formed a perfect picture. They talked about personal philosophies and goals they had set for their lives. Elizabeth listened carefully to every word Zachary spoke. Their ideas about life were parallel. She saw no indication that he was a fake as Cordelia Fuller implied. Things between them seemed so right.

Emma stepped outside the back door and rang the big bell calling everyone to supper.

Elizabeth had asked Emma to serve supper in the lovely dining room. The spacious room was a comforting reminder to Elizabeth of all the meals she had shared with her grandmother Savannah and Dandy over the years. The large oval oak table with fine quilted back chairs was so enjoyable with a roaring fire. A huge oak china cabinet with matching serving hutch had belonged to grandmother Savannah's mother, and was a real conversation piece.

Emma had the table spread with a white linen tablecloth. She used the willow-ware for the table setting. Elizabeth loved this dinnerware. It was a surprise gift to her grandmother from Dandy when he returned from one of his many trips. It has a story-telling design featuring a large willow tree by a little bridge done on bone china in green.

When everyone was seated around the table, Elizabeth welcomed them again to her home. She said, "Today, March 2nd, 1856 will always be important on my calendar of memories. My only regret is that my Grandmother Savannah and 'Dandy' are not here with us. They would be just as happy as we are and they would love John and Catherine Morgan . . . and you too, Zachary!"

They all laughed.

She continued, "Grandfather, would you please say grace?"

"Thank you Elizabeth, Emma, Sadie and William for your warm hospitality. Please bow your heads with me. Thank you, Heavenly Father for your many blessings on our lives. Continue to bless this home. We humbly thank you for the food before us. Let us always remain thankful. Amen."

Emma had prepared a feast. For dessert she had made one of her buttery pound cakes, with plenty of hot coffee.

The conversation was lively around the table. John and William had really taken to one another.

"William, how long have you lived in Richmond?"

"All of my life, Mr. Morgan."

"Then you know a lot of people in this area."

"Yes sir, I do."

"Do you know many people who work for Payton Randolph at the carriage company?"

"Why yes. In talking to a friend, Jim Adams, who is the foreman there, he says they work twenty-five men. I personally know several of them. From what I hear it's a good company to work for."

"Hmm, that's good to hear from one who is not employed there."

Zachary spoke up, "How well do you know this Jim Adams?"

"Oh, I know Jim well. He is a fine man. He was very helpful when Mr. Baldwin bought our last carriage. Mr. Randolph had him explain the workmanship on it to Mr. Baldwin. I was with him when he bought it. He is a real craftsman in the carriage making business."

Elizabeth interjected, "I forget to tell you, grandfather, that my best friend, Jane Adams, is Jim Adams' daughter."

"Well, well. That is very interesting," her grandfather mused.

"William, these might seem like strange questions, but not when I tell you that we are here to purchase the carriage company. It is certain that we will. We will meet in the morning to sign the papers and finalize the purchase."

"Grandfather, that reminds me. I thought your attorney was to have come with you to Richmond."

"He actually came the day before on Wednesday. He needed to meet with Mr. Randolph's attorney to go over the legalities."

"To change the subject Elizabeth, I've never seen such lovely dinnerware. It is almost as if you had it specially made featuring willow trees. Wherever did you find it?"

"Grandmother, I felt the very same way when I first saw it. Grandfather Baldwin brought it back from Washington after one of his trips there. You should have heard Grandmother Savannah squeal with delight when she lifted the first plate from its packing."

They began to get up from the table. Each of them told Emma and Sadie how delicious the meal was.

It was time for William to take Zachary back to the hotel, so he went for the carriage. John shook hands with Zachary and said, "I'll see you at the hotel at 8:30. We are due in Payton's office at nine."

Elizabeth told Sadie to show her grandparents to the parlor. Then she walked with Zachary to the front porch.

Zachary looked at Elizabeth from the reflection of the gaslight and caught his breath at her beauty. He was trying hard to move slowly because he knew this is what Elizabeth wanted. But the time he had spent with her since November 16th made him feel he knew her as well as he needed to. She was everything . . . no, she was more than everything he had ever hoped her to be.

He pulled her close to him. Looking into her face, he stroked her soft, black hair, and then put his face next to her cheek and lamented, "Elizabeth, Elizabeth, how long must I wait for you? If it were left to me we would never spend another day apart. I'm trying so hard not to rush you, but my resolve is weakening."

Again Elizabeth leaned against him and let his strong arms hold her up. The desire to tell him she loved him ever bit as much as he loved her almost prevailed. But she must not let her heart overrule her head. She still needed time. Marriage was forever to her. It was too serious an issue to take a chance. She had to somehow find out the truth about what she had been told.

She heard the carriage coming.

Zachary gave her a quick kiss, stepped away from her, then pulled her back into his arms and kissed her more passionately than ever before. He released her and said, "Goodnight my princess."

He disappeared down the steps and into the waiting carriage. She watched until she could see it no more, then slowly turned and walked inside.

She found her grandparents in the parlor looking very contented.

"I realize it has been a long day for you two. Do you think you will be comfortable here at Willow Place?"

"Elizabeth, without any reservation we can say this day and evening will always stand out in our minds. We can't remember when we've enjoyed fellowship and food more than here in your home. You seem to have figured out what is important in life. That can be summed up in one word . . . people. You have surrounded yourself with three lovely people, genuine people, without pretense. How comfortable they are to be with."

"Yes grandfather, they are the same dependable people every day. After the death of my grandparents they were the only family I had. I love each of them very much."

"Your grandmother and I have always been civic-minded. We've spent a lot of our lives championing causes that were important to us, but I think we might have been too busy sometimes to get as personally involved with people on a daily basis as we should. I am impressed with what I have witnessed here in your home."

"Grandmother, you've been awfully quiet."

"I've just been listening and agreeing wholeheartedly. We will be very comfortable here, Elizabeth, as long as you will have us."

"And that will be as long as you need to stay."

Chapter 33

MARCH 3

*M*arch had come in like a lion! The wind was blowing the white clouds through the sky very rapidly. The surface of the water on the lake was ruffled from the wind.

Elizabeth wondered how the business meeting was going. It was 9:30. She breathed a prayer for the whole process to go smoothly.

"Good morning, Elizabeth. I'm making some French toast for breakfast with hot maple syrup and coffee," Emma said cheerfully.

She heard footsteps. "Good morning, grandmother. Did you rest well?"

"Indeed I did. You must have had an interior decorator to coordinate your guest room. It is so tastefully decorated. I particularly liked the dusty rose chintz bedspread and matching draperies. They go perfectly with the color of your walls. Is the dresser with the side-wing, moveable mirrors a family heirloom?"

"As a matter of fact it is. Grandmother Savannah's mother passed it down to her," Elizabeth said with pride.

They had breakfast and then took a grand tour of the home inside and out. The day passed quickly.

Her grandfather and Zachary came back about 5:00 in the afternoon in their own buggies . . . from their own company! They had also purchased a Morgan horse each. It looked as if they were set for business.

"Since Grandfather Baldwin raised Morgan's and quarter horses for several years, he had the big barn built. You will have room for your horses and buggies here," Elizabeth said.

"I planned to ask you about that. Also, I wanted to ask about getting William some help. Would you object to my doing that?"

"Certainly not. It's a good idea."

They talked about the day's negotiations over supper. Her grandfather said he was very impressed by this young attorney representing Payton Randolph. His name is Phillip Gregory Maxwell III.

Elizabeth exclaimed, "What?! You don't mean it. Phillip is engaged to my very best friend,

Jane Adams. And remember the foreman at Randolph's Carriage Company is Jane's father, Jim Adams. How ironic."

"Indeed it is, Elizabeth. Indeed it is."

———

MARCH 5
SUNDAY

Elizabeth and her grandparents arrived at church the same time as Jane Adams and her family. Introductions were made all around. John and Zachary had met Jim at the carriage company the day before.

Jim shook hands heartily with John and Zachary. "I would like for you two to meet my family. This is my wife, Mary Beth, our oldest daughter, Jane, Jim Jr., Joe and Josh and our youngest, Jenny."

John extended his hand to Mary Beth graciously saying, "I'm John Morgan and this is Zachary Bainbridge."

"My pleasure."

"Welcome to our city and certainly to our church," Mary Beth said.

"We look forward to getting to know you better," Jane chimed in.

John turned and said, "This is my wife, Catherine" who extended her hand to Jim and Mary Beth.

"We are so happy to meet friends of Elizabeth. You two are blessed to have such beautiful children."

They walked to the church steps where Pastor Will Davis and his wife, Madeline, were greeting members and friends at the door. Elizabeth introduced everyone.

"Your reputations have preceded you three. We heard so many good things about you from Elizabeth," Pastor Davis remarked.

"We are happy to have you worship with us," Madeline said warmly.

The service was very uplifting. The title of Pastor Davis' message was: We have been left an example of learning . . . a legacy by the Word.

His sermon pointed out that ignorance is not bliss. The pastor quoted Paul from Romans when he wrote, "I would not have you ignorant." We have a responsibility to seek the knowledge of God's word and His will in our lives.

During the message, Pastor Davis recalled how the people in Moses' day were given the truth of God in tablets of stone, and later penned on sacred scrolls that they and their children might know the right way to live.

He also talked about Daniel and the three Hebrew children, and how God gave them knowledge and skill in all learning and wisdom, far greater than King Nebuchadnezzar's astrologers and magicians.

The pastor ended his sermon by reading II Timothy 2:15.

Elizabeth was very reflective as she listened to Pastor Davis. His remarks paralleled the message she heard in Williamsburg when she went to church with her grandparents. Maybe the Lord was trying to tell her something. Perhaps she needed to study, really study His word more. The congregation stood and sang the familiar hymn "Nearer My God to Thee."

Pastor Davis asked everyone to be seated for an announcement.

"We have special visitors with us today. They are John and Catherine Morgan and Zachary Bainbridge from Williamsburg. I have asked their permission to tell you they are the new owners of Randolph's Carriage Company. It will begin operation tomorrow as Morgan-Bainbridge Carriage Company.

"Of course, the Morgan's are the grandparents of our own Elizabeth Baldwin Morgan. As we dismiss the service, please make them feel welcome."

There was a buzz of conversation as the church folks gathered around to shake hands and speak to the visitors. These three were made to feel at home at First Wesleyan.

MARCH 6
MONDAY

Elizabeth said goodbye to her grandparents. They were riding in to Richmond to catch the 10:30 A.M. train back to Williamsburg. Zachary was taking them to the train depot. But, as planned, he would be staying in Richmond to attend to the new business.

Before they left, her grandfather said, "Elizabeth, we don't know just when we will return. We think Paul Chambers is the man who will buy the shipping business. He has also expressed an interest in buying our home. We will have to decide about our furniture. There will be packing to do. But we will be in touch and let you know. Take care of our boy, Zack, okay?"

"Yes, grandfather. I hope you will be back soon."

He climbed into Zachary's buggy and they rode off.

Chapter 34

MARCH 8
WEDNESDAY

*I*t seemed like a year since Elizabeth had been to the hospital, although it had only been a week. The first thing she did was go to the little burn victim's room to check on her.

"Good morning, Rachel. How's my girl doing? Did you miss me?"

"Oh yes, Miss Morgan. No one can read like you. I am doing better. It doesn't hurt so much now."

"Well, I've brought you a new storybook. I'll come back to read to you after they give you your bath and change your bandages."

"Can't you read to me now? Please! Please!" she said, begging.

"I saw your nurse in the next room when I came in. By the time we just got started reading we would have to stop. I *promise* I'll be back when she is finished."

"Alright Miss Morgan. Thank you for the book."

Elizabeth saw Kim walking down the hall. She caught up with her and asked how last week had gone in her absence.

"We had another busy week. Several older patients with breathing problems, and a few broken bones. Two breaks were compound fractures requiring surgery. We have one man with a very serious ax wound to his foot. And two patients were admitted with heart problems."

"Kim, I would like to be of more service than I have been in the past. Do you think I could be taught some nursing skills? I'm sure I could help with baths, and with proper training I could perhaps change bandages. What do you think?"

"I don't have to think! I know you can help more. I just didn't know if you would want to. We will begin training and you can let us know when it's enough!"

"That sounds great . . . What's the report on your dinner date with Dr. Blake?"

"Look at me, Elizabeth. Do you have to ask? Don't you see the sparkle in my eyes? Don't you see the smile on my face? Oh Elizabeth, I had such a good time. He acts like he is really interested in me. We've been so busy and overworked here at the hospital since that date that neither of us has had any personal time. But he smiles at me sweetly when we are working together. I'm happy, can't you tell?"

"Gracious me, I'd say things are progressing nicely between you two!"

Elizabeth went back to Rachel's room. She was through with her bath, and her bandages had been changed. She had her good arm curled around her new book and she was watching the door. When she saw Elizabeth she smiled.

"I told you I'd be back. You choose the story and I'll read it."

"I'd like to hear about Cinderella."

"Once upon a time . . ."

At the end of her four-hour shift, Elizabeth was putting on her coat and bonnet to leave.

"Hello Elizabeth, leaving so soon?" Dr. Blake said striding toward her.

"It's the end of my shift, David. By the way, how are little Rachel's burns healing?"

"I'm very pleased with her progress. We feel the hospital is the best place for her as we want to prevent any infection from setting in. We are also hoping there will be very little scarring. She should be able to go home in a week. For a little girl just seven years old she has shown a lot of courage. We could learn a lot from her."

"She has touched my heart for sure."

"Have you seen Kim lately? I've been looking for her."

Yes, as a matter of fact I just saw her in room 101 with that handsome Robert Watts who has the compound fracture in his left arm. I can tell you now, there is nothing wrong with his right arm."

"What do you mean by that?"

Well, as he was moving from his bed to a chair he was holding on to Kim rather tightly. He looked pretty helpless to me. You're not jealous are you?"

"It all depends on his motives. She's my girl, you know."

"No, I didn't know. More importantly, does she know?"

"Well, she ought to know."

"I wouldn't take someone like Kim Thomas for granted if I were you. She's too special and there are a lot of men who would love to have a Kim in their lives."

"Elizabeth, you sure know how to put pressure on a man."

"I must go. See you on Friday."

Hmm, Elizabeth thought as she was walking toward her buggy. *For the first time David didn't call her "beautiful woman." This is good!*

Elizabeth rode by the school to see Jane before going home.

"Tell me, Jane, what do you think of Zachary?"

"First, let me say I loved the Morgan's. You are very blessed, Elizabeth, to have them as your Grandparents. It is obvious they adore you. My dad is so impressed with Mr. Morgan and Zachary. He feels the company is in good hands.

"Now, about Zachary. What little I've seen of him I like. He comes across as being genuine. I don't have to tell you how handsome he is. He looks at you, Elizabeth, with his heart in his eyes. Anyone can see that."

This made Elizabeth feel good. She needed to hear this from her best friend and was beginning to feel very good about who Zachary really was.

"Thanks Janie, my sweet friend. I needed to see you today and to hear what you've just said."

"Elizabeth that is a rather odd statement. Why would you need reassurance about Zachary from me or from anyone? Surely you, of all people, are aware of his love for you."

Yes, yes I am aware. He has told me often enough. But I am glad you can see it, too."

"By the way, Elizabeth, I want to invite you to our spring assembly program here at school next Tuesday morning at ten o'clock. A lot of my students will be in it. I guarantee you will enjoy it. I've been put in charge of the entire program and will be working with all the children. It will be an exciting time for them and the parents as well."

"I'd love to come. Thanks for inviting me."

"I must go now, Janie girl."

"By the way Elizabeth, I almost forgot to tell you that Phillip heard from William and Mary College yesterday. They said the teaching position is his! So that means our wedding will be June 3rd! I'm so thrilled. How did I forget to tell you something so important? Mercy me!"

Elizabeth gave Jane a big hug and they laughed together.

"I must go, Jane. See you later."

Chapter 35

MARCH 11
SATURDAY

*I*t was late in the afternoon when Zachary arrived at Willow Place. Elizabeth had only seen him once since her grandparents left on Monday, and then only briefly for lunch. He had been going in early and working late.

Elizabeth ran down the front steps to greet him. William was there to take care of the horse and carriage.

"What is your horse's name?" she asked Zachary.

"Honey."

"Honey?"

"Yes. The man John and I got her from said his daughter named her Honey the day the horse was born. He says the name fits. He called her a 'honey of a horse!', and her coat is just as golden."

"What is grandfather's horse named? I forget to ask him."

"Her name is Maude."

"Oh, I sure like Honey better!"

The March wind had died down. The afternoon was warm and balmy. Elizabeth and Zachary walked toward the lake. The willow trees were almost fully dressed in their summer leaves. There were tulips and jonquils blooming wild around the lake as well as in several flowerbeds. Today there was a burst of glorious color to compliment Elizabeth's beloved willow trees.

They sat quietly and still.

Finally Zachary spoke.

"It's good to sit and reflect on such beauty, all of it God's creation. I can't help but think of God's artistry. His creation shows Him to be the master of it all. The stars, points of light too numerous to number, are indescribably awesome. The full moon belies all description, but was partly created for lovers, no doubt. I am convinced that above all, His greatest handiwork and joy was in creating a man and woman. And that makes me think of you, Elizabeth. Your beauty is not surpassed by anyone I have ever known."

Elizabeth again thought as she listened to him, *how can he say these things and be the monster Cordelia made him out to be? She simply has to be wrong.*

"You have spoken such beautiful words, Zachary. I am very touched."

"Elizabeth, I am very excited about this new venture. I really do like the city of Richmond. Most of all I like the idea of living the rest of my life here with you, and now, I am going to let my heart rule my head, and ask you to be my wife. Will you marry me, Elizabeth?"

He took her so by surprise that she caught her breath. She wanted to scream the answer yes, yes, yes to him. But she had to pursue the plan to find out the truth and she must do it quickly.

"Zachary, my love, will you give me just a little more time? Be patient with me and trust me.

I will give you an answer soon. I promise."

"Yes, Elizabeth, I'll wait for an answer. What more can I do? Let's ride into Richmond for dinner at the Candlewick Café. I hear it is splendid dining."

"I'd like that. Let's go inside so I can tell Emma and get a cape and bonnet."

What a romantic evening it turned out to be. Elizabeth had never dined at the Candlewick. It was a relatively new establishment. They had gourmet food. Their seafood was second to none. Near the end of their meal a group of strolling musicians, two trumpeters, two violinists and a guitarist, came around their table. They played some romantic Spanish songs. The harmonious sounds of trumpets sent chills up Elizabeth's spine. They, as if arranged, began to play their song, "To Each His Own."

As they were playing it, Zachary reached for her hand, looked into her eyes and said, "Won't you please say yes?"

She looked back at him and responded, "You promised."

He smiled, squeezed her hand and replied, "You are right, I did."

Elizabeth lay awake for the longest time remembering the events of the past two days, easily the greatest time they had ever spent together.

MARCH 14
TUESDAY

Elizabeth arrived early at the school for Jane's spring assembly program. She surely had some precious children at her school. One little girl named Lee, about six years old, sang a solo. She was so afraid but very determined. She would sing a verse, then cry a few seconds, then sing a few more lines and cry again. But she got through it. When she finished everyone clapped so loudly she was all smiles.

Jane's youngest sister, little Jenny Adams, only eight years old, recited all six stanzas of the poem "Mary Had a Little Lamb," and then told that it was written in 1830 by Sarah J. Hale. Elizabeth was impressed.

Then there were the Bishop boys, Zack, Greg and Levi. Their mother and dad were accomplished singers in the Richmond area. They were six, eight and ten years old, but could they ever sing. Zack was the serious one and took the lead. Greg was hard to corral. Zack had to keep tugging at his sleeve to keep him still. Little Levi, with his gorgeous blue eyes, was the shy one but had unbelievable rhythm. However, he wanted to hide behind Zack. They sang a song their mother had written for them called "Boys, Toys and Tricks." It just brought the house down!

They ended their program by having a history student, Isaac Jordan, tell about how the song "America" came to be written. The children's choir then presented a rousing rendition of the beloved favorite.

Jane was right. It was a wonderful program that showcased a wealth of talent.

Chapter 36

⌘

*T*he month of March was almost gone. Elizabeth was staying busy at the hospital learning everything she possibly could. Kim had shared some nursing books with her. She had learned techniques about turning patients properly, bandaging and therapy. She had also become more familiar with medications and how they were administered.

Elizabeth wanted to be useful and East Richmond Hospital was short staffed. Her services were much appreciated.

She saw Zachary when she could. On Friday, March 24th, he received a telegraph from John. He needed him to come back to Williamsburg for a few days. He and Elizabeth had lunch together that day. He told her he would leave Jim Adams in charge of things and would catch the early train to Williamsburg Saturday morning.

MARCH 27
MONDAY
WILLIAMSBURG

John had made the decision to sell Morgan Shipping as well as their home on Warthen Street to Paul Chambers and his wife, Pat. He had met with them on numerous occasions. They were people of integrity and character in their early fifties. Paul had been in administration at William and Mary College. Both he and Pat loved sailing. He loved the waterways, was not afraid of hard work, and was eager to learn. With the good employees at Morgan Shipping he would not have any trouble learning the ropes. John and Zack were acting consultants and had been in the planning stages all weekend with Paul. They found Paul absorbed things like a sponge. The company they worked so hard to build was certainly in good hands now.

"Zack, my boy, I'm going to need your help. I know that Elizabeth has asked us to stay with her. But if we did, we would have to store our furniture in a warehouse and it might get ruined. We will be better off to rent a house until we can build a home of our own on the lakefront at Willow Place. I want to get a contractor on that project immediately. The sooner we can get it finished the better."

"Okay. Where do I come in?"

"I will need you to locate a house for us. I don't know about rental property in Richmond. Would you mind explaining to Elizabeth why we've decided to go this route?"

"Not at all. Storing your furniture would not be wise. She will understand."

"Also, ask her to proceed with the deed work at Willow Place so we can get started with the house. I will come back to Richmond probably on the 30th for a couple of days. Perhaps by then you will have located a renter house which we can look at."

"Consider it done."

"Also, Zack, I am going to move Mike to Richmond with us. He is 58 years old, and has worked for me for 29 years. He came to work here in 1826. He is one of the best workers I've ever had, and I want to offer him the option to live on our place. He is a trusted friend with no family.

"Remember the new man who has only been with us for a year named Max Hammond?"

"Yes. He is the strong, lean 21-year old who doesn't know when to stop working!"

"You're exactly right. Well I've talked with him about coming to Richmond to be trained in the art of carriage making and told him some of my dreams, really *our* dreams, of improving carriage travel. I explained that we would like to train him for a responsible position as the company grows. He said he would gladly make the move. Is this alright with you, Zack?"

"It's an excellent idea. This Jim Adams is a master at carriage making. He will be glad to have a young man like Max come on board. As an apprentice his coming will not threaten anyone's job, so there should be no problems with the other workers."

"Max will have to have a place to live, so check into the local boarding houses in Richmond. This sale will be finalized on April 3rd, and Max can come to Richmond then.

"We are already packing and will have movers come as soon as you can find us a house. Looks like we've got things squared away. You can head back to Richmond tomorrow, unless you have other things to do before going back."

"I really do need to get back, so I'll pull out on the 1:30 train tomorrow afternoon."

Simpson came into the library where Catherine was having the packers' box up their books for shipping to Richmond.

"Yes, Simpson. What is it?"

"There is a Miss Cordelia Fuller to see you, madam."

"Oh? Hmm. Show her into the parlor and tell her I'll be right there."

"Yes, madam."

Catherine wiped her hands on her handkerchief, smoothed her hair, walked through the foyer into the parlor.

"Good afternoon, Cordelia."

Cordelia quickly jumped to her feet from the parlor chair and said, "Good afternoon Mrs. Morgan. Please forgive my intrusion but I came to ask a favor."

"My child, you certainly are not intruding. May I ask how Judge Fuller and Rose are doing?"

"Oh, they are fine. Just fine. I'll tell them you inquired about them."

"Could I have Martha bring you something to drink? I know she has some hot apple cider."

"Why thank you, Mrs. Morgan. That would be delightful."

Catherine rang for Martha and requested the cider for her guest.

"Everyone is talking about Morgan Shipping being sold and that you two will be moving to Richmond along with Mr. Bainbridge. It makes your friends very sad. We will really miss you."

"Why thank you, Cordelia. We are keeping the beach house and will come for visits from time to time.

"You said you needed a favor?"

"Yes. I was so impressed by your granddaughter, Elizabeth. I have written a letter telling her how nice the party was and how much I enjoyed meeting her. Of course, I need her address and hoped you could give it to me."

"I will be happy to. But Zachary will be going back to Richmond tomorrow and I'm sure he would be glad to take her the letter personally. In fact, I have a little package, including a letter that I'm sending her myself. If you'd like, I'll put your letter in with mine."

"Oh, would you Mrs. Morgan? That would be perfect," Cordelia said with a knowing smile.

She handed Catherine a sealed envelope with Elizabeth Morgan boldly written on the front.

"I really must be going now. Thank you, Mrs. Morgan. Give my best to Mr. Morgan. I will let myself out. My carriage is waiting."

What a sweet child Cordelia Fuller is, Catherine thought.

Cordelia, meanwhile, was pondering how Elizabeth will feel having her precious Zachary hand deliver her "thank you" letter. As she climbed into her carriage, she said to herself, if Zachary thinks he can brush me off with "Don't you go near Elizabeth," he's got another thought coming.

Catherine was sending a book to Elizabeth that she said she wanted to read. Catherine had found it at a small bookstore in Williamsburg. She would write her a note telling her of Cordelia's visit, put both letters in with the book and wrap it as a gift.

MARCH 28
TUESDAY

Elizabeth met Zachary at the train depot at 3:00 P.M. She had to go into Richmond to the mercantile for Emma anyway, so she thought she would surprise him. She was standing in the shadows out of the bright sunlight and he didn't see her at first. When he did, he smiled that captivating smile that made her knees weak.

"Elizabeth! What a surprise! To what do I owe this honor?"

"I had to come into town today so I timed it to be here when your train arrived."

"I've missed you. I have a lot to tell you. Let's go to the sandwich shop."

They each got a cup of hot chocolate.

"Elizabeth, your grandfather sent you a message. He has sold the shipping company and their home on Warthen Street to the same man. The sale will be final on April 3rd.

"You might not be too happy about this part of his message, but I believe you will realize it is for the best. He said if they stay with you at Willow Place, they would have to store their furniture in a warehouse, which could ruin it. He wants me to look for a house for them to rent until they can build at Willow Place. What do you think?"

"I am terribly disappointed to say the least. But with all the nice furniture they have, I can see why they would not want to store it."

"Now the question is, where am I going to find a nice house for rent?"

"There is something worth checking into. Old Dr. Samuel Browning's home in Fair Oaks is standing empty. He and his wife are deceased. He was 95 years old. They had an estate sale and sold all of the contents. But so far, they haven't put the house up for sale. His son is also widowed and has a room at the Richmond Hotel. He is a retired banker. You might contact him to see if he would rent it. His name is Ben Browning."

"That is at least a lead. Also, John asked that you initiate the deed work for the acreage at Willow Place. He wants to get started as soon as he can find a contractor. He is coming to Richmond on March 30th for a few days. If I've not been able to find him a house to look at by then, he will take up the search himself."

"It will surprise him to know that I have already deeded twelve acres to him on the west bank of the lake. It will be perfect for the Morgan home. I have the deeds ready for him to sign. I cannot wait to know my grandparents are so near to me. It will be a dream come true."

"I must be going Zachary. It's getting late. William brought me into town. I'll walk back over to the mercantile where he will be waiting for me."

"I'll go to the hotel and see if I can contact Mr. Browning. Oh yes, your grandmother sent you a package. It is in my grip." He opened a side pocket and said, "Here it is. I'll see you this weekend. I'll be very busy until John gets here on Thursday. Goodbye, sweet Elizabeth."

She smiled and said goodbye.

Chapter 37

Elizabeth was ready for bed when she remembered she had laid the package from her grandmother on the table in the foyer. She ran down the stairs and retrieved it. Hurriedly she opened the gift-wrappings to see what was inside. It was the book about Florence Nightingale's life! This was so like Grandmother Catherine.

She opened the book and inside there were two letters. She recognized her grandmother's handwriting but didn't recognize the writing on the other envelope. She opened the one from her grandmother first.

Dear Elizabeth,

I found the book you wanted at a small bookstore in Williamsburg. I hope you enjoy reading it. I am sending it by Zachary. Things are moving right along here. Zachary will fill you in on all the details. By the way, do you remember Cordelia Fuller who was at your cotillion? She came by the house this afternoon. She had written you a letter and wanted your address so she could mail it. I told her Zachary would be going to Richmond the next day and could bring it to you. I explained that I had a package and letter for you and would include her letter in with mine. So here it is.

She seems to be such a lovely young lady.
We will see you soon.

Love always,
Grandmother

Elizabeth felt sick inside. She could not believe she had received a letter from this person who had already caused her so much grief. Should she open it or burn it? Perhaps it was a nice letter, even an apology. But suppose it was more accusations?

She could not bear to open it. Holding it in her hands she felt as if she held a serpent! Was it poisonous? Her penmanship was remarkably good. She used pastel pink stationery. But what was inside the envelope?

After at least an hour she decided this was ridiculous. The only way to know what the letter said was to read it. So she tore the seal loose.

MARCH 27
WILLIAMSBURG

Dear Elizabeth,

I have been thinking about you since hearing that your grandparents and Zachary Bainbridge are moving to Richmond. You remember my conversation with you at your party, don't you?

Yesterday I was doing my daily devotion and felt so impressed to write you. "Do unto others as you would have them do unto you" was part of my devotion. So I felt I needed to warn you again, hopefully, to spare you what I suffered at the hands of Zachary Bainbridge.

I even talked to my mother about this. I had never revealed all that he did to me before. She encouraged me to write you and tell you the whole story.

Remember I told you he tried to force himself on me? Well, he went so far as to strike me down and almost tore my dress off. Somehow I managed to get away from him. But he caught me again and choked me until I could hardly breathe. I struggled and managed to get away. I was absolutely terrified he would come after me again.

To escape him I went to Norfolk for a while. Sophie Springer is the name of the other girl that suffered some of the same things I did at his hands.

I am sorry to have to tell you this, but I will risk your being angry with me rather than not warn you of such a man.

Sincerely,
Cordelia Fuller

Elizabeth sat motionless. She felt like she had turned to stone. It would be easy to be angry with Cordelia. But she remembered their short encounter at her party and how she had wiped away tears as she told her story about Zachary. It made no sense at all for her to tell this if it were not true. And if her mother suggested that she write this letter, then it must be true.

For her, it seemed like a hopeless situation. If she revealed this to her grandparents they would be devastated. They loved Zachary. He was in their lives long before she was.

If she told Zachary, all he could do would be to deny it, which he surely would do.

Her plan had been to try and contact Rebecca and Steve Wilson to see what they might know about Cordelia. They were two of Zachary's best friends. But now, in light of this letter, she might as well forget Zachary.

She saw no other way. She could not take a chance on having the same thing happen to her that happened to her mother. She would rather suffer this alone than to spread such a story about Zachary and hurt so many others. In spite of all this, she loved him with all of her heart.

She was so wounded in spirit she could not even pray. She did not realize she had sat all night in the chair until the sun broke through her bedroom window. She was stiff with the chill of the night air and had a dull headache.

Elizabeth splashed cold water on her face, dressed and went to the kitchen.

"Good morning, lassie. 'Tis a glorious morning out. Would you like some hot coffee?"

"Yes, Emma, and that's all I want. I need to get to work early. I'll eat some muffins at the hospital if I get hungry."

Zachary went straight to the hotel. He found Mr. Browning's room and knocked on his door. He answered.

"Good afternoon, Mr. Browning. My name is Zachary Bainbridge. I am in the room just across the hall. I would like to talk with you. May I come in?"

"Please do. I've seen you coming and going."

"I am a partner of John Morgan who owns Morgan Shipping of Williamsburg. Do you per chance know him?"

"No, I don't know him personally but I am acquainted with his shipping company."

"Well, Mr. Morgan is presently negotiating the sale of his company. The deal will be finalized on April 3rd. He and I have just purchased Randolph Carriage Company here in Richmond."

"I've heard that Payton has sold out. Welcome to Richmond. Best of luck in your new venture."

"Thank you, sir. I am here on behalf of Mr. Morgan. He is looking for a home to rent. I have been asked to begin the search for him. He will be coming to Richmond Thursday for a few days. I was told your father's home is vacant and you might possibly put it up for rent."

"Well now, I haven't given it any thought. What are Mr. Morgan's future plans?"

"His granddaughter, Elizabeth Baldwin Morgan, owns Willow Place. She insists that they build across the lake from her. He will be looking for a contractor to start his home immediately."

"Those Baldwin's. Mighty fine people they were. I knew David for forty years. He was a circuit court judge. Mighty fine one, too. Well respected. Does Mr. Morgan have a contractor in mind?"

"No sir. He doesn't know any in this area."

"Well, I can help him out there. Tell him I said so."

"Yes sir, I will. He will appreciate any help you can give him."

"Now, about that house. I've not made up my mind just what I'm going to do with it. But I see no reason to let it stand empty when it could be of service to someone in Mr. Morgan's predicament. Say he'll be in town Thursday? Well, have him come by and we'll discuss the terms."

Zachary stood to go.

"Thank you, Mr. Browning. This is a great relief to me."

"It's nice to meet you, young fella."

Zachary left with a spring in his step.

Elizabeth threw herself into her work at the hospital. She was so numb she didn't even feel tired. She avoided Kim and David. There was no way she could talk to anyone. Three rooms that were empty needed cleaning. The beds had to be scrubbed to sterilize them. Orderlies usually did this work. But they, too, were overworked. So Elizabeth chose to help in this way. She knew it would allow her to be alone for a while.

Her little friend Rachel had gone home from the hospital a week ago. She was one happy little girl when she left with her mommy.

Six-year old Andy Gladden, who had broken his arm when he fell from a cottonwood tree, was now in the room Rachel had been in. He had a nasty break on his left arm just above the wrist. She would have to check on him today. He loved trains, so she had found a storybook about trains and wanted to read it to him. Elizabeth planned to go by his room before she left work that afternoon.

She must not think about the letter. Staying busy was the answer. She needed to eat something but she knew she could not swallow a bite of food.

Elizabeth emerged from the last room she had cleaned and ran into Kim.

"So there you are, Elizabeth. It's good to have volunteer help that's not afraid of work! I see you've prepared those three rooms for patients."

"Yes, Kim. They are thoroughly cleaned. I like to keep busy."

"Turn around here, Elizabeth. Look at me. You look like you've seen a ghost! What ever is wrong with you?"

"Oh, nothing Kim. Just a little headache. Didn't sleep too well. You know how it goes sometimes."

"Yes, I do know. But you certainly didn't have to come in today."

"Is that what you do, Kim, when you have a restless night? No, I think not. I'll be fine. How are you and David, er, Dr. Blake doing?"

"You know, the strangest thing happened when the patient in room 101 was here with the compound fracture. His name was Robert Watts. Remember him?"

"Yes. He was the real handsome young man. I remember him."

"Well, he's gone home now, of course, but would you believe that Dr. Blake took over with all his care? When time came for his bed to be made and he had to be assisted to a chair, Dr. Blake appeared out of the blue to help him. I thought he acted a little protective of him. Being put to sleep with ether and the serious surgery left him a little unsteady on his feet for a few days. I began to wonder if Dr. Blake doubted my nursing skills."

"Oh, Kim. You are so naive! He was jealous. Just plain jealous!"

"Jealous? Of him? Why on earth would he be jealous of him?"

"Maybe someone just planted a little seed."

Chapter 37

"Elizabeth, you didn't. Did you?"

"Didn't I? I must go read to little Andy and then I'll be through for the day. Kim, don't question things. Just count your blessings."

Chapter 38

MARCH 30
THURSDAY

John Morgan knocked on Ben Browning's door at the Richmond Hotel.

"Come in."

"Good afternoon. Mr. Browning, I presume. I'm John Morgan. I believe Mr. Bainbridge spoke with you about my renting your home."

"Yes, yes sir, he did," Mr. Browning replied standing to his feet and extending his hand. "It's nice to meet you. Mr. Bainbridge tells me you are interested in renting the old Browning place, that's what I call it. Well, I think we can do business. Just when will you want to move in?"

"I hope we can be ready to move from Williamsburg by April 10th. We will ship our things by railcar. Most everything is packed. We've lived in a very large house, had lots of furniture. We plan to scale way back when we build, so I disposed of a lot of furniture we won't be needing."

"Let's go look at the house to make sure you will be happy with it."

"Yes sir. We can do that. I might add that I will be sending two men ahead to clean the house and make it ready to move into when the furniture arrives. Their names are Mike Kelley and Max Hammond. Mike has been with my shipping company for twenty-nine years. He has been a trusted employee and friend. Max is a young man, smart as a whip with energy galore. I plan to use him prominently in the carriage business. I just wanted you to know who they are when they begin work at the house."

"Thank you for telling me Mr. Morgan. However, I have had cleaners in the house every two weeks. I want to keep it in mint condition. It is old but has been well taken care of.

"Say the old fellow's name is Mike Kelley? I once knew a man by that name. He would be about fifty-eight or sixty years old. He lived here in Richmond. He left these parts in his mid twenties. This man made a loan from our bank. It was a small loan but he left town without paying it. The reason it stands out in my mind is about a year later he sent me the balance that he owed plus three percent interest."

"That sounds like Mike. Come to think of it, I remember him saying that he once lived in Richmond."

"This Mike Kelley was a big ole Irishman, full of humor and wit."

"I believe we have a mutual friend, Mr. Browning. I think this must be the same Mike Kelley."

"Does he have a family?"

"No. He lived with his parents in Williamsburg until their deaths. His dad died about ten years ago and his mother a couple of years ago. He looked after them as a dutiful son. He never married."

"I remember he sparked a pretty little girl here. I thought they might get married. He worked at a planning mill outside of Richmond. The next thing I knew he was gone. I don't know what ever happened to his girl."

"Zachary said you could recommend a home building contractor, Mr. Browning."

"Yes, I've talked to Clarence Cleburne who is one of the best in these parts. He has about two more weeks of work on his present job and says he can start your home immediately there after. He does quality work. I have his name and address written down for you. I have it here somewhere. Let's see, it was on this table. Oh yes, here 'tis."

"How can I ever thank you, Mr. Browning?"

"Well, no thanks necessary. You have spent time talking to a lonely old man and that's thanks enough. You probably wonder why I am living in a hotel instead of the old home place. When my beloved Mary died, I could not stand living in our big old house alone and did not want the responsibility of looking after the place. So I sold our home and have been very content here at the Hotel Richmond. This way I see people. I eat downstairs and have daily maid service. I am very happy here. Thanks for listening ."

Standing to go, John shook hands with the old gentleman and said, "It's been my pleasure. Do you think we might look at the house in the morning?"

"You just name the time and I'll be ready."

"How about ten o'clock? I'll pick you up then."

Elizabeth knew her grandfather had arrived in Richmond today. She also knew he had lots of business to take care of and would be staying in town tonight. Elizabeth stayed in her room most of the morning. She still did not have an appetite. But she ate some chicken broth that Emma had seasoned lightly. Telling Emma that she did not wish to be disturbed she went into the library.

March had indeed come in like a lion but was going out like a lamb, true to form. The weather was sunny and warm and the wind was hardly stirring. She opened the draperies in the library and opened the window. Sitting at her grandfather's desk, she leaned back in his big leather chair.

A spirit of melancholy had enveloped her, sort of a sad thoughtfulness. She really needed her Grandmother Savannah's arms around her!

She looked around the big old library, so many familiar things in this room. There was the long-case grandfather clock. It's tick-tock sound had been here as long as she could remember.

On one end of the room were the massive leather sofa and cushioned barrel-backed chairs, all so comfortable. The large Persian wool rug with its colorful design was one of her favorites.

She had to come to grips with what had happened in her life. Zachary deserved an answer to his marriage proposal. She had promised. Maybe there was still a way for her to find out about Cordelia, her background, and her believability. Perhaps she was taking a defeatist attitude. Had she sought guidance from the Lord as to what she should do? Her heart began to quicken. What was the scripture she had read just this past Sunday in first John? It had to do with trying the spirit of God. She picked up her grandfather's Bible from the corner of his desk and quickly turned to first John. She flipped the pages until she came to the fourth chapter. There it is!

"Beloved believe not every spirit, but try the spirits whether they are of God:"

She had accepted a girl's word that she did not even know against someone she loved. Just because she cried when she first talked to her and then quoted a scripture in her letter did not mean she was telling the truth.

Elizabeth was still letting the past haunt her and was living her life in the shadow of what had happened to her mother. She could not be forever suspicious.

She made up in her mind to go back to Williamsburg, look up Steve and Rebecca Wilson and talk to them about Cordelia, and ask if they know Sophia Springer. She would go before her grandparents moved to Richmond. If the Wilson's didn't know anything about Cordelia, perhaps together they could find out if she had credibility. For the first time in a long time she had peace about what she had to do.

Chapter 38

Elizabeth prayed, "Thank you, heavenly Father for your gift of peace. Even in the midst of a storm, you are there giving us shelter. Sometimes, Lord, we wander off on our own, failing to depend on you. But you never leave us nor forsake us. Praise your name. Amen."

Chapter 39

MARCH 31

$\mathcal{G}$randfather, may I come in?

"Well, well, look who's here. Of course you may. I'm looking forward to many visits to my office from you, Elizabeth," he said as he gave her a hug. "What brings you by? Anything special?"

"Since I didn't see you after you came back from Williamsburg yesterday I just wanted to stop in and see what's happening."

"Well, I've accomplished a lot yesterday and today. I checked with Mr. Ben Browning about renting his father's house in Fair Oaks. He took me over to see it this morning. It's in mint condition, Elizabeth. He said his parents were very particular people. It seems they entertained a lot over the years. They had lots of servants who kept the place clean. Your grandmother is going to be pleased."

"What about the size of the house?"

"Surprisingly, it isn't all that large and I'm glad."

"Will all your furniture fit into it?"

"Yes, I think it will. We have disposed of quite a bit of the furniture as we plan to build a much smaller house at Willow Place.

"Did Zachary tell you that I had twelve acres of land deeded to you?"

"Yes he did. Elizabeth, I wanted to talk to you about that. You know that everything we have will be yours one day. This land you've deeded to us is just a formality. The house we build will be yours when we are gone. I want you to fully understand that. And while we are talking, when the sale of the business is finalized I will open an account in your name. The money deposited will be yours to do with as you please.

"There is one other thing I want to mention. In conjunction with our Carriage business, in order to use a carriage you have to have a horse. I know your Grandfather Baldwin raised horses at one time. You have the pastureland for it. I believe it would be a good investment to raise Morgan's and quarter horses again. Would you agree?"

"Grandfather, if this is what you want to do, you know that I agree."

"We won't get into raising horses right away but I wanted to check with you about the prospects when we are ready."

"I also came to ask you when you are going back to Williamsburg."

"I have a return ticket for in the morning. I am anxious to get everything done there so we can get moved."

"Would you mind if I go back with you and stay a few days?"

"I would be delighted for you to come with me. And it will be good for your grandmother as well. We'll be staying at the beach house when we go back since most everything is packed at Warthen Street. May I ask why you want to make this trip?"

"I'm glad you asked. I'm really going on a fact-finding mission. I want to get in touch with Zachary's friends, Steve and Rebecca Wilson. I do not want Zachary to know this. I will tell him I'm going to visit with you and grandmother for a few days. Trust me on this grandfather.

It is something I must do."

"I am intrigued by this conversation, Elizabeth, but I will respect your wishes."

"I will have to depend on you to help me get in touch with the Wilson's. Will this be a problem?"

"Not at all. Steve has finished seminary and was appointed shortly thereafter to the Wesleyan church at Poquoson right on the coast. He is doing quite well there. I will see that you are taken to where they live. It will not be a problem. By the way, Zachary is out in the factory. Would you like to see him? I'll send someone for him."

"Yes, I need to tell him I'll be going back with you tomorrow. I won't plan on seeing him tonight because I must get ready for the trip."

Zachary came into the office looking a little disheveled but was grinning broadly. His eyes never looked bluer. His shirt was open at the collar showing off his golden tan. Elizabeth had never seen him look more rugged nor more appealing than at this moment.

She could feel her heart beating rapidly and wondered if he could hear it! Her face must surely be flushed. She felt like a traitor because of what she was going to do, but she simply had to know the truth.

"What brings you here to a working man's domain?" he said, totally oblivious to his charm.

"I needed to see you, Zachary, to tell you I've decided to go back to Williamsburg with grandfather for a few days. We will be leaving in the morning. I will need to pack for the trip so I won't be seeing you this evening."

His countenance changed immediately. Those happy, blue eyes turned sad almost at once. The smile disappeared. He had a questioning look in his eyes.

She could hear the disappointment in his voice when he said, "What brought this about?"

"I just feel the need to spend some time with my grandparents in Williamsburg before they come to Richmond. This has to be hard on them, even though they are happy about coming here. They will be leaving a host of friends behind. Maybe I can be of moral support to them by just being there a few days."

"When will you be coming back?"

"Probably next Thursday the sixth."

"As much as I hate to see you go, even for six days, I think you might be right. It will be a big change for them. You are a very thoughtful person, Elizabeth."

"Zachary, I think it is fair to say when I return, I will have an answer for you."

The sparkle came back in his eyes and he said, "Then may I plan on our having dinner together at the Candlewick on Saturday the eighth?"

"Yes, I'll look forward to it. "But she thought . . . *what if I don't like what I find out?*

She was trying to be positive, however.

The train ride to Williamsburg was very enjoyable for grandfather and granddaughter. Elizabeth had a chance to ask some interesting questions. She had begun to think of her forefathers.

"Grandfather, what did your father do? How did he earn a living? Where did he come from?"

"My father, Clarence Lee Morgan, was born in England in 1768. He and his parents came to America in 1788. My father was twenty. He married my mother, Emily Ann Baxter, in 1789. They both were twenty-one years old. My grandfather was an attorney, and my father was a teacher. He met my mother at a boarding house that her parents owned in Maryland. She was the love of his life he often said."

"We lived near the Chesapeake Bay waterway. This is how I came to love the water so much and became interested in shipping at an early age. I worked with every boat crew that would let me during the summer. I was industrious. No job was too hard nor beneath my dignity. It was only natural for me to go into shipping. The Lord blessed the business which 'made it big' as some might say."

"Grandfather, how fascinating, because of all these people, I am here today. Tell me, how did you and grandmother Catherine meet and fall in love?"

"Believe it or not, we met at church. Catherine lived in Williamsburg. I was working with a small shipping outfit there. I had been raised around church. When I came to Williamsburg the first thing I did was find a church. It happened to be First Wesleyan. When I saw this tanned, blonde-haired girl with the brownest eyes and cutest little figure, I was hooked for life. I met her in 1808. We married in 1809 and your dad was born in 1810."

"Grandfather, I want the same kind of marriage you and grandmother have had. I want deep, uncompromised love and complete trust. I simply cannot settle for anything less. Do you think it's possible for me to find this?"

"Yes, indeed I do. I've never asked you, Elizabeth, but you and Zachary have known each other for almost five months and have been seeing each other regularly. It appears that you two have fallen in love."

"Grandfather, I do love Zachary. Very much. But I am so afraid."

"What is there to be afraid of child? I haven't asked Zachary if he loves you, but it is evident that he does. He is a fine man, Elizabeth. We've worked together for six years now. I would trust him with my life. I know him well. He is solid. He is certainly honorable. What is there to be afraid of?"

At that time the train whistle sounded alerting them they were pulling into the depot.

She looked at her grandfather and said, "I'm here to find out if I have reason to be afraid."

She stood to her feet and walked toward the door of the train.

When they were seated in the carriage for their ride to the beach house, her grandfather held up a handkerchief and asked, "Is this yours?"

She laughed as she reached for it and said, "Zachary would love this! He says I always drop my handkerchief."

Chapter 40

Catherine looked up from the book she was reading when Elizabeth and John walked into the beach house sitting room. She heard the front door open but knew Simpson would announce whoever it was. John wanted to surprise her, so he sent Elizabeth in first.

"Elizabeth!" her grandmother exclaimed, jumping up from her chair. "Dear Elizabeth." And she gave her a warm embrace. Still holding her shoulders, she pushed her back at arm's length and said, "Let me look at you." Then she pulled her close once more and said, "I am overjoyed at seeing you again my dear."

"Grandmother Catherine, I'm *just* as happy to see you! You are such a young grandmother. I can see us now, riding all over Willow Place on Blazer and . . . and, we'll have to get a quarter horse for your very own!"

John had stood back drinking in this scene, thinking he's just about the luckiest man in the whole world.

He spoke up and said, "Well, don't I count at all?"

Catherine walked over to him. John was leaning against the fireplace mantle with his arms crossed over his chest. His blue eyes were still very bright, despite his sixty-five years, and still twinkled as they did the first time she ever saw him. She loved him so much.

"Of course you count, my dear. I've missed you terribly. Welcome home." And she gave him a quick kiss.

"What's for lunch?" John asked. "We're starved!"

"Let's go to the kitchen and see what Virginia has prepared."

"I know she's fixed apple dumplings for dessert," John said as he winked at Elizabeth.

"Just how would you know such a thing?" Elizabeth retorted, just as she knew he expected her to.

"Because I smelled them cooking when we left Richmond!"

"Oh grandfather!"

Virginia had prepared baked Atlantic salmon, asparagus with her special lemon flavored cream sauce, and baked yellow squash halves with seasoned bread crumbs. She had buttered yeast rolls and hot tea. And yes, she had made apple dumplings for dessert!

"Why, Virginia, you fixed all my favorite dishes," John remarked. "It's like Christmas instead of April first."

"Mr. John, you make this household seem like Christmas all the time. It's my pleasure to prepare what I know you like.

"Martha is setting the table on the sun porch. Lunch will be served in fifteen minutes," Virginia announced.

This was the first time Elizabeth had been to the beach house. She was surprised at how large it was. The sitting room was spacious. She counted three sets of parlor furniture plus two federal-style Boston rockers and three stool window seats. Plus, it had three sofa tables, two tea tables and a Massachusetts Federal card table that she especially liked. She surmised they must do a lot of entertaining here. This room alone could accommodate at least twenty-five people comfortably. The room fronted the James River where there was a manmade sand beach. The view was spectacular. There were three bedrooms, a dining room, kitchen and the glassed-in sun porch. Their big house on Warthen Street had four water closets and this one had three.

Her grandparents had to be extremely wealthy. Of course, her grandfather had earned his wealth by hard work and good management. He had depended on the Lord's guidance, as he had mentioned to her more than once. She was happy for them, but she still preferred her more subdued lifestyle at Willow Place.

After a big lunch they remained on the sun porch enjoying the view. A foghorn sounded and Elizabeth saw a big steamship passing by with the lettering "Morgan Shipping" on the side. A couple of crewmen waved toward the Morgan's beach house as they steamed by.

Her grandfather said, "They always sound the fog horn when they know we are here. This is the last shipment the company will make under the name of Morgan Shipping. They are heading up to the Chesapeake Bay area with several stops to unload freight. I could feel a little sad if I weren't so excited about the carriage company.

"Catherine, this is a beautiful afternoon for sailing. I'm going to take the dinghy out for an hour or so. Either of you girls want to go along?"

"Not I," said Catherine.

"Nor I," said Elizabeth.

"We will watch you. Have fun!" Catherine called out as John disappeared out the door and down the steps.

"Grandmother Catherine, I talked to grandfather on the train trip here about his family. Now I'd like to know about my maternal grandparents. Where did your father and mother come from and what did your father do for a living?"

"My father was Thomas Andrew Hamilton. His parents came to this country from England when he was a little boy. They finally settled in Annapolis. My grandfather was a merchant as was my father. They were good at their trade. They worked long, hard hours and established themselves well in the merchandising business.

"My mother was a lover of music. She had a magnificent voice. Her name was Rose Marie Grayson. She sang for a brief period of time with the Maryland Symphony Orchestra. She and my father met after a performance and fell madly in love. They were married six months later.

"The Hamilton's decided to open a store in Williamsburg, so father and mother moved here where I was born in 1790. I've lived here all my life."

"Did you really meet grandfather at church?"

"Is that what he told you? Yes, we did meet at church, but I first saw him on the river sailing his sailboat. My father had taken me out. It was a clear, lazy Saturday afternoon. There was a brisk wind blowing, so we were moving at a fast clip when I saw this sailboat come by us with the most gorgeous man I had ever seen steering the boat through the water. He really never looked our way. He was very intent on navigating his craft. I think I held my breath for five minutes. Then I gasped to my father, 'Who was *that*?' Of course, he didn't know.

"Then, low and behold, he turned up at church the next morning. When the pastor introduced us, we both were smitten. It didn't take us long to know we were meant for each other."

"Oh grandmother, I'm so glad we had this talk. I feel that I 'know' my beginnings now. I have such a desire to find the right person to spend the rest of my life with."

"What about Zachary, Elizabeth? It is obvious that he is madly in love with you. I thought you felt the same way about him. Don't you?"

"Yes, in all honesty he affects me like grandfather affected you. I came here to get some information. I plan to meet with Steve and Rebecca Wilson tomorrow, if possible, to try and get some answers to some questions. When I do, I will share my findings with you and grandfather."

Chapter 41

After church the Morgan's went straight home and ate lunch so Elizabeth could go see the Wilson's. Since it was Sunday they felt sure she would find them at home.

"Elizabeth, do you want me to go with you?"

"No grandfather. I need to do this alone."

"Then I will have Giles take you and wait for you till you finish your meeting."

Elizabeth knocked at the front door of the parish house. Then she knocked again. She waited, breathing a prayer that they would be home. The door opened and Steve said, "Why, Elizabeth Morgan. What a pleasant surprise. Do come in."

She hesitated, then asked, "Is Rebecca at home?"

"Yes indeed. Rebecca, look who's here."

Rebecca came to the living room from the kitchen and smiled warmly when she saw Elizabeth. "What in the world brings you here to Poquoson?"

"I've come a long way to see you two. I apologize for coming without an invitation and without proper notice."

"Then it must be something important," Steve remarked as they were seated in the living room.

"Yes. To me it is and I hardly know where to begin. It involves Zachary. He has often told me that you two are his very dearest friends."

"We feel the same way about Zack," Steve replied.

"Then please tell me he is not the monster that Cordelia Fuller has told me he is."

Rebecca looked at Steve knowingly. She started to speak but Steve shook his head ever so slightly.

"Tell us, Elizabeth, exactly what you are talking about?" Rebecca inquired.

"First, do you two know . . . *really* know Cordelia Fuller?"

"Yes. We *really* know her."

"Well, at my Valentine's party she was talking with Zachary at the punch table. He had his back to me and didn't know I had walked up. I got there just as Zachary said, 'Cordelia, don't you go near Elizabeth. Do you hear me?'

"I asked Zachary who she was and if she was a friend of his. He said, 'No, she is not.'

"Then just before the party ended, Cordelia asked to speak with me. She said she wanted to tell me something for my own good. She told me I really did not know Zachary. According to her they had courted six months earlier. He told her he loved her and wanted to marry her. She felt like he was rushing things. He told her he would have her one way or another, she said. He became angry and abusive and tried to force himself on her. She was horrified but was able to escape. To recover from this ordeal she was forced to go stay with out-of-town relatives for four months.

"Needless to say I was stunned. It made me very ill. But I did not want my grandparents to know because they love Zachary as a son. They told me so. This would have devastated them.

"I didn't want to tell Zachary. Suppose it wasn't true. How could he prove to me that it was a lie?

"I've struggled with it. Zachary has never shown me anything but gentleness and tenderness. However, this is exactly the way my mother was treated by my father. Then he turned into a monster. Zachary said he has told you about my parents."

"Yes, he told us and we can understand your concern," Steve said.

"Is this the whole story, Elizabeth?" Rebecca asked.

"No." She laid the letter she had been holding in her hand on their coffee table. "I received this letter dated March 27th. You two can read it."

When they had finished, Elizabeth asked, "Do you know a Sophie Springer?"

"No, and we doubt her existence. Rebecca, you tell Elizabeth about Cordelia's threat to us the night of the party."

"She came up to us also at the punch table. She said, and I quote, 'Well, I see Zachary is leading another girl astray. This Elizabeth really thinks she has herself a catch. I think I'll just break up this little romance. I can make up a story about me and her precious Zachary that would fix his wagon for good!'

"I told her she wouldn't dare do such a thing. Cordelia said she guessed she wouldn't and asked us to forget she said anything. Steve and I discussed it. We knew Zachary had never had a thing to do with her, even though she chased after him. We both decided it was an empty threat."

Steve said, "But she left us, went directly to you and made up this sordid story as she went along. If the truth be known, she threatened Zachary that she was going to tell you a lie about them. That is probably why he told her she had better not go near you."

"If only we had told Zachary what she told us, you might have been spared this anguish."

"The important thing, Steve and Rebecca, is that the truth of what this seriously mixed-up person has done is finally being revealed to me."

Steve chuckled and said, "I suppose we could apply what Christ taught the Jews in the temple when he said, 'Ye shall know the truth and the truth shall make you free.'

"This truth has certainly made me free. Zachary asked me to be his wife on March 11th. I wanted desperately to say yes. But I felt I needed to know the truth about Cordelia Fuller first. Then on March 27th I got this letter from her. That is when I decided to come to

Williamsburg to talk with you. I felt like you could help me. I told Zachary when I came back to Richmond I would give him my answer. Now I am completely free to follow my heart without any reservations!"

"Elizabeth, are you willing to face Cordelia with what she has done? Are you willing to talk with her parents, Judge and Mrs. Fuller about this?" Steve asked. "Of course, we will go with you because of our involvement."

"I never thought about it but you are right. She does need to be confronted. Do you think we might be able to see the Fullers tomorrow? I must get back to Richmond."

"I'll do my best. We will go to their home early to find out if they can see us. If so, we will come and pick you up."

"I am at the beach house. I'll be ready early. Rebecca and Steve, how can I thank you for revealing this to me. You have been an answer to prayer. You are truly the good friends that Zachary has boasted you to be."

"The feeling is mutual. We will see you tomorrow," Rebecca said, "and we will put this behind us for good," as she gave Elizabeth a reassuring hug before she left.

<hr />

Elizabeth's grandparents were anxiously awaiting her return.

Elizabeth changed clothes, putting on a loose-fitting housedress, washed her face and asked for a cup of hot chocolate. Then she settled down in a comfortable chair in one end of the long living room. She asked her grandparents to come sit with her so she could tell them what her life had been like since the night of her cotillion.

They sat in a state of shock as she related the story to them. She had been very fair to Zachary, as well as them. She bore this alone until she could find out the truth.

"Elizabeth, I remember Mary Parks asking me if I intended to invite Cordelia when we were planning the party. We all had a question about her. I remember that she would show up in places Zachary would be and he would always leave. She seemed to make it a point to be where he was. But her parents are friends of ours. We have attended the same parties and been involved in civic affairs together. I knew they would expect me to invite her. I am so sorry you have suffered so at her hands."

"Grandmother, you didn't know the kind of person she is. Don't fret over it. The truth has surfaced and I am one of the happiest people in the world."

"Elizabeth, you know the truth but you can't let her get by with this. There has to be some accountability. If not, she could do this to someone else," her grandfather cautioned.

"Yes, grandfather. Steve said the same thing. He and Rebecca are going to the Fuller's home in the morning and ask them to see the three of us. Since Cordelia told them she was going to 'fix Zachary's wagon for good,' they feel involved in this too. If they can set up an appointment, they will come and get me."

"We are signing the papers in the morning to finalize the sale of Morgan Shipping or I would go with you," her grandfather said.

"I will be fine. I intend to ask God's wisdom and guidance before I attempt to talk with them."

Her grandfather added, "I have found Judge Fuller to be a man of integrity in my dealings with him. I do not believe they know any of this."

"If we can see them tomorrow I want to be on the train to Richmond on the fifth. I came here with a heavy heart. But I will be going home with a burden lifted knowing that my love for Zachary isn't in vain. I cannot wait to see him!"

⸻⁕⸻

With much anxiety the next day arrived with an appointment to visit the Fullers.

Judge Fuller invited the three of them into his study. Rose Fuller and Cordelia were seated when they entered. Steve walked over and shook hands with them. Rose asked them to please be seated.

Judge Fuller turned to Steve and asked, "What is so urgent that you asked us to meet with you?"

"I'm afraid it isn't a very pleasant subject that has brought us here, Judge. Perhaps Cordelia would like to tell you what this is all about," Steve said looking at her inquiringly.

"All the color drained from her face but she said, "I don't know what you mean, I'm sure."

"Then maybe I can refresh your memory, Cordelia," Elizabeth said boldly.

"I am here to ask you why you discredited Zachary Bainbridge to me at the cotillion on Valentines, and then followed up with a letter of further character assassination on March 27th? None of what you told me is true, yet you plotted the whole thing. You confessed to the Wilson's that you were thinking of making up such a story.

"If the lies you told me about Zachary had become public knowledge, it could have destroyed people's confidence in him. What you did was mean-spirited, and I don't think you realize the seriousness of what you have done.

"It might interest you to know that Zachary and I love each other very much. He has asked me to marry him. What you did almost destroyed our relationship. He knows nothing about any of this. I have wrestled with it alone. I finally came back to Williamsburg seeking the truth and I have found it.

Elizabeth continued, "What I am asking of you is to admit to me and these witnesses that all you said was a made-up story without a shred of truth to it. Then I want you to tell your parents what you have done. They should hear it from you."

By this time Cordelia sat with her head bowed. She took a deep breath and began to speak.

"What you have said Elizabeth, is true. All of the things I said about Zachary were lies. There's not a word of truth to any of it. Do you have the letter I wrote you? If so, it pretty well explains what I have done."

"Yes, here it is."

Cordelia read the letter aloud. Then she told how she had lied to Elizabeth at the cotillion.

"You are right, Elizabeth, I did not realize the seriousness of my actions. I had a crush on Zachary. He was not interested in me at all. I wanted to get back at him. I realize what I did was unscrupulous beyond words and I am so ashamed!"

Judge Fuller cleared his throat and with a look of total disbelief said, "Cordelia, you have not only shamed yourself but you have shamed your mother and me. How on earth have we failed you so miserably that would cause you to do such a thing?"

"It is bad for you, and it is bad for us. But you almost ruined Zachary's reputation with this, young lady. If this had happened, you would have gone on your merry way but two beautiful young people would have lost each other because of your lies. Do you really see how destructive lying is, Cordelia?"

"Yes, father, I do. You and mother are not responsible in any way. It is entirely my doing, caused by a selfish desire for something I could not have."

"Mother, I will make this up to you. I really will. I see a need to change. I want to change. I will regain your confidence and make you proud. You will see."

"Elizabeth, Steve and Rebecca, will you forgive me? I humbly ask your forgiveness."

Rose Fuller, looking very pale and shaken, was crying quietly.

"Cordelia, I believe you are sorry. You seem to be truly repentant," Elizabeth said. "All three of us wanted this meeting to have you admit the truth, but we also wanted to help you. We wanted you to see the seriousness of your actions so it would never happen to anyone else. I accept your apology, and you are forgiven."

"I do however, want all of you to know how happy I am. I feel as if a chain of bondage has been broken and I am free, free to marry the dearest man on earth to me."

Steve stood and said, "Christ said in his sermon on the mount, 'Therefore if thou bring thy gift to the altar, and there rememberest that thy brother hath ought against thee; leave there thy gift before the altar, and go thy way; first be reconciled to thy brother, and then come and offer thy gift.' It seems this scripture has been fulfilled between you two young ladies, and you have followed Christ's example admirably. Oh that all ministers' jobs could be this easy!"

"Judge and Mrs. Fuller, Cordelia, we thank you for your time. If Rebecca and I can ever be of assistance to you we are available."

Rebecca, the sweet-spirited person that she was, walked over to Cordelia and gave her a big hug and said, "I am proud of you. You showed great courage to all of us by doing what is right and repenting."

She went over to Rose and hugged her as well. Rebecca said, "Don't worry, Mrs. Fuller, Cordelia's good upbringing has shined through. The Lord hath wrought a change and she will be alright, and so will you."

Elizabeth shook hands with the Fullers. They told her how sorry they were for the pain she had suffered.

Elizabeth looked at Cordelia. She was a naive, very insecure young lady who felt a need to be accepted.

Cordelia looked at Elizabeth. She saw a person with great strength of character and maturity beyond her years, traits to be desired.

They both walked toward each other with outstretched arms and embraced. You could feel the presence of the Lord and a spirit of peace and forgiveness.

Chapter 42

APRIL 5

The train pulled into Richmond depot right on time. Elizabeth had telegraphed Zachary to meet her. She gathered up her purse, a book her grandmother had given her, and her hatbox and hurried up the aisle to the door. She stepped down onto the platform and saw Zachary striding toward her. She began running to meet him shouting "Yes! Yes! Yes!"

Zachary grabbed her and swung her around and around. Elizabeth was crying tears of joy. She began looking for her handkerchief and exclaimed, "Oh Zachary, I've lost my handkerchief! I must have it. I must have it." She was frantic.

He said, "Wait right here." He bounded back to the door of the train and up the stairs. He began searching between the seats. Then he spotted it four seats down on the right near the aisle. He picked it up and rushed back to where Elizabeth was waiting.

"I found it! Here it is."

"Oh Zachary. This is the handkerchief I had the first day I met you on November 16th right here at the train depot. I took it with me to Williamsburg so I would have a part of you with me. At least it represented you to me on a very difficult mission. I will always keep this handkerchief. I'll place it in our family Bible."

Zachary noticed the seriousness in Elizabeth's voice and refrained from teasing her about the lost handkerchief.

"Elizabeth, you have said 'yes, yes, yes.' Does this mean what I think it means? That you *will* marry me?"

Elizabeth had laid everything down she had been holding. She took Zachary's face between her hands and looked into his precious blue eyes, "Yes, Zachary, I will be honored to be your wife." She stretched to her tiptoes and gave him a kiss to seal their engagement.

"I could think of no better place to accept your proposal than at the train depot where I first saw you, the man who has changed my whole life."

"Needless to say, I don't understand the change in you, but I'm sure looking forward to finding out what brought it about."

Elizabeth had been very reserved about her feelings for Zachary because of her father's treatment of her mother, and because of the episode with Cordelia. Now she felt totally free to share her true feelings!

She took hold of Zachary's arm and said, "You aren't going back to work are you? Please don't. Stay with me. Let's do something crazy. Let's go to the livery stable and rent a couple of horses and ride to Willow Place. I have so much to tell you. It is so good to be free, to be in love, to be loved."

Zachary didn't have a clue what had happened to Elizabeth but he caught her spirit. They picked up her baggage and drove his carriage to the livery. They left it with the proprietor, rented two horses and rode side by side with the wind blowing in their faces. They rode to the west side of the lake at Willow Place where there was an extra large willow tree. They dismounted, laughing exuberantly after such an exhilarating ride. Zachary reached out to Elizabeth and she walked into his open arms. He put his cheek next to hers and whispered into her ear, "I love you, Elizabeth Morgan." Then he kissed her with such sweet tenderness that his lips trembled softly against hers. They stood holding each other for ever so long.

Elizabeth finally said, "Let's sit down, Zachary. I have so much to tell you."

They sat underneath the large weeping willow. She leaned against it, spreading her full skirt around her. Zachary sat with one knee bent and his forearm resting on it.

Elizabeth started with the Cordelia incident at the cotillion, then the letter which he had inadvertently delivered to her himself. She told about going to see his friends, the Wilson's, and then the meeting with Cordelia and the Fullers.

As the story unfolded, they began to walk hand in hand. At times they just stood and faced each other. He kissed her eyes when she wept. She held his face between her hands, looking into his eyes filled with love for her, and apologized for ever doubting him for one moment.

When all the story was told they both felt such peace. They felt as if they had been through the fire, tested, and had emerged totally refined. They both sensed their love was boundless and could never be confined.

They remounted their horses and Elizabeth exclaimed, "I'll race you," as she rode off at a full gallop.

When they had returned the horses to the livery and picked up the carriage, Elizabeth remarked, "You know, Zachary, I've had a long day but I don't even feel tired. Life is good" she said as she slipped under his comforting arm and once again returned to Willow Place.

Zachary, very quietly, said, "Elizabeth, I want to protect you from as many hard places in life as I possibly can. And there *will be* other hard places. I am so sorry you walked the path you have walked without my knowledge of events and, consequently, without my support. But I am impressed with the way you handled the entire situation. From here on we will share everything. No secrets. Together, and certainly with God's help, we can weather any storm. Agreed?"

"Yes, oh yes, Zachary."

Chapter 43

April 14

The Morgan's were moved into the old Browning home in Fair Oaks and had everything in place as if they had lived there for months.

Simpson, Virginia and Millie had moved with them. Simpson and Virginia had no immediate family in Williamsburg. Neither one had ever been married. Millie was only nineteen and liked working for the Morgan's. She felt the move to a new place would add some adventure to her life.

Mike Kelley had consented to come with Mr. Morgan. He would be his well-respected handyman both here and at the new house when it was finished.

He had also brought young Max Hammond along. Mike and Max had been a big help in orchestrating the move so smoothly.

Catherine absolutely loved the Browning house. Its elegant interior enhanced the choice of furniture she had kept from the big house on Warthen Street. The window dressings were in the best of taste and blended perfectly with her upholstered furniture. She did miss her sunroom, however.

Virginia had no complaints about her kitchen. She found it was quite satisfactory with plenty of cupboard space.

Martha had stayed behind in Williamsburg. She had a family of her own. They would miss her.

~~~~~~

The work at Morgan Carriage Company was moving right along. Jim Adams proved to be a first-rate foreman. He was easy going but demanded first quality work. He got along well with the workers.

John went out into the factory on Monday morning, April 17th. He spotted Max and motioned for him. He said, "Good morning, Max, I'd like to have a word with you in my office." John draped his arm around Max's shoulder as they approached the office door.

"Have a seat. I've already talked to you about my plans for you in this company. And I have observed your work at the shipyard. You are very energetic and productive. I've noticed you work particularly well with your hands. You have a good sense of humor, which always helps. Tell me a little more about yourself and some of your interests."

"Well, sir, I like what I see here at the carriage company and agree with you that we can improve on their comfort. The physical workings of the carriages and buggies seem pretty sound to me. I'm pleased you are interested in helping me develop my skills in this new field of work. I realize it is a great opportunity for me and I'm indeed grateful for your confidence in me."

"Well said, young man. Well said."

"When you aren't working do you have any hobbies?"

"Well sir, my most prized possession is my guitar. Playing it fills up a lot of my spare time. I sing a little and write a lot of my own songs. Reading western books intrigues me. I wouldn't mind working on a ranch part time. That about sums me up, I guess."

"You sound like a well-rounded young man to me. I want you to know we will give you every opportunity here at Morgan Carriage. If you come up with some good ideas, don't hesitate to let me know."

He shook hands with Max and patted him on the back as he left his office. He looked at his vest pocket watch and walked down to the small office where Zack was working on the books and knocked on the partially open door.

"Good morning, John," Zachary said as he leaned back in his old worn chair. "Come in. Here, let me move those books out of the way so you'll have a place to sit."

"Thank you, Zack. You hardly have enough room to work in here."

"It's fine. I can make do until we can get a handle on the business."

"Zack, my boy, I can't tell you how thrilled Catherine and I are over yours and Elizabeth's engagement. It is hard for us to comprehend what has happened in our lives since we met Elizabeth. You are two of the people we love most in the world. To think you will truly be a part of our family brings great joy to our hearts."

"Well, the feeling is certainly mutual. Isn't Elizabeth something, John? She is really quite a girl. I can promise you I will take care of her. Our love for each other is something we will nurture and cherish and protect."

"I believe that, son. Now let me tell you why I came. You have been working with me for almost six years. You invested your time and much-needed talent in Morgan Shipping. I consider this as stock in the company. I told you I would make it worth your while if you would come here with me. I made a handsome sum on the sale of Morgan Shipping. I have put money in the Citizens Bank here in Richmond in your name. It represents the stock you had in the company. Here is your bank passbook. It is your money. You earned it."

Zachary looked at the amount and whistled. He was shocked. "Are you sure you want to do this, John? This is a lot of money."

"As I said, it is yours. You earned it. Now I must get busy. You are a very fine young man, Zachary Bainbridge."

Chapter 44

APRIL 28

Elizabeth had been back in her routine at the hospital for three weeks now and had learned a lot about nursing. She still did a lot of reading, not only to the children but also to the older patients. They loved to see her come into the room with a book. She also helped to cool fevered brows, helped with baths and could change a bed in record time.

Nurse Kim Thomas and Dr. David Blake had become a "couple". They were very comfortable in each other's presence. They consulted with one another about their patients and made a very good professional team.

Elizabeth's engagement to Zachary was common knowledge now. Her friends were pleased and happy for them, especially Kim and David.

As she was getting ready to leave the hospital for the day, Kim came up to Elizabeth and said she had a question. They stepped into Kim's office.

"Elizabeth, do you know a young man who is working for your grandfather named Max Hammond?"

"Yes and no, Kim. Yes, I've heard my grandfather sing his praises and no, I don't know him personally. Why?"

Did you know this young Max is living at the Butts Boarding House?"

"Yes, it seems this was the plan for him."

"Well, my sister, Jo Anna, who is eighteen, is a friend of Annette Butts. Her parents own the boarding house. Jo Anna spent last Saturday night with Annette. She came home talking about Max. She says he plays the guitar and sings. He has such a great personality that a crowd gathers around him in the sitting room. They listen to him sing and before long, he has them singing along with him.

"Max asked her name and said he would like to see her again. Needless to say she is smitten by him. Of course, mother and father will have to meet him and find out more about him before they will permit Annette to go out with him. What do you think?"

"My grandfather is so 'smitten by him,' as you call it, that he had him move here from Williamsburg to continue working for him. He has plans to train him for a good position with Morgan Carriage. But your parents are correct in wanting to meet him. I'm sure if young Max is really interested, he will do whatever is required to please Jo Anna's parents. You can count on that."

"Well, I must run. See you next week."

Elizabeth had a dinner date with Zachary at the Candlewick Café this evening. They had invited Phillip and Jane to go with them. She was anxious to get home and prepare for the evening. What a relief to be rid of fear and so many disquieting questions. She felt such a great inner peace.

Their dinner date was at eight o'clock. As they were being seated at their reserved table in an alcove of the café, they heard the strollers' music. Zachary had pre-arranged as soon as they were seated that the strollers would come to their table and play *their song*, 'To Each His Own.' Then they presented Elizabeth and Jane with a red rose. The musicians played two more Spanish songs in wonderful harmony just for them.

As the strollers left them and went to other tables, Elizabeth took Zachary's hand and said, "I feel just like a princess."

Zachary replied, "And you look like one, my dear."

Jane looked at Phillip and said, "And what, my dear Phillip, do I look like?"

He replied, "Remember how I described you the day I asked you to marry me?"

"Yes."

"What did I say?"

"You called me your little pixie and said I was petite."

"And why did I say I liked your being petite? Do you remember?"

"You said it meant you could easily sweep me into your arms and carry me."

"And what else did I say?"

"You said I was exactly the kind of woman you wanted to be the mother of your children and that you could not live without me."

"You would make a very good witness, my dear. I still feel the same way about you, my little pixie. Enough said."

"Oh Phillip, you are a lawyer first and foremost!"

"Not for long. I'll soon be a college professor!"

The waiter appeared to take their order. They had fun making their selections. They each tried something different so they could sample from each other's plate.

Zachary liked Elizabeth's choice of friends. He felt they could all four become very close over time. He looked forward to it. He was sorry that Phillip and Jane would be moving to Williamsburg so soon, but they could visit back and forth.

The food came, and it was delicious. They talked and laughed a lot and enjoyed one another's company. The strollers came back and played for them again just before they left.

On their way home Zachary asked Phillip to tell him more about his teaching job at the college, and why he wanted to change professions.

"I just don't care that much for the courtroom scene. I enjoy teaching college students the science of politics much better than the argument in the courtroom. If we are motivated by right principles then we can teach them to others. Hopefully, some of those we teach will build on a right foundation. But we must teach by example and not purely by principle.

"Confucius said . . . 'To put the world right in order, we must first put the nation in order; to put the nation in order, we must first put the family in order; to put the family in order, we must first cultivate our personal life; we must first set our hearts right.'

"Besides, Jane is a school teacher. We will have the same interests . . . The love of children and the desire to influence them for good. Does that answer your question?"

"It certainly does, Phillip. I am impressed. If I had children I would like to know they were being taught in school by folks like you two."

Elizabeth said, "You can see, Zachary, why these two people are so special to me."

"Jane, how are you coming with the wedding plans? Today is April 28th. June 3rd will be here before you know it."

"I meant to tell you, Elizabeth, we have changed the date to Friday night, June 2nd. Will that be a problem for you?"

"Not at all."

Phillip spoke up and said, "Zachary, would you mind standing up with me? Our wedding party is going to be mostly family, but since Elizabeth will be the maid of honor, I'd be grateful if you would be my best man. There will be four other groomsmen, plus the best man, and of course the groom makes six. What do you say?"

"I would be honored."

"We decided to make this day one to remember for the rest of our lives," Jane said. "Of course, it will be held at First Wesleyan."

They had arrived at Willow Place. Jane was spending the night with Elizabeth. Zachary and Phillip would have to drive back into town. They helped the girls out of the carriage, kissed them goodnight and left.

Elizabeth and Jane walked arm in arm across the porch and into the house. Elizabeth looked at Jane and said, "I'd call this a perfect evening."

Chapter 45

APRIL 29

SATURDAY

Elizabeth saw Sara, Emily and Julie playing in the backyard of the Everette home as she drove up in her buggy at mid-morning. When they saw her they ran to meet her.

"Good morning Miss Morgan," Sara called out.

"Good morning Miss Morgan," Emily and Julie echoed.

"Well, good morning. How are my favorite girls this beautiful Saturday morning?"

"Fine, Miss Morgan," young Emily replied. "I haven't been sick in a long time."

"I know you haven't, Emily. You look strong and healthy."

Elizabeth had picked up four-year old Julie who was small for her age. She put her little arm around Elizabeth's neck.

Elizabeth sat down on a comfortable old tree stump, which had been left for that very reason.

"Tell me, did your Easter dresses fit?"

"Oh yes, Miss Morgan," Sara answered enthusiastically. "We wore them to church Easter Sunday and to the Easter egg hunt that afternoon."

Emily spoke up, "Our shoes fit us, too. Granny Smith gave us straw bonnets."

"I'm sure you all three looked very pretty dressed up in your new clothes," Elizabeth said as she gave Julie a hug.

Julie mimicked, "We looked very pretty."

Maggie Everette came outside the back door. "Good morning, Miss Morgan. I thought the girls had grown awfully quiet for some reason."

"Yes, they were telling me about their new Easter outfits and the egg hunt."

"I found three eggs,' Julie said, her big brown eyes looking very serious.

"We appreciate the nice clothes you brought the girls, Miss Morgan. You have been very kind to our family. Because of you our lives have completely changed. We are so thankful.

"Sara, could you tell Miss Morgan what you learned about Easter in Sunday school?"

"We learned that Jesus was crucified on Good Friday and was buried in a tomb. Then on the third day he arose from the dead. That is why we celebrate Easter."

"Very, very good Sara. I'm so proud of you. It shows you listen in Sunday school."

"I will be six years old in June, Miss Morgan, and then I can go to real school when it starts in September. My mommy told me so," Emily said, stretching to stand just a little taller.

"I found three eggs," Julie repeated again."

"You girls run along now. Go play some more hopscotch, or jump rope" Maggie suggested.

"Jim is plowing the field for spring planting. He has regained the self-esteem he had when we were first married. The Smiths have given us a real chance here on the farm and we have such a good relationship. Jim feels very protective of them. They needed someone to look after them and we are thankful that God allowed us to come here" Maggie said to Elizabeth.

"I am so happy for all of you, Maggie. Where are the Smiths? I had hoped to see them also."

"They rode into Richmond to the mercantile for some supplies. I'll tell them you came."

"I must go now. I like to stay in touch with two of my favorite families,' Elizabeth said as she turned to leave. "Goodbye girls."

"Goodbye Miss Morgan," they all three sang out.

May 5
Friday

Kim greeted Elizabeth when she got to the hospital that morning. As they were talking, Dr. Blake walked up.

"Good morning ladies. Elizabeth, we've got one crotchety old guy in room 106. He would try the patience of a saint! He has blood poisoning in his left leg from stepping on a rusty nail. His foot and leg are swollen and have to be packed in ice and he is resisting. Would you look in on him with some of your bedside manner, please?"

"David, before Elizabeth goes, would you please tell her about Max?"

"Oh, yes. This young man is very talented. He needs to be on the stage. You might have forgotten, Elizabeth, I am staying at the Butts Boarding House. Of course, this is where Max is 'bunking down' as he calls it. Why, he has made that place come alive. He keeps everyone laughing."

"After being around him and seeing his serious side, we convinced Mr. and Mrs. Thomas that it would be okay for Jo Anna to see him. They consented to let them go out to dinner with Kim and me. Jo Anna has a great natural talent for singing, same as Max. You ought to hear them sing together. Max has taught her some of the ballads he sings. I really do like Max."

"And so does Jo Anna!" Kim chimed in.

"This is very interesting. I'll have to share this with grandfather and Zachary," Elizabeth mused. "Now I'll go check on Mr. 106. Does he have a name?"

"Yes. It's Jake Smart. Wait just a minute," David said. "I'll be right back."

He returned with a book entitled "The Lonesome Cowpoke" by Luke Chaps.

"Max let me borrow this book. See if the old codger will let you read it to him. If he will lie still and keep that foot and leg in ice it will help him get well quicker. He doesn't need to be moving around. He needs to lie quietly. See what you can do."

Elizabeth walked into Mr. Smart's room. The door was wide open. A nurse was pleading with him to keep his leg still. They had a cradle made of oilcloth filled with ice that wrapped around his foot and leg.

"Mr. Smart, good morning!" Elizabeth said with as much authority as she could muster. "I see you have a very serious problem with blood poisoning. Now you are a very smart man. Why, your name is even "Smart". You do want to go home don't you?"

He lay perfectly still and looked at her steadily. "Why sure I want to go home!" he snapped.

"Then I suggest you cooperate with the doctor and nurses of this hospital who are trying to get you well so you can do just that. How did this happen to you?"

He began to stir and attempted to move his leg.

"Lay still, Mr. Smart. This is part of the treatment that is going to get you well. If you insist on moving around this blood poisoning could travel to your heart and you are smart enough to know what that might mean, aren't you?"

He looked at her again, very steadily.

"Well aren't you?"

"Yep, I guess so."

"Then I suggest you act like the tough hombre I've heard that you are and get yourself well so you can get back in the saddle and take care of business.

"Now while you keep perfectly still I've brought a book to read to you. It's called 'Lonesome Cowpoke' a western that you should really enjoy."

Elizabeth began to read . . .

"The snow was blowing down the collar of Slim's heavy buffalo hide coat as he pressed his horse on through the snow. The sagebrush was blowing in the stiff wind that was to his back. He had been riding for two days. He should be reaching the fort by nightfall . . ."

After four chapters she paused and looked at Mr. Smart. His eyes were closed. He was breathing deeply. He was sound asleep. She tip-toed out of the room behind nurse Brown.

"I don't think we've been using the right tactics with the old man. You simply out-witted him. I hope it lasts." Nurse Brown smiled as she patted Elizabeth on the shoulder.

"I'll be back in a little while to check on him," Elizabeth said.

Chapter 46

May 9

Tuesday

The Morgan's had started their home on the northwest side of the lake at Willow Place. There was a knoll with a plateau at the top just perfect for the house. They would be high enough to look down on Willow Place from their front porch.

The house was going to be one level with a wrap-around porch. John decided to make it a brick house since Willow Place was brick. Their contractor, Clarence Cleburne, was known to be one of the best brick masons in the entire area. And he loved laying the brick himself on the jobs he contracted that called for brick work. The porch banisters would be painted white to match the white trim of Elizabeth's house.

They would have a living room and parlor combined and a formal dining room, a large kitchen, a small study, a sewing room and three bedrooms. Each bedroom would have a water closet with the new style bathtubs that were plumbed in.

They also planned to build a servants quarters behind the big house for Simpson, Virginia and Millie with water closets and bath areas.

The plan was to have it all completed by the last of August.

Elizabeth's grandparents had come to Willow Place to check things out at the building site. They were pleased with the progress.

They walked back down to the east side of the lake and were sitting on the benches close to the water.

"Elizabeth, the dogwood trees have about lost their blooms now. But on Easter Sunday, just three weeks ago, they were filled with pink and white blossoms. I can see why you love this place so much. The dogwood trees enhance the beauty of the weeping willows," her grandmother commented.

"Yes, Grandmother Catherine. And all of the dogwoods are natural. They've just always been there. We could say they are the creation of the Master Artist. Of course, we have had gardeners come in and landscape the area to control undergrowth. They also planted shrubs and seasonal flowers. I can't tell you, even though I've tried, about the attachment I have for this place. My Baldwin grandparents held my hand as a little girl and walked me all around Willow Place, from the stables to the pastures to the lake, even to the plateau where your house will sit. They showed me the beauty of nature. Scampering squirrels, baby rabbits, deer, birds' nests, and wild flowers. They took time with me. In doing so, they made me feel complete and not neglected or abandoned because of the loss of my parents."

"This place represents good memories," her grandfather said. "We hope to have the opportunity to do the same for a grandchild some day. Our lives seem so unfulfilled in those areas because of losing our son, John Lee. But we have our future to look forward to with any grandchildren you and Zachary may give to us, should we be so blessed."

Elizabeth smiled at the very thought of it.

"Grandfather, you are the best!

"By the way, I've been thinking about something lately. I'd like to have a big picnic here at Willow Place sometime in June before it gets too hot. I have mentioned it to Zachary. He likes the idea. I'd like to invite a few of the couples that were at my party in Williamsburg. What do you think?"

"It's a great idea. I've wanted you to get to know some of those young people better anyway," her grandmother said.

"How many people are we talking about?" her grandfather asked.

"I've counted eight couples including Zachary and me, and of course, there would be the two of you as chaperones. These are the ones I have in mind . . . Steve and Rebecca Wilson, Scott and Libbi Dixon, Matthew and India Jones, Andrea Ashton and Ben Bainbridge, Rebecca Bainbridge and Robert Thomas, a local boy; Phillip and Jane, Max Hammond and Jo Anna Thomas. What do you think? Would they all come?"

"If we provide places for them to stay and send them train tickets, I don't see how they could refuse," her grandfather said.

"Steve and Rebecca could have a bedroom at Willow Place. Andrea and Rebecca Bainbridge could share a room here," Elizabeth said thoughtfully.

"Matthew and India, and Scott and Libbi can stay with us," her grandmother added.

"We could get a room at the Richmond Hotel for Phillip and Jane," her grandfather suggested,

"And the rest all live here."

"The next question is choosing a time. What about the weekend of June 17th? That's about six weeks away. That will give us time to contact everyone and make all the plans," Elizabeth remarked.

"Sounds good to us," her grandparents agreed.

With a spark of excitement in her voice, Elizabeth added, "I will get invitations in the mail tomorrow."

"Your grandmother has the addresses of all those in Williamsburg. Let me send them a telegram. When they reply I'll get their train tickets and send them by mail. That will be the quickest way to handle it. Catherine has Ben and Rebecca's address in Norfolk."

"Grandfather, you just take care of everything."

"I'm trying to make up for lost time," He said with a smile.

When John and Catherine returned home, Mike met them at the front drive to take the horse and carriage to the stables. The living quarters were very nice at the north end of the stables where Mike lived. Simpson, Virginia and Millie were living in the servants' quarters attached to the old Browning home.

"Mike, when you finish I'd like you to come up to the big house. I want to talk with you," John said.

"Be right there, Mr. Morgan, sir," Mike replied jovially.

John was waiting in the library when Mike was shown in by Simpson.

Mike stood a little less than six feet tall. His hair was thick and gray as were his eyebrows. His skin was leathered tan from the sun, wind and seawater. He was broad-shouldered and strong from hard work. His eyes were blue as the skies of Ireland. His smile was broad and contagious.

John, having observed Mike over the past thirty years, knew he was well liked by his peers and felt as if he were a better person for having known him.

"Sit down, Mike."

"Don't mind if I do."

"Mike, I'd like to ask you some personal questions if I may," John said leaning forward in his chair.

"Fire away, Mr. Morgan."

"Tell me about your life as a young man. Where were you born? How did you wind up in Williamsburg?"

"Well sir, I was born there, and grew up there. When I was in me early twenties I came here to Richmond to find better work and get ahead in life. All I could find here was work in a planing mill. And I did that for a while. Then I decided I could do better if I went somewhere else. So I went to Norfolk and worked on a steamer."

"What brought you back to Williamsburg?" John inquired.

"I came back to visit me parents. Twas good timin'. Me father was riddled with arthritis and me mother was in failing health. It was not the time to be goin' away again. That's when I went to work for Morgan Shipping. I was able to look after them till they departed, may God rest their souls."

"Was there ever a young lady in your life?" John asked. He watched Mike's face carefully. He saw a softness appear there.

"Yes, I had a girl once. She was a sweet bonnie lass. I loved her. I did, at that. But I had nothing to offer her. She twas a lass I met right here in Richmond. I would have loved to marry her. But twasn't to be. Circumstances prevented me coming back," Mike said regretfully.

"Did you ever hear from her again?"

"No sir, never did."

"Do you remember her name, Mike?"

"Forget her name? Never! Twas Emma O'Reilly. She was an Irish lass. She had reddish blonde hair and green eyes and twas wispy thin. I can still see her in me mind's eye, Mr. Morgan. A fella could never forget a lass like Emma."

John almost fell out of his chair with surprise. Could this Emma O'Reilly be Elizabeth's Emma? It would have to be because of his description of her. But he dare not say anything now. He needed time to think about this. He remembered the things Ben Browning had told him about a young Mike Kelly who lived in Richmond about thirty years ago. Hmm.

"Mike, I appreciate your coming in to talk to me. I like to know about people who are important to me. We will talk again later. I'm sure you've had a long day as I have. I will see you tomorrow," John said.

Standing to leave Mike said, "Goodnight Mr. Morgan," as they walked together to the side door.

Chapter 47

MAY 10

WEDNESDAY

Today was Elizabeth's day at the hospital, John remembered, as he sat in his study. Maybe she would come by the factory on her way home. He would sure like to talk to her about his conversation with Mike last night.

When Mike brings the carriage around I have another question for him, John thought. He drank his coffee and read the Richmond Daily News. He then tiptoed into the bedroom and kissed Catherine goodbye. She stirred, gave him a smile and wished him a good day at the office, then turned over and snuggled back into the warm quilts. He looked down at her and thought; *I can't imagine my life without her.*

He heard the clop-clop of Maude's hooves on the drive and the creaking of the carriage wheels. He went out the side door and Mike was waiting for him, prompt as always.

As John was getting ready to take the driver's seat, he liked driving himself to work these days, he said, "By the way, Mike, have you ever thought of trying to find this Emma O'Reilly to see what has become of her?"

"Well sir, yes and no. If I found her and she is married, what good would it do? She was such a bonnie lass. I'm sure someone snatched her up!" Mike said.

"But what if she is still around and never married? Would you still be interested in her?"

John inquired.

"Tis a good question. Twould be interesting to see her again. I'd like that. Tis only wistful thinking, I'm sure."

"Maybe not," John said as he drove off.

———◦———

Elizabeth entered the hospital singing softly to herself. She felt unusually good this morning. She had a deep sense of happiness. Her grandparents were so excited about their new house being built. The picnic was a good idea, something to look forward to. That reminded her, she had forgotten to include Kim and Dr. Blake. They were a must to be invited.

She stuck her head in the door of Kim's office, after knocking, and greeted her warmly.

"You seem to be in a good mood this morning," Kim remarked.

"I am indeed. We are planning a June picnic at Willow Place. It will be on Saturday the seventeenth. You and Dr. Blake are invited. I hope you can work out your schedules to be able to attend. We are inviting several special couples that came to the Valentine's party in Williamsburg. We want Max and Jo Anna and Robert to come. We would like Robert to meet Zachary's sister, Rebecca. Would you talk to Jo Anna and Robert for us? It is going to be a "couples" thing. Also, ask David to tell Max about it. It is going to be an informal affair. We want to get together for some fun and fellowship."

"Sounds like a great idea to me. There aren't that many things happening for the young people around Richmond. From what David and Jo Anna say, there's more fun happening at the Butts

Boarding House than anywhere in town. Max has orchestrated some Friday and Saturday night sing-a-longs," Kim replied.

"Have you checked on Jake Smart this morning?" Elizabeth asked.

"Yes, and he's waiting for you. After reading half of the western book to him, he can't wait to hear the rest of it. You have a gift, Elizabeth, for helping sick people. Your volunteer work these past five months has been a real blessing to this hospital. One thing's for sure. You settled Jake Smart down! Keeping his foot and leg iced has really improved his condition. He sees that it doesn't hurt as much as it did."

"Then I best get on down to room 106.

"Good morning, Jake. How did you rest last night? Here, let me look at that foot and leg. Why, the swelling has gone down considerably and it isn't as red as it was."

She walked around the bed and fluffed up his pillow.

"I see you've had your bath and your bed's been changed. Are you ready to hear some more of 'Lonesome Cowpoke'?"

"Yes ma'am. I'm real anxious to hear what happened to that young whipper-snapper Jesse. Did anyone ever tell you how purty you are?"

"Are you trying to bribe me so I'll finish this book today?" Elizabeth asked.

"No ma'am. I'm just tellin' the truth. And you are real tough to be so purty," Jake remarked.

She began to read . . . "Jesse saw that he was surrounded, so he climbed quickly and quietly on up the rocky hillside to higher ground. He figured if he could circle around to their left he could pick off at least three of these hombres before they knew he was there."

—◁◁◁▥◁▷▥▷▷—

At the end of her day Elizabeth decided to ride Blazer over by the carriage factory to see her grandfather and Zachary for a few minutes. She loved these spring days so that she could ride Blazer to work.

She walked into her grandfather's office. He wasn't there. She then went down the hall to Zachary's cubbyhole. He wasn't there either. She walked to the small landing that perched above the carriage shop area. She saw Zachary, Max and her grandfather standing at a long table looking over some prints. She waited a few minutes. Zachary was facing the landing and glanced up. He smiled and waved. He and her grandfather came to join her. Max threw up his hand.

They walked down to her grandfather's office. She said, "I just wanted to come by on my way home and say hello."

"I'm glad you did. I was hoping you would come by. Sit down Zack, I have something mighty interesting to tell both of you.

"Last night I had a conversation with Mike Kelly. I asked him some personal questions because of something old Mr. Ben Browning said to me. He mentioned that a Mike Kelly used to live in Richmond about thirty years ago, and that he had a girlfriend. Everyone who knew them thought they would get married. However, he left town and wasn't heard from again. I was curious about this. Come to find out Mike did live here and was interested in a 'bonnie lass' as he called her. He left Richmond to find a better life and planned to come back for her. But circumstances prevented it. I asked him if he remembered her name. He said he would never forget her or her name."

"Did he tell you what it is?" Elizabeth quizzed, putting two and two together by this time.

"He said it was Emma O'Reilly! Can you beat that! Elizabeth, it would have to be your Emma. Wouldn't you agree?"

"It certainly sounds that way. What should we do?"

Zachary spoke up and said, "Why, we play cupid, that's what we do!"

"After Grandmother Savannah died, Emma and I had a talk about Mike Kelly. She still cares for him, for his memory, even though it's been so long ago."

"We should try to bring the two of them together again. We need to have Mike make a trip out to Willow Place to see Emma. We will tell him she will be there, but for her it should be a surprise. She could be sitting out by the lake on a bench when he drives up. Do you think it would be too much of a shock for her, Elizabeth?" her grandfather asked.

"She has a strong constitution. I think it would be a very romantic thing to do," Elizabeth answered. "The spark might not still be there, but how wonderful if it is. I get all teary-eyed just thinking about it. When can we set up the meeting?"

"What about this Saturday morning? Do you have some mending you could ask Emma to do sitting out in the sunlight by the lake?" her grandfather plotted.

"Yes, and that's one of her favorite places to sit while she sews, so she would not be suspicious."

"Then I will have Mike drive me and your grandmother out to Willow Place about 10:30. You can have her out by the lake by then. We will come inside. Then Mike can ride around to where she is sitting."

Elizabeth looked at Zachary and said, "Why don't you ride Streak out about 10:00. I think we all ought to be a part of such a wonderful surprise."

Chapter 48

May 13
Saturday

*E*verything was set for the meeting between Mike and Emma. Everyone was in the house and Emma was sitting on a bench facing Willow Lake. She was busy hemming some new table napkins she had cut out a few weeks ago.

Mike had let the Morgan's out of the carriage in front of the house, and was now circling back around heading out. He stopped the carriage near the bench where Emma was sitting and stepped down.

Emma looked up but the sun had her blinded. Mike approached the bench and said, "Tis gorgeous weather we're havin'. Tis altogether marvelous."

Emma closed her eyes and listened.

"I say, 'tis altogether marvelous weather."

There was only one person she had ever heard who talked like that, with such an Irish brogue.

"Mike Kelly, is that you?" she asked as she stood to her feet.

"Tis me, bonnie lass. Tis me alright."

She looked into his rough but handsome face. He still had the head full of thick hair, although it had changed from brown to gray. Those were the same blue eyes she remembered well. He still had the same fine build.

"Well, may I ask where you've been?"

"Tis a long story, Emma. Would you be willing to listen if I told you?"

"I will be glad to listen, Mike Kelly. But I have a family to take care of. Miss Elizabeth's grandparents just came up. I need to take care of lunch. Say, is that Mr. Morgan's carriage you are driving? It sure looks like it."

"Yes, it tis. The family knows about this. It was their idea. They wanted me to surprise you. They are inside waiting on us."

"I'm confused. How do you know the family? How do they know you?"

Mike took her hands in his. "Emma, I can't believe me good fortune to see you again. Tis like a dream, it tis. But it will take some time to make myself clear to you. Just be patient, lassie. We will have a chance to talk before the day is done."

When they got to the front door, Elizabeth opened it wide. She said, "Come in, Emma, and introduce your friend to us."

They all gathered around the couple, talking excitedly. Mike met Elizabeth, Sadie and William. They treated him like a long lost friend.

Emma had a big pot of Irish stew on the stove. She served it up, piping hot. They all gathered around the kitchen table and ate and laughed heartily.

That afternoon Elizabeth and Zachary rode horseback. Mike took the Morgan's back home. He told Emma he would be back late in the afternoon so they could have their talk.

Sunday morning Emma told Elizabeth that Mike had explained about his parents being sick for so long. He never felt he had done well enough to come back for her. He said he realized what a mistake he had made. He had wasted so many years.

"How do you feel about Mike, Emma?" Elizabeth asked.

"It might sound strange to you, lassie, but my feelings for Mike have never changed. It is like he never went away."

"I saw the way you looked at each other, Emma. I could see the love and respect in your eyes."

"We talked at length yesterday. We felt very comfortable together. I am fifty-six and Mike is fifty-eight. We do not have any more time to waste. We plan to keep on seeing each other and talking and sharing what has happened in our lives since he left in 1822. We plan to spend as much time together as we can, and we shall see what becomes of it." Emma declared.

"I know you will depend on God for guidance. I will support you in your decision where Mike is concerned. Grandfather knows Mike as I know you. He calls him a friend. That is a good enough reference for me."

"Thank you, lassie. I am happy, truly happy. The way our lives have come together again after thirty-four years can't be just a coincidence. Just think, Mike will be working right here on Willow Place where I work. We consider it a miracle. Neither of us ever married. We don't have children, so we have no one to consider except each other. I believe that true love will stand the test of time and that is what has happened between us. By the way, Mike is going to meet me at church Sunday. We want to spend the afternoon together if that's alright with you, lassie."

"That's fine, Emma. I am so happy for you and Mike."

Chapter 49

JUNE 2
FRIDAY

*F*ormal invitations had been sent out for the wedding of Jane and Phillip Maxwell. Their families had gathered in for the special event.

Phillip's parents, Greg and Ann Marie Maxwell, his grandparents the senior Maxwell's, and his grandmother, Mrs. Annette Van Pelt, all came up from Petersburg, Virginia for the ceremony.

The Maxwell's close friends, Charles and Helen Parker, where Phillip is boarding, were there.

Jane's family including both sets of grandparents, the Adams and the Tice's, her aunt Genia Barnette, and aunt Maye Tice on her mother's side of the family, attended. They all live in Richmond.

The church was filled with friends and relatives. Jane's brothers, Jim, Joe and Josh, were ushers and seated all the guests. They looked particularly dashing in their black cutaway coats and black ascot ties.

The organist played softly. On cue, she began to chord "Nearer My God to Thee." The congregation stood and sang the first verse and chorus.

Daniel and Ann Bishop sang, "Lord, We Ask Your Blessing."

Pastor Davis and Phillip were standing on the platform awaiting the entrance of the attendants, groomsmen and the bride.

As Elizabeth was escorted down the aisle by Zachary, the Bishops sang "Today, Tomorrow and Forever."

Elizabeth and the attendants were wearing rose-colored summer voile dresses with portrait necklines. She had her black hair fixed in an upsweep. She carried a bouquet of yellow roses and baby's breath.

Zachary and the groomsmen were wearing black cutaway coats, white ruffled shirts and black ascot ties.

Elizabeth and Zachary joined the pastor and groom on the platform. Phillip sported a traditional tuxedo with tails, white shirt and white ascot tie.

The processional of the attendants and groomsmen was a lovely sight. Rose petals of red and yellow were scattered by the flower girl, and the ring bearer made his way down the aisle cutting his eyes first right then left.

The moment had come. The traditional bridal march was played as the radiant bride entered the sanctuary on the arm of her father.

Jane's wedding gown was a brilliant white with a sheer overlay and long sleeves that came to a point. There was tear drop lace at the neck which also trimmed the sleeves and hem. Pearl beads highlighted the neckline and sleeves, and a back bustle was garnished with a train that flowed down the aisle behind her. An elbow length veil finished the lovely bride. She looked like an angel.

The bridal bouquet was made up of beautifully arranged yellow roses and baby's breath framed with lush greenery.

You could tell by the look on Phillip's face, he was awed by Jane's beauty.

Pastor Davis performed the traditional wedding ceremony. It was simple but beautiful.

Chapter 49

Following the morning ceremony, the wedding party and out-of-town guests were treated to a lovely reception in the fellowship wing of the church.

That afternoon Phillip and Jane left in a decorated carriage with the traditional "Just Married" sign, tin cans, and a cow's bell dangling from the rear of the carriage. The couple headed to Hopewell to spend a week at a lakeside cottage for their honeymoon.

Chapter 50

*J*ane, we've been married three days now and I can hardly remember my life without you. I feel so blessed to have found a girl
like you. I've watched you as you move around the cottage. You
have such a smooth, easy way about you. You make things seem
effortless. You know how to do so many things, Phillip said as he
stood behind Jane with his arms around her waist and his cheek
next to hers.

She almost had their breakfast ready to put on the table. She
made bacon and pancakes, Phillip's favorite.

"Remember," she replied, "I'm the oldest of five children. I had
to learn how to do a lot of things, like getting a fire going in a
stubborn stove, and putting a meal on the table for six hungry
mouths, by myself when my mother was away. I'm thankful for
knowing these things. It has helped me become more independent. I like to think I am a survivor."

"You are a very strong person, admirably so. But I want to make
life easy for you. I hope I can provide for you in a way that will
shield you from hard places. I never want to fail or disappoint you."

Jane turned around in his arms, traced his strong jaw line with
her finger and said, "Phillip, my Phillip! You fail me or disappoint

me? That will never happen. I've met my match when it comes to strength. Besides, where you are concerned I want to be as weak as a little kitten and let you be my strength. Remember when you told me you liked my being petite so you could sweep me up in your arms? Well, here I am!" she laughed playfully.

He scooped her up and swung her round and round in the small kitchen, then put her down in front of the stove and exclaimed, "I'm starved!"

Jane put breakfast on the table. They held hands and Phillip offered thanks for the food, and they both enjoyed a hot breakfast.

"Tell me Phillip, are you nervous about your new job?"

"No, not at all. I am rather looking forward to it. I hope we can locate near the college. John Morgan said he had a friend in real estate he was contacting to help us find a suitable place. As soon as I get settled in the new job, we will look for a small house to purchase.

"Do you dread moving from Richmond to Williamsburg, Jane? Are you afraid?"

"No, quite the contrary. I am looking forward to broadening my horizons. I will miss my family and friends, but I'm looking forward to making new friends. Elizabeth met some fine people at her Valentine's party. She mentioned many of them to me. She's inviting several of these couples to the picnic on June 17th. We will have a chance to meet them.

"Let's get the table cleared and the dishes washed. I'd like to drive into town and visit some of the shops," Jane said.

They finished the dishes and Phillip went out to hitch Betsy up to the carriage. He spotted a patch of white and yellow daisies growing on the back side of the cottage. He picked a bouquet and carried them in to Jane.

He smiled and handed them to her, except for one. He began pulling off the petals one at a time saying, "She loves me, she loves me not. When he pulled the last petal off the daisy it came out . . . she loves me not. "Well we will just have to do something about that now, won't we?" He reached for her. She eluded his grasp and ran around the table and out the door. He was right behind her.

She reached a thick grassy area and laughingly fell to her knees just as he got to her. He leaned over and pulled her to her feet and smothered her with kisses.

"Now, do you love me, little pixie?"

She was out of breath from laughing so hard. She exclaimed, "Yes, my sweet husband, I do love you."

They both stood very still holding each other tenderly.

Tears welled up in Jane's eyes. "Oh Phillip, we are no longer two, but we are one. We have our whole life ahead of us. Let's cherish every single day of it."

"Yes Jane, just like our song says, 'Today, Tomorrow and Forever'" Phillip said and kissed her upturned face on the forehead, nose, cheek and then her perfect lips.

Chapter 51

JUNE 10
SATURDAY

*C*atherine and John were having a leisurely breakfast. They enjoyed their late mornings on Saturdays. She set her coffee cup down and said, "John, I've never seen Elizabeth so happy and excited as she is over this picnic at Willow Place next Saturday. I've been thinking, she really needs some tables and chairs placed around under the willow trees so guests can sit down to eat their lunch. What do you think of renting some tables, white tablecloths and chairs from the Richmond Hotel? They usually have extras in storage for special occasions. You have come to know Donnie Tyson, the proprietor, quite well haven't you?"

"That's an excellent idea, Catherine. I've been thinking of something else. You know how much we've enjoyed going to the Candlewick Café since Zachary and Elizabeth told us about it. Their strolling musicians are fantastic. They work nights at the café. What if we get could get them to play at the picnic for a couple of hours?" John asked.

"I think Elizabeth would be thrilled to have them. Let's ask her and let her decide, however," Catherine said thoughtfully. "We don't want her to think we are interfering in her plans."

"Good idea, good idea," John reflected.

JUNE 17
SATURDAY

Elizabeth was so excited about the picnic she could hardly sleep and was awake at dawn. She had bought a new violet blue cotton dress just for the occasion. It had short puffed sleeves, round neck and tiny covered buttons to the waistline. The full gathered skirt was ankle length. She wore her white, eyelet pantalets, which were so comfortable.

Her hair looked especially nice she thought. When she was completely dressed she leaned close and looked into the mirror. The color of her dress matched her eyes exactly! Would Zachary notice?

Elizabeth hoped everyone rested well last night.

She hurried down to the kitchen, poured herself a cup of coffee and went outside to check on things. The tables her grandfather had rented from the hotel were perfect. They looked so pristine placed underneath the willow trees and overlaid with the white linens. It would be nice to have a comfortable place for everyone to sit while they ate lunch. Her grandparents were so precious, so unselfish. They had such a desire to please her. She wanted to be careful never to take advantage of them and their generosity. She could not believe they had engaged the strollers to be there for a couple of hours for the picnic! This would be a grand day.

She saw William standing out at the small pier at the south end of the lake. She walked down to where he was.

"Good morning, William. Whatever are you doing?"

"Miss Elizabeth, I got the flat bottom boat down from storage. Your Grandfather Baldwin wrapped it up good and I found it to be in mint condition. It has no leaks. The oars look like new. I thought some of the young folks might like to paddle around the lake. I also found two canoes he had stored away. So I have all three of them ready to go," William said smiling from ear to ear.

"Thank you, William. What would I do without you?"

She went back to the house and into the kitchen. She found Steve, Rebecca, Andrea and Rebecca B. all sitting at the table drinking coffee and eating bran muffins.

"Well, good morning! How did you all sleep last night," Elizabeth inquired.

Andrea said, "Just like babies!"

Rebecca replied, "I did fine until Andrea almost rooted me out of the bed!"

"Rebecca, you're the one who crowded me to the edge of the bed!" Andrea giggled.

It was obvious to Elizabeth that these two had hit it off.

Steve said, "We certainly slept well. We've been looking forward to this day for weeks."

"As I told you last night, Elizabeth, this is the nearest to a perfect place I've ever seen. I can't imagine awakening to this every morning," Rebecca added.

"I am so happy to have all of you in my home. I really want to get to know each of you better, especially Rebecca B. since she is going to be my sister," Elizabeth said. "It's about time for everyone to be arriving. Why don't you all go on outside and I'll be right with you. I need to speak to Emma first."

Emma and Virginia had become good friends since the Morgan's had moved to Richmond. They had worked together to prepare the food for the day.

Emma came into the kitchen from the outside. She had been buzzing around all morning getting everything in place for the picnic.

"There you are, Emma. Is there anything you need? We can send William into town if you need anything special."

"No, lassie, I have everything under control. You go enjoy yourself. Let Sadie and me take care of things. Virginia and Millie will be here any minute. They are coming with Mike. They will be bringing what Virginia has prepared. I hear them now out back. Shoo now!" Emma said waving her apron at Elizabeth in a mock scolding manner. "Go on. Off with you!"

Chapter 52

*E*lizabeth walked across the front lawn and joined Andrea and Rebecca sitting on the grass underneath a tree.

"Since we didn't have a chance to talk much last night, Andrea, tell me a little about yourself," Elizabeth said.

"Well, if I stretch it, I'm five feet three inches tall, I have dark brown eyes and blonde hair."

"Andrea, silly girl, we can see that!" Rebecca chided her.

"Well, let me see. I love to eat!"

"You don't look like you eat at all," Elizabeth responded. "You are so small. What are some of your favorite hobbies?"

"Seriously, I love working with children. I teach the six-to-eight year olds in Sunday School.

Since I was fifteen I have written stories and illustrated them with pencil sketching and watercolors. I have quite a collection," Andrea said.

Rebecca spoke up, "What a coincidence, I too write and illustrate. Can you believe it?" She looked at Andrea and asked, "Have you ever thought of trying to get your work published?"

"Yes, I have. But I've never looked into it. I would certainly like to. Why do you ask?" Andrea inquired.

"Well, my older brother Thomas has encouraged me to submit my work to a publisher. It would be nice if you and I could look over each other's collection. Maybe by combining some of our work we could succeed in getting it in book form," Rebecca suggested.

"Yes, that might be a good idea. We could use the name Ashton and Bainbridge, Authors and Illustrators," Andrea said with a gleam in her eye.

"Bainbridge and Ashton has a better ring to it, don't you think, Elizabeth?" Rebecca retorted.

Elizabeth replied, "I think I see a real kindred spirit between you two girls!"

They heard the carriages rolling in.

Andrea piped up, "Your brother, Ben, had better be good looking with a great personality or I'm going to pair up with Robert Thomas and leave you stranded."

"Well, I feel really sorry for you, Andrea. Zachary got the good looks in the family. Poor Ben got the brains and that's about all," Rebecca quipped.

They grabbed each other by the arm and began strolling toward the carriages, giggling and making plans all the way.

Elizabeth shook her head and smiled. *What great friends,* she thought.

Steve and Rebecca had walked almost all the way around the lake and returned just as the carriages arrived.

John, Catherine, Scott, Libbi, Matt and India climbed out of the first carriage. Dr. Blake, Kim, Max, Jo Anna, Ben and Robert arrived in the second. Zachary, Phillip and Jane pulled up in the third carriage.

The fellas began shaking hands. Introductions were made for those who did not know one another. Zachary took Ben to where Elizabeth was standing and said, "Elizabeth, this is my brother, Ben. Ben, this is your soon-to-be sister-in-law, Elizabeth Morgan."

"I'm very pleased to meet you, Elizabeth. Father and Thomas both said you were attractive when they came home from your Valentine's party, but you are truly lovely," he remarked as he gave her a hug.

"I'm glad to finally meet you too, Ben. It's amazing, you and Zachary could almost pass for twins! Thank you for making the effort to come to my picnic," Elizabeth said warmly.

"I wouldn't have missed it! Now where is this Andrea Ashton I'm supposed to escort at this affair?"

Elizabeth guided him over to where Andrea and Rebecca were standing. She made the introduction.

Rebecca B. said, "Well, didn't I warn you?"

Andrea's face turned a bright red as she blushed and said, "Remind me never to trust her!"

Ben reached for her hand, "Let's take a stroll around this gorgeous place and see what we can find."

Andrea looked at Rebecca. "So all he got were the brains huh?"

Elizabeth said, "Let's go find Robert Thomas, Rebecca."

She looked everywhere for him. Then she spotted him backing out of one of the carriages.

"There you are Robert. I want you to meet Rebecca Bainbridge. She will be your date for today," Elizabeth declared.

Robert flashed a dazzling smile and, with a twinkle in his eye, bowed from the waist and said in the most pleasing voice she had ever heard, "I'm delighted to meet you, Rebecca Bainbridge. Would you do me the honor of wearing this pink rose? I grew it myself. It matches your dress."

Rebecca's hair was a rich deep auburn. The rose was perfect!

Scott, Libbi, Max and Jo Anna were down where the boat and canoes were tied to the pier. Max was laughing boisterously. He and Scott were good friends and both had great senses of humor. When they got together, laughter abounded.

Steve and Rebecca, Matt and India were sitting on the grass under a sprawling willow tree. Phillip and Jane walked up about the same time as Zachary and Elizabeth.

Steve spoke up and said, "Phillip, we've been told you and Jane are moving to Williamsburg. This is great news. We live about thirty miles south of there in a coastal town called Poquoson. Matt and India live in Williamsburg. So do Scott and Libbi. This will give us an opportunity to all spend some time together."

"Sounds good to us. We really don't know anyone there. Jane will be leaving a teaching position here. We don't know if she will seek another teaching job, but she's looking forward to making new friends," Phillip said.

Elizabeth asked Matt, "What kind of work are you in?"

"My father owns Jones Mercantile as did his father before him. It's located near the heart of the city of Williamsburg. A very good location. I am the buyer for the store. India, tell Elizabeth about your job, or should I say hobby."

"I have a very interesting hobby. It gives me a lot of pleasure and brings happiness to a lot of others. I design and make dolls and their clothes," India announced very proudly.

"And we have the perfect place to market them. She has a featured section up front in the store. We call it 'India's Adorables.' At Christmas time it's the busiest place in the store!" Matt explained.

"Most of my dolls are soft and cuddly. They are made of cloth. I paint their faces, from newborns to little girls. I use yarn for their hair. I pay a lot of attention to details in their clothing. I've loved dolls all of my life, so I've never called it a job. It truly is a hobby," India said.

"India, you look like a doll yourself with those big blue eyes and dimples," Zachary chimed in.

Scott, Libbi, Max and Jo Anna joined in laughing.

"What's so funny?" Elizabeth wanted to know.

"It's that crazy Max," Scott explained. "He's been down at the south end of the lake trying to call up some wild turkeys he thought he saw."

"So that's where all that gobble-gobble noise was coming from," Matt said with a chuckle.

"Yep, that's what you heard alright," Scott said.

"Speakin' of gobble-gobble, when do we eat?" Max asked. "I'm a growin' boy, you know. It takes vittles and lots of 'em for a growin' boy!"

Max was wearing western clothes. He ordered them from a catalog. He loved the boot cut of the pants and the simple lines of the shirts. He especially liked his Wellington boots and Stetson hat.

Scott said in a very serious tone, "Why Max, meal time is not till three this afternoon, didn't you know? It's only 11:45 now. I tried to get you not to stop at six eggs this morning at breakfast! We might find a cow you can milk if you just gotta' have something."

"Aw Scott, cut it out now!" Max replied laughingly.

"It really won't be long until we eat," Elizabeth commented. "In the meantime we've been trying to find out a little about each other. You people are special to my grandparents and therefore I want to get to know you better. So Scott, tell us what you do for a living."

"I'm a newspaper man. My father and I own the Williamsburg Gazette. It's been in the family for years. I really like my work. If you ever get ink in your blood it's there to stay. I kinda like what Oliver Wendell Holmes once said, 'A page of history is worth a volume of logic.' I sort of think of our newspaper as a page of history."

"Goodness, Scott, you sound so professional!" Elizabeth exclaimed.

"Not at all. Now, Libbi is the professional in the family. Tell them about your interior decorating talents.

"Oh yes, I am very interested in that. I've redesigned and redecorated our home inside, then tackled two rooms in my parent's house. Two of mother's friends had me help them, and a local dress boutique had me redesign their shop. I've been busy and I love it," Libbi said.

By this time the rest of the picnickers had all gathered around.

Elizabeth told them she was a volunteer at East Richmond Hospital where Dr. David Blake was resident surgeon and Kim Thomas was head nurse.

They all knew Max because he had worked at Morgan Shipping and lived in Williamsburg before coming to Richmond.

She introduced Jo Anna and Robert Thomas, explaining they were Kim's sister and brother.

Elizabeth asked Robert what he did for a living.

"I'm a farmer, lover of the land if you please. If it's a seed, I can grow it! I see the sun come up and watch it set at night. I walk in the rain when the good Lord sends it for my crops, lookin' up and thanking Him who is the giver of every good and perfect gift. Then I pace the floor when the rain is slow in coming and remind the Lord just how needy we are. It's a good life! And one of these days I'm gonna' find me just the right woman to share it with." He cast his eyes in Rebecca B.'s direction.

Rebecca's face turned crimson but she still managed a broad smile.

"Jo Anna, what are some of your hobbies?"

"Singing . . . I love to sing. Mother says I was born singing, at least my cooing sounded like singing to her!"

Jo Anna was a lot like Jane Adams Maxwell. She was funny and fun-loving. Her hair was light blonde, thick and curly. She had gorgeous brown eyes.

Libbi had a personality that was bubbly and friendly. Her ash blonde hair was shoulder length. Her eyes were as green as the dress she was wearing.

Elizabeth looked around at all these wonderful new friends. She believed the future for her and Zachary would be a good one surrounded by friends like these.

"And what line of work are you in?" Elizabeth asked Ben.

Ben spoke up and said, "I'm just a beach bum. I work in a ship-yard in Norfolk. I'm a planker. I do the finish work on the planks that form the hull of ships. It has to be done just perfectly. When I'm not doing that, I'm sailing, sailing, and sailing. And I doubt I'll find a girl who would want to settle down with a beach bum like me!" as he looked flirtingly at Andrea.

"Don't be too sure" Andrea said. "There are probably some female beach bums out there who would like nothing better than to sail around the Atlantic all day," she came back wittingly.

They heard the ringing of the lunch bell along with a shout of "It's about time!" from Max.

—◦◦◦◦—

Chapter 52

The long table was laden with all kinds of delicacies from stuffed chicken, roast beef, and Virginia ham to colorful vegetable dishes, yeast rolls, cornbread, cakes and pies. There was also an abundance of sweet tea and lemonade.

Elizabeth had asked her Grandfather Morgan to get everyone's attention and welcome them to Willow Place.

"Ladies and gentlemen, this is a grand day here at Willow Place. You graciously accepted our invitation to this picnic and put forth an effort to come. We thank you. Catherine and I have walked among you today, listened and observed. You are an outstanding group of young people.

"I will ask my good friend, Steve Wilson, a young Wesleyan minister, to say grace for us."

"Please bow your heads," Steve said.

"Heavenly Father, we look around us and see the evidence of your creation, both in the landscape and in the people here today, and we are awed by it. Our hearts overflow with thanksgiving to you. Bless the lives of those who are here, our families, and friends. We thank you for the bounty spread before us. We thank you for those who prepared it. Bless all who partake. Amen."

It didn't take long for everyone to fill their plates and find seating around the tables.

Elizabeth, Zachary, Jane and Phillip were sharing a table. All of a sudden they heard a carriage approaching. Quickly, out of it stepped the strollers from the Candlewick Café. They began playing as they walked toward the gathering. The guests were spellbound by the music of the instruments. The trumpets' sounds seemed to echo harmoniously off the lake.

Even though everyone was hungry, they could hardly concentrate on their food for watching and listening to the strollers. They went from table to table charming their audience. Max was excited with admiration for their talent!

They came to Elizabeth's table and began to play "To Each His Own." Zachary reached for Elizabeth's hand as they played.

When they finished Phillip asked them to play "Today, Tomorrow and Forever." The strollers obliged without even a break in the music.

They left as subtly as they came. The music truly added a touch of perfection to a wonderful day.

When everyone had finished eating, they paired off and strolled around Willow Place. The boat and canoes made a big hit as couples paddled around the lake. There was a joyous atmosphere in this enchanted setting.

John and Catherine sat on a bench with a full view of the beauty surrounding them. The summer flowers were abloom with a variety of colors. The trees had never looked greener, nor more majestic. The summer breeze moved their branches rhythmically.

Catherine said, "John, just think, this is soon to be our home."

"Yes, thanks to our adorable granddaughter," John reflected. "God's blessings have truly been poured out on us."

They watched the young people all around them. They were in their early to mid-twenties, such versatile personalities and talents.

In the late afternoon they all gathered around the lakeside and began playing some childhood games like drop-the-handkerchief. When they started playing, Zachary announced Elizabeth was a professional at dropping *her* handkerchief! They played two-man tag and then had a three-legged race.

Emma and Virginia had collected all the food and put it away right after lunch. Around 5:30 they rang the dinner bell. They had made roast beef and ham sandwiches, sliced cake and lemonade. After all the activity everybody was ready to eat again, and Elizabeth's grandfather said grace.

"Heavenly Father, this has been a good day here at Willow Place. Old friends have come together. New friendships have been formed. Proverbs tells us 'a friend loveth at all times.' And another ancient proverb says, 'Hold a true friend with both your hands.' We pray there have been these kinds of friendships born here this day. We thank you for this food that has been set before us. Amen."

Then John said loudly enough for all to hear, "I suggest you put Max at the end of the line if the rest of you want some food!"

There were loud hoots and cat calls from all of the fellas as they pushed Max to the back of the line.

Max laughed good-naturedly and said boisterously, "That's okay. I know the cooks!"

After a good meal everyone sat around in a semicircle and shared stories.

Robert, who had a deep resonant voice began telling a ghost story.

"When I was a kid about seven years old, we lived near a grave-yard. There were two ways to get to the country store from our house. One road passed on the back side of the graveyard, but the shortest way led you in front of it and through a small pine thicket. When it was bright and sunny mother would send us for a spool of thread or something she had to have from the store.

"On this particular day my five-year old brother, Layton, went with me to get some soap. It was late and by the time we started home Layton was whining because he was tired. I decided we would take the short cut home through the pine thicket. I heard a sound like someone was behind us getting closer and closer. I took Layton by the hand and said, 'Let's run!'

"We got to the edge of the graveyard so we could see all the grave stones in the dusky dark. They all looked like someone was hiding behind them. About that time something white ran by us so fast it almost knocked us down. By this time Layton was crying. Then something dark blew by us into the graveyard! An owl began to hoot as a rotten tree limb fell in the thicket."

Suddenly, Scott Dixon jumped up in the group and shouted, "Gotcha!"

All the girls including Grandmother Catherine shrieked. The fellas all fell over laughing and rolling in the grass.

Everyone sang out, "What happened? What was it?"

Robert continued, "Well, the next day father found a large, shaggy white dog lying dead in the graveyard. A neighbor had shot at a red fox on his place near his hen house. We figured that had to have been the two 'ghosts' we thought were chasing us."

Max had brought his guitar to the picnic. He walked over to a tree where he had it propped in its case. He took it out and motioned for Jo Anna to join him. They began singing several songs with a western flavor. They sang some funny, catchy tunes they had written together. Then they sang some sing-a-longs so everyone could join in. William had made a campfire which was now crackling, and by this time the moon was shining full.

As things grew quiet Steve and Rebecca began singing "Amazing Grace" with unparalleled harmony. They sounded like angels. After the first verse they signaled for everyone to join them. It was the perfect ending to a perfect day.

The train would be leaving the depot going back to Williamsburg at 10:30 A.M. Sunday. Everyone agreed to meet for breakfast at the Richmond Hotel at 8:30 so they could have more time together before departing.

The carriages were lined up to take those staying in Richmond back into town. But before departing the couples paired off and took one final stroll around the lake.

Phillip and Jane sat at one of the tables. The moonlight was streaming across the water on the lake like choreographed ribbons of light. Phillip took one of the daisies from the small bouquets that served as the centerpiece for the table. He began pulling off the petals, "She loves me, she loves me not, she loves me, she loves me not, she loves me!" he said triumphantly as he pulled off the last petal.

David and Kim had walked hand in hand nearer the lake. Kim leaned up against a willow tree. Her long, light brown hair curled over her shoulders and formed a halo around her pretty face. David had never seen her look lovelier. She looked soft and vulnerable. He was used to seeing her at the hospital with her hair tucked underneath a nursing cap, decked out in a starched white uniform with an authoritative air about her.

They had dated several times and she had worn her hair down then. But tonight she just looked especially angelic. He wanted to take her in his arms and hold her and tenderly kiss her sweet lips, which he had not done before. But she moved away and said, "We must be going back to the carriage."

Kim felt tingly all over. Her heart was pounding. This Dr. David Blake made her feel so vulnerable! She didn't want things to move too quickly. She liked him very much but she certainly did not want to be just a passing fancy to him. He was so appealingly charming she wondered if he could be trusted with her heart.

Ben, Andrea, Max and Jo Anna had walked down to the pier where the boats were tied up. The katydids and tree frogs were competing with each other. Max said, "Wonder what tune they are playing?"

"Oh Max, you can hear music in anything!" Jo Anna exclaimed.

"Yep, it's just in my soul."

Ben spoke up and said, "Girls, we fellas could get used to this. It's a pity we live so far away from each other. We need to get together again soon."

"I'm lucky. I've got my girl right here in Richmond," Max said and reached for Jo Anna's hand.

"That's right, both of you do live here. Norfolk and Williamsburg is another story, right Andrea?"

"If you say so Ben," Andrea muttered with a tinge of regret in her voice.

Robert and Rebecca B. were sitting on the porch steps of the stately old home.

"You really do love farming, don't you Robert?" Rebecca said.

"For sure. We have sixty acres of land. We plant half of it in cotton and the other half in corn. Our soil is rich and we take good care of it. My father has raised a big family working the farm. We are a close-knit and loving family. I believe farm life helps to foster good family values," Robert responded.

"I need to work on a children's book with illustrations depicting farm life. Sounds like a good project," Rebecca mused.

"Rebecca, I like you. You are genuine and down to earth. Since your brother, Zachary, is engaged to Elizabeth perhaps you will be visiting here a lot. I hope we can see each often."

"Thanks for your vote of confidence," Rebecca said teasingly. "I like you, too. I do plan on coming back as often as possible."

Matt, India, Scott and Libbi had walked to the north end of the lake near the spot where the Morgan house was going up. They were on their way back toward the carriages.

"This is a picture perfect place alright," Scott said. "I can see why Elizabeth would love it here. But I like city living. I like the hustle and bustle of Williamsburg. Living close to my work

is necessary. I have to be where news is happening to run a newspaper."

"I like city living, too. I guess it's because we've always lived in the city. Marketing is in my blood like newspaper ink is in yours Scott," Matt remarked.

"I will have to say Willow Place can be described as traditional, old southern living and a very romantic place and I love it here. But I also love my opportunity to sell my dolls at the mercantile. And I *love* Williamsburg. I suppose we could say "To Each His Own," India said thoughtfully.

"Elizabeth is very attached to Willow Place and I can certainly see why. It is one of the prettiest places I have ever seen," Libbi added.

They arrived back where the carriages were waiting. Goodbyes were said and with contentment and good memories the guests of Willow Place started toward Richmond in their carriages.

Chapter 53

August 24

The summer had been a rather lazy one. Elizabeth was still volunteering at the hospital. Things were progressing nicely for Kim and Dr. Blake. She suspected they would probably become engaged before summer ended.

Her grandparents' new home would be ready by the first week in September. What a comfortable feeling for her to look out her bedroom window each morning and see that big, red brick house sitting on top of the hill across the lake. It was beautiful. The wrap-around porch trimmed in white made it highly visible.

Sometimes she felt like all of this was a dream. She often thought about where her life had come since the day her Grandmother Savannah had died. She realized more and more each day how God provided for His own.

Elizabeth went down to the kitchen in her robe. She had slept late. It was raining steadily. It had been hot and dry during the month of August. She was looking forward to staying inside and catching up on some reading.

Emma was sitting in her chair in the kitchen stringing and breaking green beans.

"Good morning, Emma. I'm sure everyone has had breakfast already," Elizabeth said.

"Yes, lassie. Yours is in the warmer. It's been a good morning for sleeping late."

"I kept meaning to get up but the sound of rain against my window kept lulling me back to sleep."

"Lassie, I have something to tell you. Mike and I are engaged and are going to be married on Saturday, September 14th."

"Why Emma, that is wonderful! Where will the wedding be held?"

"We have asked Pastor Davis to marry us in the small chapel at the church. We plan to keep it simple, just family. At our age we feel this would be proper. We have asked Sadie and William to stand up with us. It would please us if you and Mr. Zachary would be there, as well as the Morgan's. Mike is going to ask them to come."

"It is an honor to be included in your special day. Zachary will feel the same way. Grandmother and grandfather wouldn't miss your wedding, I'm sure. Oh, dear sweet Emma, I am so happy for you.

"I remember last fall when I asked you why someone as lovely as you had never married and you told me briefly about Mike Kelly. I saw that special look of love in your eyes then that I see now. I believe God must have meant this to happen," Elizabeth said as she gave Emma a heartfelt hug.

"I have something else to ask you, Elizabeth. I will soon be fifty-six years old. Mike and I are going to want to spend as much time together as possible. I have put some savings back for retirement. So what would you think of my training someone else for my job here?"

"Emma, I have never even thought about a time when I might not have you here at Willow Place. It saddens me to think of it. But I respect your feelings. Do you have someone in mind or should I begin to look for someone?" Elizabeth inquired.

"Well, I do have a person in mind. My Sunday school teacher, Sybil Dyer, mentioned to me a couple of weeks ago that if I ever decided to retire she knew of a young lady in her early thirties who was very good at domestic house work. She must have an idea that Mike and I might be getting married,' Emma said with a grin.

"Did she tell you anything about this person?"

"When she told me her name was Sara Bradley, I knew exactly who she was talking about. The Bradley's are very fine people. They are clean as a pen. Sam Bradley works at the carriage factory. Sara is an excellent cook already. She's shy and a little bit chubby, minds her own business she does. She would respect this household, I believe."

"Then I will be happy to speak with her about this position. But Emma, what *will* I do without you? By the way, where do you and Mike plan to live?"

"Well lassie, Mike has found us a small house to rent. It is on this side of Richmond. He won't be far away from his work for Mr. Morgan."

"It sounds like you two have done some good planning, Emma."

On Tuesday, September 3rd, Elizabeth met with Sara Bradley. She was very impressed with her. She explained what her duties would be. She would work with Emma the rest of the week so she would be able to assume the duties after Emma and Mike were married.

Elizabeth would miss Emma but she liked Sara immediately.

SEPTEMBER 14

Emma and Mike had decided on a morning wedding. Elizabeth, Zachary, John and Catherine arrived together. William and Sadie were already in the chapel. Pastor Davis' wife, Madeline, had added her personal touch to the chapel by placing a tall basket of fresh cut flowers on the altar. She had three white candles on a table near where the couple would be taking their vows.

The chapel door opened and Emma and Mike came in. What a handsome couple Elizabeth thought.

Mike had on a black waistcoat and fitted black pants with a tiny gray pin stripe. He had a white shirt with a pleated front and a black bow tie. He was smiling as someone who had received the grand prize at the county fair!

Emma was wearing an ivory-colored lace dress with a round neck bordered by a narrow standup lace ruffle. It had long fitted sleeves and a simple a-line skirt with satin lining. She was wearing a cameo pin at the center of the neck of the dress. Elizabeth remembered admiring that beautiful pin which had belonged to Emma's mother.

Both of them looked younger than their years.

The couple had chosen the traditional wedding ceremony. They repeated their vows, "for richer, for poorer, in sickness and in health, till death do us part."

When they were pronounced man and wife, Pastor Davis lit the three candles, prayed a prayer and ended with, "In the name of the Father, the Son and the Holy Ghost, amen."

Congratulations were bestowed upon the couple by all those who attended. Emma and Mike left in an unmarked carriage to begin their life together.

Chapter 54

⌒◡

The Morgan's had moved into their Willow Place home on September 6th. The movers had everything in place. They spent their first night there with excitement yet feeling completely at home. Zachary had a room with them at their insistence.

In her grandparents' bedroom Elizabeth saw that they had chosen the Queen Anne style of William and Mary furniture. She liked it because it emphasized the quality of the mahogany wood grain. The simple lines added to its elegance Elizabeth thought. This was the only new furniture they had bought. They had done a real good job with the color schemes and placing their furniture in their new home.

Elizabeth was happy for her grandparents. The look of contentment on their faces told the whole story.

—◄▰▰▰►—

Zachary received a letter from his brother, Ben, from Norfolk dated September 10th. It read:

Dear Zack,

I've had you on my mind lately, brother. The picnic at Willow Place was a real treat. I like who you've picked out to be my next sister. There's Rebecca of course, Tom's wife Joyce, a neat sis, and then there's Elizabeth. She's a real looker.

This Andrea Ashton that I met there has become the object of my affection! I've sailed up to Williamsburg to see her several times since June. We have great fun together. I just might have finally met the one to tie the knot with.

I'd sure like to see you. Would it be possible for you to come to Norfolk for a few days? We could do some sailing. I have access to a new cruiser. It's a great boat. Let me know when you can visit.

Affectionately,
Your Brother Ben

John had been back to the shipping company in Williamsburg twice to help Paul Chambers solve some problems. Paul had been in touch just last week with some government requirements they didn't fully understand. John had spoken with Zachary about making a trip to help them out. This trip would be a perfect time for him to untie his sailboat he had stored at the Morgan's beach house and head to Norfolk for a few days.

Arrangements were made by telegraph to go to the shipping company on September 19th and then head for Norfolk the next day. Zack was excited.

Elizabeth went to the train depot to see Zachary off. This had become a special spot to them since it was the place they first met. He teasingly called it "hallowed ground."

They sat on "their bench" and talked as they waited for the train.

"Zachary, I'm glad you are going to see Ben. It's good to know you are a close family, but I worry about you sailing from Williamsburg to Norfolk alone. Sometimes in September the winds are rough. Will you take the time to telegraph me each day after you finish your sailing? You will surely be through by dark. I'll check with Mr. Farris at the telegraph office each day," Elizabeth said.

"My dear, nothing is going to happen to me. I've got too much to come back to!" Zachary reassured her. "But I will telegraph you every day if that's what you want."

"I don't mean to be difficult but the dearest person to my heart will be sailing in those waters."

"Elizabeth, remember the dress you wore the day of the picnic, the violet one?" Zachary asked. "You've worn it only twice since that day."

"Yes, I know the one," Elizabeth answered.

"Will you wear it the day I come back from Ben's? I remember it is the exact color of those unbelievably beautiful eyes of yours."

"Yes, I'll be sure to wear it," Elizabeth replied smiling to herself.

They heard the all-too-familiar whistle of the train as it approached the depot.

She walked with him to the loading platform. He leaned down to her upturned face and kissed her expectant lips. This lovely creature held him captive. He was so thankful the Lord allowed him to find such a wonderful person to be his wife.

He looked more closely into her face and saw tears in her eyes.

"Please, please don't cry, Elizabeth. I will be back on Tuesday the twenty-fourth. You will be at the hospital tomorrow, church on Sunday and back to work on Monday, so you will be busy. Please don't cry," Zachary said imploringly.

But Elizabeth was sobbing by this time. She thought, *what is wrong with me? Why do I feel such apprehension?*

She finally got control of herself. She wiped her eyes with her handkerchief.

"I'm so sorry, Zachary. I don't know what came over me. I'll be fine. But I feel compelled to tell you that I want us to set our wedding date as soon as you return," Elizabeth said with such an urgency in her voice.

"If it took this trip to cause you to make that declaration, it is worth it," Zachary said, and kissed her one more time.

The conductor was bellowing "All aboard!" He had to run!

"Don't drop your handkerchief!" he yelled as he disappeared through the train door.

Chapter 55

SEPTEMBER 19

Zachary met with Paul Chambers early Thursday morning. By lunchtime they were through with business. He left there and went directly to the Morgan's beach house. He got his sailboat out of storage and readied it for the water. There was a nice stiff breeze blowing out of the southeast. With that kind of tailwind, he knew he could get to Norfolk before dark. He was anxious to get going and didn't realize he had missed sailing so much.

He made it to Norfolk with time to spare. He tied up at the familiar pier. After all, this was his home most of his life until he moved to Williamsburg. He hired a carriage and went straight to the telegraph office and sent Elizabeth a message that he had arrived safely.

Zachary then headed straight to his parents' house and surprised them a day early.

When Rebecca saw him she gave him a big hug and immediately asked, "Why didn't you bring Robert with you?"

"Little sister, why would you want Robert Thomas when your big brother is here?!"

"It *is* good to have you home again. How is Elizabeth? I'm surprised and disappointed that she didn't come with you," Rebecca said.

"Well, this is the tail end of the business trip, and Ben and I plan to spend most of our time sailing," Zachary replied.

Steven and Barbara Bainbridge were overjoyed to have their son home for a few days. Steven was a designer at the shipyard where Ben worked. Their family had salt water in their veins. Sailing was second nature to them. Steven was highly acclaimed for his designs of sailboats and steamers. His admirers said he had a natural talent.

Barbara was an artist in her own right. She was a talented pianist. Music was as much a part of their household as sailing.

When Thomas and Joyce saw that Zachary had come a day early, they came over and brought Joey and Heather. They lived next door to their parents.

Everyone was laughing and talking all at once, a typical family get-together.

Zachary looked at little four-year old Joey and said, "Come here, Joey, and let me see what you have there. Here, sit on my knee. What's this?"

"It's a sailboat, Uncle Zack. Grandfather made it for me. Can I go sailing with you and Uncle Ben?" Joey asked wide-eyed.

"Tell you what, Sunday afternoon Uncle Ben and I will take you for a ride in the boat," Zachary answered.

"May I come too?" six-year old Heather asked politely.

"We wouldn't think of going without you, little angel," Zachary said, picking her up high above his head and giving her a big hug.

They enjoyed a good meal together, then gathered around the piano and sang some favorites.

Zachary's mother, Barbara, looked at everyone in the circle and said "What a good feeling to have all our children together again. This is like Christmas in September."

"Yes, we are blessed to have all our family close by except for you, Zachary," his father Steven said. "It looks as if we've lost you to Richmond and that beautiful Elizabeth."

Zachary held out his cupped hand and said, "Yes, she holds my heart in the palm of her hand."

Rebecca spoke up very honestly and said, "Richmond would also have me if Robert Thomas felt the same way about me that Zack feels about Elizabeth."

"You've only seen him that one time at the picnic, Rebecca!" Zachary exclaimed.

"Oh no, Ben and I have sailed up to Jamestown three times since then and met with Robert and Andrea at the Ashton's. And we have also been exchanging letters. You can learn a lot about people by letter writing, especially when distance prevents you from seeing one another on a regular basis," Rebecca explained.

"Ben, what about Andrea?" In your letter you sounded kind of serious about her," Zachary inserted.

"I've talked with mother and father about her. She's different than any girl I've ever met. She's a real challenge with a spirited personality. I really do like her. And I will soon be twenty-four years old. She is the first for which I've cared enough for to ask her to marry me. But I don't want to rush her," Ben admitted.

"Son, how's the carriage business going? Do you like it? Do you find it challenging?" his father inquired.

"I miss the water and sailing more than I care to admit, but I do not miss the rigors of the shipping world. I really am intrigued by the carriage business. John, Max Hammond and I have put our heads together. We have a dandy of a carriage on the design board. We believe it will be very marketable when we fully develop it," Zachary said.

"John Morgan has been very good to you, Zack. He sees in you what your mother and I know you possess. I know he hasn't misplaced his trust in you," his father commented.

"John and I have a very good relationship. I respect him, father. He is a man of principle and a fine Christian example to those around him. I owe him a great deal," Zachary replied.

"Changing the subject if I may," Rebecca interjected, "do you think Elizabeth might consider inviting me, Andrea and Ben back to Willow Place again, Zack?"

"Are you saying, little sister, that you want me to ask her to invite you three back?" Zachary said teasingly.

"Since you put it that way, yes that's exactly what I want you to do," Rebecca replied emphatically.

"Well, I think I can arrange a visit," and he gave her a big hug.

They talked and laughed and sang around the piano. It was a wonderful family gathering.

Chapter 56

Zachary and Ben were at the dock early. It was a splendid day for sailing. The brand new Cruiser sailboat belonged to a close friend of Ben's who insisted that Ben and Zachary take it out for the day.

They spent some time going over it, admiring its rigging and equipment. Ben was familiar with the boat. He had been out on it several times with his friend. It was well equipped. They checked everything out to make sure all was in order. It had a new brass barometer, compass and all the latest equipment. They had drinking water, a couple of blankets, and they had packed their lunch in a tin pail.

When they set sail the wind was at twelve knots, then increased to twenty knots. They glided along effortlessly feeling the wind against their faces. They felt like kid brothers again! They headed up the Chesapeake Bay.

Zachary said, "Ben, you'll probably never leave this area, will you?"

"Not on your life, Zachary my boy!"

In the early afternoon a northwest wind blew in at thirty-five knots and was dead against them. The gale had come up from out of nowhere. The waves were eight to ten feet high. They were surfing on the crests of the waves. When they would sink into the troughs of water, the wind would ease off. Then when they would rise they would take a beating. The wind increased from thirty-five to forty-nine knots and they knew they were in trouble. With the wind had come a pelting rain.

Gale force winds had come up suddenly in Norfolk with a driving rain. Steven looked out the window of his office, which overlooked the ocean. His two boys were out there somewhere in all this mess. The sky was dark and ominous looking. It was 3:30. They said they would be in no later than 5:00. They were both good sailors, but even so he felt a little uneasy.

By 6:30 they still had not gotten in. The wind and rainstorm was still raging.

Thomas and Joyce and the children had come over to their parents' home. Each of them was walking from window to door checking on the weather every few minutes.

They tried to reassure each other that Zachary and Ben were seasoned sailors. They could handle themselves. Besides, maybe the storm was more inland and they might be out beyond its fury just waiting it out.

By 11:00 P.M. there was still no sign of them. Their mother, Barbara, would weep silently and then pray audibly for the Lord to be merciful to her sons and take care of them and bring them home safely. She reminded the Lord that his word said He was a strength to the needy in distress and a refuge from the storm. She prayed, "My boys, whom you know so well and who know you, are both in distress and are engulfed in a storm. We have to believe you are there with them supplying them with strength. And we thank you for the comfort we can draw from this. Amen."

Everyone in the room said "Amen."

Morning came and the wind and rain were still battering the coast. Steven said it was time they notified the Coast Guard. They had a station at Norfolk. He went there and filed a report. They said they would send a steamer out to look for them.

Steven also telegraphed John Morgan.

―◄═══►―

Elizabeth received Zachary's telegraph on Thursday night and he said:

"Sailed from Jamestown to Norfolk on Thursday the 19th. No problems. Will telegraph you on Friday as promised. You can count on it. Love, Zachary."

There, he had made it fine. But why did she feel so uncertain about this trip?

Elizabeth stayed at the hospital later than usual this Friday. Then she went by the telegraph office to see if she had received word from Zachary. It was 4:00 P.M. and there was no message. She went home in the buggy, ate supper, then saddled up Blazer and rode back to see if perhaps her telegraph had come. She waited around until 6:00 but still no message.

She rode hard and fast, back to Willow Place and up to her grandfather's house. She rang the doorbell several times. Simpson opened the door and she brushed past him and went through the house calling, "Grandfather, where are you?"

"My goodness child, what is wrong?" her grandfather asked striding toward her.

She threw herself into his arms and said, "It's Zachary. There is something wrong. I know it. I just know it! When he left on Thursday I knew something was going to happen!" Elizabeth sobbed.

"What on earth are you talking about, Elizabeth? What makes you think something is wrong with Zachary?"

"Because I didn't get a telegram. He promised. See, he promised!" Elizabeth said waving his telegram in the air.

"Elizabeth, calm down and tell me what you're talking about," her grandfather insisted.

"Oh grandfather, I'm so scared. You see, when Zachary left to go to Williamsburg he said he would telegraph me *every day* he is gone to let me know he had finished his day of sailing safely. This is the telegram I got yesterday. He ends it by saying, 'Will telegraph you on Friday as promised. You can count on it.' I just left the telegraph office and there was no telegram. Grandfather, he would not still be sailing this late. There has to be something wrong."

"Elizabeth, anything could have happened to prevent him from sending a telegram. He could have gotten in later than he planned. Sometimes the wind doesn't cooperate with a sailor.

"You just don't realize what good sailors Zachary and Ben are. I have sailed with both of these young men. They are not reckless. They are serious when sailing. Now dry your tears. In the morning I will send a telegram to Steven Bainbridge and ask him to wire me back right away," her grandfather reassured her.

"I still don't feel good about it. Zachary does what he says he will do. I asked him to *promise* me he would send me a telegram every day he was gone. All I know is he *promised!*" Elizabeth replied in despair.

"Elizabeth, stay with us tonight. I'd feel better if you would."

"Oh grandfather, could I? Could I please stay in Zachary's room? Do you think he would mind? I need to feel close to him. I knew I loved him, but I don't think I could live if something happened to him," Elizabeth said.

Her grandmother had been listening quietly in the next room. She chose to let Elizabeth have this time alone with her grandfather.

She walked into the sitting room and said, "You most assuredly can stay in Zachary's room. His bed has been freshly made. I have a pair of his pajamas if you would like them. I'm sure he won't mind. Now let's have a cup of hot chocolate in the kitchen."

"Grandmother and grandfather, I am so glad you are here at Willow Place. Since Emma is gone I feel so alone in my big, old house sometimes. I needed you tonight.

"Tell me, do you really think Zachary is alright?" Elizabeth asked.

"I can't imagine that he wouldn't be. Perhaps when I get to the telegraph office in the morning there will be a message there for you," her grandfather said.

Elizabeth went into Zachary's room and closed the door. This house was so well made. It had all of the latest conveniences. There was a nice closet for clothes. Zachary had his things arranged so neatly. Grandmother Catherine had laid out a pair of Zachary's blue pajamas. She had to roll up the pants legs and the sleeves, but they would do nicely. She turned back the covers and slipped between the smooth sheets. She laid her head on his pillow, then she began to cry great heaving sobs of disappointment because she had not heard from him. She felt almost foolish, but she could not escape this foreboding feeling that something was wrong.

She cried out to the Lord, "You know me, Lord. You know my unrest. You know my frailty, my weakness at this hour. I need your help. I need strength that only comes from you. Help me *now*, Lord. Amen."

She laid there for perhaps another hour before blessed sleep came over her.

She was up early Saturday morning, bathed and dressed. She went to the kitchen. Her grandfather was ready to go into Richmond. He said he would get a telegram off to Steven immediately and would return as soon as he heard anything.

Elizabeth went to the Morgan stable, saddled Blazer and rode him around the lake to her house. William was in the kitchen along with Sadie and Sara. She smelled the delicious aroma of breakfast food.

Even though she was still troubled, she decided she needed to eat with her little family. She felt better after she had some hot coffee and a fresh berry muffin. She complimented Sara on the good job she was doing. She asked William if he would take care of Blazer for her.

Sadie said, "Miss Elizabeth, I have washed and ironed the blue dress you wore to the picnic. It is hanging in your closet."

"Thank you, Sadie. You do an excellent job on my dresses."

Elizabeth decided to go out and sit on the front porch. She thought about the dress Zachary had asked her to wear when he returned on Tuesday. She remembered the anguish she felt at the train depot. Why could she not shake the feeling that something bad would happen on this sailing trip? Maybe it was because she did not know anything at all about sailing.

Waiting was so hard for Elizabeth. She did not like having to wait. She heard the clock strike ten. Then she saw her grandfather's carriage coming. Mike stepped out of the carriage. She knew immediately something was wrong. Her grandfather came up the steps and handed her the telegram. She read: "Zachary and Ben are lost at sea. Coast Guard is searching for them. Storm came up suddenly Friday afternoon. Will keep you posted. Steven Bainbridge."

Elizabeth's shoulders slumped as she leaned forward in the chair, burying her face in her hands. "No, no, no," she sobbed. She began to tremble. She raised her tear-stained face, looking at her grandfather and said, "What are their chances? I don't know anything about sailing. Do they have a chance to survive?"

"Yes, Elizabeth, they certainly do. Man has been battling the elements of the ocean for centuries. The weather determines what happens in a sailboat. Too much wind can toss it about, but good sailors know how to compensate for such problems. I believe Zachary told me Ben had access to a Cruiser sailboat. If they are in that type of sailboat, then they will have some protection from the elements."

"Oh grandfather, you make it sound so simple, like everything will be alright."

"I am not scolding you, Elizabeth, but you must have faith and hope. Remember in Hebrews it says, 'Now faith is the substance of things hoped for, the evidence of things not seen.' All we have in a situation like this is hope. We can't do one thing to help or change things." He knelt down beside Elizabeth's chair, looked her in the eyes and proceeded, "But we personally know the *One* who can! Let's pray in faith believing that God is with Zachary and Ben now, at this very moment.

"Lord, give us strength and courage, hope and faith to believe that you are guiding the boat that Zachary and Ben are in out in your big ocean. Amen."

"Grandfather, thank you for your words of wisdom and prayer. I'm sure I will be fine now. I think I am going to ride Blazer for a while. It seems strange that we are having beautiful, sunshiny weather here in Richmond and the weather is so bad and stormy on the coast. But it is a good day for riding," Elizabeth said.

"I think it will do you good, Elizabeth. I will go and tell your grandmother about the telegram."

"Do you think I should go with you?"

"No, you go ride. Your grandmother will be fine. She has strong faith at times like these. I will go back into town at five to see if there is any more news. You be careful riding."

"I will, grandfather."

Chapter 57

Come on, Blazer boy, let's ride like the wind! Elizabeth said as they headed south into wide open spaces. Blazer seemed to sense her mood. She let him have full rein. After a few miles they headed back to Willow Place. She went to her favorite place under the big willow tree on the back side of the lake. This was the place she read her first letter from Zachary, where he said she was like an elusive butterfly.

She stretched out on the ground on her back with her hands clasped under her head. She closed her eyes and visualized Zachary's familiar face. In her mind she traced the outline of his strong jaw line, his laughing blue eyes that were so warm and tender when he told her that he loved her, his perfectly shaped lips, his beautiful white teeth, and his thick, sun-bleached blonde hair. She knew every feature by heart. And she loved him so.

She could almost hear him call her his "princess."

Surely memory would not be all she was left with. God must have a plan in mind for their life together. She must believe that He did.

"Heavenly Father, please let us hear from Zachary and Ben this very afternoon. I can only imagine how his family must feel. Comfort them I pray. Lord, give me a feeling of assurance that my Zachary is safe."

She laid there for a while with her eyes still closed. She heard a gentle fluttering overhead. She opened her eyes just in time to see three doves fly out of the willow tree and soar heavenward. She felt her heart leap. Were not doves a sign of peace?

She got up quickly, mounted Blazer and rode him to the stable. She brushed him good, fed him and then went inside. It was 3:00 P.M. and she realized she had not eaten. In the kitchen she found a plate of food Sara had fixed and left for her. She had no appetite, but ate what was prepared to gain her strength.

———◅▥◯▥▻———

Ben and Zachary had been battling the rough seas for hours. It seemed more like weeks! Their bodies ached with fatigue and their minds were worn thin with anxiety. The overwhelming noise of the storm did not allow them to communicate very well with each other. Each was left to battle internally with his own thoughts and dreads.

Zachary recalled the first part of the day. It had started out so gloriously. Their twenty-one foot cruiser cut through the water effortlessly. They watched waves of white water peeling away from the hull. The reflection of the sun on the water formed the colors of the rainbow.

They had watched the seagulls and albatross fly over, gliding with their long, slender wings. The two of them were enjoying a world they loved, sailing on God's big ocean! They didn't even feel the sting of the wind and water against their faces. They felt no hunger pangs. They were in their element.

Zachary realized that Ben was the more experienced sailor. In the summer months he lived on the water when he wasn't working. Ben knew the Chesapeake Bay area well.

It was when they came upon Hoopersville Island that Ben said they should start heading for home. That's also when the gale winds started blowing. Within minutes they were in the middle of this full-blown storm.

The barometer had dropped considerably. The wind had shifted from the northwest to southeast, and the waves were heeling them over on their starboard side. There was no way for them to tack against the waves and wind.

Ben yelled to Zachary, hoping he could hear him above the storm, "There is a small island I think they call Fishing Creek. We should be very near it. Help me keep an eye out. If we don't get to it before dark, we could be in for a long night!"

"If the wind would quit swirling, and blow steady in that direction," Zachary yelled back. Then he prayed, "Lord, we need your help *now* just as the disciples did when you came walking to them on the water. You are a shelter in the time of storm. We *need* your help. Amen."

"Amen to that, big brother," Ben echoed.

It wasn't long before the wind was to their backs pushing them on a straight course. Looming ahead was Fishing Creek Island. It took some maneuvering to get the cruiser to shore. That's where their experience paid off. Darkness fell as they made landfall.

It seemed to be a deserted island. They had dry matches sealed away in their lunch pail, which had been protected underneath their now-soaked woolen blankets. Of course, they had nothing dry to help them start a fire, but there were candles in the cruiser cabin.

They thankfully ate the food packed in the lunch pail. They were soaked to the bone. The wind and rain didn't help matters any. It was a miserable night.

Morning dawned through cloudy skies, wind and more rain. But by ten o'clock the storm moved out and the sun broke through. They noticed the wind coming out of the northeast at about twenty knots. If it held, they could be back to Norfolk by mid day.

As they set sail their thoughts turned to family and how worried their loved ones must be. Zachary could only imagine Elizabeth's anguish. If he ever got back to Richmond . . .

At three o'clock Saturday afternoon Ben and Zachary tied up to the dock at Norfolk. Zachary went straight to the telegraph office and sent this message to Elizabeth:

"I once was lost, but now I'm found!
God heard all our prayers.
Meet me at the train depot Sunday afternoon.
Love, Your Zachary."

Then the boys took a carriage to their parents' home. They were greeted with shouts and laughter, many tears and a few "praise the Lord's."

They understood Zachary's desire to go back to Richmond on Sunday morning.

John Morgan leapt from the carriage and ran up on the porch at Willow Place where Elizabeth and Catherine were sitting.

"They are safe! They are safe!" he exclaimed as he hugged both of them excitedly.

"Are you sure? Are you sure?" Elizabeth asked.

"Here is Steven's telegram. It says, "Ben and Zack arrived home around 3:00 P.M. Saturday. They are safe now. Prayers have been answered. Zack will tell you all about it. Kindest regards, Steven.' And Elizabeth, here is a telegram for you from Zack," her grandfather said triumphantly.

She opened it quickly and read it out loud.

Elizabeth laughed and cried as did her grandparents. This began as a nightmare, but from the time she saw the doves the Lord had given her a sense of peace. Tomorrow could not come soon enough, and her prayers had been answered!

Chapter 58

Elizabeth dressed carefully in the violet blue "picnic dress" that Zachary wanted her to wear. She felt like wearing her hair in an upsweep. He liked the curly tendrils that framed her face when she wore it up. She used his favorite perfume. She checked herself in the mirror a dozen times. She was as nervous as if this was their very first date.

She arrived at the depot thirty minutes early. She sat inside on "their bench." She thought back to their first meeting in this very room, the handsome, debonair stranger wearing a yellow scarf.

She remembered how she felt when he touched her. A man she did not know, yet his very touch made her knees weak.

She relived the train ride to Williamsburg, the electric feeling in the air when their eyes met. The time they spent together in Williamsburg was fresh in her mind, especially the time in the garden on the James River when he told her how he felt about her, their very first kiss at the train station, the first time he said "I love you."

The sounding of the train whistle jarred her back to reality. She stood to her feet and walked to the station door and out onto the platform.

The train rounded the bend and came into full view. The person she loved most in the world was on that big iron machine headed toward her. It came to a full stop, seemingly relaxing as it released a billowing blast of white steam.

The train door opened and out stepped Zachary, the first one off the train! She stood very still and let him come to her. He lifted her up into his big, strong arms and held her close for a few seconds. Then he put her down gently, kissed her tenderly, held her back at arms length, looked into her violet blue eyes and said, "I love you desperately, my princess. Let's go somewhere private so we can talk."

"The only place I can think of that is fitting is Willow Place. I can ask William and Sadie to sit in the parlor as long as you are there. We will have a comfortable place for a private conversation. We can talk in the library," Elizabeth said.

They walked to the carriage where William was waiting. He had already loaded Zachary's baggage.

When they arrived at Willow Place, Elizabeth saw that Sadie was still cleaning in the downstairs area. She asked that she and William remain in the parlor while Zachary was there.

They went into the kitchen to get a sandwich. It was two o'clock. They decided to go out on the front porch where they could look out across the lake.

"Elizabeth, this weekend I had a harrowing experience. I have sailed on my own since I was about fifteen. But the weather has always been good. The few times we've sailed when the weather turned bad my father was always along and we were close enough to shore to come in quickly," Zachary said. "But this time the storm came up so suddenly."

"Zachary, it must have been difficult and scary. You don't have to tell me about it if you would rather not." Elizabeth said sympathetically.

"No, Elizabeth, just bear with me. I must talk about it, especially to you.

"The day began perfectly. Ben's friend wanted us to use his new cruiser sailboat. It was a magnificent boat! We had at least four hours of ideal weather conditions. We could not have ordered a more perfect day. Then Mother Nature's fickle ways changed everything. The storm became violent almost immediately. We were sailing north up Chesapeake Bay and were getting ready to turn around and head back to Norfolk. But the wind and rain were blinding. The boat was being tossed about like a toy. We were unable to make any headway in that kind of weather. We really had no control over the boat," Zachary recalled.

"I can imagine how helpless you and Ben must have felt. Surely you were both terrified. What on earth did you do?" Elizabeth asked.

"This went on for at least three hours. All we could do was sit tight, pray and wait it out. Finally, Ben said he remembered an island called Fishing Creek that should be nearby. We simply had to make it there! We prayed and asked for God's help. The swirling wind would have to stop. We had to be pushed in a more direct line. In about thirty minutes the wind came from the southeast and literally pushed us right up to Fishing Creek Island," Zachary explained as he leaned forward in his seat.

"Then you were able to get help on the island?"

"No, the island was deserted. After a long struggle against the unyielding wind we did finally get the boat secured.

"Our blankets were soaked but our lunch pail underneath them had been spared. We had packed matches, along with something to eat. By this time it was pitch black dark. We ate our sandwiches, which helped. Everything was soaking wet. We couldn't build a fire. Besides, it was pouring rain and windy. So it was candles in the cruiser cabin rocking with the pitching waves all night."

"Oh Zachary," Elizabeth cried. "No wonder I was so distraught when you left me, and when I did not receive a telegram on Friday night."

"My dear, sweet Elizabeth, I did not understand your crying at the station. I was the one going to do something I loved and you were left behind with such misgivings. I am truly sorry. I knew in the midst of all of this that you would be in such anguish. My heart cried out for you," Zachary said, visibly shaken.

"What happened next?"

"We shivered and shook all night. Ben and I huddled close to each other trying to keep warm. As brothers we have always been close but we really bonded during this difficult time. I found out he is a real tough kid. Well, he's really not a kid at twenty-three, but he's my 'kid brother!

"Elizabeth, I learned many things on this sailing trip. I hope to never take things for granted again.

"I learned how insignificant we are in the grand scheme of things. It's kind of like putting your hand into a bucket of water and then removing it. You can't tell your hand was ever there at all.

"It really puts your life into perspective. I realized my gains in life. I've worked hard and steady and I've applied myself to learning. And some might say I've done well. But, more importantly, I realized what I almost *lost*. My life was hanging by a thread. I could easily have lost it, and that would have meant losing you. I would have never known our love fulfilled. I would have never known what it was like to have a child, to be a father. I learned what a precious gift life is," Zachary said, having shared his innermost thoughts with his precious Elizabeth.

She was so moved that Zachary permitted her to see inside his very heart. She was awed by his revelations. She knew she had not misplaced her deep affection for this prince of a man to whom she was betrothed.

"Zachary, my dearest Zachary, my eyes have seen deep into your soul today. How blessed I am to be loved by you. Regardless of what comes our way I know our love for each other will always endure. What I feel for you is so deep and strong. You fill my heart with a wondrous joy that will always be with me. I know *this*, my Zachary, you are always where I want to be!" Elizabeth said almost in a whisper.

"Tell me, Elizabeth, did you ever doubt that I would come back to you?"

"My emotions were on a roller coaster. When I did not receive a telegram on Friday night after you promised me faithfully you would send one, I feared the worst. I went to my grandparents' home for reassurance. I spent the night with them and even slept in your bed, and wore a pair of your pajamas! And I was in anguish."

Zachary interrupted her by saying, "You slept in *my* bed and wore *my* pajamas? Oh my, where ever will I sleep now!"

"Oh Zachary! Anyway, the next morning we got the telegram from your father saying you and Ben were lost at sea. I felt as if the same black sea had crashed in around me.

"Grandfather reminded me that I needed to exercise faith and hope in a situation like this. He prayed for God to guide your boat at that very moment. He gave me encouragement when I really needed it. And you know what? A strange thing happened. After we talked I took Blazer out for a ride. I came back to my private spot on the lake. I laid down on my back underneath my favorite willow tree, closed my eyes and visualized your face. I saw every precious detail of it.

"Then I prayed that we would hear from you and Ben that very afternoon. I asked for God's comfort and that He would give me assurance that you were safe. After I prayed, still with my eyes closed, I heard a gentle fluttering overhead. I opened my eyes and saw three doves fly heavenward. I knew that dove's are a sign of peace!

"I got up, rode Blazer home, went inside and it was three o'clock. I had a true sense of peace about me. Then we got your telegram at five o'clock," Elizabeth said.

"Elizabeth, do you know what time we tied up at the dock on Saturday afternoon? It was three o'clock. Do you think it was a coincidence that those doves flew overhead when they did, just when we were safe? I don't think so."

Chapter 59

Elizabeth, there is something else we need to talk about. Remember the very last thing you said to me at the train depot on Thursday, September 19th the day I left? Zachary asked taking hold of her hand.

"You tell me, Zachary," she replied.

"You said, and I quote, 'I feel compelled to tell you that I want to set our wedding date as soon as you return.' I heard this over and over in my head after we survived our terrible ordeal. So, let's talk about it."

"I, too, have thought a lot about it, Zachary. After the wonderful cotillion that grandmother and grandfather Baldwin gave me, I don't think an extravagant wedding will be necessary. I simply do not want a lot of pomp and circumstance. All I want is something simple, and then time with you. You are the object of my affection not a big, expensive, wedding. Does this surprise you? To tell you the truth I would like to elope."

"Knowing you, Elizabeth, it doesn't surprise me. I sensed at the cotillion that you didn't like being the center of attention. You are a born Cinderella, a fairytale princess with exquisite beauty. And your inner beauty even exceeds what people see on the outside. You are more interested in giving than receiving. People have seen this in your character.

Now, where does this leave us? John and Catherine will not like the idea of not giving you the finest wedding of the century. They are proud of you, and would want to honor you in this way because they love you. If we elope, how do you think they will react?" Zachary asked.

"I've also thought a lot about that. When they wanted me to come and live with them I explained my feelings about Willow Place. I went into great detail. When they saw how I really felt they understood. Look how things turned out. They are *here*. We are together. They have a new business that is less stressful for Grandfather. They are very happy, and their happiness is very important to me. But I have to make my decisions on what I think is right for me, for us.

"We will leave a letter for them. In it I will explain my feelings to them. They love us enough to respect our decision, I feel sure. What do you think?"

"I have to admit that slipping away, just the two of us, is exactly what I prefer. You know, the more I think of the idea, it will be fun and exciting. Let's do it!" Zachary declared emphatically. "What about setting a date?"

"I have one in mind, but I'd like to know if you have a preference."

"How about yesterday?! No, seriously, I have thought of a date. However, the final decision will be left up to you, Elizabeth."

"Suppose I count to three and we say our dates at the same time. Agreed?" Elizabeth asked.

"Agreed." Zachary answered.

"One . . . two . . . three."

"November 16th," they both said in unison!

"See, we are already thinking like one," Zachary exclaimed.

"Tell me, Zachary, why did you choose November 16th?"

"Because, my dear, it was the first time I saw this apparition that turned out to be real, that turned out to be you. I almost feel as if my life began on November 16th last year. To me that is truly *our* day."

"So why did you choose November 16th, Elizabeth?"

"Because it was the day I fell in love with you, a perfect stranger." Elizabeth answered.

"Did you really, Elizabeth? It seemed like you had a hard time acknowledging your love for me," Zachary said reflectively.

"I know. I let fear of the past and seeds of doubt, planted by someone I did not even know, cloud my senses. But that is in the past. I feel now that our lives are so perfect. Let's always keep this joy and contentment alive in our life together. We will have hard places, and difficult times, but together with a unity of mind and spirit we can overcome anything and still be happy. I know this is true because my 'Dandy' Baldwin taught me that it was."

"November 16th is exactly eight weeks away. We will have to work out the particulars you know," Zachary mused. "And could I ask a favor of you? Since we plan to elope we will be going wherever we choose for the honeymoon by train. Would it be asking too much of you to wear the same green velvet dress you wore on November 16th last year?"

"I'll wear my same outfit if you will wear the same thing you wore on that day, especially the yellow scarf. Agreed?"

"Agreed!"

Again they gave each other a warm hug and he kissed her sweet lips quickly.

"Now let's walk around the lake and up the hill to your grandparent's and let them know I'm home safe and sound," Zachary suggested.

"Okay, I'll tell William to take your baggage around," Elizabeth said, "and remember, not a word of our plans!"

What a difference a few hours can make, Elizabeth thought.

———◦⊙⊙◦———

The Morgan's were so happy to see Zachary. He went over the whole story of the weekend's events. They listened attentively, not wanting to miss a single detail.

John shared with Zachary their great concern. They even laughed, after the fact, at how upset Elizabeth was. They all chuckled at Elizabeth's wanting to sleep in Zachary's bed. But they certainly understood her desire to feel near him.

Virginia had prepared a delicious supper and they continued to share and fellowship into the evening. The discussion turned to the Morgan's new home. Granted, it was smaller than their home in Williamsburg, but it still had an elegant charm to it. And it had a sunroom on the south end of the wraparound porch. Catherine insisted on that because Elizabeth once said everyone needed a sunroom. Since it was a one level home, Catherine's one regret was it did not have a staircase with a banister for Elizabeth to slide down!

They walked through the house admiring the workmanship. Their furniture from Williamsburg fit nicely in each room with the addition of a few new pieces.

One thing Elizabeth particularly admired was their American banjo wall clock. It had a Giltwood case with inset reverse mother of pearl panels. The colors matched those in the formal part of their large sitting room, especially the gorgeous wool needlepoint rug.

Also displayed in the dining room was a treen wassail bowl and dipper with goblets made from burr walnut. A very fine collection, Zachary noted.

All in all it was a very good evening. The Morgan's were proud of their new home. They both said they hoped one day to have grandchildren coming in and out of their house.

John spoke up and asked, "Have you children discussed wedding plans yet?"

Elizabeth and Zachary exchanged glances.

Elizabeth quickly answered, "Yes, we have talked some about it, but we haven't made all the decisions yet. We will be discussing it more as time goes on."

"Oh yes Elizabeth, I almost forgot," Zachary said. "My sister Rebecca has this big crush on Robert Thomas. And my brother Ben is crazy about Andrea Ashton. Robert has made three trips from Richmond to Williamsburg to see Rebecca, Ben and Andrea at the

Ashton's home. Rebecca asked if I could get them an invitation to come back to Willow Place for a weekend soon. What do you think?" Zachary asked.

"By all means Zachary. But I need to see a calendar if I may. Grandmother," Elizabeth called out, "do you have a calendar near?"

"Virginia has one in the kitchen just inside the pantry door on the wall" her grandmother answered.

Elizabeth returned with the calendar and said, "Zachary, you can ask Robert if Friday, October 11th would be a good weekend for him. If so, we can telegraph Ben, Rebecca and Andrea an invitation. It would be nice to include Max and Robert's sister Jo Anna. The girls could all stay with me . . ."

Before she could finish, her grandmother said, "The fellas can stay with us!"

Elizabeth's grandfather said, "I'll bet old Max could plan a great Saturday night hay ride."

"It sounds like cupid shot some of his arrows at your picnic, Elizabeth. It will be interesting to see if anything permanent comes from any of them," Catherine said smiling.

Chapter 60

September 23
MONDAY

So much had happened that the weekend seemed to have been a month long. But Elizabeth was glad to get back to work on Monday.

"Kim, I was checking the list to see who was admitted to the hospital Sunday and I saw Jake Smart's name. What's wrong with him?" Elizabeth asked.

"We aren't sure that anything is wrong. He came in late last night saying he just didn't feel well. At first he said it was a pain in his side. Then he said it was chest pains. Dr. Blake came in and checked him over and couldn't find anything wrong. But when we suggested he could go back home he began saying his chest was hurting real bad. Dr. Blake decided he better keep him for observation. This morning, early, he asked where you were. Then he asked if you had any more of 'them western books' around here. We think he is here to get you to read to him! You better go check on him. Yes, he's back in room 106," Kim said. "And I'm sure he's watching the door for you."

"What if he *is* here just because he wants me to read to him?"

"We will let Dr. Blake deal with him. He will see him this morning for another consultation,"

Kim replied.

———❦———

"Good morning, Mr. Smart. What are you doing back in the hospital?" Elizabeth asked as she fluffed up his pillow.

"Well, you see, it's my old ticker I'm a thinkin'. I'm hurtin' in my chest. They jest might have to keep me here fer a good while. Say, do you have any more of them western story books you could read to me?" Jake asked with a twinkle in his tired old eyes.

"No, I don't have any more books. But I'll tell you what, if Dr. Blake thinks it will be all right for you to go home, I'll see if I can't find another western storybook. If you will come into the hospital lobby on Mondays, Wednesdays and Fridays at 2:30, I will read the book until we finish it. Do you think you can do that?" Elizabeth asked.

"Yes 'um, I could do that I reckon. You shore do read them books real good," Mr. Smart said grinning toothlessly.

"Dr. Blake will be in to check you over really well in a little while. You just be patient until he comes," Elizabeth advised.

"I'm already feelin' a right smart better," Jake said as Elizabeth left the room.

She went back to Kim's office and found David going over some patients' charts with Kim. She told them of her conversation with Jake.

"I figured as much. But I'll give him another good going over and let you know what I find," David said. "By the way, has Kim told you that we are going to be married? We just got engaged last night at the Candlewick Café."

"Well, congratulations to both of you. I'm so happy for you. Have you set a date yet?" Elizabeth asked.

"It will be sometimes next May. We aren't sure about the exact date yet," Kim said as she looked adoringly at David.

"We heard about Zachary and Ben being lost in the storm. We were very concerned for them and so relieved to hear they were safe. It makes you think how uncertain life really is, so we decided we didn't want to wait any longer than necessary. We want to have our home and have it furnished when we get married. We should be able to have everything in place by next April or May," David said. "I must be making my rounds now. See you two later."

Kim hugged Elizabeth and exclaimed, "I'm so happy Elizabeth! David is not only a fine doctor but he is a tower of strength to me. He has a wonderful sense of humor. I've learned so much about him since we have been dating. We both have the same values. I feel like the luckiest girl in the whole world. I feel so *blessed* that David loves me."

"And David is equally blessed to have your love Kim," Elizabeth assured her.

Later in the morning David told Elizabeth he had sent Jake Smart home, but Jake would meet her in the lobby Wednesday at 2:30. "And I'll get another western book from Max and have it here," he promised.

It was a busy Monday at the hospital but Elizabeth was glad for the work. Otherwise, her thoughts would stray to her beloved Zachary and she would while her time away daydreaming.

On her way home she went by to see Emma. She missed her desperately. Emma had been a blessed fixture in her life as long as she could remember. Her home at Willow Place seemed so empty without her. William and Sadie stayed in the little house at night. Of course, Sara went home to her family after work. But all this would change in only eight weeks!

Mike and Emma's house was extra nice. It had just become a renter house. An older gentleman had lived there alone after his wife died. His children lived in Petersburg. Recently they took him to live with them and they planned to rent it until they found a buyer. Mike and Emma were fortunate to find this place.

Elizabeth knocked on the door and Emma appeared.

When she saw Elizabeth her eyes lit up with delight.

"Come in, Elizabeth, lassie. How good to see you. I just happen to have a fresh kettle of hot chocolate and some bran muffins just out of the oven. Come sit at my table. My, my lassie, how I have missed you!" Emma said giving Elizabeth a warm hug.

Elizabeth told Emma about the past weekend and Zachary's harrowing sailing trip.

Emma lamented, "And I wasn't even there to comfort you, lassie."

"Yes, and I missed that, Emma," Elizabeth said.

"But I'm so glad for you and Mike. You seem so happy Emma, and it shows. Of all the people who deserve to be loved and cherished, it is you. You have spent so much of your life giving to others. Now, show me through this doll house."

Emma had very good taste. She and Mike had decorated very well. The Morgan's had given them several nice pieces of furniture they didn't need in their new house, as well as quite a few linens and dishes.

"I am impressed with all you have done to make this house a home in such a short time, Emma. Your sewing talents are evident in the curtains you've made. It's a pity this house is not yours. It is all you two would ever need," Elizabeth said.

"Well, Elizabeth lassie, it just could be that we will buy it. Mike sold his parents' home after they passed away and put the money back. He also has some savings. He is going to talk with the owners about buying it. Of course, it is according to what they ask for it, you see."

"All things work together for good to them that love the Lord," quoted Elizabeth from apostle Paul's writings. "Things will work out for you two, I'm sure! I must be going. Say hello to Mike for me."

Chapter 61

The builders at the carriage factory had almost finished the new carriage that John, Zachary and Max had designed. There was a lot of excitement over it. John had wanted special emphasis placed on comfortable seating. He wanted the seats well upholstered. They opted for the highest quality material and leather they could buy. Max had been very instrumental in the exterior design, with extra springs for the axle, and a new ball joint on the team hitch. John and Zack had focused on the interior with extra brass trim and durable oak and walnut finishing's. It should be ready for showing by the third week in October. They were anxious to see if it would be a good seller. The men in the factory all liked it. John just beamed with pride as he stood back and watched its progress.

Zachary was glad the carriage would be finished before the wedding in November. He wanted to have his desk cleared by then. He wanted at least two weeks for their honeymoon.

Zachary drove out to the Thomas farm to talk with Robert about having Rebecca, Ben and Andrea come for a weekend visit to Willow Place on October 11th. Robert was very pleased at their thoughtfulness.

This was the first time Zachary had visited the Thomas farm. He knew little or nothing about farming but it was obvious Thomas did. Robert talked about the land with great fondness. He respected the cycle of preparing, planting, growing and harvesting the fruits of their labor.

"I have to tell you Zack, when I look out over this land it is a daily reminder to me of the creator of it all. I think of what comes from the earth. Adam was formed from the dust of the earth. That's where we had our beginning. What we eat comes from the soil. In the book of Job it says there is a vein of silver and a place for gold in the earth. Iron, coal, precious stones such as sapphires, onyx and diamonds come out of the earth. So a lot of what we are comes from the soil.

"I think of the beautiful story of Ruth and Boaz and his love of the land. I hope one day to find me a Ruth to share my life with," Robert expounded in that deep resonant voice of his.

"Robert, you've given me a completely new perspective and respect for the land. And whoever turns out to be your Ruth will be a very fortunate young woman," Zachary said.

"Then I would like to tell you that I am indeed fond of your sister, Rebecca. Our means of travel prohibits us from getting to see those we care for as often as we would like. So we can't always have long courtships. We have to make up our minds in a hurry when we find the right person.

"Rebecca has indicated to me that she shares my feelings. I'd like for us to be able to settle down together right here on the farm. I just wanted to let you know how I feel," Robert told him, looking him straight in the eyes.

"Robert, I don't have a problem at all with your feelings for Rebecca. It did not take me any longer to know that I loved Elizabeth. As far as I am concerned you and Rebecca have my blessings," Zachary said draping his arm around Robert's shoulder as they walked to Zachary's carriage.

Since Zachary was living with the Morgan's, he and Elizabeth saw each other every day when Zachary got in from work. They walked all over Willow Place. Some of their walks were pretty long hikes but they liked exploring the whole of it.

Zachary knew how Elizabeth felt about this place. He knew they would live here after they were married. She had made this clear a long time ago, but he did not feel comfortable about it. He wanted to feel like the provider and he really needed to talk with her about his feelings. He would do so this afternoon.

When he drove into the driveway he saw Elizabeth sitting on a bench next to the lake. She had on a black pants-skirt, her riding boots and a violet blue sweater. She had just returned from riding Blazer and was waiting for him.

Zachary climbed down from the carriage, tied Honey to the hitching post and walked over to where she was sitting.

"How's my favorite girl today? And how was your day at the hospital?" Zachary inquired.

"We had a busy day. Remember the old cowpoke I told you about named Jake Smart? He's the one who stepped on a nail and got blood poisoning all the way up his leg. He was in the hospital back in May."

"You mean the one you read the western book to?"

"Yes, he's the one. Well, he came back to the hospital Sunday complaining of chest pains. Come to find out he's just a lonely old man that wanted some attention. He actually wanted me to read him another book! We've made arrangements for me to read to him in the hospital lobby on my workdays. It takes so little to please some people. Sometimes it requires us to give of ourselves," Elizabeth said.

"And how did your day go?"

"Well, our dream carriage is soon going to be a reality. And . . . I went to the Thomas farm to talk to Robert. He said October 11th will be fine for the weekend visit. I also talked with Max at work. He said that he and Robert could handle the hayride. Tomorrow I'll send a telegram to Ben, Rebecca and Andrea.

"I am really impressed with Robert. He is a fine man. You should ask him sometimes what he thinks of the good earth. His reply is worth hearing. He also told me he is serious about Rebecca.

"Changing the subject, Elizabeth, but I want to talk to you about Willow Place," Zachary said with a thoughtful look on his face.

"About Willow Place? What do you mean, Zachary?"

"I know how you feel about Willow Place, Elizabeth, and I respect your feelings. In fact, I can't imagine us living anywhere else but right here in this lovely country home. You don't know how many times I've stood and looked at this house. I've pictured you and me walking up the steps, me picking you up and carrying you through the door as my bride.

"I've pictured a sign in the front yard . . . 'Bainbridge House.' Our house, with our children. I consider the lake and trees as Willow Place. I've even pictured a small boy and girl running and playing on the lawn. So you wonder what my problem is, right?" Zachary asked.

"Yes. Yes I do," Elizabeth said with a puzzled look on her face.

"The problem is that it is *your* home. A man is supposed to provide for his wife, for his household. But this house is a legacy of yours from your Baldwin grandparents. I'm in a dilemma trying to feel like the provider that I should be."

"Stop right there, Mr. Bainbridge! If you think for one minute I'm going into a marriage with a mind set that this is mine and that is yours, you are mistaken." She had jumped to her feet with a spark in her eyes.

"When we take our marriage vows we will no longer be two but we will become one. As far as I am concerned there will be no 'this is mine and that is yours' in our relationship. Everything will be *ours*. This house will be *ours*. I would hope that you would feel the same about whatever you have being *ours*. Remember, a house divided against itself cannot stand. Now other people may not feel this way but I do. So there!" Elizabeth said. By this time she was crying.

Zachary gathered her up in his arms and kissed away her tears. He didn't care who might be watching!

"Zachary, I do love Willow Place. But your coming to live here will make this place a real home. I can't imagine my life without you in it. Since my grandparents have been gone, and with Emma now gone, this house has been so big and empty and lonely. But in eight weeks this brick and mortar house will come alive again! That will happen because of you. It is an overwhelming thought to imagine what it will be like to awaken each morning with you beside me. To sit across the table from you at meal times. To spend Christmas with you and winter evenings in front of our fireplace. And most overwhelming of all is to have you hold me in your arms each night as I fall asleep."

As Zachary held her close they looked across the lake where the heavens were aflame with a spectacular sunset.

"What a glorious way to end the day, this is *our* Willow Place Elizabeth" Zachary whispered against her cheek.

Chapter 62

OCTOBER 2
WEDNESDAY

*H*ave you seen Elizabeth? Kim asked nurse Louise.

"Yes. She is down in the lobby reading to Mr. Smart. He got here early, sent word to Elizabeth that he was here, so she went right down."

"Thank you, Louise."

Kim walked to the lobby. She saw the old man giving his rapt attention to Elizabeth as she read to him. He looked old and worn sitting there she thought. Kim moved a little closer so she could hear.

"Marshall Bosworth took off his gun belt and laid it on Sheriff Cassidy's desk. He removed his Marshall's badge and laid it beside the gun.

"Sheriff Cassidy said, 'I shore wish you wouldn't do this, Hank. You know the town of Mineral Wells won't be the same without you.'

"'Well now, Sheriff Cassidy, I'll be leavin' things in good hands. I come here to git a job done and I've finished what I started. It's time fer me to be movin' on. I've straightened out a lot of trouble in my time, but now I kinda feel like the old eagle. I'm not afraid of the storms, but I think it's time I jest soar above 'em.'

"With that said, Bosworth mounted ole Blackjack and rode off headin' south."

Elizabeth closed the book and said, "Well now, Mr. Smart, that's the end of 'Marshal Bosworth of Mineral Wells.' Did you like it?"

"I shore did, Miss Elizabeth. There's jest nothin' like them western stories. I thank you fer readin' to me. I shore do," old Jake said with a twinkle in his eyes.

"Would you like for me to carry you home now," Elizabeth added.

"No ma'am. I see my neighbor Hank comin' in the door now. He brung me and said he'd be back for me. But thank you jest the same. You'll read some more to me sometime, won't you?"

Jake asked.

"I sure will, Mr. Smart. Goodbye now," Elizabeth said.

She turned to go back to the main floor and saw Kim waiting for her.

"You made a lonely old man happy today, Elizabeth. I came to tell you there is a new patient I want you to meet. She's going to need some tender loving care," Kim said.

On Friday morning, October 4th, when Elizabeth got to work Kim met her in the lobby.

"I have some bad news for you, Elizabeth. Old Jake Smart died in his sleep last night. His neighbor, Hank, found him this morning early. I wanted to be the one to tell you," Kim said.

"Oh Kim, I'm so sorry to hear this. How sad. He was such a lonely old man. I wonder if he had family?"

"We don't think so. His neighbor seemed to be the one who cared for him. Mr. Smart paid cash both times he was in the hospital. We never saw any family when he came here, just the neighbor he called Hank," Kim replied.

"Those western books meant a great deal to him. Beneath his crusty old ways was a sweet man. I can truthfully say I will miss him," Elizabeth said.

As it turned out, Jake Smart had no one except Hank. They did find a considerable amount of

money in an old, stained envelope with the name Hank printed shakily on the front of it. Inside was a scrawled note asking Hank to pay for his burial. He said he had a grave plot already paid for in East Richmond Cemetery. He told Hank to keep the money that was left. It was signed "Old-timer Jake Smart."

He was buried on Saturday morning. Hank had found Jake's old worn Bible on the table beside his bed. He had a piece of red ribbon in the opening of the 23rd Psalm. He had underlined "The Lord is my shepherd."

Dr. Blake, Hank and several of the staff from the hospital including Kim and Elizabeth were the only ones to attend the short graveside service.

Dr. Blake read the 23rd Psalm, prayed and then asked Elizabeth to read what he had marked in the western book she had just read to Jake. He handed her the book. She took it with trembling hands and began to read . . .

"It's time fer me to be movin' on. I've straightened out a lot of trouble in my time, but now I kinda feel like the old eagle. I'm not afraid of the storms, but I think it's time I jest soar above 'em."

There wasn't a dry eye among them.

They all prayed the Lord's Prayer together and then sang the old familiar hymn "Amazing Grace."

Jake Smart would have been proud.

Chapter 63

OCTOBER 11
FRIDAY

*T*he train pulled into Richmond right on time. Ben, Rebecca and Andrea were the first ones off the train. There to greet them were Robert, Max, Jo Anna, Elizabeth and Zachary.

They were all talking at once, shaking hands, hugging each other and exclaiming, "We're starved!"

They loaded up in the carriages and rode out to Willow Place.

Catherine had insisted on having a meal prepared for them at her house. Virginia had outdone herself this time. She prepared a roast with her special seasoned gravy and mashed potatoes creamed as only she could do. She had made crowder peas, green beans and cranberry salad. Of course, she had her famous apple dumplings.

Virginia told Catherine, "You are feeding four men with hearty appetites. They need some stick-to-the-ribs type of food."

They all ate around the big round kitchen table. They were mannerly, yet lively. The comradery was contagious. Everyone was relaxed. It was as if they had all been together just yesterday. Catherine beamed as she saw such warm companionship flowing around her table. This brought her great joy. She marveled at how the Lord had blessed them to be able to be here with their precious Elizabeth.

When they were finished the fellas brought their baggage in and were shown to their rooms. Robert and Max were going to be guests of the Morgan's along with Ben so they could all be together for the weekend.

Mike took Rebecca, Andrea and Jo Anna over to Elizabeth's to get settled in. Then they all gathered in the parlor for some conversation and music.

Max played his guitar and Jo Anna surprised them all with an old banjo Max found for her. They both had a natural ability for music and learned to play without any formal training. They made up catchy tunes and began to put words to them. Max would look around the room and include everyone in the song he made up as he went. Some lines were funny and some serious, but everyone seemed to enjoy the moment.

When they finished singing their tune, everyone applauded and asked for just one more song.

It had been a good evening for all of them. They left the parlor, put on their coats and went outside. Moonlight accented the romantic glow of gaslights that encircled the drive.

Each couple found their own spot for some private conversation.

Robert and Rebecca were seated on the porch, and Ben and Andrea had walked to a bench near the lake. Max and Jo Anna were laughing playfully and chasing one another up and down the driveway. They seemed to have more fun than anyone. Zachary and Elizabeth were strolling hand in hand across the front lawn.

Robert turned to Rebecca and said, "I had a talk with Zack last week about us, Rebecca. I told him how we feel about each other. At least, I think you love me like I love you."

"Do you realize Robert, this is the first time you have said that you love me? *Do you?*" Rebecca asked.

"You mean I haven't ever told you? Well, it's all I think about. I guess that's why I thought I had told you. Then I guess that means you've never told me that you love me either, right?" Robert asked.

"No, I haven't told you," Rebecca agreed.

"Well then I'm going to start all over. Rebecca, my dear Rebecca with the auburn hair and dark brown eyes, I want to tell you that I am madly in love with you. It all started back on June 17th, the first day I ever saw you. My love has grown every day since then. It has been four months and that is enough time for any harvest. Before I ask you to marry me and move to the Thomas Farm, I'd like to ask you one question. Do you love me?"

By this time Rebecca was laughing and crying all at the same time.

"And what if I said no?! Just teasing, just teasing! The answer is yes, of course, yes I do love you with all of my heart. Now could you ask me the second part of that question?"

Robert got down on one knee, took her hand between his big, farm-worn hands, looked into her eyes and said, "Rebecca my love, will you marry me?"

"Thank you for asking me, and yes, my darling, I will marry you," Rebecca responded.

Robert stood to his feet, pulled her into his arms and kissed her for the very first time, but it felt so natural.

From nearby they heard a "Hmm . . ."

They jumped apart and saw Zachary and Elizabeth standing on the steps.

Robert looked at them with a grin from ear to ear and said, almost in a whisper, "She said yes!"

Rebecca looked at her brother and wondered what he would say.

Zachary extended his hand to Robert and said, "Congratulations, Robert. She's our princess, you know. You'd best treat her like one." Then he reached out to Rebecca and said, "You could not have found a finer man. I have no doubt he will make you happy."

By this time the others had gathered in, sensing something was going on.

Zachary spoke up and said, "Robert has an announcement to make," and he looked at Robert.

"Well, on September 23rd Zachary came to the farm to tell me of his plans to invite all of us to Willow Place for this weekend. I sort of got carried away telling him how much the land means to me. Then I reminded him about how Boaz had a great love for the land and that Ruth came along and felt the same way he did. Theirs was a beautiful love story. I told him I hoped someday to find me a Ruth to share my love, and my love for the land. Tonight I found 'my Ruth,' and her name is Rebecca. I asked her to marry me and she said yes!"

There was a round of applause and everyone wished them well.

"When will the wedding be?" Andrea asked.

"I can tell you now, I didn't ask Rebecca to marry me to have to *wait!* I don't believe in long engagements, so I hope it will be within the month!" Robert said boldly.

"We will look at the calendar and decide. We have to talk to my parents, of course," Rebecca said.

Elizabeth added, "I guess there is something magic about Willow Place. This is the third engagement that has happened here in the past eight months!"

It was getting late. Zachary and the boys went around the lake and up the hill to the Morgan's home for the night. Of course, there would be a bedtime snack waiting for them.

The girls all went inside with Elizabeth where Sara had baked a chocolate cake before she left. Elizabeth served cold milk along with the cake.

They were all a buzz over Rebecca's engagement. Rebecca was still in a daze but it felt wonderful!

Saturday morning they were all up early. They knew their time together was limited. Again, Virginia fixed breakfast for everyone. When they had finished all the fellas gave Virginia a big hug and told her she could cook better than anyone. Each of them picked up all the plates from the table and stacked them neatly while the girls collected the silverware and cups.

Max picked up his guitar which he always had close by. He propped his foot on a chair and began to play and sing another catchy tune.

He slung his guitar over his shoulder and danced Virginia all around the kitchen singing, "Ginny, Ginny, won't you marry me," over and over.

Virginia's face was blushing but she loved every minute of it.

Catherine told John later she had never seen such a charming personality as Max had.

The day was filled with fun things. They paddled the boats and canoes around the lake and went horseback riding. Some of them walked along the fences and watched the young colts frolic.

They paired off in the early afternoon.

Ben and Andrea sat near the lake under a sprawling willow tree.

Andrea said, "Ben, I am so glad I did not know you and Zachary were sailing and lost in a storm. I would have been so upset. Your poor family must have been frantic."

"It wasn't easy for them, I'm sure. It was a very sobering experience, Andrea. I hope I am never caught in another situation like that. As much as I've sailed, I have never been in very bad weather. Oh, I've been caught in a little rough wind and pelting rain, but never when I had absolutely no control over the boat. We felt like a cork being tossed about in the sea," Ben remarked.

"Were you terribly frightened? I guess that's a foolish question. Of course you were," Andrea said.

"We were both scared to death. If you ever thought you were invincible something like that will humble you really fast. I can tell you now, I thought about God and my relationship with Him, and did a lot of praying. I don't think I measured up too well, so I decided then and there things would be different from then on.

"And Andrea, my pretty little Andrea, I thought about you. I thought about how much I respect you, the worthwhile things you are doing in your life, especially working with the little kids in church. I wondered if I would ever see you again. I'm glad someone planned this weekend. It's been great seeing everyone," Ben said, "and especially you."

"Ben, you talk so easily about your innermost feelings. To me this shows your inner strength. I'm glad I came to your mind during the storm. If I had known you were in such danger I would certainly have prayed for you. But I have thanked God that He took care of you and Zachary. I, too, am glad for our time together."

Max and Jo Anna were hanging over the pasture fence admiring the horses. He was surprised by how much Jo Anna knew about them. Being raised on a farm, Jo Anna knew a lot about animals.

"You are quite a girl, Jo Anna, did you know that? You have a great personality and you're no softy. You're just my kind of girl. I always have a good time when I'm with you," Max said as he playfully nudged her under the chin.

"We do make a pretty good pair, don't we?" Jo Anna replied.

"I know I'm a big cut-up and most people think of me as a clown. But I have a serious side. I have values and a standard that is important to me. I know what I want from life and I'm willing to work to achieve my goal. My goal is to be independent, stand on my own two feet, and pull my own weight. I know a Higher Power that can help me do just that. If I put my priorities in the right place nothing is impossible. But I intend to have fun along the way. I intend to laugh and I intend to make others laugh!" Max said emphatically.

"Max, you are my idea of what a man ought to be. I appreciate your serious side and I love your humorous personality! I think we make pretty good music together!" Jo Anna said, and then exclaimed, "See that bay mare? She is as frisky as she can be, and that colt must surely belong to her. Horses are my favorite animals. They have such a free spirit. That mare reminds me of my sorrel. She's a great quarter horse. Her name is Ginger," Jo Anna said.

They heard the big dinner bell ringing to gather them in for lunch. They had beef stew, sandwiches, milk and chocolate cake for dessert.

The whole gang loaded up in one carriage to ride into Richmond. Max and Ben sat up in the driver's seat with Max at the reins. The others rode inside. They took a tour around the city looking at some of the beautiful and older landmarks. Ben, Rebecca and Andrea had not seen down town, and wanted to do some sightseeing.

They went to the shops in downtown Richmond. All the fellas bought their girls woolen mittens. They told them the mittens were to keep their hands warm this winter when they weren't around to hold them.

At five o'clock they drove to the Candlewick Café. John Morgan had made reservations for them. He had also arranged for the strollers to come in early to play for Elizabeth and her guests. Then they were going on a hayride around seven-thirty.

As soon as they were seated in an alcove area, the strollers came to their table. Their music was so perfect, so romantic that they were held spellbound. Elizabeth wondered where the inspiration comes from to write music that reaches to one's very soul. The strollers were certainly gifted musicians, but they also had engaging personalities. Their eyes almost talked to their listeners. They were wearing black pants and white ruffled-front shirts with long puffed sleeves. As they neared the end of their command performance, they all faced Elizabeth and Zachary and played "To Each His Own." They were definitely crowd pleasers.

The group left the café at six forty-five, loaded up and rode out to the Thomas farm. Robert's brother, Layton, had the wagon filled with hay and the big Morgan's were hitched up and ready to go.

Max and Jo Anna provided the music. They all sang together from Sunday-School songs and hymns to personal favorites. Of course, Max sang some of his impromptu songs. They rode all around the rolling acres of the Thomas farm.

They came back to a crackling fire outside the Thomas home and enjoyed hot, spiced apple cider.

Robert and Rebecca excused themselves, went inside and told his parents about their engagement. It was the first time Rebecca had met his parents. Rebecca was warmly accepted. They had some wedding plans to talk about!

The group got back to Willow Place about eleven o'clock. Their train would leave at eight-thirty in the morning. It had been a memorable fall weekend.

Chapter 64

OCTOBER **14**
MONDAY

*E*lizabeth spent time Monday morning in the hospital room with Julia Anderson. She was seventy-six years old and had a serious heart problem. She was restless and anxious. Elizabeth spent most of the morning with her. By lunchtime her daughter had come. Julia settled down after she arrived.

Finally, Kim and Elizabeth had a few minutes to talk. They both were excited that Robert and Rebecca were getting married. Kim said she had never seen her brother so happy.

"We have a small house on the farm where father and mother started when they were first married. After the fourth baby came, they had to build a bigger house. Father said they had kept the little house in good shape for just such an occasion as this. Very little will have to be done to make it ready to occupy. I have a feeling those two will be married by Christmas," Kim declared.

"You and your family seem to be very close. I see a great spirit of unity among you," Elizabeth said.

"When you have a large family it means everyone works together to survive. We were taught as small children to respect each other and to love each other. We saw this example in our parents, so I suppose we thought it was the only right way to live. Even though we had a large family with ten of us living under one roof, father has done well enough on the farm for us to have a large house so we each have our own measure of privacy. They all are very dear to me," Kim said with feeling.

"You need to know that Zachary is very fond of Robert and believes he is a man of integrity. He is looking forward to having a 'brother' living here in Richmond, and he's especially glad that his sister will be close by," Elizabeth said.

"I need to check on my patients. We'll talk more later," Kim said as she picked up a chart and headed down the hall.

Elizabeth got home early. She was rather tired after the weekend.

She looked on the table in the foyer to see if there was any mail. William had checked the mailbox for her. There was a letter from Jane Adams Maxwell. She went into the parlor, curled up under a lap blanket on the sofa and hurriedly opened the envelope . . .

October 4, 1856
Williamsburg

My Dear Elizabeth,

I received your last letter dated September 1st. It is always a joy to hear from you. However, your account of Zachary's sailing experience was most unsettling to Phillip and me. We are grateful he and Ben made it safely back to Norfolk. We both felt your anguish as we read your description of the event.

Your hospital "experiences" sound intriguing! We are both pleased that you find your volunteer work so fulfilling.

So the Morgan's house is all finished and they've moved in? This is so good for you to have your grandparents there with you. You need them and they need you as you well know.

We can feel your deep affection for Zachary as you write to us about him. Phillip and I have found that love is a thing of splendor. We marvel from day to day at the new experiences we feel because of our great love for each other. It simply transcends the ordinary and takes us to heights almost inconceivable and certainly beyond our ability to explain. Love blends two into one and makes us stronger and better. No wonder love is so strong because we both know that love comes from God. My, oh my, did I get carried away! You and I are very fortunate to have found Zachary and Phillip.

Speaking of Phillip, we love living in Williamsburg. We have cultivated new friends. We have spent a lot of time with Matt and India Jones and Scott and Libbi Dixon. We have had a lot of fun with them. We sit up until the wee hours talking and laughing and playing games, and eating . . . I can't forget eating!

We also see Steve and Lee Wilson as often as we can. Steve's church work keeps him very busy. We feel he will be moving up quickly. Wouldn't it be great if he were sent to Williamsburg to pastor? Reverend Perkins might be pretty near retirement age. Steve has such great support in Rebecca. She is by his side whenever he needs her. When they come up from Poquoson and the eight of us are together we have such a wonderful time. The only thing that would make it better would be if you and Zachary were here.

Phillip absolutely loves his teaching job. He has a great group of students, most who are eager to learn. He has not regretted his career change thus far.
He loved William and Mary College when he was going to law school here.

We are looking to buy a house. We have found two possibilities. One is near the college and is owned by an older professor. We shall see. I'm sure in time we will find the one that meets our needs.

I've saved our most important news for last. We are going to have a baby!

Isn't that wonderful? It is due next May. We are so excited. You are the first

I've told except for our parents. This will add another dimension to our lives. Phillip is absolutely walking on air.

Do write me again soon. We love your letters.

Affectionately,
Jane

Elizabeth was thrilled at the thought of Jane having a baby. She knew she would make the perfect mother. Elizabeth purposed to write her soon and congratulate them.

———

Elizabeth realized it was one month and two days until their wedding day. She wanted to keep *her* bedroom as *their* bedroom. The view over the lake and the willow trees from her window was perfect. She would like to add a small balcony outside the window at some point. The window could be made into a glass door for access to the balcony. She would talk to Zachary about it.

When Zachary came in from work she was waiting. She was looking forward to making plans for the future.

Sadie put supper on the table which Sara had prepared before she left. Elizabeth, Zachary,

Sadie and William ate together enjoying each other's company. It was at mealtime that Elizabeth missed Emma the most.

While Sadie was cleaning up, Elizabeth and Zachary went into the parlor.

"Zachary, I want us to make my bedroom into our bedroom and I want it to be ready when we return from our honeymoon. What do you think?" Elizabeth asked.

"What do you have in mind exactly?"

"For one thing I would want new bedroom furniture. Could we go this Saturday and choose some from Breckenridge Furniture?" she asked.

"I don't have a problem with that. We are really pressed for time now, so we need to act quickly," Zachary said thoughtfully.

"I also want to have the room freshly painted and the wall behind the bed wallpapered. Of course, I'll want new curtains. Do you think we could get all of this done before the wedding?" Elizabeth asked reluctantly.

"I don't see why not. I'll talk to the contractor who did John's house. He should be able to help us out. I like the idea of making your bedroom ours. I love the view out the window of the lake and the trees. You know what would be nice, Elizabeth? If we could put a balcony off the bedroom so we could sit out there during the spring and summer months. It shouldn't be too difficult to do. We could make the window into a glass door. For privacy we could have a drapery that we could pull when the door is closed at night. If you agree I can also speak to Mr. Cleburne about this as well. Even if it wasn't finished by the time we are married, perhaps it could be by the time we return from our honeymoon. What do you think?" Zachary asked.

"Why, I think that's a great idea!" Elizabeth responded, smiling to herself. She would let him think it was his very own idea to build a balcony.

"Elizabeth, we also need to think about where we want to go for our honeymoon. I am going to try to have my desk cleared by Friday, November 14th. I want us to take two weeks. What are your thoughts about where we should go?"

"To tell you the truth, I planned to leave that up to you," she answered.

"I've been thinking about going to the beach house in Williamsburg. After a week we could go to Norfolk for a couple of nights to visit my family. I want them to get to know you. What do you think about those plans?"

"I think it's a wonderful idea, Zachary. The view of the James River from the beach house is so romantic, especially when the sailboats pass by. There should be some sailing if the weather isn't too cold, right?"

"Oh yes, sailors are on the water year round if the sun is shining and the wind is right," Zachary assured her.

"I just thought of something, Elizabeth. Suppose John and Catherine are planning on going to the beach house during this time. Do you think you could ask if they will be going to Williamsburg in November? If so we can make other plans."

"Sure, I can do that. You know, Thanksgiving is November 28th. I know my grandparents will be expecting to spend it with me. One thing we could do is go visit your parents on Friday through Sunday before Thanksgiving, come back to the beach house on Monday, return to Richmond on Wednesday the 27th, and be here for Thanksgiving on the 28th. What do you think?" Elizabeth asked.

Zachary laughed and said, "I have an idea we will be juggling holidays for a long time to come! But that sounds like a great idea to me. Then we would have Friday through Sunday to ourselves at Willow Place . . . *our* place! Oh, Elizabeth, I'm as excited as a little boy at Christmas time!"

Chapter 65

October 19

Saturday

Elizabeth ate breakfast with her grandparents and Zachary. They explained about the changes they were going to make in Elizabeth's bedroom and that they were going to select furniture today at Breckenridge Furniture store.

"It's a good idea to get this taken care of ahead of time," Elizabeth's grandfather said.

"Yes, I spoke with Clarence Cleburne on Tuesday about doing the work. They are going to start on the project this Monday. He says the bedroom work will move quickly. I also spoke with him about building a small balcony outside the bedroom. He says he can do it without compromising the looks of the house. It will have a wrought iron railing, which will blend nicely with the brick. We will probably want a matching balcony on the south end of the house when they finish with this project," Zachary said.

Catherine spoke up and added, "You will really enjoy the balcony because you can look down on the lake just as we do here from our vantage point. Your home is very beautiful, Elizabeth."

"Indeed it is, and it is well built. Your Grandfather Baldwin did well when he purchased this property," said Elizabeth's grandfather.

"We need to be on our way. Thanks for such a delicious breakfast, grandmother. I agree with 'the gang,' Virginia is the best cook ever."

She gave her grandmother a hug and her grandfather a kiss on the cheek as they left.

—⫸⫷—

Elizabeth and Zachary walked and walked through the large furniture store. When they had looked at all the bedroom suits they came back to the one they had both liked from the start. They chose a Chippendale tall chest of drawers of red maple with simple lines. The matching dresser had a large arched crescent-form mirror that swiveled between columnar supports. The bed had a deep headboard and a low footboard with high posts. They selected two matching Chippendale maple armchairs. The seats were upholstered in needlepoint tapestry of rose, ivory and green.

Elizabeth had a round maple lamp table that belonged to her Grandmother Savannah that she would use between the chairs, plus she had a maple bedside table that would complement the rest of the furniture.

They were pleased with their choices.

Next, they went to pick out the wallpaper for the wall behind the bed. They chose the ivory background with stripes of rose and green, which would match the colors of the tapestry in the chairs. They chose ivory paint for the other three walls.

Then they went to a drapery shop to select material. Their draperies would be the same shade of ivory as the paint. The tiebacks would be rose, green and ivory stripes.

This had been a profitable day. They had hopes the room would be completed by their wedding day.

"Elizabeth, let's go by the Sandwich Shop and have lunch," Zachary suggested. "There are some other plans we need to make."

They were having their last cup of coffee and Elizabeth said, "Now about those other plans . . ."

"Yes, I am thinking we need to talk with Pastor Davis about the ceremony. The train to Williamsburg will be leaving Saturday morning the sixteenth at 8:30 A.M. We will have to meet him at the church chapel by 7:30 for the ceremony and go from there to the train depot. We will need two witnesses. Madeline Davis can be one. And Elizabeth, William is going to have to be our confidant in this. He will have to load our baggage and take us to the chapel as well as to the station. He can be our other witness," Zachary said.

"Oh Zachary, this is exciting to me! I feel almost like a little girl slipping her hand into the cookie jar. Maybe if we ride over to the Davis house now we can tell them our plans."

They made all the arrangements with Pastor Davis and Madeline. The Davis' just shook their heads and smiled at these young people. They had to admit the plans sounded romantic. They assured Elizabeth "mum's the word."

When they left the pastor's house, Elizabeth and Zachary felt they had accomplished a lot. They agreed they would talk with William about his role in all of this just a few days before the sixteenth. Zachary said he was going to have to figure out how to get his baggage out of the Morgan house without being seen. He would choose his time.

The contractor, Mr. Cleburne, and his workers came early Monday morning to begin work on redecorating Elizabeth's room. She, Sadie and Sara had moved all of her personal belongings into the guest bedroom where she would stay until they came home from their honeymoon.

Elizabeth had William and Mike Kelly to load her bedroom furniture onto the wagon to take to the Everette's. She knew they had a bedroom sparsely furnished and would welcome it. She would go see them tomorrow.

The next two weeks transformed a young girl's bedroom into a bridal suite. All the work was done, the furniture had been delivered. The glass door leading to the yet to be constructed balcony had been installed. The draperies were hung. Elizabeth caught her breath in disbelief at the transformation. She could not have been more pleased.

She went into the room that had been her Dandy's and Grandmother Savannah's bedroom for so long. Everything had been removed except the furniture and a cedar-lined Chippendale blanket chest at the foot of their bed. In it was an ivory-colored, heavy cotton bedspread. It had a two-inch thick crocheted border and, just as Elizabeth remembered, in each corner were three small doves in flight about three inches high done in needlepoint the same colors as the spread. You had to look closely to even see them. It was elegant. It had never been used. Her grandmother had shown it to her and said she was saving it for some special occasion. She asked Sadie to hang it outside to let it air out and then place it on her bed.

Chapter 66

The weekend of October 25th and 26th the Carriage Company put their newly designed carriage on display. They called it the MBH Carriage for Morgan, Bainbridge and Hammond. There was a logogram stamped into a black and gold embossed emblem that was attached to the front of the carriage.

A seat sample was broken down to show the five-inch coil springs, heavy-duty padding and the quality of leather used in construction. Samples of the parts and materials used for the main body of the carriage were also on display. All in all it was a very successful weekend. They were surprised at the amount of interest it generated. There was a constant flow of men coming to look at it on both days. Two orders for the MBH were taken on Friday and three on Saturday.

John's dream of giving people a more comfortable means of travel had come true. He was glad to be out of the shipping business and into the fun of carriage making. He loved the hands-on working conditions. He had great respect for all of their craftsmen, especially Jim Adams who was a true leader and had knowledge and skills that were amazing. John thanked God for his packed down, heaped up and running over blessings!

Zachary went in to work on Monday with an eye toward getting everything in order for the biggest event of his life. When he really stopped to think about Elizabeth becoming his wife, his companion, his partner for the rest of their lives, he could scarcely comprehend it. The sweetness of this angelic creature's soft skin touching his took his breath. He knew he dare not go there in thought.

He had to begin balancing his ledgers for the end of the year inventory. All invoices had to be reconciled. He was a stickler for keeping good, current and accurate records, but there were always problem areas with which to deal.

Before she left for the hospital on this crisp October 28th Monday morning, Elizabeth went one more time to look at the bedroom. She could hardly stay out of it. Zachary loved it as much as she did. She could picture the two of them sitting at the maple table having coffee and fruit muffins for breakfast, just the two of them. Should she let her mind wander any further? Certainly not.

It was a busy day at the hospital. Elizabeth was glad for the diversion. She knew it was only nineteen more days until their wedding but it seemed like an eternity. She needed to stay busy to make time pass more quickly.

Elizabeth left work right at two o'clock. She went into Richmond to several stores looking for more items for her trousseau. She had almost everything she would need but wanted another extra special nightgown and robe. She had seen one in Abney's Department Store last week but thought perhaps she might find one she liked better. Elizabeth checked at the Boston Store and found one she liked, and decided to buy both, so she bought it and then went to Abney's to buy the other set as well. She rationalized that a girl could always use nightgowns.

When she got home, Elizabeth added her new purchases to the trunk she would be taking to Williamsburg.

Tuesday she rode Blazer to the Smith farm to visit her friends Henry and Bessie and the Everette's.

"It shore is good to see you, Miss Elizabeth," Henry said when he opened the door.

"Come in," Bessie said, drying her hands on her apron and then reaching out to Elizabeth. "We always like it when you come to see us."

"How have you two been doing?" Elizabeth inquired as she and Bessie walked inside arm in arm.

"We've felt might near better'n we've felt in a few years, ain't we Bessie?" Henry said as he kicked his heels up a bit.

"That we have! The Everette's have brought life and joy with them to the farm, Miss Elizabeth. Why, them little girls beg to spend the night with us every chance they get," Bessie said proudly.

"I'm going now to check on them. You two take care of yourselves. I'll see you again soon," Elizabeth said as she walked to the door.

Maggie Everette was all smiles when she asked Elizabeth into their home. She had worked wonders with the place. They had some extra money since coming here to live and could afford a few extra things now and then. Elizabeth had provided gifts of what she knew the Everettes were in need of from time to time. It warmed her heart to see them healthy, well fed and happy.

"Come in, come in. Girls, look who's come to see us!" Maggie said.

Emily and Julie came running. "Hello Miss Morgan. Look at my dolly!" Emily held her doll up so Elizabeth could see. "Granny Smith made her dress."

"Look at my dolly. She has a new dress, too," Julie said.

Elizabeth gave the girls a hug and looked at their dolls and the adorable little clothes their "Granny Smith" had made for them.

Maggie said, "Come and see my beautiful bedroom, Miss Morgan. We are so proud of it. You can't know how happy the furniture made us. You sent everything I needed to make the room complete. The windows, the bedclothes, and the bedspread. Isn't it just beautiful? I feel like a queen just looking at it. Jim said he loved to see me so happy. How can I ever repay you, Miss Morgan? I am so helpless to do so."

"Maggie, you just repaid me many times over. The greatest gift we can know is in giving. Your thankful heart is so precious to me. You and your family have made such a difference to the Smiths. You've given them reason for getting up each day. Caring people all have their own ways of giving. To see people that matter to me so happy is all the payment I need," Elizabeth assured her.

"I'll just be going. Tell Jim I hope to see him on my next visit. I saw him way out in the field when I rode up. Bye, bye girls. Tell Sara I said hello when she comes in from school."

And with that Elizabeth was off.

Chapter 67

November 8
Friday

When Elizabeth got home from work their beautiful Romeo and Juliet balcony was finished! Oh, she could not believe it! It was perfect. She stood and gazed at it for the longest time. Then she ran inside, up the steps, into their bedroom, across the floor to the balcony door, opened the draperies and the door and stepped outside onto the balcony. It *was* truly perfect. She would get two chairs from Breckenridge Furniture to place on it. She gazed across the lake at all the beauty. She could see her Morgan grandparent's home perfectly from here. She breathed in the fresh clean air. She said out loud for any and everyone to hear, "Praise God from whom all blessings flow!" Then she bowed her head in humble gratitude, knowing she was so undeserving.

This had been her last day at the hospital for a while. She had told Kim she would need some time off with the holidays coming up.

Zachary came home a little early. He came straight to the front door and knocked. Sadie went to the door. Elizabeth heard him say loudly, "This is Romeo. Does Juliet live here?"

She rushed to the door. Sadie walked past her toward the kitchen, just shaking her head and chuckling to herself.

"No, Juliet doesn't live here, but will I do?" Elizabeth asked with a most impish smile.

"Let's go look at the balcony from the front of the house," Elizabeth said leading Zachary down the steps by the hand. "What do you think? Isn't it perfect?"

"Yes. The workmen did such a fine job. It blends with the original structure as if it has always been there," Zachary observed.

They went inside and up to the bedroom and then stepped out on their very own balcony. Zachary held Elizabeth close. They stood this way for ever so long. He then tilted her face upward. She was so beautiful. What a pleasure to just look at her. "I can imagine what our first little girl is going to look like. She will be a miniature of you. And I will spoil her to death. She will be daddy's little girl."

"Our first little boy will look exactly like his daddy. He will follow you everywhere and will be very protective of his mommy."

"Just think, Elizabeth, its one week and one day until we won't have to be apart again. And it will be here before we know it!" Zachary said.

"I want to show you something, Zachary. Have you looked at the bedspread on our bed?"

"Yes I have. It's beautiful. Where did you get it?"

"From Grandmother Savannah's cedar chest. It's never been used. She said she was saving it for a special occasion. She showed it to me several times. She would be so pleased to know it is being used on our bed. But look at it carefully, Zachary."

He looked at the whole spread. He let his eyes travel all along the border. Then he saw them. "Elizabeth, three doves in flight. *Three doves in flight!* This is unreal," Zachary gasped shaking his head. "This is what you described seeing when we were delivered from the storm!"

Chapter 67

"That's exactly what I thought when I saw it. I feel that God is sanctioning our marriage and this is a reminder of His blessings," Elizabeth said.

"So do I, Elizabeth. So do I."

Chapter 68

NOVEMBER **13**

WEDNESDAY

*E*lizabeth went to the library to write the letter to her grandparents telling them of their elopement. She almost felt like she was betraying them, but she knew this was the right thing for Zachary and her.

NOVEMBER **13**

RICHMOND

Dearest Grandmother and Grandfather,

I know no easy way to tell you this but by the time you receive this letter Zachary and I will be married. Our elopement is my idea.

But it was our choice together.

You two wonderful people gave me the party of a lifetime last Valentine's Day. Then we had the wonderful picnic, all thanks to your unselfish generosity.

In light of this I just didn't feel like a big wedding. I know perfectly well you two would have gladly provided the finest wedding money could buy. But I had to do what I felt was right for me, and this feels right.

William knows of our plans and is providing our transportation to the chapel and train station. Pastor Davis and his wife will be performing the early morning ceremony. You can ask them about it at church on Sunday.

We are on the eight-thirty train to Williamsburg. We will be spending our honeymoon at your beautiful beach house. That is why I asked if you two planned to go there in November. Please forgive us for not asking your permission to use it.

We plan to go to Norfolk November 22nd–24th to visit Zachary's parents. We will return to the beach house on the 25th and will come home on November 27th. We plan to spend Thanksgiving with you unless you have other plans.

I love Zachary with an everlasting love. I am so happy to be Mrs. Zachary Bainbridge.

You are two of the dearest people on earth to Zachary and me. Please try to understand and be happy for us.

Grandmother, if you would like you can have a reception for us later.

Love always,
Elizabeth and Zachary

She must have read the letter over a dozen times. She would address it and give it to William to deliver straight to her grandparents when he left the train depot. Zachary was going to tell William of their plans when he got in from work today. She could not think of anything else they needed to do before Sunday. She had all of her clothes ready and packed.

Friday night, November 15th, the Morgan's were invited to a friend's home for dinner. This gave Zachary his chance to get his bags out of the house. William set them inside the back hallway at Elizabeth's home along with her trunk. They would be ready to load first thing in the morning.

When they had everything squared away, Elizabeth laughed and said, "Instead of putting a ladder to my window to elope, as is customary, I need to put a ladder to *your* window so you can escape! How are we going to get out of the house that early without being seen?"

"That's easy. I am going to leave John and Catherine a note and tell them you and I have a day planned and I'll be leaving by seven in the morning. It being Saturday they will sleep in anyway most likely," Zachary replied.

"I will meet you and William at your back door right at 7 o'clock and then we'll load our baggage."

They were getting into the mood of the big event. In fact, they felt a little smug that they could pull this off!

They went upstairs and took one last look at the room they would be sharing when they returned as Mr. and Mrs. Zachary Steven Bainbridge.

Elizabeth walked to the front door with Zachary and watched as he jogged around the lake toward her grandparent's house until he was out of sight.

Chapter 69

NOVEMBER 16
SATURDAY

Faithful William was right on time. The carriage was loaded and they were on their way at seven sharp. William had dressed up for the occasion.

They arrived at the chapel at 7:20 A.M. Pastor Will and Madeline Davis were waiting when they arrived.

The ceremony was very sweet. Pastor Davis presided over the ceremony as though they were in a big cathedral. He had great admiration for this young couple and he respected their right to choose a simple service instead of an elaborate one. They congratulated them and wished them well as they left the chapel as Mr. and Mrs. Zachary Bainbridge.

William got them to the train depot with about thirty minutes to spare. When he had finished putting their baggage on the loading platform Elizabeth gave him the letter to her grandparents. Zachary shook hands with William and gave him an envelope with a sizeable sum of money in it for his faithful service to them.

Tears came in William's eyes. He thanked Zachary and said, "God bless you Miss Elizabeth and Mr. Zachary." Then he climbed up in the carriage and softly said, "Giddy-up."

Zachary told Elizabeth, "Stand right there. Don't move until you see me inside through the window. Then come to me."

He sprinted to the station door, went inside to the same place he was standing a year ago today. When Elizabeth saw him she began to move slowly toward the station door.

Again, just as last year on November 16th, he watched spell-bound at this vision of loveliness. Her hair was as black as a raven's feathers. She had a perfect widow's peak, giving her face the shape of a heart. She was wearing her deep green velvet dress, a matching bonnet and hand muff. Her green wool coat, buttoned snugly, accentuated her tiny waistline. She truly looked like a dream.

Elizabeth stepped inside the door, stopped and looked the room over just as she did the year before.

Her eyes stopped on this magnificent specimen of a man who was wearing a yellow scarf. His hair was a silvery blonde. He had a glorious tan, and gorgeous blue eyes.

She moved toward him, extended her hand just like when she first met him, and said, "You must be Zachary Bainbridge."

Again, he was staring at this lovely creature and was stricken speechless.

She said, just like last year, "Well, are you?"

Again, addled, he asked, "Am I what?"

She said, "Are you Zachary Bainbridge?"

They both laughed and then moved to "their bench."

Still playing the game, Zachary asked, "Did you have a pleasant ride into town?"

"Yes, yes I did. But an unusual thing happened to me on my way into town."

"Really, and just what would that be, may I ask?"

"Yes, you may ask. I must tell you that I got married on my way into town."

"No! You didn't."

"Yes, yes I did."

"Well, is the man you married the jealous type?"

"Yes, yes he is. Very jealous."

"What do you suppose he would think about you and me talking like this?"

"He wouldn't like it."

"He wouldn't?"

Their little game ended by the sound of the train whistle.

"May I say, Mrs. Bainbridge, I see nothing but joy and happiness ahead for you and your husband."

"Oh Zachary! I'm the happiest bride that ever eloped!"

They hurried to the passenger platform, boarded the train and went straight to the dining car for breakfast.

The train was underway. They found the perfect place in the dining car and took their seats. Almost immediately an older black server was there to take their order. He poured coffee and water. They each ordered an omelette, toast and orange juice.

The coffee was perfect, as was the juice. In fact, everything about this day was perfect.

Their server was very personable. He did everything with a flair. He made their first meal together on their wedding day one they would fondly remember.

When they finished their meal they left the dining car and took their seats in the coach.

Zachary sat beside Elizabeth, put her arm through his and laid his hand on top of hers.

Leaning over to her, he whispered, "So your husband is the jealous type? How do you know?" And their little game was underway again.

"He told me. Yes, he told me so."

"Are you jealous of him?"

"Yes, oh my, yes!"

"Do you think you have reason to be jealous?"

"No, no I don't think so."

"Married to someone like you, he would never look at another woman, would he?"

"Well, I should hope not!"

"Would you look at another man?"

"Mercy no, never!"

"Do you love your husband?"

"Yes. Oh, yes! With all my heart."

"I'm sure he loves you with all his heart."

"You think so?"

"My beautiful Elizabeth Bainbridge, I know so."

Laughing, they looked at each other hardly able to believe this day, this magical day, was finally here.

Zachary said, "All playfulness aside, Elizabeth, I am reminded of the beautiful scripture from Ruth that Pastor Davis used in our wedding ceremony this morning. It was so meaningful to me, to us . . . 'for whither thou goest, I will go; and where thou lodgest, I will lodge: thy people shall be my people, and thy God my God.' Elizabeth, this very day I pledge my love to you and you alone."

"And I make that same vow to you, Zachary, my husband. I pledge myself to 'One and Only You.' I know these pledges are easy for us to make to each other today because of the magic of the moment. The test will come in the years that follow. As I've said so often, true love *will* stand the test of time. No matter the trials, disappointments, sorrows or setbacks that *will* come, true love will survive them all and become stronger. I know this is true because my 'Dandy' taught me this by word and by example," Elizabeth said.

"I wish I could have known your 'Dandy' and your Grandmother Savannah, Elizabeth," Zachary answered.

"Look! There is the James River. We're getting close to our destination," Elizabeth said. "To think we were on this train in this very place together one year ago today. We were strangers then, but today we are one! I love this day, November 16th. Our day!"

Chapter 70

Charles Erickson, the caretaker of the beach house, picked them up at the train depot. After he and Zachary unloaded the trunk and baggage and put it inside the beach house, Zachary walked to the carriage, bowed very low and said, "Your Highness, may I assist you?" Then he very ceremoniously led her to the door, scooped her up in his strong arms and carried her over the threshold, setting her down gently.

"This will have to do until we get back to Willow Place and I carry you across the threshold of our home, my darling."

"Zachary, it is toasty warm inside. I had expected it to be cold," Elizabeth said as she walked into the kitchen where she smelled the aroma of cinnamon pastries. "Someone has been to the bakery," she exclaimed. She opened the cabinet doors and said, "There is food in here! Who did this?" she asked.

"Charles took care of all the details. I've been in touch with him, making sure everything was taken care of. John is fortunate to have such a trustworthy person to look after this place," Zachary said.

Charles' wife had sent over a small pot of vegetable soup and cheese sandwiches. It made a tasty mid-afternoon meal for them. Elizabeth made a mental note to send her a thank you letter.

The sun was bright and there were puffy white clouds drifting lazily across the November sky.

After unpacking, they changed into some comfortable clothes, bundled up and took a long walk on the beach. The cold wind against their faces put a spring in their step. This was a beautiful place, and they both were glad they came here for their honeymoon.

For her wedding night Elizabeth chose her long, white batiste gown. It had a round neck encircled with white lace. Very narrow pink satin ribbon was woven through the lace ending in streamers with love knots. The slightly gathered long sleeves had lace ruffles at the wrist.

Zachary drank in her beauty. This lovely creature was no apparition. Neither was she an elusive butterfly. She was very real. And she was his.

Her graceful movements captivated him. She stacked the bed cushions in a chair, turned down the covers, picked up her brush and began brushing her hair.

Elizabeth watched Zachary through the mirror. To be in his presence in this room was a long-awaited dream come true. He was her prince! Words could not describe her love for him. It seemed so natural to be here with him.

Zachary watched as she brushed her long, shiny, black hair. When she finished she laid her brush down, turned and walked toward him. He opened his arms and she walked unhesitatingly into them.

—◦◦◦—

The days passed quickly. They stayed busy. There was a good stage production by Belasco at the Williamsburg Opera House. It had been showing nightly for three months. They went on Tuesday evening. It was a drama but with some humor and very entertaining. Of course, they went to see Jane and Phillip. What a great time they had reminiscing! Elizabeth said on Monday night when she and Zachary returned from Norfolk she would have Steve, Rebecca, Matt, India, Scott and Libbi all over for dinner so they could all be together again.

When they were leaving, Elizabeth said to Jane, "You are my dearest friend. No matter the time or distance that may separate us, you will always remain my friend.

"A wise old man named Mencius wrote in 289 B.C., 'Friendship is merely one mind in two bodies.' I like that. I feel the two of us think alike. I know we have the same values. Another old proverb says 'hold a true friend with both your hands.' I am going to do that, Jane. Always! Zachary and I will look forward to next Monday night."

The highlight of their week was on Thursday evening. The "Classic Harmony with Strings" was at the Stratford Theater for a one-night performance. Zachary had surprised Elizabeth with reserved seats in the left front balcony. They were so close they could almost touch the group. Of course, this was the group that had played at her cotillion.

Zachary had arranged for them to play their song "To Each His Own" especially for Elizabeth.

When they did the fanfare and Kreisler, the leader of the group, announced the next song was for a newly wed couple, Zachary and Elizabeth, she gasped. She was so surprised and pleased. Then a very talented singer sang "their song." She felt so special. Zachary looked at her with love and adoration.

Chapter 71

They arrived in Norfolk at two o'clock Friday the twenty-second. They took the train from Williamsburg to Hampton and the ferry across to Norfolk.

The whole family was there with a feast awaiting them. Elizabeth had met the family except for Joey and Heather. Zachary's parents, Steven and Barbara, as well his brother and sister-in-law, Thomas and Joyce, were at the cotillion. She met Ben and Rebecca when they came to the picnic.

They went out of their way to make her feel welcome.

Elizabeth loved their time around the piano with Mrs. Bainbridge playing and all of them singing.

Thomas, Zachary and Ben kept all of them laughing. Everywhere she looked she saw love and respect. And these boys loved their sister Rebecca. They teased her unmercifully, but always in good fun!

Joyce was an easy-going, agreeable person. Elizabeth especially liked her. She knew they would become good friends.

Joey and Heather warmed up quickly to Elizabeth and wanted to sit close to her. These two stole her heart right from the start.

They asked her a lot of questions. Heather acted so grown up just to be six. She had big brown eyes like her mother, Joyce.

With a solemn and questioning look, she asked Elizabeth, "May we come to your house?"

Elizabeth picked her up and hugged her tightly just for a second and said, "You certainly may, anytime."

Late in the evening they had sung more songs, had dessert and were sitting around the dining table. So far Elizabeth had not addressed Zachary's parents by name. It was an awkward situation because she did not know what to call them. She decided the best thing to do was ask them what she should call them. When she did Zachary's mother answered, "My dear, what would you prefer to call us?"

She sat very still and silent for a long time. Everyone was looking at her. Then she said, "My real father died before I was born. My stepfather died when I was three. My mother died when I was seven. I had the most wonderful Baldwin grandparents. They nurtured me so that I never felt denied. I could not have been more loved. But after the ages of four and seven, almost the same ages as Joey and Heather, I have had no one to call father and mother. If you would have no objection, I would like to join Zachary in calling you father and mother. I will respect that privilege if you permit me to do so."

Zachary was so touched. A wonderful bond was being formed that would last a lifetime.

Steven and Barbara stood up and reached out to Elizabeth. She went to them. They each hugged her and Steven said, "I am so honored, Elizabeth, because you feel that way."

Barbara added, "Elizabeth, I can't take your mother's place but I will do my best to be a good mother to you. You are special to me."

Joyce spoke up and said, "Elizabeth, you could not have married into a better family. The whole family has treated me just as fine as they treat Thomas. I am glad to have another sister in my life." Then Joyce gave Elizabeth a big hug.

Thomas and Ben also gave her a hug and called her "sis" the rest of the evening.

Rebecca said, "I'll get to see Elizabeth all the time as I'll be living in Richmond very soon!"

Zachary thought . . . *I have never really considered Elizabeth as orphaned at such a young age.* It broke his heart. It endeared her even more to him, if that were possible.

Elizabeth said, "It is obvious this is a house of love. What has made your family so strong father?"

"I was taught by my father the concept found in Psalm 127 . . . 'Unless the Lord builds the house, they labor in vain who build it.' He said that the Lord Himself must be the center of our lives and our home. He instilled the importance of being a born-again believer and of marrying a born-again believer. This is the only way to have a stable and strong home that will withstand the storms of life. He told us this over and over again. It has worked for the Bainbridge household. Our 'boat,' if you will, has been designed by the Master Builder."

"Zachary, why haven't you told me you have a father like Solomon?" Elizabeth exclaimed.

"I knew you would find this out for yourself. Isn't he something?" Zachary replied.

"Now, now children, let's go back to the piano and sing a few more songs before we retire for the night," Steven said as he took Barbara by the hand and walked to the piano.

It has been a wonderful November 22nd!

The Bainbridge's had a lot of fun things planned for the weekend. It passed all too swiftly.

Zachary and Elizabeth left on Monday morning to go back to the beach house. Charles met them at the train depot. They went into Williamsburg to buy a few gifts to take back with them. They went first to the Jones Mercantile to get dolls for the three little Everette children and one for Jenny Adams, Jane's little sister. They wanted to see "India's Adorables" Collection. Both Matt and India were there and were delighted to see them. They described the four little girls to India and let her choose the dolls for them. She wrapped them carefully.

"We look forward to seeing you tonight at Jane and Phillip's," India said as they left the store.

Next, they went to a department store. Elizabeth's grandmother had mentioned a couple of weeks ago that she was almost out of her favorite perfume. This would be a perfect gift for her. Zachary chose a new sailing cap for John. He knew this would please him. They picked up a few more gifts for Sadie, William and Sara and all their friends back home.

They stopped at a small café and ate a sandwich with a cup of hot chocolate. It was mid-afternoon when they got back to the beach house. They rested for a while, then went to Jane and Phillip's lovely home. You could see Jane's personal touch throughout the house.

Each of the girls had brought a special dish for the evening meal. Jane had prepared a baked ham, curried chicken, yeast rolls and tea. Altogether they had English peas, potato salad, yams and fruit salad to go with the meat. For dessert they had pecan pie.

Scott said, "You ladies did an excellent job preparing the food. It was delicious." and you could hear a hearty echo of agreement from all the guys!

After dinner they all wanted to know about the wedding.

"What made you decide to elope instead of having a traditional church wedding?" India asked.

"Because my grandparents had already given me the cotillion, I just didn't feel like being put on display again. I'm really a very private person. I loved our wedding just the way it was. A sweet, meaningful ceremony with just the minister, two witnesses, and Zachary and me," Elizabeth said.

Rebecca spoke up and said, "It's very unusual for a young, beautiful girl to feel that way. Most all of us want a big wedding. It's our dream."

"I loved mine and Scott's church wedding. I wouldn't have changed anything about it," Libbi added.

"The only thing I would have changed about ours is for Matt not to have stepped on my wedding dress when we were coming out of the church!" India said laughingly.

"Mine and Phillip's church wedding was also an event that we will never forget. I thought it was just right," Jane said to Libbi.

India chimed in . . . "To each his own. It would be a dull world if we all wanted the same thing."

They all decided to play a popular game of charades. It was such fun! Steve was the action player. He chose the word "elope." He tried to form the letter "e" with his hands and then he loped around the room. They guessed deer, kangaroo, antelope and on and on. Finally, he went over to Elizabeth and Zachary, pointed to them and proceeded to lope around the room.

Scott yelled out, "Oh, you mean, "E-lope!"

Steve sank down in his chair and said, "Finally!"

They all laughed and clapped.

They each took a turn and had great fun and fellowship.

Elizabeth asked Jane and Phillip if they had thought about names for the baby. They had a few picked out but nothing definite.

They all agreed to try and get together at least once every three or four months, and then they said their goodbyes.

<hr />

Tuesday would be a day of rest and packing for the trip home.

Zachary was up before Elizabeth. He prepared fruit cereal for their breakfast, made a pot of coffee and set the table. He found white linen napkins with a small red rose in one corner. He knew a red rose was given to say "I love you." He folded the napkins so the red rose stood out and placed them beside their cereal bowls. Then he had an idea. He saw a white bud vase in the sitting room. He took the vase, got another rose napkin and tucked it down in the vase so the red rose was prominent. He folded the other three corners of the napkin over the edge of the vase. He placed it in the center of the table, stepped back and looked at it. Perfect!

He found some stationary of Catherine's and wrote a note on it to Elizabeth. He propped it in front of her coffee cup. Just as he finished Elizabeth came into the kitchen. She had on a long, straight black and gray tweed skirt and a fleecy red wool sweater with a high neck. She had fixed her hair in an upsweep. Curly strands framed her pretty face.

"Zachary, my love, you've already fixed breakfast," she said surprised.

He had folded a dishtowel over his forearm, made a deep bow and said, "Madam, at your service. Please be seated." He pulled her chair out and then took his seat across from her. He watched her face as she picked up his note and read it:

This is the true measure of love, when we believe that we alone can love, that no one could ever have loved so before us, and that no one will ever love in the same way after us.

Goethe

"My beautiful bride, this seems to have been written for us. I know that it describes perfectly the way I feel about the love we share."

Your husband,
Zachary

He had never seen this look on her face before. It was a look of wonder and revelation. She sat speechless and spellbound. She didn't respond for the longest time, but merely gazed deep into Zachary's eyes. Holding the paper in her hand, she said, "Oh, Zachary how I love thee! This is just too beautiful to spoil with words."

Finally she asked, "Where did you get this, Zachary? Who is this Goethe?"

"His name is Johann Wolfgang von Goethe. He was a German poet. He lived from 1749 to 1832. I've read one of his books. This is my favorite of his writings. I liked it so much I committed it to memory. Oh Elizabeth, isn't it a perfect description? The love a man has for a woman and a woman has for a man."

"Zachary, of all the things you have done for me in our perfect time together this past eleven days, this is the most special of all. I will always keep this note. It will be placed in our family Bible beside the handkerchief I was carrying the first day we met.

"Look at this table. You are so clever. I have roses in the beach house in November. Grandmother Catherine is going to be missing three rose napkins and a white bud vase! I must have them as a keepsake of our honeymoon!"

They had their cereal, drank their coffee very leisurely and re-lived their wedding day.

The time of seriousness passed and laughter set in. They giggled about the elopement. They loved it and would have had it no other way. They laughed that William had been in on their plans. He must have really enjoyed knowing their secret.

Elizabeth told Zachary after they were married and were seated in the dinning car she had a desire to tap on her water glass with her fork, stand to her feet and announce that they had eloped and gotten married at sixteen minutes until eight that very morning!

"There was this older, prim and proper couple sitting at the next table. Can't you just imagine their reaction to such an announcement?"

"I wonder what your grandparents are going to say to us when we get home," Zachary pondered.

"So do I. But I feel sure they will respect our decision. It will be good to get home, to *our* home, to *our* room, to *our* balcony . . . my Romeo!"

He reached for her. She dodged his grasp and ran through the house. He was right behind her. She had run into the bedroom when he caught her. She fell across the bed. He grabbed her and tickled her until she lost her breath laughing. Then she cuddled up close to him, laying her head on his big, broad shoulder.

"Zachary," she asked, "Am I your girl?"

"You surely are. And you always will be."

"Will you always take care of me, no matter what?"

"Always, my love, always."

"Tell me, Zachary, how much do you love me?"

"Why, I love you a whole sky full! How much do you love me, Elizabeth?"

"There is no height high enough, no depth deep enough, no width wide enough, and no words fine enough to measure my love for you, Zachary. But I will have the rest of our lives together to show you."

"Will you seal that with a kiss?" he asked as he lifted her face and kissed her tenderly.

Chapter 72

As the carriage pulled up in front of Willow Place Elizabeth admired her new balcony. As William unloaded the baggage, Zachary picked Elizabeth up and carried her across the threshold. He stood holding her for a few minutes looking at their new home. She smiled her impish smile and told him, "Welcome home."

They went up to their bedroom. They had forgotten just how beautiful it was. There on the lamp table was a gorgeous bouquet of red roses with a note, which read, "Welcome home children. Our love, and total support on your new journey through life. Grandmother, and Grandfather."

They stood with their arms around each other's waist admiring the roses, so pleased by the message that came with them.

Then they discovered that all of Zachary's clothes and personal belongings had been moved from the Morgan's to their room. Sadie had also put all of Elizabeth's things back in their room from the guest room. Elizabeth felt so at home!

They went back downstairs and were congratulated on their marriage and welcomed home by Sadie. She was very happy for these young people.

Elizabeth said, "Let's you and I drive up to see grandmother and grandfather."

They rang the doorbell and Simpson opened the door immediately. Usually very stoic, he smiled broadly and said, "Congratulations. I love the way you did it!" Then he snapped back into the same ole stoic Simpson. They would not have believed he said that if they had not heard it with their own ears. They knew they had at least one fan.

Her grandparents were in the sitting room and did not know they were in the house until Zachary spoke up and said, "Well, aren't you going to welcome us home?"

They both jumped to their feet and her grandfather said, "Well, see here, the elopers have returned! Welcome home grandchildren."

Welcome into our family, Zachary," Catherine said as she gave both of them a hug.

John put his arm around his beloved granddaughter, led her to the sofa and said, "Sit down here beside me and tell us all about your trip."

"First let me tell both of you how precious you are to me, to us," Elizabeth said. "Our elopement was not meant to exclude you. Please don't think it was. I thought a long time before I presented my idea to Zachary. Since I was honored at the lavish cotillion, I just didn't feel like an expensive wedding. I wanted Zachary to myself on my wedding day. I did not want to share him. To me our wedding was perfect for us.

"I knew we would be living across the lake from both of you for the rest of our lives. That is what is important to me. I want us to be close daily. I like the idea of running up the hill and dashing in your backdoor, into your kitchen to see if you have some extra goodies to eat. You will be a big part of our everyday lives. Now, am I forgiven?" Elizabeth asked looking from one to the other with those gorgeous blue eyes.

"My dear, there is nothing to forgive. Your grandfather and I know you well enough by now to know you always have a good reason for your actions. We had to admit that eloping sounded very romantic, even to us old folk," her grandmother said.

"Tell me something, Zachary. Did you put a ladder to Elizabeth's window and whisk her away?" John asked with a gleam in his eye.

They all had a good laugh.

Elizabeth and Zachary shared with their grandparents all the fun places they went on their honeymoon. They told them about the production by Belasco at the Opera House and how much they enjoyed it. They also recounted the great concert at the Stratford Theater by "Classic Harmony."

"We had a wonderful honeymoon at the beach house. Grandfather, it was an ideal place for us to have our privacy. We thought of you two and your foresight to have such a place for the family to enjoy. We knew you would not mind our using it," Elizabeth said.

"My child, it's yours and Zachary's beach house as much as it is ours. You two are all we have. What's ours is yours," her grandfather assured her.

"Let me tell you what Zachary did for me at breakfast Tuesday morning." Elizabeth proceeded to tell them the whole story. "Grandmother, you are missing three rose napkins and a white bud vase. They will be a reminder of our honeymoon forever!"

"Our modest wedding present to you" her grandmother said.

"It was such a romantic time for us. We will cherish the memories we made these last twelve days forever."

"But the happiest time for me was coming back to Willow Place as Mrs. Zachary Bainbridge. Coming into *our* home, one we will forever share as long as we live. Walking into our newly decorated bedroom and seeing those beautiful red roses with the welcome home note from *our* grandparents that made me feel so loved and special. You two are the best, always so thoughtful," Elizabeth said.

Zachary chimed in, "By the way, John, you can retire your old beat-up sailing cap. We got you a spiffy new one. It looks just like you! Catherine, we got you a bottle of your favorite perfume. We will unpack and bring them over tomorrow."

"What are your plans for Thanksgiving tomorrow, grandmother? I smelled some wonderful cooking when we came in. What time are we eating?" Elizabeth asked.

"We will gather for Thanksgiving at 1:30. We can all eat light for breakfast. There will be a lot of delicious food for lunch and plenty of leftovers for supper.

"Your grandfather and I decided we should include everyone. We will have Simpson, William, Sadie, Mike, Emma, Millie, Virginia and us four. This has been a good year for all of us. It will be a day of thanksgiving for God's abundant blessings to us all," Catherine said.

Elizabeth and Zachary said goodnight and rode back down to the stable. Zachary took care of Charlie and parked the carriage. They walked up to the house and went in through the backdoor, put out the lights and went upstairs to their room.

Holding Elizabeth close Zachary said, "It is still very hard for me to believe we are married. Marriage is wonderful. One day you are two and in love. The next day you say your wedding vows and your whole world changes. You two become one! This is God's plan for man. He is the giver of perfect gifts. Elizabeth, I will cherish you always."

It seemed words were not needed at this moment. They stood holding each other for the longest time.

Elizabeth said, "Zachary, let's start a tradition this first night in our home. Let's read a Bible scripture each night. We can alternate. I'll begin tonight. Let's be faithful in doing this. This was something Grandmother Savannah and Dandy did. I would like to continue this tradition in our marriage. What do you think?"

"Elizabeth, I love tradition. It played a great part in my life growing up. This is a wonderful idea."

They sat in their chairs. Elizabeth picked up the Bible and began to read from Ruth, "Whither thou goest I will go . . ."

Thanksgiving Day was one they would all long remember. It was filled with good food, good fellowship and many testimonies of God's blessings.

Chapter 73

*Z*achary was happy to get back to work. Things were going well at the carriage factory.

Elizabeth and her grandmother began doing lots of things together.

The church was working on projects to help the poor at Christmas time. They were very much involved in this effort. The lives of Elizabeth, Zachary and their grandparents began to merge.

Elizabeth stayed in touch with the Smiths and the Everette's. They were dear and special people to her.

She and Emma set aside one day a week to visit each other. Elizabeth wanted to learn as much as she could from what Emma knew about her Baldwin grandparents and her mother, Victoria. Their time together was top priority for both of them.

She and Sadie also spent quality time together. Sadie and William were able to tell her many interesting things she did not know about her grandparents and her mother.

Robert and Rebecca were married on December 14th in Norfolk. Rebecca was a radiant bride. Her coloring, especially her dark auburn hair, was stunning with her ivory lace wedding dress. Elizabeth learned that Rebecca got her gorgeous hair from her maternal grandmother. She had wondered about this since her brothers all had blonde hair.

It was a nice wedding and well attended. Robert just beamed each time he looked at Rebecca. They had Max and Jo Anna play their stringed instruments and sing at the reception. The people in Norfolk loved their talent and Rebecca's parents wanted to adopt them!

Robert and Rebecca opted to come to their home on the Thomas farm for their honeymoon. The Thomas' all worked together to have it in perfect shape for the newlyweds.

Several inches of powdery snow fell on December 18th. It was beautiful. Zachary came in from work early and surprised Elizabeth with a new horse drawn sleigh he had bought. He knew she loved sleigh rides. The horse's leather rigging was laced with sleigh bells. They made their own music as they rode through this "heavenly white stuff" as Elizabeth called it.

The new sleigh glided over the landscape. There was magic all around them it seemed. Things looked different in the snow. The birds' feathers looked more colorful. The red berries on the holly bushes sparkled like rubies.

"Oh Zachary, just look at this wonderland of beauty!"

Zachary had never seen Elizabeth more radiant and lovely. She was so much fun and she laughed often and said some of the funniest things. She kept him laughing with her quick wit and was his greatest fan.

They finished decorating the big evergreen tree that William had cut for the living room. It was beginning to look a lot like Christmas around the Bainbridge house.

Elizabeth went upstairs ahead of Zachary. When he came up he found she had opened the draperies and was sitting on the balcony wrapped from head to toe in a blanket.

There was a perfect full moon casting shadows over the lake. The moonbeams threaded across the lake like a wide yellow ribbon rippling in the movement of the water. The branches on the willow trees were wispy white with snow and swayed slightly in the breeze. The stars glistened like diamonds in the sky. It was truly a winter wonderland at Willow Place. He had never seen such beauty. If he were only an artist he thought.

"You love your balcony, don't you, my princess?"

She turned smiling and said, "Oh, Zachary, the balcony was a perfect idea. I feel like it is our little corner of the world. It is a perfect corner!"

He leaned down and kissed the tip of her very cold nose. She was just like a child when it snowed.

Chapter 74

In a couple of days the snow almost melted. The weather was crisp but the sun was shining brightly in a cloudless sky. It was the weekend before Christmas, their very first to be together. Elizabeth had not committed herself to anything at the church. She and Zachary went to the children's program on Saturday night, sat back and enjoyed it. It was good for once to watch without any responsibilities.

Sunday morning the choir performed a cantata entitled "Holy Child of Bethlehem." It was enchanting. The story in song, interspersed with recitations, was beautifully presented. They had chosen Robert Thomas as their narrator. His resonant voice gave an air of reverence to the program.

Max and Jo Anna sang a duet "O Holy Night."

Elizabeth and Zachary left the service with their spirits lifted.

Monday afternoon they visited the Everette's and Smith's. They gave Sara, Emily and Julie their "India's Adorables" dolls. India had chosen well for them as each one liked their own doll the best.

Emily crawled up in Zachary's lap and leaned against his chest. He stroked her hair and talked to her. Elizabeth imagined that he missed Heather and Joey this Christmas season. Next year they would spend Christmas with his family.

They had brought presents and fruit for Maggie and Jim as well as for Bessie and Henry.

These folks were special to Elizabeth. It was obvious they were contented. This made Elizabeth very happy.

They left and stopped by to see Emma and Mike. They gave them the gifts they had bought for them in Williamsburg. Emma had baked them a fruitcake.

She served them a cup of eggnog and a slice of her wonderful pound cake. It was so good. They realized just how hungry they were!

The Thomas' had invited them to the farm for the evening. What a treat it was. They were such fun to be with. Jennifer and Allison were smitten by Dr. Blake. He loved to tease them! The thirteen-year old twins, Trey and Andrew, played in such a rough-house way. Layton had invited his girlfriend, Laura Baker, to join them.

Max and Jo Anna played and sang. Max kept everyone laughing as he usually did.

They ended the evening by singing "Silent Night," everyone's favorite.

"Good morning, my love. Do you know what today is?" Elizabeth asked excitedly. "Do you?"

"Let me see. Is it Tuesday?" Zachary answered.

"Yes. Yes, it's Tuesday. But what *day* is it?"

"I just told you. It's "Tuesday," he said again.

"Zachary Bainbridge, you know fair well its Christmas Eve. Grandmother Savannah and

Dandy always exchanged presents on Christmas Eve. Do you have a present for me?"

"Well now, I just might have."

"Tell me, Zachary, *do you? What is it?*"

"It won't be a surprise when you open it if I tell you. Besides, in the Bainbridge household we always open presents on Christmas morning. Now, whose tradition are we going to follow?" Zachary asked, goading her on.

"Oh, Zachary, don't tell me that. How can I wait another day?"

"Come here little girl. If it means that much to you, we will do both and open one tonight and the rest Christmas morning. Now does that make you happy? Now give me that Elizabeth smile. Let me see those laughing eyes and those dimples."

She gave him a dazzling smile and said, "You really don't mind if we open just one tonight?"

"Of course not" Zachary chided. "We will enjoy Christmas Eve and Christmas morning and create our own traditions. Do you want to open our gift now or tonight?" Zachary asked.

"Oh, most definitely tonight. But I can hardly wait" Elizabeth said.

They dressed for the day and had coffee and some of Emma's fruitcake for breakfast. Then they went into town.

Elizabeth loved the hustle and bustle of the shoppers on Christmas Eve. She always had last minute gifts to buy. She loved going to the Sandwich Shop for hot soup at lunchtime. Zachary was learning the mind of a woman.

They went to the mercantile. It was filled with scurrying shoppers and excited children. She loved to buy gifts for children she knew would not have much of a Christmas. It was her favorite thing to do on Christmas Eve. There were several families she always bought gifts for.

She and Zachary were making some selections when she noticed a young couple talking very seriously and looking troubled. She casually drew a little closer so she could hear.

"But Marie, we are going to have to make some other choices."

"Joseph, you know what the children asked for. I thought we had saved enough to pay for this doll and this wagon. These are the ones Sally and Bobby said they wanted."

"I know, Marie, but I had to buy that part to fix our wagon. That was an unexpected expense. We don't have the money for these. We will have to choose something else for them. I don't like it any more than you do, but we don't have any other choice. It's what we must do."

Elizabeth felt sure she would never forget the resigned look on that young couple's faces. She called Zachary to one side and told him what she had heard.

"We must do something to help this family. Oh Zachary, we must."

"Let me think, Elizabeth. I wonder where he works? We are in need of a couple more men at the carriage factory. Maybe I can offer him a job. The new carriage design has increased our production because of more orders. We pay better wages than any place in the Richmond area. Let me talk with him," Zachary said.

He walked up to the man and introduced himself.

"Excuse me, sir. I am Zack Bainbridge of Morgan Carriage Company. We are in need of an employee for the factory. I wonder if you might be interested in coming to work for our company?"

The man looked astonished. He stood there staring at Zachary and it took him a moment to respond.

He extended a calloused hand and said, "I am Joseph Jordan. This is my wife, Marie. Did I understand that you just offered me a job?"

"Yes I did. Are you working anywhere now?" Zachary inquired.

"I work at the Sawmill. It's hard work with low pay. I would like the opportunity to work at the carriage factory. I hope you are serious about the offer. If you are you won't be sorry," Joseph said.

"I am serious. Could you come to work on December 30th at 8:00 A.M.? We will talk about your salary then. I can assure you it will be a living wage," Zachary told him.

"I really can't thank you enough," Joseph said with another firm handshake.

"May I now ask a favor of you two?" Zachary asked.

Joseph looked hesitant. "Yes, if I can help you I will."

"Well, my wife and I don't have any children to buy Christmas presents for. One day we hope to have a family. Do you have children?"

Marie spoke up and said, "Yes sir. We have two, a little boy, four, and a little girl, seven."

"Would you give me the privilege of buying some things for their Christmas? It would really add to my Christmas spirit to do so," Zachary assured them.

"We really don't know what to think or what to say. I have always worked to support my family. It's been meager I'll admit, but I don't want charity," Joseph said emphatically.

"Joseph, please," Marie said in a whisper, "please, it's for the children."

"Let me remind you that I will receive far more from this than you will. The Bible says it is more blessed to give than to receive. The time will come when you can pass this blessing on by doing something special for someone," Zachary reminded him. "And remember you will be earning a fair wage when you come to work for Morgan Carriage Company!"

"In light of what you say I will accept your kindness," Joseph said.

"Since you know what your children like, would you help me pick some things out for them?" Zachary suggested.

He made sure they got the doll and wagon. He had Marie to choose some much needed clothes and some fruit and candy for the children.

Elizabeth watched from a distance and was so pleased that all worked out well.

When the Jordan's left the mercantile, Zachary and Elizabeth felt like they had really celebrated the true spirit of Christmas.

"I've been thinking, Zachary. You know God *gave* His only Son. Then His Son *gave* His life. In doing so, He *gave* us eternal life. So Christmas should be a celebration of *giving*. Giving to others makes me happier than anything," Elizabeth declared.

"Very well said, my dear. Those are my sentiments exactly."

They finished buying the gifts for the children on Elizabeth's list. They chose what they purchased carefully, making sure they included needed items as well as toys, fruit and candy.

"Let's go to the Sandwich Shop for a bowl of hot soup, and then we will deliver our gifts," Zachary said.

Chapter 75

They got home around five o'clock and found two plates of baked ham, potato salad, green beans and spiced apples covered on the kitchen table. A note from Sadie said they had left at 4:30 to spend Christmas Eve with Emma and Mike.

Sitting down to eat Zachary said, "This food looks delicious! The soup at the Sandwich Shop this afternoon was good but it didn't last very long."

"After we finish eating let's go change into our robes and sit by the fire and our beautiful Christmas tree," Elizabeth said.

William had banked the fire well in the living room. Zachary laid a couple more logs on it, stirred the embers a little and in no time there was a roaring fire with flames leaping high in the fireplace.

Elizabeth curled up on the sofa and cuddled up very close to Zachary. She laid her head on his shoulder and watched all the characters she could see dancing in the flames. She felt so contented, so very blessed.

"What are you thinking about, Elizabeth?" Zachary asked.

"Oh, a lot of things. About you and me, our first Christmas together. The church services and the visits with friends. The mercantile experience. Just a lot of things," she replied.

"You seem a little melancholy tonight."

"Sometimes I have a hard time accepting that we have so much and there are others who seem to have so little. I'd fix everyone's problems for them if I could," Elizabeth said rather sadly.

"But you can't do that. So you do what you can when you can. Today you made a difference for a lot of people and we must be content with that."

"Today *we* made a difference, not just me. I'm so glad I have you, that we have each other," Elizabeth said as she moved just a little closer to him.

"I notice you haven't said anything about wanting to open your gift and it's almost midnight!" Zachary exclaimed.

"I know. After today, a gift for me seems so unimportant," she murmured.

"Well now, just wait until you see the gift before saying it's unimportant." Zachary lifted a small, beautifully wrapped gift from the pocket of his robe. "This is just for you, my Christmas angel."

She held it and looked at how it was wrapped.

"It's almost too pretty to open," she said.

Elizabeth carefully untied the red satin ribbon and removed the shiny gold paper. She lifted the lid from the box. Inside was a beautiful gold locket. She took it out of the box and examined it closely. In the center of the heart was a blue sapphire. The back was engraved with her initials and their wedding date. He included a note, which read:

"This heart represents my love for you. The blue sapphire reminds me of your beautiful blue eyes. Someday you can pass this on to our daughter. I give this with my love to 'One and Only You.' Zachary."

"Oh Zachary, I love it! It's a perfect gift and very special because you chose it. As you say, one day I do hope to pass it on to our daughter. Thank you for making our first Christmas one I will always remember."

She went over to the Christmas tree and picked up the smallest gift from under the tree and gave it to him with a smile.

"Well, I've heard it said that good things come in little packages. We shall see."

Zachary noticed the detailed wrappings on the box and suspected she had wrapped it herself. She had chosen a printed wrapping paper in red, green and white. She had tied it with a green satin ribbon. He, too, carefully unwrapped his box. Inside he discovered an English Hunter-gold pocket watch with a hinged cover over the dial. He snapped the cover open. Engraved inside the lid were his initials, their wedding date and "To Each His Own." He had never seen such a handsome watch.

"Do you like it?" Elizabeth asked, waiting for an answer.

"Like it? I love it. I've really been in need of a new watch. Mine has been losing time lately. This is a perfect gift, Elizabeth, just perfect," Zachary said giving her a hug and kiss.

"You can one day pass that watch on to our son," Elizabeth said seriously.

"But of course" Zachary said.

Elizabeth went upstairs while Zachary tended to the fire and the candles on the tree.

Christmas day was spent with Elizabeth's grandfather and grandmother. They had gone to Williamsburg to visit friends over the weekend and had come home on Christmas Eve.

They exchanged gifts and had a delicious meal together.

The afternoon was spent talking about what brought them together and when they first met.

"I'll never forget you taking off your shoes and running up those stairs in the big house on Warthen Street to crawl into that big bed for a nap," her Grandmother Catherine said reminiscing.

"Nor when you came sliding down those long banisters, not once but twice," her grandfather added with a chuckle.

"Yes, we began to live again when you came into our lives, Elizabeth,' Catherine remembered fondly.

"Our coming here was the best move we've ever made. And having Zachary as a grandson-in-law is just icing on the cake," John declared.

Their time together was so special to all of them. This first Christmas at Willow Place would live on in their catalog of memories.

Chapter 76

The new year of 1857 brought many changes. The economy was booming. The need for more extensive travel had sparked the railroad companies to lay more tracks, bringing cities closer together.

Bigger and better steamers were being built. John and Zachary were glad to be out of the shipping business.

The Carriage Company was expanding. Max Hammond had been promoted to manager of the company. John's trust in this young man had certainly not been misplaced.

Zachary asked Elizabeth to only volunteer one day a week at the hospital. She and her Grandmother Catherine wanted to spend more time together. They were also involved in several charitable organizations.

Sara had to leave Willow Place to take care of her mother who had become quite ill. Zachary insisted on hiring a full-time live-in cook. They felt they had found another Emma when they hired Molly Thatcher. She was forty-five, widowed with no children. She had worked for a prominent pioneer family in Richmond. She came highly recommended.

Molly had a take-charge way about her. She was bossy in a pleasant sort of way and knew her business. She practically had

Zachary jumping through hoops. But with Elizabeth she was gentle and protective.

She was short with red hair and a little bit plump, and her cooking was second to none!

John and Zachary had hired a full-time gardener to keep Willow Place well manicured year round. Since they were raising more and more horses, they had also hired two men to help William with the spring foals.

Springtime at Willow Place had never been prettier.

Zachary and John had just left on a buying trip to New York. They would be gone a week. It was the first time Elizabeth and Zachary had been apart since they were married.

Elizabeth sat on the balcony in a reflective mood. The morning sun was shining its rays on all the beauty of her beloved Willow Place.

She thought back to her childhood. She could almost see her Dandy holding her hand as they walked around the lake. In her mind she could hear her Grandmother Savannah reading to her. She remembered her beautiful mother, Victoria, brushing her hair.

She could almost feel the rocking motion when she and her Dandy rode double on his big quarter horse, Thunder. He was so proud of her when she learned to ride. The scriptures they taught her came to mind as well as the sage instructions they taught her. The wonderful times they shared helped her get through the sad times of losing them.

Her mind traveled back to November 16th, 1855, to the first day she ever saw Zachary. Her life began anew on that day.

To think, she let a stranger, Cordelia Fuller, make her doubt Zachary when he had told her, "I have never been frivolous with my emotions toward women. When I marry I want it to be for life. So I have guarded my feelings for just the right person."

She learned from Zachary's father how he was raised and how he had raised his children. Their faith was strong. She repented again, as she had often done, for her misjudgment of Zachary. She should have listened to her heart.

Oh, how very much she loved Zachary. Her love for him had no limits.

She reflected on how she came to know her adored Grandfather John and Grandmother Catherine. When they came into her life God knew how desperately she needed them. Their deep love for her was evident in all they did. The respect, trust and love they had for Zachary endeared them to her even more. And she would never forget, because of them she met Zachary.

Hers and Zachary's life together for the past five months had been fulfilling in so many ways.

Physically it was as Goethe had described. This was a part of their life no one else could ever enter, their own private world.

The comradery they shared was unbelievable to her. They thought alike about things. One would start a sentence and the other would finish it. Sometimes she felt they even breathed at the same time.

Spiritually they were in perfect harmony. They knew who their Creator was. They knew their strength came from Him.

She thought, *I wonder what our future holds? How will the generations to come feel about this beloved Willow Place? Will they love it as I do?*

She stirred a little from her reflective mood and breathed deeply the fresh clean air. She shifted in her padded wicker chair and watched as a mother duck and her ducklings swam in a straight line on the lake. She smiled a knowing smile.

Her thoughts returned to her beloved Zachary. There was something she should have told him before he left, something he did not know about. It would change their lives forever. She could hardly wait for his return.

In the quietness of the morning she heard horses' hoofs thundering in the distance. She leaned forward on the balcony as she saw a rider approaching. She recognized Mark from the Western Union Office as he approached the house. She immediately hurried downstairs to the front door and was waiting when he dismounted and bounded up the steps.

He handed her a telegram saying, "Mr. Ferris told me to make haste in delivering this to you, Mrs. Bainbridge."

Elizabeth reached for the telegram with a trembling hand. Her heart pounding within her caused her breathing to become labored.

She leaned back against the door post as young Mark said goodbye and rode off. She looked down at the familiar yellow envelope of the telegram in her hand once again . . . Dare she open it?

The End

To order additional copies of

Willow Place

JOAN CLINTON SCOGGINS

Have your credit card ready and call:

1-877-421-READ (7323)

or please visit our web site at
www.pleasantword.com

Also available at: www.amazon.com
& www.barnesandnoble.com

Printed in the United States
23706LVS00002B/106-183

9 781579 217075